the OUTLAW
TAKES *a* BRIDE

the OUTLAW
TAKES *a* BRIDE

SUSAN PAGE DAVIS

SHILOH RUN PRESS

An Imprint of Barbour Publishing, Inc.

Print ISBN 978-1-63058-259-3

eBook Editions:
Adobe Digital Edition (.epub) 978-1-63409-251-7
Kindle and MobiPocket Edition (.prc) 978-1-63409-252-4

Cover design: Faceout Studio, www.faceoutstudio.com

Published by Shiloh Run Press, an imprint of Barbour Publishing, Inc., P.O. Box 719, Uhrichsville, Ohio 44683, www.shilohrunpress.com.

Our mission is to publish and distribute inspirational products offering exceptional value and biblical encouragement to the masses.

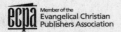
Member of the
Evangelical Christian
Publishers Association

Printed in the United States of America.

CHAPTER 1

Early May 1885, Colorado Plains

Johnny Paynter slung his saddle over his chestnut gelding's back. He and Reckless would work alone today, repairing the ranch's roundup pen. Johnny didn't mind being up here at the line shack all alone—it was better than fighting for elbow room in the bunkhouse. Especially when he was on the foreman's bad side. Still, he couldn't help remembering that today should have been his day off.

Frantic hoofbeats pounded in the distance. Johnny dropped the girth ring and walked around his horse to stare down the trail. His friend Cam Combes was riding hard.

"What's your hurry?" Johnny called as the other cowboy drew near.

"Get your gear. You've got to get out of here." Cam pulled his horse to a stop.

"Why?" Johnny asked. "What's happened?"

"It's the foreman. Somebody shot him. And Johnny—they think you did it. You got to run for it!"

"What on earth?" Johnny stared at him. The Lone Pine foreman was known to be harsh and short tempered, but Johnny had mostly managed to stay on his good side—except for the words they'd exchanged right before Johnny came up here to the line shack, but that wasn't serious. "Are you telling me that Red Howell is dead? How did it happen?"

"Nobody knows." Cam swung down out of the saddle and dropped his pinto's reins. "Ike found him this morning, on the trail about a half mile from the ranch. You were the only one unaccounted for when he rode in with the news. Red had told us he was riding up here to see you this mornin'. Wanted to know how you were doing with the roundup pen. Now I guess they think you ambushed him or something."

"That's crazy," Johnny said.

"Some of the boys heard you the other night, when Red told you to come up here. They're sayin' you had a fight."

Johnny shook his head in protest. "That wasn't any fight. I told Red it was my Sunday off this week, and he said too bad, and I said I really needed a day off, and he said—"

"No time to argue. Get your stuff. You've got to go."

"What, go down and talk to the boss?"

"No!" Cam frowned. "If you do that, they'll turn you over to the law."

"But I didn't do anything." Johnny glared at him. "I didn't even know Red was coming up here. Don't you think I should just go and tell them that?"

"No, I don't. You need to lie low. Better yet, get out of Colorado. Before the sheriff rides up here to take you in."

Johnny's stomach felt hollow. "I'm not going to run. I didn't do anything." He went back to his horse and tightened the cinch strap.

"I believe you, but I'm not so sure they will. I heard some of the boys talking about a necktie party."

Johnny froze. "Are you serious? You mean they'd string me up?"

"You know I always give it to you straight. Remember when Buck Higgins blamed you for lettin' the remuda loose during the roundup?"

"Yeah."

Cam nodded. "I told the boss you wouldn't be that careless. Turned out Buck was to blame. I've got your back, Johnny, and I'm just saying you'll be safer if you make a run for it now. Some of them are pretty hotheaded. If I were in your boots, I'd want to get out of here and not take the chance."

Cam marched into the cabin, and Johnny followed, puzzling over what he had said. It wasn't Cam's fault. He was only delivering the news.

"I don't know what to do—where I could go. . . ."

"There must be someplace you could hide out for a while, until things quiet down." Cam grabbed Johnny's extra shirt from a peg on the wall. He spotted Johnny's saddlebag on the cot, picked it up, and stuffed the shirt into it. "What else you got here?"

His urgency ignited a flame under Johnny. He shoved the rest of his few belongings into the saddlebag, his mind racing as fast as his pulse. "I guess I could head down to Texas. My brother's got a little spread there."

"There you go." Cam smiled. "That's what you need—someplace where you can go and take it easy for a few weeks. When things quiet down, you can come back if you want to, and see if the boss will hire you on again. Give the sheriff time to sort out this shooting and find out who really did it."

"I don't know, Cam. Just take off without knowing—"

Cam shook his head. "They said the sheriff had gone to the other end of the county, and they don't expect him back for a few days. Come on! I'll ride with you. I admit, I'm worried about you. The fellows at the ranch are real riled. If you don't get out of here soon, you'll be dangling from the nearest cottonwood."

"You'd go with me?" Johnny asked.

"Sure. You're my friend."

Relief at not having to go alone washed over Johnny, yet at the same time he hated to get Cam more involved than he already was. But that was Cam's way, he supposed. It wasn't just little things like the incident with the remuda. Johnny also recollected the time he'd been thrown from a green cow pony and landed on a barbed-wire fence.

Cam had wrapped his cuts and ridden back to the ranch house with him, to make sure he got there without passing out, and he'd given up a night off to stay with him at the bunkhouse. He rubbed his forearm through his sleeve and could feel one of the jagged scars he still bore from that. Even though Cam could get a little wild sometimes, he had proven himself a true friend.

Cam rested a hand on his shoulder. "I'm not going to let them lynch you for something you didn't do. Besides, I've never been to Texas. I wouldn't mind seeing some new country."

Three minutes later, the two men were riding hard down the trail away from the ranch. Johnny's mind still whirled. His life was in danger. He could do nothing less than ride away, even though it went against every impulse.

"You said you have a brother in Texas?" Cam asked.

"Yeah. It's a long ways. And I haven't seen him for a couple of years."

"Should be all right," Cam said. "And it's only for a little while."

St. Louis, Missouri

"Seems that feller's awful persistent."

Sally Golding jumped and took her hands from the dishwater. Effie Winters, her hostess and her pastor's wife, stood in the kitchen doorway, scowling down at the letter in her hand.

Sally hastily wiped her hands on her apron. "For me?"

"What's that make—seven? Eight?" Effie held out the envelope, still eyeing it as though reluctant to hand it over.

"Thank you." Sally took it, slid it into the pocket of her threadbare black dress, and turned back to the sink. She wouldn't open it in Effie's presence. While the Reverend and Mrs. Winters had shown great kindness in taking her in, their hospitality seemed to be growing a little thin. Effie made no secret of the fact that she felt Sally had overstayed her welcome.

But what else could she do? Not many places of employment were open to a respectable widow in St. Louis. Sally had tried to live frugally on her sewing skills, but she hadn't earned enough to pay rent and buy food for herself. When she had appealed to the minister a year ago, he had spoken to his wife and they had offered her a tiny room in their attic until she could get her feet under her again. It was their duty to help widows, the reverend had told her. The next Sunday, he had announced her move into their home to the congregation, a bit pompously, Sally thought.

"You about done with those dishes?" Effie eyed the clean skillet and saucepan waiting to be dried and put away.

"Almost."

"Hmpf. I've got some stitching for you when you're through." Effie's heavy footsteps echoed as she walked away.

Sally bent once more over the dishpan. She worked hard in the Winters home—as hard as a hired maid might do, but without wages. While Effie led the churchwomen in organizing efforts for charitable causes, Sally felt she could show a little more kindness at home.

Sally continued doing whatever sewing jobs she could get from other people, but her time was limited, as was her means for advertising her services.

At first she'd tried to save enough to take her back to her parents' home in Abilene, Texas, but after a few months, she'd had several broad hints that contributing to her hosts' funds would not be amiss, since she ate out of their larder. Giving most of what she earned to Effie to supplement the pastor's meager salary meant Sally had saved less than five dollars in the past year. She wasn't sure the minister even knew of her contributions, but she didn't dare ask.

She finished the dishes, dumped the water, and hung up the pan and her apron. She longed for a cup of tea but didn't dare fix herself one. Effie Winters would accuse her of shirking. She went to the parlor, where her hostess sat on the horsehair sofa with her lap desk before her.

"You had some mending?" Sally asked.

Effie pointed with her pen. "My shirtwaist. Heaven knows I need a new dress, but it's hard to come by enough money for one."

Sally hesitated. Was the woman hinting that she should give her more money? If Effie could buy the fabric, Sally could sew a dress for her in a couple of days. But that would take all her time, and if Effie wasn't pleased with the result, she'd never hear the end of it.

As she picked up the bundle of mending, she realized it included several items besides the shirtwaist. "I should be able to get to these this morning, after I finish Mrs. DeVeer's skirt."

Effie nodded absently and continued her writing for a moment. "Oh, do you have any scraps for the quilting bee? We're making that flying geese quilt for the missionary who was here last month."

"I may be able to come up with some."

Sally climbed the narrow stairs and entered her bedroom, thankful for the one small window at the end of the chamber. In summer, this room became a kiln, nearly stifling her, and in winter she all but froze. But now the cool spring weather kept the attic tolerable, and the window gave her adequate light so that she could do her sewing up here in private and not have to put up with Effie's sighs and innuendos. Her hosts seemed to be eager for her to move out, yet Sally couldn't imagine what Effie would do if she left. She certainly wasn't used to doing heavy housework anymore, though she did some of the cooking and made an effort to help the ladies in her husband's congregation and nurse the ill when needed.

After closing the door, Sally sat down in her straight-backed chair near the window. She put the bundle of mending on the small table before her. The letter crackled as she took it from her pocket. This was letter number eight, but she hadn't liked to give Effie the satisfaction of saying it. The nerve of that woman to count her letters! Did she keep as close track of how many Sally's mother sent?

Her seam ripper worked fine as a letter opener, and she carefully slit the top fold of the envelope. Tears filled her eyes as she read the first page. Her many prayers had been answered.

It had taken him long enough, but he had finally proposed marriage. She could leave St. Louis, the city that held so many bad memories.

She had never had the courage to tell her parents how things really were during her marriage to David Golding, or the manner of his death. She had no desire to disgrace them with the knowledge of the pain and degradation she had suffered at his hands. When she was notified of his death, she wrote to her parents that he had died suddenly, but not that he was shot in a saloon brawl.

To her shame, Sally had stayed in St. Louis and scraped along for nearly two years after her husband's death, rather than admit to them how bleak her life had become. What had happened to the courage she'd had as a girl? She didn't like hiding the truth from her folks. Had she become so beaten down that she couldn't face those who loved her?

Now God was giving her the chance to return to Texas and be near them again. Oh, not very near—she would still be a couple of hundred miles from her parents' home—but close enough that she might visit them after a while. She longed to see her mother's dear face and feel her father's strong arms around her. And this time, she would visit as the wife of a respectable, hardworking rancher.

It would also be a second chance for her at having a family. Maybe this time she would get it right. She had answered the rancher's advertisement with trepidation, but his letters showed him to be a caring, thoughtful, and generous man. Life with him could only be better than what she had endured with David, and for the last year with the Reverend Winters and Effie. That thought gave her the courage to seek out a new course. Perhaps if all went well, she could finally have the family she had longed for so many years. Children.

Since David's death, she had come to think she would never be a mother. The memories of the two babies she had never held in her arms always darkened her mood, and she tried not to dwell on them. She had accepted that she would never know a husband's true love or the joy of raising a child. But now. . .now perhaps God was smiling on her. Three or four days of travel would take her to the man who said he loved her and would take care of her for the rest of her life. The man she had never met but had fallen in love with.

Mark Paynter.

Johnny and Cam rode together down the dusty lane, looking for Mark's ranch. The road hadn't been used much, and they hadn't met anyone else since leaving the last town behind.

"It can't be much farther." Johnny rose in his stirrups and peered ahead.

"You don't think we took the wrong trail?" Cam asked.

"Not a chance. That big rock was the landmark. He said turn right at the rock that looks like a bread loaf."

"Right."

Weeks on the trail and scanty food had worn Johnny down. He leaned over to one side and tried to watch his horse's feet, but he couldn't see much from the saddle. "I think Reckless is limping."

"Wouldn't surprise me. He lost that shoe a good five miles back." Cam gazed at the chestnut's hooves as they ambled along. "Well, we'll be there any time now."

The sun beat down with no compassion, and the horses' heads drooped low. Johnny opened his canteen and took a swig. If they didn't find water for the horses soon, they'd be in trouble. He ran his hand over his beard, wiping away a few stray drops of water. At the line shack, he hadn't had a razor. He and Cam hadn't shaved since they lit out. It would feel good to get cleaned up again.

"Hey, look." Cam pointed, and Johnny sighted in the direction he indicated.

Over the top of a small rise ahead was something that might be a ridgepole. They urged the horses to a trot, but at once Reckless's limp became more pronounced, and Johnny let him fall back to a walk.

Cam rode on ahead to the top of the knoll and turned and waved his hat. "Come on, boy! We're there!"

Reckless had a hard time navigating the hill, and Johnny swung down and led him the last few yards. They were at the edge of a yard flanked by a small cabin on one side and a large corral on the other. Beyond the corral stood a barn of sorts. Apparently its main use was for hay storage, though one part seemed to be walled in, probably so Mark could secure his saddles and tools.

"Funny," Johnny said. "The corral gate is open."

Cam frowned. "I don't see any horses."

Johnny looked closer at the house. No smoke rose from the chimney, but a man might let the fire go out in this heat. "Think there's anyone here?"

A cow bawled pitifully, and Johnny spotted her in a small pen near the barn. He led Reckless down the hill toward her, looking about as he walked. He spotted a few head of cattle grazing several hundred yards away on the fenced range.

Cam rode ahead. At the corral fence, he dismounted and eyed the cow.

"She looks like she needs to be milked."

Johnny walked over and stood beside him. One glance confirmed Cam's assessment—the cow was uncomfortable, all right.

"Something's not right."

"I saw some cattle off over there." Cam jerked his chin toward the grassy range.

"Yeah, I saw them, too. Come on." Johnny left Reckless ground-tied and walked toward the house. He was bone tired, and he didn't want to sleep on the ground again tonight.

The cabin door was shut, and he knocked on it. "Mark?" Silence greeted him, so he knocked again. "Anybody home?"

Cam sidled up to him and reached for the latch. The door opened under his touch. "H'lo, the house!"

They looked at each other.

Cam hopped over the threshold, and Johnny hesitated only a moment before following him.

Lying facedown on the floor of the one-room cabin was a man dressed in twill pants and a frayed chambray shirt. Johnny's stomach flipped.

"Well, you said it," Cam said. "Somethin' ain't right."

Johnny stooped and grasped the man's shoulder and rolled him over. Staring sightless up at the ceiling was his brother, Mark Paynter.

CHAPTER 2

———◆———

Sally trudged to the post office through the rain, holding her black umbrella over her head. On most days, Effie or the pastor went for the mail, but on miserable cold winter days or ones where a body could drown by stepping off the sidewalk into a pothole, Sally had the privilege.

She didn't mind going out in the rain, though it meant she would have to change her entire outfit on her return. The umbrella did little to protect her black bombazine skirt as it billowed in the wind. However, making the unpleasant trek herself meant she would see the letters before Effie and the Reverend Mr. Winters did.

She had received only one additional letter from Mark since his proposal. It arrived a fortnight past, and in it he had said he would await her response before writing more about their future. He sounded as though he wasn't confident that she would accept his offer.

Sally prayed that he had received her answer soon after penning his doubtful thoughts. She had sat down as soon as possible and answered that hesitant missive, of course, and assured Mark that he possessed her heart and she now waited only for his word to leave St. Louis and join him in Beaumont, Texas.

At the post office, she opened the door, stepped into the doorway, and turned so she could stand inside while collapsing her umbrella. She slid it into the holder inside the door and glanced about. Two people stood at the counter, awaiting their mail. When they had finished their business and left, she smiled at the postmaster.

"Good afternoon, Mr. Beamus."

"Hello, Mrs. Golding. It's a pleasure to see you, though I suspect getting here was not very pleasurable."

Sally laughed. "You're right. It's coming down pretty hard out there."

"Let's see. . . ." He turned to the rack of cubbyholes behind him. "I know there's something for the minister. Oh, and here's one of those Texas letters for you."

Sally schooled her features so that she wouldn't show her elation when Mr. Beamus turned back toward her and held out the two envelopes.

She glanced at them just long enough to assure her that her own letter was from Mark, not her mother, and tucked the letters into the deep pocket of her cloak.

"Thank you very much."

"Anytime."

The door opened behind her, and she left with a nod to the newcomer, plucking her umbrella from the stand as she passed it. She opened it and plunged into the downpour again, after closing the door firmly behind her.

When she got back to the parsonage and slipped in the back door, the kitchen was empty. She had time to slip her own letter into her dress pocket and was hanging up her cloak when Effie entered.

"Heavens, that umbrella is dripping all over the floor, and your tracks—why, your shoes must be soaked."

"I'm afraid you're right," Sally said serenely. "I'll mop the floor after I've had a chance to put on some dry clothing." She held out the reverend's letter. "Here you go, for Mr. Winters."

"Hmpf." Effie eyed her shrewdly. "Is that all?"

"I've nothing more for you." Sally positioned her open umbrella the right distance from the cookstove, so it would dry out while she dashed up to her room but would have no chance of being singed.

"Nothing from Texas today?" Effie persisted.

"My mother seems not to have written this week. They're probably busy with the garden and the livestock. Excuse me." Sally made a bee-line for the stairs before Effie could press her on the issue.

In her attic room, she sat down near the window. With trembling fingers, she tore open Mark's letter. Folded inside his message was a bank check. Sally's heart raced. She held it up near the window and looked at the amount. It was more than she had earned in the past year.

She turned to the letter.

> *My dear Sally,*
>
> *It was with great joy that I read yours of the 3rd. I trust the enclosed funds will cover your expenses to get here. Please write as soon as you know when you expect to arrive, or if there is no time for mail, send a telegram. I will be getting things spruced up at the ranch. I cannot tell you how happy I am that you have agreed to come and be my bride.*
>
> *With great anticipation,*
> *Mark Paynter*

She clutched the letter to her heart and blinked back the tears that welled in her eyes.

"Oh, thank You, Lord! Thank You!"

She sat another minute, reveling in her boon, then quickly pulled off her damp clothing and put on her only other dress, a faded calico. She always wore the black outside the house since David's death, but she donned the older dress often while doing Effie's housework.

An unpleasant task awaited her. She would have to tell the minister and Effie that she was leaving. She wished she could go and buy her train ticket before telling them, but she didn't see how that would be possible. Effie would be angry if she left the house without telling them.

Sally smoothed her hair and turned to the stairs. Maybe she should just tell them that "friends in Texas" had sent her the money for the trip. Perhaps they would assume the gift was from her family.

No, Effie would never think that.

Sally raised her chin. She would proudly tell them that she was leaving them to marry a respectable Christian rancher. She sent up a prayer for strength and walked down to the parlor.

"Somebody shot him." Johnny stared down at his brother's body. For weeks he'd tried to imagine what his meeting with Mark would be like, but this had never occurred to him.

"I'm sorry," Cam said. He crouched on the opposite side of Mark's body and studied his face. "He looks like you."

"Cam, who would do this?"

"How should I know?"

Johnny sat back on his heels and wiped his sleeve across his brow. "I can't believe it. Mark was always the steady one. Everybody liked him."

"You don't know that," Cam said. "You haven't been around him for a long time."

Slowly, Johnny stood and walked to the open door. "Whoever did it took his horse."

"We oughta look around the corral and see if there are hoofprints. He mighta had more than one horse. And there could be other people. Did he have any ranch hands?"

"I don't think so."

Cam got up and stepped over the body. "We'd better check the barn."

"Yeah. And we need to bury Mark." Johnny's throat was dry, and he swallowed hard. "I reckon we need to get the law out here, too."

"No!" Cam whirled and glared at him. "How do you think it would look if you got a lawman to come here?"

"What do you mean?"

"He'd think we did this."

Johnny shook his head. "Cam, he's my brother. I wouldn't hurt Mark."

"No, but the sheriff don't know that. And if he started asking around, he might hear you was wanted in Colorado. He might even have a wanted poster on you by now."

For a second, Johnny thought his heart had stopped ticking. "Do you think so?"

"I dunno, but I don't think you should chance it. We ran away after Red was killed. We're as good as outlaws now."

Johnny clenched his teeth. He'd tried not to think of it that way. Cam had said he had no other course but to run and that things would get straightened out.

"Come on," Cam said. "We'll look around and make sure no one else is needing us, and maybe we'll see some clues to who did this. When we're sure the coast is clear, we'll tend to your brother."

Johnny followed him outside, his steps dragging. He wasn't sure Cam was right about the law. It seemed to Johnny that if he rode to town and told the local sheriff he'd just arrived and found his brother dead in his own home, the sheriff would believe him. But what if he didn't? He looked around the barnyard. This was a nice little spread. The sheriff might think he and Mark had fought over it.

Cam had located the well, which had a stone berm about two-and-a-half-feet high, and was hauling a rope up from it. Johnny walked over and watched him pull out a wooden bucket full of water and set it on the edge of the wall.

Cam cupped his hands and took a drink. "That's good water. Drink up, boy, and wash the dust off your face."

Johnny scooped up some water for a drink and splashed his face and beard. He felt somewhat better with his parched throat eased and a soft breeze cooling him. Until he thought of Mark, still and growing cold while he and Cam stood here making themselves comfortable.

"Come on." He strode toward the corral. The rail fence ran right up to the barn. Around the open gate, he searched the ground. Boot prints. Shod hooves.

Cam stepped forward, but Johnny held up a hand. "Wait. See that? We need to get one of Mark's boots and see if he made those footprints."

"Why? It's not like we'll know who did, if they aren't his."

Johnny gritted his teeth and didn't respond. He crouched down and ran his finger around the crescent of a hoofprint. "At least one horse wasn't shod."

"Right. How many shod, do you reckon?"

Johnny studied the other prints, inching through the open gate and into the corral to see more, but most of them were marred, overlapping each other in the dry dirt. He could make out the impressions of some rounded forehooves, and a few were definitely from slightly narrower hind feet.

"Hard to say, but I think at least two."

"So. . ." Cam straightened. "Either someone walked in here and left with three or more horses, or they rode in and took their mounts and your brother's horses."

Johnny nodded. "Let's look in the barn."

The open structure held no stalls, the way a barn would in cold-weather country. The lower level held a pile of loose hay in the back corner, and the mow overhead was stuffed with it. Johnny approached the door to what he assumed was the storage room.

"Hey, look."

Cam came to his side. "Someone broke the lock."

Johnny frowned at the hasp that had been pried from the doorjamb. He pulled open the door and peered into the small, dark room.

Cam shoved past him. "Two barrels of oats. Harness. One saddle."

Johnny stepped in and joined him. A spade, an ax, a hammer, and several other tools hung on the wall. "Somebody stole his working saddle." The one that was left was an old, dried-out, cavalry-issue rig with a thick coating of dust. "That one hasn't been touched for a while."

"I think you're right," Cam said. "They're long gone, whoever done it."

"Not too long," Johnny said, thinking of his brother's body. "Mark hasn't been dead a whole day." Suddenly doubting his own judgment, he looked at Cam. "Do you think?"

Cam shook his head. "He ain't stiff, and if it happened yesterday, there'd be. . ." He made a face. "You know how it is when we find a dead cow."

"Yeah." Johnny preferred not to think about the aftereffects of death—the bugs, the bloating, the stench. . . "We'd best get him underground as quick as we can."

"All right." Cam took the spade from the wall. "Do you want to get him ready, or you want me to do it?"

"I will," Johnny said. As hard as it would be, he wanted to spend these last few minutes with Mark and examine his wounds again.

"I'll find a likely spot to dig, then. Water the horses first, eh?" Cam shouldered the spade and went out.

Johnny's steps dragged as he went out into the brilliant sunshine. The cow lowed piteously. He almost ignored her, but after taking buckets of water to Reckless and Cam's pinto, he went to the barn for a milk bucket and to see if Mark had a stool. Mark would wait another twenty minutes, but this cow needed relief. Besides, the milk would come in handy.

He let the motions of routine take over, numbing the jagged pain that tore at him. As he sat rhythmically milking away, leaning back a little so he didn't contact the cow's hot side, sweat trickled down his back and off his face. He laughed out loud. Grief would hit him soon. It was sure to. But this was too absurd. His brother lay dead a few yards away, and here he was milking a stupid cow.

As though she heard his thoughts, the cow flicked him in the face with her tail, the coarse hairs flogging him like tiny whiplashes.

"Is that all the thanks I get?" His thoughts turned back to his brother. If he'd been shot today, it must have been early morning, or else Mark would have milked the cow. So, around sunup. That was probably as close as they could come to pinpointing the time.

Johnny didn't bother to strip the cow dry. When the bucket was two-thirds full, he stood and set it away from the reach of her feet. He untied her and gave her flank a swat. "Go on now."

She eyed him balefully for a moment then ambled away. Johnny picked up the pail and walked to the house. Inside the doorway, he set the bucket down and went to Mark's side.

Drying blood soaked the front of Mark's shirt. The only comfort to Johnny was that it probably happened quick. He doubted his brother had lain there long, knowing he was dying. Nothing about the body or the floor around it suggested he had moved at all after he was shot.

Johnny walked slowly around the cabin. The kitchen area was in disarray, with a few supplies strewn about. Whoever killed Mark must have helped himself to the foodstuffs. They didn't take everything, though. A barrel half full of flour stood open below a worktable, and though the shelves had some empty spaces, several jars of preserves sat there intact, waiting for a hungry man to open them. A little more snooping revealed cornmeal, salt, and a small amount of dried peas.

Johnny walked over to the bunk built onto one wall. The covers were neatly spread, and his heart spasmed as he recognized an old patchwork quilt their mother had stitched. She had promised Johnny one, but it wasn't half finished when she died, so he never got his quilt.

He reached to pull it off the bunk and hesitated. Should he bury Mark in it? He hadn't seen any lumber lying around, from which he could make a coffin. But it seemed wrong to bury Mama's quilt. Maybe there was another blanket he could use.

A few garments hung from nails in the wall, and Johnny examined them. The white cotton shirt must be Mark's Sunday best. He could put that on him and remove the bloody chambray one. If he washed the blood off, Mark would look almost natural.

He got a basin of water and a rag and steeled himself to remove Mark's bloody shirt. He unbuttoned it and laid back the front pieces of the shirt. Two bullet holes. They had shot Mark twice in the chest. Johnny tried not to think too closely about that as he dabbed the blood away, but he couldn't help the pictures forming in his mind.

Cam walked in as he finished and was easing the ruined shirt off over Mark's lifeless arms. He stopped in the doorway.

"Did you milk the cow?"

"Yeah."

"Good. We can have some milk with our dinner." Cam stepped closer, frowning. "What are you doing?"

"Dressing him nice."

Cam squinted at the basin of bloody water and the clean white shirt Johnny had brought over.

"You're going to change his clothes?"

"Thought I would."

"You might want his things later on. He's not going to care what he has on."

Johnny paused in his ministrations. "Cam, he's my brother. I want to bury him nice."

After a moment, Cam said, "Sure. You do whatever you want. I'm gonna see if ol' Mark had any coffee."

"He never liked it," Johnny said.

Cam grunted and moved toward the kitchen area. Johnny decided to let him worry about what food was left. All he cared about for the moment was that his brother was going to be buried in a clean shirt, with his blood washed off him.

Sally waited until suppertime to break the news. Her stomach fluttered during the minister's blessing over the food. Effie would complain that the vegetables were cold after the lengthy prayer, but that was hardly Sally's fault.

After the *amen*s, the Reverend Mr. Winters reached for the meat loaf, and Effie pounced on the nappy filled with mashed potatoes. Sally had resisted the temptation to bake the potatoes, though it was much easier. Effie preferred them mashed, with plenty of butter, so Sally had taken the extra time to peel and mash them. She waited until the couple had heaped their plates and then helped herself to modest servings of meat loaf, potatoes, and squash. She doubted she would be able to eat much.

She watched Mr. Winters take a few bites. He didn't offer compliments, but his face relaxed into satisfied folds as he chewed the meat loaf. She had cooked it just the way he liked it, crispy around the edges, but well-done and juicy in the middle, with plenty of onions. Sally reached for her water glass and took a quick sip to moisten her dry mouth. When she set the tumbler down, it clunked on the table, earning her a scowl from Effie.

Sally quaked inside, but she didn't dare hold off until Mr. Winters's plate was nearly empty. Then he would launch into a discourse on next Sunday's sermon, or the reprobation of today's youth, or the greedy landgrab of the Europeans, who were carving up Africa however they pleased.

"We had a good meeting of the Ladies' Aid," Effie said.

Her husband swallowed. "How many were out?"

"Twelve. And we'll have another quilting tomorrow evening."

"Good, good."

Effie took a bite of the meat loaf then wiped her lips with her napkin. "Mrs. Haven's time is near. I told her I'd take a turn helping out after."

Cooking and keeping house for new mothers was one of the good works Effie seemed to enjoy. Sally wondered if it was because she had no children of her own. However it was, she always took a turn, and that had endeared her to some of the parishioners. Sally also volunteered for that duty, though handling the infants scraped a raw place on her heart.

She cleared her throat and looked toward the minister, not Effie. "It seems I shall be leaving you soon, sir."

Both the preacher and his wife stopped chewing. Mr. Winters froze with a forkful of potatoes in midair, and Effie's hand hovered over the salt cellar. Sally couldn't resist a quick glance, revealing Effie's gaping mouth.

"Yes." Sally decided the safest place to turn her gaze was her own plate. "I'll be returning to Texas straightaway."

"To Texas?" Mr. Winters stared. "This seems rather unexpected."

"I'm surprised you have the means to travel," Effie said.

Sally took a deep breath. "As you know, I've been corresponding with my family and—"

"And a man."

Effie made it sound tawdry, but Sally kept her chin up, though it may have trembled a little.

"Yes, a fine Christian man. I shall be married soon. My parents will be so pleased."

"Don't they know of your plans yet?" Mr. Winters cocked his head to one side.

Sally's cheeks heated. She would shamelessly dodge that question. "I meant, sir, that they will be pleased to see me settled. My intended is, as my father would say, all wool and a yard wide." She pushed back her chair. "Excuse me. I'll get the coffee."

She stayed in the kitchen longer than she had to, but her absence seemed prudent. Effie made no attempt to modulate her voice in the dining room, and Sally could hear their words clearly.

"I knew it! I knew she was up to no good."

"What do you mean?" The pastor's voice was less strident. "I thought you wished to see Mrs. Golding settled."

"Of course," Effie said, "but not like this." The minister murmured something, and Effie went on, "I shouldn't be surprised if she's never met the man! She's been writing him letters since way back before Christmas, but who knows how they made the connection? The newspapers have lurid advertisements almost every day for women to go and marry these rough miners and ranchers. He could be anyone. She could be walking into a life of slavery. Or worse. I wouldn't want to be too near the Mexican border, myself."

"But she said he's a fine Christian," the minister said. "And you've remarked on the lack of privacy since she came here. You'll have the freedom of your home back, my dear."

"We shall have to hire a girl to come in and do the heavy work, and that will mean wages." Effie made this sound like a dire thing.

"Perhaps we can find another woman who needs room and board. It's worked out well with Mrs. Golding, hasn't it?"

"Hmpf."

Sally smiled grimly to herself. More than ever, she was convinced the minister knew nothing of the small amounts of money she gave Effie. She poured out their coffee and set the cups on a tray with the cream pitcher. The sugar bowl stayed on the table next to the spoon holder, so she needn't worry about that. As she entered the dining room with the tray, Effie fixed her malevolent eyes on Sally.

"Does this *gentleman* have a name?"

"He does. Mark Paynter. He owns a cattle ranch." Sally was proud of herself for keeping her voice level, and she hoped they didn't ask how many cattle Mark owned, as his herd was yet very small. But it would grow and he would prosper, she was sure.

"I suppose he has half-a-dozen unruly children he wants you to raise for him." Effie's tone had turned a bit smug.

"Actually, no." Sally set the cups and saucers carefully onto the tablecloth. "He has been a bachelor up until this time."

"Oh, an older man," Effie persisted. "Set in his ways."

Sally shrugged and managed a slight smile. "I don't know all his eccentricities, of course, but he is two years older than I am." Effie opened her mouth again, but Sally said, "I see you're nearly finished with the main course. I've baked an apple pudding, and I'll bring it in directly." She tucked the tray under her arm and made herself walk slowly back to the kitchen, though she wanted to flee.

"Apple pudding," Mr. Winters said behind her. "That sounds very nice. We'll miss your cooking, Mrs. Golding."

Sally turned for a moment in the doorway. "Why, thank you, Reverend. It's kind of you to say so."

The skin around Effie's eyes contracted in wrinkles as she glared at Sally.

CHAPTER 3

Johnny rose when the first light of dawn crept through the one window in the cabin. Cam still slept on the floor. He had insisted Johnny take his brother's bed. Johnny stepped over him and tiptoed outside.

The sun was still below the horizon, and the air smelled sweet—breathably cool. He walked slowly around the yard and leaned on the corral fence. His horse and Cam's came over, gazing at him with large, hopeful eyes. Reckless nickered and snuffled his sleeve.

"Yeah, yeah," Johnny said. "I'll put you out in the pasture now." They hadn't dared turn out the horses the evening before—not with murderous robbers in the area. Keeping them close was their only defense, short of sleeping outside to guard them, and neither Johnny nor Cam wanted to do that. They'd slept in a house for the first time in weeks.

Johnny opened the gate between the small corral enclosure and the field. The days of open range were gone in Texas, and Mark had fenced quite a chunk of his land. Johnny couldn't help but be impressed with his brother's hard work.

He walked slowly behind the barn and up a gentle knoll to the spot Cam had chosen for Mark's grave. They hadn't marked it yet, but the newly turned earth showed where Mark lay. Johnny promised himself he would take care of that soon. A cross, at least. Maybe later he could have a stone made, but he was capable of putting together a decent cross and carving Mark's name on it.

He hauled in a deep breath as he stared at the burial plot. It wasn't right. Mark had never hurt anyone, and so far as Johnny knew, everybody liked him. It just wasn't right.

He turned back to the cabin. A few chickens flitted about the barnyard. Johnny approached them carefully and watched where they skittered off to.

Cam was standing in the cabin doorway, stretching, when Johnny ambled across the yard with four eggs in his hat. "What do you reckon?" Cam said.

"Gonna be hot again."

"I mean, what do you think we ought to do."

Johnny shrugged. "I still think we should ride into town and talk to the sheriff."

"I thought we settled that." Cam eyed him as if he were a six-year-old. "You're a wanted man, Johnny. This is a good place for us to lie low. If anyone comes around, we just tell them you're Mark's brother, and he's out tending his stock at the moment."

"We can't keep that up forever."

"We won't need to. And if it'll make you feel better, after a while, we can tell the town folks that Mark died and we buried him. We just won't say when."

Johnny let out a long, slow breath. He didn't like lying, and he was pretty sure it wasn't legal to dispose of a body without telling the authorities. He looked down into his hat. "I got four eggs."

A grin split Cam's tanned face. "Now you're talking. I'll bet we can scare up a real breakfast."

As they worked together to prepare the meal, Johnny mulled things over.

"Do you really think we're doing the right thing?" he asked as he fried the eggs.

"Seems to me like the only thing we *can* do." Cam eyed him keenly. "I thought staying around the Lone Pine would be a big mistake. I still do. And this isn't such a bad place. No one from Colorado will bother you here."

Johnny nodded. After all, they had come to Texas at his own suggestion. "It just doesn't feel right, you know?"

Cam set two forks on the table. "Look, Johnny, I don't really know what's best for you. If you really want to turn yourself in, maybe you should, so it won't eat at you."

Johnny swallowed hard.

"Of course, there's no guarantee you'd get a fair trial," Cam said. "Especially in a place where nobody knows you."

Johnny broke the yolk on two of the eggs before turning them. He like his cooked firm. What would happen to Mark's ranch? He was Mark's only living family, and he figured he was his brother's heir. But not if he wound up being hung for a murder he didn't commit. "What would you do if I did go to the law?"

"I don't know." Cam rubbed his jaw. "I suppose I'd go looking for a job."

"You wouldn't go back to Colorado?"

"Maybe. I'd have to do something. We're both flat broke."

Johnny blew out a deep breath. They hadn't found any money in their quick search of the house. Whoever killed Mark must have taken any cash he'd had. The supplies were minimal. If he and Cam stayed on, they'd have to go to town soon. But the small herd of cattle—mostly breeding cows and their calves—looked healthy. Besides that, Mark had provided a sturdy cabin; a small garden growing out back, though most of the plants were beginning to die off; and a flock of chickens scratching about the yard. Increasingly, keeping his head down made more sense. The two of them had everything they needed, and nobody would look for them here. No one in Texas knew about the killing. There was no reason to keep running.

The eggs were done, along with what bacon they'd had left in their saddlebags. Johnny took the frying pan over to the table, where Cam had set two plates and was pouring milk, their one plentiful commodity, into the only cups they'd found—one tin cup and a thick, ironstone mug.

Cam gave Johnny the mug. "We need to get some coffee soon."

Johnny grunted and slid the eggs and bacon onto their plates.

"What?" Cam asked.

"Nothing. You're right. We'll need some other stuff, too. And you're right that we don't have much money."

"Too bad those robbers got whatever your brother had."

They sat down and began to eat. After his eggs and bacon had disappeared, Cam said, "So, what do you think? I'll go along with whatever you decide."

Johnny clenched his jaw for a moment. "I reckon we should either stay here or keep moving. I'm sort of leaning toward staying."

Cam nodded. "The way I see it, we're broke, but we'd be worse off if we tried to move on."

"Guess so." Johnny picked up his last piece of bacon. "I reckon we can stay a few days, anyhow. Sort things out. Let Reckless rest his foot."

"Hey, maybe we could sell his cattle. That'd give us a stake."

Johnny didn't like it. Yes, Mark was dead, but did he have a right to sell off his brother's property? Next Cam would want to sell the whole ranch.

"Let's not be hasty," he said.

"Right. We may wind up eating those cattle." Cam rose and took his dishes to the worktable and set them in the empty dishpan with a clatter.

Johnny leaned back in his chair while he chewed the bacon and thought over their situation. "Cam, I'd like to clear my name in Denver, but I'm not sure that's possible."

"Likely not, unless you could show 'em something that would prove someone else killed Red Howell."

"Don't know how I could do that."

"You can't. Seems to me, disappearing is still the best solution, like you said. And here, you can ease into the countryside. We can work this ranch and make it pay, like Mark wanted." Cam eyed him closely. "We can do it, Johnny. I know we can."

Johnny tried to make that fit over his grief, but the hard knot still sat in his chest. Having a small ranch of his own was every cowpuncher's dream. But building up Mark's ranch wouldn't bring him back, and hiding from the law to do it. . . He tried to push that thought away. He hadn't done anything wrong.

From outside, a distant bellow wafted to them. Johnny shoved back his chair.

"I forgot about the cow. She'll need milking again."

Cam joined him and puttered about the barn, taking stock of their new assets. When Johnny had milked the cow, he let Cam turn her out while he carried the bucket of milk to the house. He set it in a corner with a dish towel draped over it. Mark must have had a springhouse, or a root cellar. Or maybe he kept things like milk down the well to keep them cool. He would have to explore those possibilities.

He noticed a drawer on the front of the worktable. He and Cam had missed it last night. Johnny pulled it open. A jumble of small items lay inside, and he took them out, one by one, in the dimness and held them up toward the window.

Two sheets of writing paper and an unused envelope he set aside. A pocket knife. A carriage bolt. A key, but to what? It looked too small for a door key.

The next item he recognized immediately. He'd seen the miniature portrait of his mother many times. Pa had insisted she have it made before he went off to fight in the war twenty-four years ago. Someone musthave sent it to Mark after she died. Johnny gazed at it for half a minute. He had no family left. Even after Ma and Pa died, he'd had Mark out here, where he could reach him if he really wanted to. He wiped a tear that trickled down his cheek and set the portrait on the table.

The drawer was nearly empty, and he fished out two horseshoe nails and a few coins totaling forty-five cents. Those he slipped in his pocket. Spending Mark's spare change didn't rankle him nearly as much as the thought of selling the herd or the land. He heard Cam's steps on the stoop and scooped the things back into the drawer and closed it.

"Bossie's all set. Now what?" Cam asked.

Johnny turned to face him. "I was wondering if Mark had a root cellar or anything like that. Maybe we should do some more looking around outside. And if we want to keep cooking, we need to find out where he got his firewood. Or maybe he burned mostly coal in that stove. There was some coal in the barn."

"All right. I guess there's plenty of work to do around here." Cam smiled at him. "Before you know it, this will feel like home sweet home."

―――――

Sally settled into her seat on the train, her heart pounding. She had actually done it.

She scooted over to the window and gazed out at the back of the station and the freight cars standing in the rail yard. She hoped she would never see St. Louis again.

Face turned to the window, she waited for the wheels to turn, taking her to her new life.

"Beg pardon," a man said. "Might I sit here?"

Sally looked up at the middle-aged gentleman. He had a large mustache, and his sack suit, felt hat, walking stick, and folded newspaper told her that he wasn't wealthy but at least a part of the respectable middle class. A quick glance about revealed that the car's seats were filling fast, so she didn't suspect he had ulterior motives.

"Of course." She shifted her handbag to the window side and made sure her skirt didn't spill over onto his part of the seat. She had worn her mourning gown but had a new traveling dress in her luggage. She had been able to purchase cloth for the new dress with the money she'd received for making Mrs. DeVeer's outfit. For the last two nights, she had sat up stitching it. She hoped she'd find an opportunity to change shortly before they reached Beaumont. She wanted to arrive looking fresh, not rumpled and dusty. She hoped Mark would like the new dress.

The man removed his hat and stuck it and his stick in the rack above the seats then sat down with a sigh.

"William Thormon," he said with a brief smile.

"Oh, Sally Golding." She extended her gloved hand, and he took it for a moment.

"Traveling far?" he asked.

"Yes. Beaumont, Texas."

"Texas?" He eyed her keenly. "And I thought my jaunt to Tulsa was a wearisome distance. Whereabouts is Beaumont?"

"Southeastern Texas."

"Near the coast?"

Sally nodded. "It's east of Galveston and Houston. Not far from the Louisiana line, actually."

"Hmm. It'll be hot down there." He eyed her black dress and shawl.

"Yes." Sally didn't think she owed him an explanation of why she was going. He could plainly see that she was widowed. But he seemed like a decent man, and she didn't want him to think otherwise of her. "I have family there."

"Of course." He seemed relieved and opened his newspaper.

Sally folded her hands demurely in her lap. Through the black cotton of her gloves, she could feel her thin, gold wedding band. She had almost discarded it after David died but thought better of it. She was glad she'd kept it when she moved into the Winterses' home. The reverend would surely have disapproved if she'd stopped wearing it.

She had held on to it for the journey, too. All along she had known that somehow she would leave St. Louis, and whether she returned to her parents' home or went elsewhere to make a new start, the ring would lend her a modicum of respectability, and perhaps even protection. Predatory men would think twice about pursuing a woman who wore a wedding ring.

She glanced at Mr. Thormon. He seemed engrossed in his newspaper, but he looked up and smiled, as though he had sensed her gaze upon him.

"May I offer you my paper when I've finished with it?"

"Oh, well—yes, thank you. When you're done. That would be nice."

He nodded and went back to his reading.

Sally felt her face flush. She certainly didn't want the gentleman to think she was grasping or flirtatious. She turned toward the window. They had left the city behind and were hurtling across the plains. The trees and fence posts in the foreground whipped past so fast, her stomach started to lurch. Better to focus on something more distant. A herd of cattle, gently sloping hills.

After a few minutes, she closed her eyes and leaned her head against the window frame. Soon she would be with Mark. Though she had never met him face-to-face, she knew he was one of the kindest, most considerate men on earth. And he knew so much about ranching and cattle. They would make a success of the ranch—she knew it. Mark had written to her that the last winter had been hard, and rain was scarce this spring. But God would provide what they needed. He would sell off his steers, and together they would subsist in the snug little house Mark had described in detail.

Even living frugally on an isolated ranch would be better than life with the Reverend and Mrs. Winters. Effie's disapproval had turned to hostility during the past week after Sally announced her departure. When her husband wasn't around, she had begrudged Sally every mouthful of food and berated her for leaving them without a housekeeper. Sally had set her jaw and completed the long list of chores Effie gave her each day. Telling herself she was doing it for Mark and for their future together helped Sally get through it. She had found it hard to squeeze out time to go and purchase her ticket and collect her pay from Mrs. DeVeer.

"Shirking your tasks," Effie had scolded when she returned to the parsonage.

"I had to finish up some business and buy my ticket," Sally had replied.

Effie eyed the package that held her dress goods. "And what's that? Surely you're not taking on more outside sewing when you should be tending to things here."

"No, it's not outside sewing." Sally had scurried up the back stairs and out of earshot, but the last few days of her visit were almost unbearable under Effie's mean eye and sharp tongue.

But Sally was here now, on the train to Texas, and the man she loved was waiting for her.

The man she ought to have married the first time, she thought, and then stifled the notion. If God had wanted her to marry Mark back then, He'd have brought him across her path before she became attached to David. Which wasn't to say God had wanted her to marry David Golding. Sally now believed that was the worst error of judgment she had ever made. But God had smiled on her now. He was giving her a second chance with Mark Paynter.

———

For the next two days, Johnny and Cam worked around the ranch. Johnny found a few extra horseshoes and tools that allowed him to replace the shoe Reckless had lost. They patched the roof over the bunk and then checked the forty-eight cattle to make sure they were all healthy and properly branded with Mark's MP brand. They discovered the root cellar, which contained a few potatoes and turnips. Johnny made a batch of butter by shaking cream in a jar until his arm ached. Cam heated a big kettle of water over an open fire, and they washed their clothes. They went through Mark's small wardrobe and decided what things each of them could use.

On the third day, they knew they couldn't put off going to town any longer. Cam was getting antsy for coffee, and the other supplies were running low. They ate eggs and pancakes at every meal. Johnny finally admitted he was hankering for something sweet, and they saddled their horses and rode the way they'd been headed when they came to the ranch.

The sun beat down on them. Johnny hoped it wasn't too far. They crossed over a plank bridge that spanned a trickle of water. He took that as a sign of civilization. About five miles out from the ranch, they topped a slight rise in the nearly flat range, and Beaumont spread before them.

They rode in at a slow trot, taking in the offerings of town. To Johnny's surprise, most of the businesses sat within a hundred yards of a river, and despite the recent hot weather, it flowed along with an impressive water level. Stock pens covered at least an acre of ground, and a large building near the waterfront bore a sign declaring it a rice mill.

"Rice?" Cam shook his head. "Who'd have thought it was wet enough to grow rice here?"

They let the horses plod along until they passed a sawmill and came into the retail district. The main street boasted a mercantile, a haberdashery, a bank, a hotel, a boardinghouse, a bakery, and farther along, a train station. Johnny counted three saloons, and he was sure there were others down the road, but Cam had pulled aside and dismounted in front of the first saloon.

Johnny hitched Reckless to the rail before the building and followed Cam into the low-ceilinged twilight. He let his eyes adjust for a moment and joined Cam at the bar.

"Them fellers didn't care who got in the way," a man was saying to the bartender, who nodded sagely while a few other men leaned on the bar and listened.

"I feel bad for Frank Simon, getting shot like that," another man said.

The bartender nodded. "We all do. The doc says it'll take him a month or two to get back on his feet." He sized up Johnny and Cam as he spoke. "You new in town?" he asked Cam.

"Yeah, I'm out to Paynter's place," Cam said with a nod toward Johnny. "What's going on?"

"Oh, it was three or four days ago now," the bartender said. "Half-a-dozen hooligans rode in and tried to rob the bank. The fella what owns the grocery came out with a gun to help stop 'em, and they shot him. The sheriff came along then, 'cause he'd heard the gunfire, and he and a couple other fellas ran 'em off, but old Frank won't soon forget it."

"Outlaws," Johnny looked at Cam.

"I'm surprised you hadn't heard about it out to your place," the first man said, eyeing Johnny.

The bartender slid two glasses of beer toward them. Johnny put some coins on the bar, and he and Cam carried their refreshment to a table. Johnny hated beer. He'd tried it once, in Denver, and swore he would never drink it again. His mother would be happy if she'd known. But he didn't want to cause a stir by refusing it today.

"They must be talking about the ones who killed Mark," he whispered to Cam.

Cam nodded. "The timing's right." He took a big swig of his drink.

"We should tell the sheriff."

"No," Cam said. "We can't. Didn't you hear? They think you're Mark."

"You think so?" Johnny glanced toward the cluster of men at the bar.

"Hey, Paynter," one of them called, "You sure you didn't see nothing out your way? The sheriff thought they rode in from the north."

Johnny opened his mouth. Now was the time to set the matter straight. And the time when Cam kicked his ankle under the table.

"No," he said.

He'd done it now. He had lied. Whether out of shock, reflex, or intent to deceive, it was done.

"We should go," he said to Cam in a low voice.

Cam picked up his half-empty mug. "Hold on." He glugged down the rest of his beer and eyed Johnny's full glass. "You leavin' that?"

Johnny nodded. Cam reached over and picked it up. He drank half of it down and set the glass on the table.

"All right. Come on."

Outside, Johnny turned on him.

"Now what do we do?"

Cam eyed him critically in the harsh daylight. "You do look like him. 'Course, Mark didn't have a beard. But I'll bet you could pass for him even if you shaved. Maybe better'n now."

"Stop it. We need to straighten this out."

"Too late."

Johnny's stomach heaved, even though he hadn't drunk anything.

"I want to see the sheriff."

"I thought you'd changed your mind about that."

Johnny didn't know what to say. He couldn't think straight.

Cam stepped closer and put a hand on his sleeve. "If that's what you really want to do, I'll go with you."

Johnny looked up at him. "Really?"

"Sure. I told you the other day, it's up to you. Of course, even if the sheriff believes our story, he's going to wonder where we came from, and how we just happened to show up at Mark's place the same day he was killed."

Johnny's throat squeezed so tight he could hardly breathe. "Those outlaws. They came into town after they killed Mark."

"That's right." They stood for a moment, gazing at each other.

Johnny lowered his voice. "They couldn't suspect us of committing this robbery in town, could they?"

"I dunno." Cam glanced back at the saloon door. "For sure they'd realize whoever shot up the town killed Mark, too."

"It might sway them to think we did it all." Johnny stared into Cam's troubled brown eyes. Would confessing who he really was put his friend in danger of hanging? Cam had stuck by him through thick and thin. Johnny couldn't cast suspicion on him.

He could feel his friend's agitation, and he didn't like it. At last he ripped his gaze away. "Come on. We've got to get some supplies."

"That's right," Cam said. "And we'd best not stay in town too long, or people might start asking more questions. You go to the feed store for a sack of chicken feed, and I'll see if the mercantile across the street has got coffee."

"Get some bacon, too," Johnny said, "and a little bit of sugar."

"I've only got fifty cents."

"Yeah. Well, get what you can."

Johnny mounted Reckless and rode down the main street. He wasn't sure where the feed store was, but he hated to ask anyone. They would think it odd that Mark Paynter didn't know his way around town. Johnny wasn't comfortable letting them think he was his brother, but he was now more afraid of telling them he wasn't Mark.

He reached the end of the business district. The buildings got farther apart, and houses scattered out into the countryside. He turned back and headed Reckless down a side street, toward the river. He was rewarded by the sight of a livery stable with a smithy attached, and beyond it a feed store. He tied the horse out front and stepped inside.

Two men were talking near a rough counter. The man behind it looked up and said, "Morning."

The second man turned toward him with the nonchalant air of one curious to see who the wind blew in. Johnny stopped and tried not to stare at the shiny star glinting on his vest.

The sheriff frowned at him. "Paynter, that you?"

CHAPTER 4

O f course it's him," the store owner said. "Mark's just growed a
beard." He nodded at Johnny, smiling.

"Sorry," the sheriff said. "Didn't recognize you with the whiskers."

Johnny's heart pounded. "I, uh, was out on the range for a few days
without my razor and decided when I got home to keep it."

His gut wrenched. He couldn't undo it now. He'd lied to the sheriff, and he couldn't take it back. He felt sick. This was worse than having a glass of beer, and he knew it. Ma would be so ashamed of him.

"Well, I'd best be getting on," the sheriff said, picking his hat up off
the counter. "See ya, Mel." He nodded at Johnny. "Stay alert, Paynter.
Some raiders are on the loose."

Johnny swallowed hard. "Do you think they've left the area?"

"Hope so, but you never know."

"I'll be careful." Johnny felt like a traitor. He made himself turn
away and not watch the sheriff walk out.

"What can I get ya, Mark?" the owner asked.

"Sack of chicken feed," Johnny said.

"Coming right up." Mel walked around the end of the counter and
over to a stack of full feed sacks.

"Uh, I've only got my horse today," Johnny said, eyeing the hundred-
pound burlap sacks. "No wagon." A buckboard sat beside Mark's barn,
back at the ranch.

"You want a fifty-pound sack instead?"

"Probably best. I'll come in with the wagon soon and get some more. And some oats."

"Whenever you're ready." Mel brought over the smaller sack, which was still plenty big. "You want that on your tab?"

"Uh. . .sure."

Johnny took the sack and carried it out on his shoulder. He eased it up onto Reckless's haunches and tied it in place, feeling even worse. He'd gotten this feed under false pretenses—and how big a tab did Mark have?

He rode slowly back toward the mercantile on the main street. Cam was just stowing some parcels in his saddlebags. He looked at the sack of feed behind Johnny's saddle and nodded.

"Good, you got it. I got the coffee, some bacon, and some beans and cornmeal. And the sugar you wanted."

"You had enough money, I guess?"

Cam shook his head. "When I told the storekeeper I was Mark Paynter's new hand, he offered to put the coffee and other stuff on Mark's account."

"The same happened to me," Johnny said.

"Seems we've stumbled onto a good thing." Cam grinned and swung into the saddle.

Johnny didn't like it, but he didn't say anything, as other people were going in and out of the mercantile.

When they had left the center of town, Cam glanced around and said, "This is great! You can pick up your brother's life, assuming no one in town knew Mark too well."

"I don't think that's a good idea. Besides, the sheriff was in the feed store."

Cam's features sharpened. "Oh? Did he speak to you?"

"Yeah."

"Did he know you? Or think he knew you?"

"Not at first, but the owner said I'd grown a beard, and then he seemed to accept it."

Cam laughed. "People see what they want to see."

Johnny shook his head. "I don't like it, the whole idea of it. I don't want to live a lie."

Cam sat back in his saddle. "Well, let's just think about it for a while and see what develops."

They rode back to the ranch in near silence. Johnny put the coffee and other supplies away, while Cam stowed the chicken feed in a barrel in the barn. With sundown, the temperature cooled, and for the first time, Johnny didn't mind making a fire in the stove. He stirred up some corn bread to go with their bacon and beans.

Cam smacked his lips over the corn bread. "Nice to have a hot meal."

Johnny grunted. "You can cook next time. I made plenty, so we can have some tomorrow without heating up the place again."

"Good strategy." Cam reached for another slab of corn bread. "Your johnnycake's almost as good as my stepmother's."

Johnny smiled at that, but he hoped Cam wouldn't somehow rope him into doing all the cooking. Cam had a way of doing the chores he wanted to do and getting someone else to do the rest. But now Johnny was the only other person around to take up the slack. He liked Cam, mostly, but some of his friend's quirks grated on him. He recalled that back at the Lone Pine, Cam had often come in two-thirds drunk after his evening off. When that happened, it was best to stay out of his way until he'd slept it off. But no one could handle a branding iron as well as Cam, or string wire as tight.

When they had finished eating, Cam took his plate and flatware to the dishpan and tossed it in with a clatter.

"Hey! Easy on the dishes," Johnny said. "We'll be eating off our tin camp plates next thing you know."

"Sorry." Cam put on his hat. "Guess I'll mosey out and see how the cattle are doing."

"What about the dishes?"

"What about 'em?"

Johnny frowned. "Well, I cooked. Seems as if you'd oughta wash the dishes tonight."

"There's hardly any."

"There's plenty. Cooking makes dirty dishes, you know. Besides, they'll dry on and stick if we don't wash them up now."

"You sound like an old woman," Cam said.

Johnny glared at him, feeling the heat in his face. "Sorry, but I like to eat off clean dishes, not ones full of cockroaches and mold."

Cam laughed and walked out the door.

Johnny huffed out a breath in frustration. He felt the way he had when his big brother had teased him or told him he wasn't "big enough" to do something. Only Mark had always come back and made things up later.

Mechanically, Johnny poured what hot water was left in the teakettle into the dishpan and ladled in enough cold from a bucket so he could put his hands in it. Mark had left scraps of soap in a mesh cage on a dish nearby, and Johnny swished it through the water until a satisfying skim of bubbles had formed on the surface. With a sigh, he sank his plate and Cam's in the soapy water.

By the time Cam came in, the dishes were put away and the kitchen was tidy. Johnny kept the fire going just enough to keep the cabin comfortable and heat a fresh pot of coffee. Cam stood in the doorway and looked around, nodded, and closed the door behind him.

"Why you burning candles?"

"Forgot to get lamp oil."

"Hmpf." Cam sat down on the bench near the stove and pried his boots off. "I woulda done those dishes."

"I know," Johnny said, and he realized he was lying again. Would it get easier every time he did it? He didn't want to be a liar. Ever. But he was. Today he had lied at least three times. "I don't want to do it," he said with sudden decision.

"What? The dishes?"

"No. Pretend to be Mark."

"Kind of late now, Johnny."

"Maybe if I shave, we can start over. Go into town tomorrow and tell them Mark's dead."

Cam shook his head and set his boots aside. "They'd know right away it was you they saw today."

"All right then, we wait a few days. A week, maybe. Next time we need supplies."

"It won't work. How would you say he died? If you tell him the outlaws did it, they'd know we lied today."

"We could say he got sick."

"What kind of sickness takes a man that fast and ain't catching?"

"I don't know."

"You've gotta have a better plan than that." Cam got up and walked over to the cupboard. He took out the pan of corn bread and lifted a slab.

"Hey, that's for tomorrow," Johnny said.

"Just one piece." Cam took it and slid the pan back into the cupboard. He took his clean coffee cup from the shelf and poured himself a cupful then ambled back to the bench and plunked down. "You can't let your guilt get the best of you."

Johnny fell silent. He sat for a long time on the edge of the bunk, watching Cam eat the corn bread, brush the crumbs off his shirt onto what had been a clean floor, and guzzle the coffee.

"There's one thing keeping me from telling the sheriff," he said at last.

"What's that?"

"I don't want him to think we're both outlaws. I'm sorry I brought you here, Cam. I've put you in a bad place."

"No," Cam said. "Don't feel like that."

"It's true. If I start telling the truth now, the whole town will think we're both killers."

"Hey, cut that out." Cam went to the cupboard and got the other cup. He filled it with coffee and brought it over to Johnny. "Here, drink this. We're going to make a new start."

"We are?" Johnny eyed him doubtfully.

"Sure we are. You're right that you can't tell the sheriff about Mark. That chance is gone now. But we can both go on from here and make a good, honest go of it. We'll be the best ranchers this town has ever had."

———

The train slowed, and Sally braced herself against the seat ahead of her. They were stopping, and she ought to get out and walk around.

"This is my stop," said the portly woman next to her. "I hope the rest of your journey is pleasant."

"Thank you," Sally said with a wan smile.

"You should eat something," her seatmate recommended, fumbling for her shawl, handbag, a parcel, and a parasol. "I don't believe you've eaten a thing since I boarded this morning."

Sally ignored the last remark and waited until the passengers disembarking had gathered their belongings and left the car. Slowly, she stood, clinging to the seat back. Her head swam. She closed her eyes and waited for the dizziness to pass.

"Are you all right, ma'am?"

She opened her eyes. The dark-skinned porter stood in the aisle, concern written in his features.

"Just a little woozy," she managed. "Stood up too fast, I imagine."

"We'll be here a half hour, if you'd like to have a stroll or get something to eat."

"Yes, thank you. That would be nice." Clutching her handbag to her side, she stepped cautiously into the aisle. The porter nodded and moved on down the car. When she reached the steps, Sally had a moment when she feared she would pitch down them headlong, but another uniformed man appeared at the bottom, extending a hand.

"May I assist you, ma'am?"

"Thank you." She plummeted down the last step, which jolted her, and the man steadied her.

"All right?"

"Yes. How long until we reach Beaumont?"

"Beaumont? Let's see. . . ." He rolled his eyes upward for a moment, as if the line's timetable were written somewhere up there. "Not until tomorrow morning, about ten o'clock, I'd say."

"Thank you." Another night on the train. At least the seats on this one leaned back. Sally tried to console herself with the thought that in less than twenty hours, she would be with Mark. She hoped they would have another stop long enough for her to get her valise and change clothes. She didn't want to spend the night in her new dress. The black would do for a few more hours, though it had grown rather grimy.

She walked slowly toward the station. To one side of the ticket window was another where people could send telegrams. She wished she had enough to send Mark a message confirming the time of her arrival, but telegrams cost thirty cents a word. Her meager funds had dwindled to eighty cents. That was plenty for food between here and Beaumont if she continued to eat sparingly, but it wasn't enough for even three words in a telegram, so that option was out. She hoped the information she had sent him when she posted her final letter in St. Louis was accurate enough for him to know he should meet her at the station in Beaumont tomorrow. She would have to trust the Lord that everything would work out.

The smells from a luncheon counter inside the station made her stomach clench. The lady on the train was right—she should eat something. Maybe that would take care of this lightheaded feeling.

Fifteen minutes later, Sally settled back into her seat on the train. She could have lingered a few more minutes, but she wanted to make sure she had no chance of missing the train and that no one else claimed her familiar seat. She had drunk a cup of lukewarm tea and eaten a sandwich, and she had an apple in her handbag, along with a biscuit stuffed with cheese and sliced ham, wrapped in a napkin. She would eat those later today, and maybe that would get her through to Beaumont, where Mark would be responsible for her welfare. She hoped so, because food at the train depots cost much more than it would in other places, and she now had only twenty cents left. If she could just get through today and tonight, Mark would take care of her.

———

Rain at last. Not a hard, soaking rain, but at least it came down. Johnny had feared they were in for a first-class drought.

"What should we do today?" Cam asked.

"I brought that harness in," Johnny said.

"What good will that do? My horse never pulled a wagon before. Did yours?"

Johnny shook his head. He'd never tried to hitch Reckless to anything, and the cow pony probably wouldn't like it. "Sometime we'll want to use that wagon. Stockpile some horse feed and some coal."

Cam shrugged. "Fine."

"And I've been thinking we could build another bunk in here. There's a couple of boards out in the barn. It's not enough, but it would be a start."

"I am tired of sleeping on the floor." Cam sighed and shoved himself to his feet. "All right, I'll oil the harness if you want to work on that."

Johnny gazed up at the rafters, but he couldn't see anything useful above them. "Maybe if I poke around, I'll find a few more pieces of wood." That would mean going out to the barn, but the rain would let up after a while. In the meantime, he could clear the space where he'd been thinking of putting Cam's bed. They'd be squeezed for floor space, but they'd worry about that later. If they stayed very long, they could add on to the cabin. But he didn't want to think that far into the future.

They puttered around, and the day dragged. When he went out in the drizzle to fetch more water, Johnny thought maybe a windlass for the well should be his next project.

That afternoon, while Cam sat at the table, humming and rubbing neat's-foot oil into the leather, Johnny took the broom and swept the side of the room farthest from the stove. He figured he had found enough boards now for a bunk frame. Might as well sweep up and start building Cam's bed.

He poked around under his bed with the broom and was rewarded with a nail and a penny, both useful items. He prodded farther into the corner beneath the bed with the broom. It thunked against something back by the wall. He turned the broom around, poked it again with the handle, and got a hollow thud.

Johnny lay on his stomach and peered under the bunk. Way back against the wall was a box of some kind. He wriggled under the bed until he could grasp it and pulled it out.

As he emerged backward from beneath the overhanging quilt, Cam said, "What on earth are you doing?"

"Found something." Johnny slid the small wooden box out the last foot and studied it. Made of pine, the lid was intricately carved, and he was certain Mark had crafted the box. Both brothers had developed a talent for woodcarving at their grandfather's knee.

Cam came over and gazed down at the geometric pattern. "Nice box."

"Yeah." Johnny picked it up and set it on the bunk. A small lock was set into the front of the box. He tried to lift the lid.

"Locked?" Cam asked.

"Yeah." Johnny got up and walked over to the worktable, where he opened the drawer and rummaged through the small items there. He came out with the key.

"What's that?" Cam asked.

"A little key. I found it a couple of days ago, but I didn't know what it went to." He fitted it into the lock and turned it. It gave a satisfying click. He opened the lid. "Papers."

"Any cash?" Cam leaned in close to look.

Johnny lifted the items out—a loose envelope and a packet of letters tied together with a short piece of twine. On the bottom were a few folded sheets of paper. He smoothed out the creases on the first one.

"This is the deed to the ranch."

"Let me see."

Johnny passed it over, and Cam carried it near the window. "Looks like he owned it free and clear."

"That's good." Johnny fished out the last item. "This looks like a receipt for fifty head of cattle. Bought last fall."

"Better and better," Cam said. "Your brother did things nice and legal, and he kept his business tidy."

"Yeah, seems like it." Johnny had never had papers to keep track of. He just went from job to job and punched cattle. Mark had really started to make something of himself, as a landowner and a ranchman. He'd always been a big brother to look up to. Johnny wished he had stayed closer to Mark and learned his steady ways.

He studied the receipt. "If he bought fifty head, where are they? There's not that many now, unless you count every calf, and they're mostly only a few weeks old."

"I dunno. Maybe some of them are in another pasture, or maybe he sold them already. What's the rest of that stuff?" Cam asked.

"Well, here's another receipt. . .for the cookstove." He wondered why Mark had spent so much on a fancy kitchen range. He could have gotten along fine with a smaller heating stove for the short Texas winter and a bachelor's cooking needs.

Johnny picked up the loose envelope. "Huh. This is from me. I remember I wrote to him a year or so ago, to tell him where I was at." He took out the scribbled note and gazed at it. He had never been much of a correspondent. But Mark had thought enough of him to keep his note, with the address on it—the Lone Pine Ranch, where Johnny was accused of killing his foreman.

Cam reached for the letter, and Johnny gave it to him. Cam glanced at it. "We should probably burn this."

Johnny swallowed hard. Cam was right—if he never wanted anyone here to know Mark had a brother. If anyone saw that note, they could connect him to the ranch in Colorado—and Red Howell's murder. He gave a curt nod. Cam walked over to the stove and fitted the handle into one of the round lids on top. He lifted it and tossed the letter into the firebox. Johnny shuddered and turned back to the treasure trove. The packet of letters was the only thing left.

He picked up the whole bunch and squinted at the handwriting and the postmark on the top one. He didn't recognize the hand, and he didn't know anyone in St. Louis. He slid the twine off and fanned out the letters. Must be a dozen or more, and all from the same person. The writing was gentle and curly. Cam walked over beside him.

"Well?"

"I don't know," Johnny said. "They're all letters from St. Louis."

"Anyone in your family there?"

"No."

Cam took the top one. As he removed the missive from the envelope, Johnny studied the others.

"He stacked them with the newest ones on the bottom. That would be the oldest."

Cam shook out the sheets of paper. "*Hmm.* Whoever it's from had a lot to say. It was written in December." He flipped to the back page. "Sally. Who's Sally?"

Johnny's throat went dry. Mark had a whole life he knew nothing about. "I dunno."

Cam went back to the front page. "Dear Mr. Paynter, I take pen in hand—"

"Hold on," Johnny said.

"What?"

"Do you think we ought to read those?"

"Why not?" Cam sounded slightly annoyed.

"Well, you know. They're private. This Sally person didn't expect anyone but Mark to read them."

Cam sighed. "Johnny, listen to me. Mark is dead. This is sort of a relic. It may help us know more about him. You want that, don't you?"

"Well. . ."

"It can't hurt anyone if we read them now."

Johnny wasn't sure about that. But if this Sally was a good friend of Mark's, maybe someone should write and tell her he was dead. Cam wouldn't like that, though, he was sure.

"Pen in hand"—Cam scanned the words and found his place—"with great hesitation. I am a widow now living in St. Louis, where my late husband and I resided. He passed away more than a year ago, and I have lately resided in the home of a kind minister and his wife. I have never replied to an advertisement before—"

Johnny reached over and grabbed Cam's arm. "Good night! Mark placed an ad for one of those mail-order bride women!"

"Sounds like it."

Johnny's stomach felt a little dodgy. He would never have imagined Mark doing such a thing.

Cam cleared his throat. "But I summoned courage to do so when I saw that you live in Texas, which is where I grew up. My family lives to the north of you, near Fort Belknap. You describe yourself as a starting rancher. Sir, I assure you that I am capable of making a ranchman a good wife. I was raised practically on horseback, and I often helped out with the livestock on our small holdings. My father has a freighting business, and two of my brothers are now partners with him. It would give me great joy to return to Texas and make a home there." Cam looked up. "Sounds a little desperate, don't you think?"

"Hard to tell." The more Cam read, the more wrong it seemed to be reading this and witnessing the poor woman's exposure of her personal life.

"Let's see. . . . She says, 'You've probably received many replies to your advertisement. I don't know what to tell you that would keep you from passing over mine. You are thirty years old. Well, I am twenty-eight. Some women might shave off a few years in the telling, but I feel honesty is the best foundation for a relationship. Sir, I have no children and would expect nothing from you other than a home and a chance to begin a new life. I tell you frankly that I have few assets. My husband left me nothing, and I am now earning my keep by cooking and keeping house for the minister. I also do some sewing for people, and I could stitch clothing for you and any ranch hands you might have. I am in good health and used to hard work.' "

Johnny felt his face flush at the revelation of these intimate details. The whole thing made him feel a bit sad.

"Finally, sir, if you see fit to answer, please direct your letter to the address below. Very truly yours, Sally V. Golding, in care of the Reverend Mr. Elijah Winters, General Delivery, St. Louis, Missouri."

Cam lowered the letter, and they stared at each other for a long moment.

"Quick," Cam said. "Give me the newest one."

Johnny fumbled with the stack of envelopes and gave him the bottom one. Cam whipped a single sheet out of the envelope.

"Dear Mark, I cannot express my joy and delight on receiving your last letter. I know it is not the fashion to appear too eager, but if the truth were told, I do not wish to put off for one unnecessary minute being at your side. Yes, dear man, I happily will be your wife. It pains me to have to accept your offer of train fare, but I have been completely honest with you about my circumstances. I assure you, I shall make a frugal housewife, as I have had to learn those lessons in a hard school. As soon as you send it, my dear, I shall buy my ticket and let you know when to expect me in Beaumont. And now I must get to my sewing. Farewell, dear heart, and with God's blessing we shall soon meet face-to-face. Sincerely yours, Sally Golding."

Johnny's jaw had dropped halfway through this recital, and it was all he could do to draw breath. His ribs squeezed his lungs too tight, and he thought he might never recover.

"Sounds like he's gone and done it," Cam said.

Johnny nodded slowly. Mark had planned to be married. And soon.

CHAPTER 5

"This could ruin everything," Cam said, scrutinizing the final letter.

Johnny stood and strode to his side then snatched the letter from his hand. "When did she write this?"

"About two weeks ago."

"Two weeks?" Johnny's breathing came fast and shallow. "Cam, what do we do?"

"Calm down." Cam paced to the stove and back. "First of all, are you sure that's the latest one?"

Johnny went back to the bunk and riffled through all the letters. "Pretty sure."

"It takes a while for a letter to get to St. Louis."

"Not that long with the railroad lines."

Cam snapped his fingers. "We need to check at the post office. There could be another one waiting there for Mark."

Johnny put a hand up to his thick hair and grabbed onto a lock, tugging it until it hurt. "Why didn't we think to check the post office when we went to town?"

"I don't know, but we'll do it today. No, wait." Cam hurried to the peg rack near the door and took down his hat. "I'll go. The postmaster probably saw Mark every single time he went to town. If anyone would know you weren't him, the postmaster would be a likely candidate."

"What am I supposed to do?" Johnny managed to breathe now, but a tight knot had settled near his breastbone.

"You stay here. Read those other letters through, so we know everything she's told him. And take particular notice of what she knows about him."

"I can do that." It made sense. Johnny walked over to the bunk and plunked down with the rest of the letters.

"I shouldn't be more than an hour or two. At least the rain's let up." Cam clapped on his hat and went out, slamming the door behind him.

Johnny's hand shook as he took the second letter from the envelope. What had they gotten into? He had finished reading it when he heard the hoofbeats of Cam's horse as he loped off toward town. Sally had expanded on her daily life and her hopes of being useful and having a family of her own one day. She sounded like a nice young woman—churchgoing, hardworking, vulnerable, but with an inner strength. He opened the next one.

I come from a large family, Sally had written. *I do miss my parents, and all of my siblings. I haven't seen any of them in more than five years. I'm glad you still have your brother, even though your parents are gone. Maybe someday I shall have the pleasure of meeting him.*

Johnny's heart raced. She was talking about him! Mark had told her that he had a brother.

He lay back on the pillow and stared up at the open rafters.

"Well, that tears it."

———

The closer they got to Beaumont, the more nervous Sally became. Her palms began to perspire, and she peeled off her gloves.

What if Mark didn't like her?

It was different, writing something in a letter and reading what someone wrote, than it was talking in person. What if he took exception to some aspect of her appearance, or her turn of speech, or the way she did things?

But no. He couldn't write the things he had and be mean or stupid or thoughtless.

She didn't need to take out his letters in order to recall what he had said in each one. She treasured them and had gone over them time after time in her attic room. Mark seemed open and eager to know everything about her. She had told him things she had never revealed to anyone else. Had she told him too much?

He had been so sweet and kind about her marriage to David. *You don't need to tell me anything you don't want to,* he had written in one of his last letters. *But I want you to know that you can tell me anything at all. I feel we are one in our hopes and dreams, in our faith and aspirations. I would not judge you harshly, because I know you now, and I am sure that you have always done what you felt was the right thing at the time. I know from things you have hinted at that you were not happy, even before Mr. Golding met his end. If you wish to tell me about it, now or later, I shall be a sympathetic listener. If not, I shall still be a staunch friend. It's true I want to know every detail of your life, but my dear, the last thing I want is to put you in discomfort. So share with me those things that you want to tell and keep the rest in your heart for later, after you know me better and trust me more.*

She smiled to herself as the train clattered onward. How could she ever trust him more? She had revealed to him her innermost secrets after that, even about the two babies. She had cried when she wrote the words and had to blot the letter before she could continue. But she had trusted him with the knowledge that each of her miscarriages had happened after one of David's fits of anger. Mark could draw his conclusions from that.

It had only been fair to tell a man seeking marriage about it, and to assure him that the doctor had said he thought she would be able to have other children. She couldn't enter into marriage without him knowing that, because most men—most normal men, she told herself—wanted children.

And how sweet and kind his reply had been! *My dearest, I have never spoken or written words like these before, but I want you near me. I want to take care of you, to cradle you in tenderness and protect you from violence. Dearest Sally, a woman like you should never have to endure those things. Yes, our life will be hard here on the ranch, but I hope and pray that it will be easier than what you have borne heretofore.*

She closed her eyes in prayer. Any man who could write a letter that sensitive must be a man of great faith and courage. He knew the worst, and he still wanted her as his wife.

"Please, Lord," Sally whispered, "don't let anything come between us now."

———

When Johnny had finished the next-to-last of Sally Golding's letters, he reread the final installment—the one Cam had read earlier. It all made so much sense now. And yet it didn't in a way. He'd never dreamed his brother could be so eloquent, or so passionate. If anyone had asked him about Mark, Johnny would have described him as a no-nonsense ranchman who knew cattle and horses. He never would have said Mark had a tender side, no siree! He supposed every man fell for a girl some time or other, but most of the cowpunchers he knew didn't act on it. They'd ride to town and ogle the saloon girls, or go to a community dance and sashay with the town folks' daughters. But how many of them would up and propose? Not many.

Of course, most of them didn't have their own spread. They wouldn't have a roof to put over a wife's head, even if they met a woman likely to say yes. Mark was different, all right. He'd worked hard and saved his money and bought his own land. He'd liked books, too, though there were only a few in the cabin. He'd wanted to be his own boss, and apparently he'd wanted a family, too. He'd never have that now.

And what about this poor Sally? She had poured out her heart to Mark, telling him things Johnny blushed to read, and some that made him angry. Mad enough to thrash this David man she'd been married to, if he hadn't already turned up his toes in St. Louis.

They would have to tell her right away. Send a telegram, maybe. Why hadn't he thought of that before Cam left for town? Because he hadn't finished reading the letters, and he hadn't known the whole story, that's why. Sally was really in love with Mark and trusting him to take care of her for the rest of her life. And from what he could tell, ol' Mark had it bad. He was just as deep in love as Sally, even though he'd never seen her.

Johnny held his head in his hands and moaned. How on earth could they fix this? Nothing popped out at him. Maybe Cam would have some ideas. Had Mark sent Sally the money for her train ticket before he died? It might be too late to stop her. That thought jolted him. He jumped up and strode outside. Reckless nickered from the corral. Johnny went over and leaned on the top rail.

"I really messed up, fella."

Reckless rubbed his head against Johnny's arm so hard he shoved Johnny off balance.

"Hey, watch it." Johnny scratched the gelding's head, under his forelock. Distant hoofbeats sounded, and he whirled toward the road, holding his breath. After a moment, he relaxed. Cam had come into view, galloping in on his pinto. They halted in a small dust cloud, and Cam hopped down.

"I was right. You had a letter at the post office."

Johnny eyed him testily. "You mean Mark."

"Right." Cam took it from his saddlebag and thrust it into Johnny's hand. The envelope was addressed in Sally Golding's distinctive writing, with a St. Louis postmark.

"Did you have any trouble at the post office?"

"Not a bit," Cam said. "I told the postmaster I was Mark's new ranch hand, and he said he'd heard from the owner of the mercantile that Mark had hired someone. Made me feel right welcome."

"Did he, now?" The guilt resurfaced as Johnny tore the envelope open. He pulled out the letter and scanned it silently. His chest tightened, and his throat seemed to close as he hauled in a new breath.

"What's it say?" Cam demanded.

"She thanks him for sending the train fare. Cam, she's on her way by now. Expects Mark to meet her at the train depot in town. And she says she's fine with his suggestion that they—" Johnny cleared his throat, but that didn't help. "That they get married right away. Sounds like Mark offered to have the preacher standing by." Johnny met Cam's gaze. "What do we do?"

"Don't panic. Remember, Mark never got this letter. So that means the preacher doesn't know."

"Right. Unless he and Mark were chums and Mark told him all about his prospective bride."

"Now there's a depressing thought." Cam scowled and reached for the letter.

"Half the town could know about Sally," Johnny said.

"Naw, I don't think so. Some of those men would have ribbed you a little the other day, if they knew Mark that well."

Johnny wasn't sure about that, and it was small consolation.

Cam's eyes darted back and forth as he read the letter. He got to the end of the sheet and flipped it over. "Hold on."

"What?"

"She says she should arrive on June the fourth."

"What day is it?" Johnny asked. Everything inside him jumped into position to run away. "Is it June yet?"

"I think so," Cam said. "It must be. Is there a calendar in the house?"

"Uh. . .I don't know. Yeah. Yes, there is. Hanging near the table, remember?"

They looked at each other for a second and hurried inside. The calendar was open to the May page. Johnny took it off its nail and turned to June. "The fourth is a Tuesday."

"Well, the postmaster said he had thought he might see you at the church service yesterday, so. . ." Cam let it trail off and stared at Johnny.

"You mean. . . . No! She can't be coming. . .tomorrow?" Johnny gulped. "We've got to clean this place up!"

Cam's face was that of a man who had been cheated out of his last dollar. "We need to stop her."

"It's too late for that." Odd though it seemed, knowing the truth calmed Johnny.

Cam, on the other hand, turned beet red. "But—but—"

"But what?" Johnny picked up the water bucket and poured half the water into a large pan on the stove. "Mrs. Golding is coming here soon, and we can't stop it. The man she loved is dead. We need to honor his memory by giving her a good impression of his place."

"We can't bring her out here!"

"There's only one northbound train out of town a day, Cam. What do you suggest? She'll probably turn around and go back to St. Louis when she finds out about Mark, but I doubt she can leave immediately. She'll need time to grieve, anyhow, and she'll probably want to see his grave. I wonder if we can find some flowers to plant on it."

Cam stared at him like some mindless lizard. Johnny tried to be patient.

"Our responsibility is clearly to make her stay as painless as we can. And that means making the ranch as tidy as Mark would have."

"She can't come out here," Cam said slowly, each word falling like a brick. "And we can't tell her about Mark."

"Are you loco? We have to!"

"No. Listen to me. When she arrives, you'll have to give her some excuse to postpone the wedding."

"Postpone the wedding." Johnny eyed him keenly. "Oh, no. No, Cam. Absolutely not!"

"Hear me out. Now, this Sally, she's going to come in on the train tomorrow."

"Right. That's why we need to—"

Cam held up a hand, and Johnny stopped. Obviously he would get nowhere until Cam had his say.

"Just listen for a minute," Cam said. "If Sally finds out first thing that Mark is dead, she'll be heartbroken."

"Naturally."

"Sure. And we'll have to make arrangements for her to stay somewhere. She's obviously broke, since Mark had to send her the fare. You know we can't afford to pay her way back to St. Louis."

"Well. . ." Johnny hadn't considered that. He couldn't stand the thought of lying to her, but Cam was right that they couldn't afford to buy her a return train ticket, or to put her up long in a hotel.

"But if Mark meets her at the depot. . ." Cam waved a hand Johnny's way.

"No."

"Think about it, Johnny."

"I won't do it."

"It's the only thing you *can* do, man!"

Johnny crossed his arms over his chest and set his jaw. He was not going to let Cam browbeat him into lying to the widow Golding and letting her think he was Mark. "I suppose you want me to think of some reason to break up with her and see her get settled in town to support herself as a seamstress, or some such cockeyed scheme."

"Hadn't thought of that," Cam said. "No, I'm afraid it wouldn't work. You'll have to marry her."

Johnny's jaw dropped.

Cam fixed him with a determined gaze. "Now, before you go getting on your high horse about lying and all of that, consider the alternative. The sheriff spoke to you in town a few days ago. Thought you were Mark. You didn't correct him. What do you suppose will happen now if you say you're not Mark?"

Johnny's heart thumped faster than a galloping horse. "I'll confess.

I'll have to. It's the only thing to do now. We can't drag this widow into a deception, Cam. You're talking about me living a lie for the rest of my life. About entering into life's most sacred bond under false pretenses. I won't do it."

"Mmm-hmm. All right. So you go to the sheriff and tell him you're not Mark. You're Johnny. What does the sheriff do then?"

"I. . .I don't know."

"Well think, man! He'll want to know why you didn't tell him at the start. And you'll have to tell him Mark's dead. And then he'll want to know when your brother died and why you didn't tell him, and why you buried him on the sly."

"I didn't do it on the sly. I never intended to hide Mark's death, and I certainly didn't set out to lie to anyone about it."

Cam nodded tolerantly. "Of course not. But the fact remains, you *did*."

Johnny's breath whooshed out of him. He ran a hand through his overly shaggy hair. It was all true. He had made the decision on his own. Cam had offered to stand by him if he wanted to go to the sheriff last week, and he hadn't taken the opportunity.

"And after he learns that you hid the body of a man who died under suspicious circumstances, he's apt to start asking around about you. And if he hears anything out of Denver. . ." Cam stepped closer and laid a hand on his shoulder. "We've been friends a long time, Johnny. I'd hate to see you hang."

Something panicky fluttered in Johnny's stomach. "I can't marry her. It wouldn't be right."

"I'll be right there with you. Your best man. And I'll help any way I can." Cam's expression brightened a little. "And you can think of it this way: everything you do will honor Mark's memory. You can take care of the woman he loved just the way Mark would have. You'll be doing it for *him*, Johnny."

Somehow that didn't seem right to Johnny. If he went through with this, he wouldn't be doing it for Mark. He'd be doing it to save his own sorry neck. He ran his hand through his beard, which was getting some length to it.

The cow bellowed. She stood waiting at the pasture gate.

"Is it that late?" Johnny squinted at the sun. It was still well above the horizon, but these June days were long on daylight.

"I'll milk her," Cam said. "You go finish redding up the cabin. And tonight you can go over her letters again and see if you can figure out anything Mark promised her that we should have ready."

Johnny went to the cabin and put on a pair of trousers and an extra shirt that had been Mark's and washed every stitch of his own clothing. As he hung them out, Cam appeared with the bucket of milk.

"New duds?"

"Mark's," Johnny said. "I saved the wash water, if you want to wash your things."

To his surprise, Cam set about to do his laundry while Johnny scrubbed and straightened up in the cabin.

"Hey, Mark," Cam called from the doorway.

Johnny looked up. "Don't call me that."

"I have to. And you'd better get used to it." Cam came in with an armful of stove wood. "We don't have much of this left."

"Yeah, we might have to spend a day up in the hills, cutting some trees." Johnny frowned. "And we'll need the wagon to haul the wood in. We've got to train our mounts to harness."

"We'll need the wagon tomorrow," Cam reminded him. "It's almost dark now. I guess we'll hitch them up in the morning and see how they do." He dumped his burden in the wood box and walked over to the table. "Hey, what's this?" He picked up a small folder Johnny had placed there.

"Mark's bankbook. I found it under the sugar crock."

Cam opened it and whistled. "Fifty-two dollars. That's not too shabby."

"He took some out last month," Johnny said. "I reckon it was for Sally's travel expenses."

Cam squinted at the bankbook. "You're probably right."

"I wish we'd come earlier," Johnny said. If they had, his brother might still be alive. He and Cam could have helped Mark stand off the outlaws. And Mark could marry his bride and have the life he had wanted.

Cam laid the bankbook carefully on the mantelpiece. "Well, that's good news."

"It's not enough to send her back to St. Louis," Johnny noted.

"No, but there will be other expenses."

"Don't forget, Mark had credit at several businesses in town. He may owe more than that fifty dollars to the shopkeepers." Johnny looked out the window to where his clothes hung limp on the corral fence. "It's so damp today, things probably won't dry out before dark."

"Do we have a flat iron?" Cam asked.

"I haven't found one."

"Huh. You don't want to meet your bride-to-be in a wrinkled shirt."

Johnny gritted his teeth. He still didn't like the idea of marrying Sally Golding, but he couldn't see a way out, short of turning himself in to the sheriff. If he did that, a marshal would take him back to Colorado to stand trial, and he didn't like his chances.

But marrying wasn't something he'd given a lot of thought. He'd never courted a girl, and he had supposed he would go on living as a bachelor cowboy for some time yet.

"Maybe I can heat up something else and smooth your shirt out." Cam opened the cupboard and scanned the contents.

"Do you think I should shave?" Johnny ran his hand through his beard. "I must look scruffy."

Cam swung around and studied him. "No, I don't think so. What if Mark sent her a picture? That beard hides a lot."

"I don't think she mentioned a picture," Johnny said. "But I guess you're right. Any differences won't be as noticeable if I keep the beard."

"Yeah, and the folks in town might be more likely to realize you're not Mark without the whiskers."

"All right." Johnny sighed. Had his fear of getting caught clouded his judgment? "I'd better trim it, though." Mark had only a small mirror, and dusk was falling.

"Wait until morning," Cam said. "I'll shave. Then at least one of us will look well groomed."

"Maybe you should marry her."

"Oh, no. I'm not the one with the brother bent on romance."

Johnny scowled. "I'm a little uneasy about that wagon business. There's still enough daylight to hitch up the horses and try them out. Don't you think we'd ought to do that? Give them a taste of the harness? And then in the morning, it will seem like routine stuff to them."

"I guess. Sure. We don't have an extra horse for her to ride." Cam headed for the door, and Johnny grabbed his hat. Their horses trotted over to the fence as soon as Johnny whistled.

The sun hung low, and they worked quickly to adjust the straps on the double harness. The fit wasn't too far off. Reckless was obviously a little smaller than one of Mark's horses had been. In less than ten minutes, the team was ready. Cam led them over to the wagon, and Johnny bent to hitch the evener to the wagon tongue.

"I'll hold 'em while you get up on the seat," Cam called. "Get the reins, now."

One rein was hitched to each horse's bridle. Johnny gathered them and climbed into the wagon. He had driven a team hundreds of times, but he wasn't prepared for the way Reckless and Paint plunged forward the second Cam let go of them. Johnny couldn't tell which horse panicked first, but they charged across the barnyard, jolting the wagon, and his sawing on the reins had no effect. Paint let out a neigh that sound like a scream, and Reckless jumped away from him, trying to elude the tornado that was strapped beside him. The noise of the wagon rattling behind them probably contributed to the alarm, and Reckless tore for freedom. Paint, on the other hand, pushed against the chestnut, forcing him too close to the gatepost at the corner of the corral. Reckless squealed, and they both crow-hopped to the right, swinging the wagon around.

Johnny realized his danger just before the impact and threw himself across the wagon seat, hoping he could jump clear. The wagon lurched and tilted on its side. He hit the ground in a haze.

CHAPTER 6

The spinning darkness in Johnny's head cleared slowly. Vaguely he heard Cam say sternly, "Ho, now! Whoa, son! Stop that."

Johnny lifted his head a couple of inches from the dirt. Pain cut through his skull like an ax blade. He closed his eyes. The horses shrieked, and Cam's voice grew more insistent. "Settle down. Easy, now."

Johnny tried to push himself up. Pain raced up his arm. He rolled over onto his back and clutched the offending limb to his side. It took several seconds for him to realize it was his right arm that hurt. Just great. What else could go wrong?

Finally, he rolled onto his left side and raised his throbbing head. The team had stopped fifty yards up the dusty road, after dragging the incapacitated wagon that far. Several sideboards and stakes had come off it and littered the ground. Cam had caught up with the horses and now grasped the bridles of the spooky cow ponies.

He looked toward Johnny and shouted, "You all right?"

The horses shied at his loud voice, and Cam struggled to hold their heads low.

"Can you help me?"

Johnny shook his head and winced. Even that hurt.

"We need to unhitch them," Cam said. "One wheel is smashed."

"Oh, great." Johnny got slowly to his feet and staggered to the team, holding his right arm tight against his side. "I think my arm's busted."

"No foolin'?" Cam asked, bending sideways to look past his pinto.

"No foolin'."

"I guess you can't hold their heads, then."

Johnny eyed the heaving, twitching cow ponies. "Hold 'em steady. I can probably unhook the tugs with one hand."

The next five minutes were the most excruciating of his life, but he finally freed the horses from the wagon, and Cam led them to the corral. Johnny sagged against the fence, panting. A breeze ruffled his hair and cooled his damp forehead. He didn't want to move again.

Cam closed the gate and trudged back to Johnny. His eyes narrowed as he sized up the damage.

"Really broke it, huh?"

"I'm pretty sure," Johnny said. "I landed on it hard."

Cam poked his forearm with one finger, and Johnny flinched.

"Don't do that."

Cam grunted and walked a couple of yards to stoop and retrieve his hat. "So now what?" He scooped it up and patted it onto his head.

"Well, we sure can't take the wagon into town tomorrow." Johnny eyed the wreckage with distaste.

Cam edged his way around the wagon, taking in the breakage. "Nope, we can't. Guess I'll have to stay home. You can take Paint and let Sally ride him."

"Oh, no," Johnny said. "With this arm, there's no way I can ride Reckless and lead that ornery pinto, too. It's six miles, Cam. I'd never get there in one piece, leading that cantankerous pony. Besides, they're so jumpy now, there's no telling what either one of them would do if a lady with skirts from here to Fort Worth climbed on his back."

"True. I don't know as a woman's ever ridden Paint."

"Not to mention that we don't have a sidesaddle."

Cam huffed out a big breath. "I guess there's nothing for it, then. We'll have to rent a rig at the livery."

Cam helped Johnny limp to the cabin and ease down onto the

bunk. The pain from his arm as he got situated almost put Johnny out, but he managed not to yell like a girl.

"I'll make you some willer bark tea," Cam offered.

"Where you going to get willow bark? I didn't see any over there."

"There's some willer trees down by the watering hole in the creek, where the stock drinks."

"Hmpf."

"If I go get it and make the tea, will you drink it?"

"I s'pose," Johnny said.

"Good. It should help you sleep. Maybe in the morning, your arm will feel better."

"I doubt that."

"It's not poked through the skin, is it?" Cam asked.

"Don't think so."

"Maybe we should get your shirt off. Let me take a good look."

Johnny flapped his good hand to keep him away. "Oh, no you don't. Just go get that bark."

Cam stepped back. "All right, then." He walked out the door.

Johnny closed his eyes and tried to relax his jaw, but he couldn't. His arm hurt so bad, he had to keep his teeth clenched. This was not good. At least he'd had Cam with him when this happened. Otherwise, he might still be lying out there in the dirt.

Cam was a good friend. Even though Johnny didn't always see eye to eye with him, Cam stuck by him. Now he was trying hard to find the best way to handle this mess. Just the thought of jogging along on a horse for six miles made Johnny's arm hurt worse. But Cam would think of something. He was out there now peeling some bark off a willow branch to dull Johnny's pain. And he had even dug the grave for Mark. Yes, Cam was about as good a chum as a man could ask for. Johnny let out a big sigh.

Of course, if Cam hadn't been here, he might not have tried hitching those cow ponies to the wagon.

"How you doing?" Cam asked the next morning.

Johnny tried to sit up and groaned. "I hardly slept all night. I think I need to see if there's a doctor in town."

Cam grimaced. "I'm sorry we've got no wagon now. That wheel is smashed to bits. You'll have to ride Reckless."

"Help me up." Johnny held out his left hand. Cam tugged him up until he sat on the edge of the bed. "Hurts like crazy," Johnny said between clenched teeth.

"It looks swollen, too." Cam looked around. "Let me find something to use for a sling. You don't want to ride a horse with it flopping all around."

"That's the honest truth." Holding on to his elbow seemed to help. Johnny sat on the bed until Cam came back with two linen towels.

"It's all I could find. Dish towels."

"Tie 'em together," Johnny said.

"We can't put it on you until you're washed and dressed up purty for Sally."

If Johnny were a swearing man, he would have cursed then. He thought about refusing to cooperate, but what good would that do? Cam had seen the train arrive the day before at about two o'clock, and they assumed it would arrive near the same time today. Gingerly, he turned toward Cam.

"You'll have to undo my buttons."

His upper arm was a tender mass of red, purple, and black, swollen to nearly twice its normal size. He tried to move his fingers, but the pain was so bad that he quelled the impulse.

"I don't know if you can even get your clean shirt on over that," Cam said.

"I guess I've got to."

Cam frowned. "Whyn't you go without it? We can bring it along and put it on you after the doc tends to you. And if it won't fit, we'll be near the haberdasher and can buy a new one."

Somehow they got him into clean pants. Cam stuck Johnny's boots on partway, and Johnny shoved his feet in the rest of the way. Cam combed his hair and buckled his belt for him.

"We'd best eat something and go into town as early as we can," Johnny said. "You'll have to milk the cow. I'll see if I can wash the dishes with one hand."

He drank about a quart of willow bark tea with his breakfast of cornmeal mush and eggs, but his arm still hurt so bad he had to stop frequently and inhale and exhale slowly. Cam scrambled around cooking, making the bed, hiding his own bedroll in the barn, milking the cow, and saddling their horses. At the last minute, he eased the left sleeve of yesterday's plaid shirt over Johnny's good arm and draped the other side of the garment over his shoulder and around him. In a moment of inspiration, Cam fastened the loose edge of the shirtfront to the makeshift sling.

"That gonna do it?"

Johnny nodded. "It'll have to. Get my hat, and bring Mark's white shirt and Sunday coat."

With the bankbook safe in Johnny's pocket, they went out to the corral where Reckless and Paint were tied to the fence. The horses looked as innocent as could be, unaware of the havoc they had caused.

Cam boosted Johnny into the saddle. Johnny nearly pitched off the far side, and he feared at first that he'd pass out, but after sitting for a minute, he got control of the pain. For once, Reckless didn't fidget, for which he was grateful.

"Look on the bright side," Cam said. "Having a busted arm could be the perfect excuse to postpone the wedding."

Johnny said nothing. He still hadn't settled it in his mind that he would marry Sally Golding, yet he couldn't think of an honorable way out that wouldn't land him on the gallows. Maybe Cam was right, and they should try to delay things. Maybe something would happen that would let him out of Mark's promises.

Finally they were on the road to Beaumont. If they found a doctor and he wouldn't give credit, they would have to go to the bank for money to pay him. So long as he could get the arm set, Johnny was past caring about money. Every step Reckless took jarred him and sent pain rioting through his whole body. Last night he hadn't thought about any damages but his arm, but now bruises on his leg, hip, and ribs served as constant reminders of the accident, and his head throbbed. Trotting was out of the question.

The sun was high overhead when they arrived at the livery stable. Cam swung down and ambled inside, while Johnny chose the easier course of staying in the saddle. A moment later, Cam and the livery owner came out the door of the large post-and-beam barn.

"I don't give nobody credit." The owner turned his head to one side and shot a stream of tobacco juice into the weeds near the fence.

"I guess we can get some cash out of the bank." Cam looked to Johnny, and he nodded. What else could he do?

"Awright then. You come back here with two dollars cash, and I'll have a rig ready for you." The owner squinted up at Johnny. "You're Paynter?"

"Yes, sir," Johnny said.

The man nodded. "I'm Benner. Guess you know that."

Johnny wanted to give an easy smile and say of course he did, and everyone in town knew Mr. Benner, but he couldn't. Between the violent ache in his arm and his aversion to lying, the reply stuck in his throat and he only nodded.

"Done something to your arm, I see," Benner said, nodding toward Johnny's makeshift sling.

"Mark had a little accident out at the ranch," Cam said. "We're going to see the doctor now."

"Oh, well, if you can find Doc Neale in, you'll be lucky. He keeps his horse here, and he came in for it about seven this morning. Haven't seen him since. Gads all over the place to tend to folks."

That didn't sound too good.

"We'll stop by his office and see if he's there," Cam said. "I'm new in town myself. What time does the train come in?"

"Two fifteen." Benner spit again, punctuating his sentence. "She's usually on time."

"Then we'll come for the rig about two," Cam told him. "We're meeting somebody at the depot."

"Fair enough. I'll have it ready to go. And you have the cash ready."

Cam laughed, but Johnny didn't feel like it. He just wanted to lie down and die somewhere.

Benner went into the barn, and Cam walked over to his horse. "Guess the next stop is the bank."

"All right," Johnny said, "but watch for the doctor's shingle on the way. I'm about done in."

The bank was easy to spot—a stone-fronted building on the main street, far grander than the mercantile on one side and the barbershop on the other.

"You'll have to go in," Cam said. "I'll help you down."

Johnny eyed the front entrance to the bank with apprehension. "Those folks in there would know Mark, at least by sight. What if they know I'm not him, Cam?"

"Don't borrow trouble. If you act confident, they won't question you. Nobody else has."

It still didn't sit right with Johnny, and he felt far from confident, but he put all his weight on his left foot and swung his right leg over Reckless's hindquarters. Hanging on to the saddle with only his left hand gave him little purchase, and he plummeted to earth. Cam jumped between the horses just in time to keep him from sprawling in the street. In steadying Johnny, he nudged his right arm by accident, and Johnny let out a tortured exclamation.

"Sorry," Cam said, standing back.

Johnny hung on to his elbow and clenched his jaw. After a few seconds he was able to breathe again.

"I can ask in here where the doctor's office is," Cam said.

Johnny nodded curtly. "Do I look decent?"

Careful not to bump his arm again, Cam straightened his shirt and the sling. "There you go."

"The bankbook."

Cam took it out of his pocket for him and placed it in his hand.

"Let's get this over with." Johnny walked slowly up the steps, still holding his arm against his side.

"Remember, we need to pay for the buggy and probably the doctor. And the preacher."

Johnny scowled at that.

"Better get ten dollars, to be on the safe side," Cam said.

Johnny paused in front of the door, and Cam opened it for him. As Johnny walked past him, Cam hissed, "Remember, you're Mark now."

A couple of other customers were inside the bank, one standing before the teller's cage. Johnny walked over and stood behind him.

"May I help you, sir?" the teller asked as the customer he'd been helping turned away.

"Yes, thanks." Johnny stepped closer. He wasn't used to dealing with banks, but he placed the bankbook on the counter at the bottom of the metal grille in front of the teller. "I'd like to withdraw ten dollars. Mark Paynter."

"Oh, yes, Mr. Paynter." The teller studied his face for a moment then smiled. "You've grown a beard. That's it."

Johnny managed to smile. "Sure enough."

The teller opened a cash drawer below the counter and took out some bills. He counted out a five and five ones and slid them through the opening at the bottom of the grille.

"Thank you," Johnny said.

"And if you'll just sign here. . ." The teller pushed a small slip of paper out. On it was written, "Withdrawal, ten dollars."

Johnny stared down at it.

"There's a pen right there," the teller said, nodding to the ledge on the counter beside Johnny.

His heart pounding, Johnny reached for it with his left hand. "I, uh. . .I can't write it with my right hand today."

The teller held up a hand. "Of course. I'm so sorry. Go ahead and use your left hand if you can. Or just make your mark, if you can't do the whole signature. I'll vouch for you."

Make your mark. Johnny almost laughed. He held his breath and concentrated as he painstakingly formed the letters. He couldn't even hold the small piece of paper steady, but the teller slid his fingers through the slot and held it down. *Mark Paynter.* It was sloppy, it was barely legible. And it was a lie on paper. That had to be worse than the spoken lie. Johnny was sure he had committed some sort of crime. How many did that make?

The teller pulled the paper back through to his side of the grille and picked it up. He smiled. "A little wobbly, but it'll do."

Johnny put the pen back in its holder and scooped up the ten dollars. "Thanks again."

Cam was waiting for him just outside the door. As soon as he was outside, Johnny handed him the money.

"Take that and get me to the doctor. Now."

"That nice lady who just went in there told me exactly where the doc's office is. We can walk if you'd like."

That would certainly be better than mounting and dismounting again. Johnny nodded.

They walked down the street and around a corner.

"It's yonder." Cam pointed, and Johnny saw the sign—DR. JOHN NEALE—before a house. Two saddle horses were hitched to a rail in front.

"I can make it," Johnny said. "You go check on the train. See how much time we've got."

Cam gave him part of the money and headed off toward the depot. Johnny hobbled to the doctor's house and up the front steps. A card on the door said, WALK IN, so he did. A man wearing a suit and high-collared shirt stood talking to another man, this one in dusty work clothes.

"I'll come by this afternoon," the well-dressed man said. Johnny's expectations rose that this was the physician. When the second man thanked him and left, Johnny stepped forward.

"Are you Doc Neale?"

"I am. I take it your arm needs attention?"

"Yes, sir."

"Step through."

Johnny followed him into another, smaller room that might have once been a dining room or bedroom. Now a high, narrow cot stood in the middle of the floor.

"Sit there."

Johnny sank onto the stool he indicated.

"What's your name?"

Johnny's throat tightened. "Mark Paynter."

"I don't think I've seen you before, but I've only been in town a few months." Dr. Neale unpinned the sling from Johnny's shirtfront and removed it gently.

"Horse get the best of you?"

"Something like that."

"Let's get your shirt off."

The doctor eased the sleeve off his left arm and hung the shirt on a peg behind the door. When he came back, he touched Johnny's right arm lightly. Johnny flinched and ground his teeth.

"Hurts, eh?"

"You said it," Johnny mumbled.

"I'll give you something for the pain. At least it's not a compound fracture." The doctor prodded gently, and Johnny made himself sit still for it. "Feels like the humerus is broken." At Johnny's blank look, he said, "That's the bone in your upper arm. The ends of the bone actually seem to be together. I think it's more cracked across, rather than snapped in two pieces."

"Does that mean you don't have to set it?"

"I'll manipulate it a little, but I don't think I'll put a cast on it. This type of fracture can usually be healed by keeping the limb strapped in place. I'll give you a proper sling, and that should work as well as anything. But you've got to keep it immobilized. No thrashing about or trying to use it too soon." While he spoke, the doctor turned away to a worktable and busied himself making notes and then shuffling a few bottles from the row at the back of the surface.

"What will this cost?" Johnny asked.

"Three dollars, if you have cash. Otherwise, we'll talk."

"I can pay."

"Good. That's mostly for the sling and the medicine I'm going to give you. It will blunt the pain and help you sleep at night."

Johnny nodded. The doctor brought him a small glass with a half inch of fluid in the bottom.

"Drink this. It will dull the pain while I treat you."

"Thanks. It won't knock me out, will it?"

"Why? You got plans for this afternoon?"

Johnny hesitated. "Well, yeah, actually. I have to meet someone when the train comes in."

"You'll be fine. But no punching steers or swinging a lasso for a month or so. You hear me?"

"Loud and clear." Johnny tipped up the glass and drained it.

"Do you have to ride horseback to get home?" the doctor asked.

Johnny shook his head and regretted it immediately as the pain launched again in his skull. "Renting a buggy. For the visitor."

"Good." The doctor puttered about for a few minutes, measuring some powder into a small vial and making some notes on a card. After a while he came to Johnny's side and took hold of his injured arm. It didn't hurt as sharply as it had when he'd mounted Reckless. The medicine must have been taking effect. Johnny stared at the opposite wall, where some kind of certificate hung in a gilt frame.

"I'm going to manipulate it just a little," Dr. Neale said. "It'll hurt, but trust me, a lot of people have it worse than you do. Your bone is mostly where it should be."

"Right," Johnny said and clenched his teeth.

The pain jolted him and made his stomach drop. He caught his breath and determined not to holler.

"You're doing fine," Dr. Neale told him. "I'm going to wrap it for now, since you'll be traveling, but you can take the bandage off in the morning."

The doctor wound the bandage snugly around the injured limb, and it did feel better. He buttoned Johnny's shirt.

"There, all done but adjusting the new sling." He brought over an item of sturdy black material and eased Johnny's bent arm into it then fastened the buckle behind his neck. Eyeing the arm critically, he adjusted it until the angle pleased him. "Remember, that's to keep you from bending it when you shouldn't. Just let it rest."

"I'll try."

The doctor held up the vial. "Stir a teaspoon of this powder into your coffee or water every evening. Not too much. You can use it during the day if the pain is severe, but willow bark may be enough. Come see me in a week. If you get a high fever or the pain seems much worse, come back sooner. If things are progressing as they ought in a week, I'll leave you alone for a month."

"Thanks, Doc. Do you happen to know what time it is?"

The doctor took out a pocket watch and looked at it. "Five minutes to two."

"Thanks." Only twenty minutes before the train pulled in.

"You're all set." Dr. Neale put the glass vial of medicine in Johnny's good hand.

"Oh, wait. The money." Johnny set down the vial and fished the bills from his pocket. "Thanks a lot."

"Anytime."

Johnny pocketed the medicine and grabbed his hat. When he reached the street and was able to walk swiftly toward the depot, he knew he felt better. He half expected Cam to be waiting outside the station, but he was nowhere in sight. A few people loitered about the train platform. One or two had luggage with them. Johnny went over to the ticket window. "Train on time today?"

"I expect so." The ticket agent glanced upward. "Eight more minutes."

"Thanks."

He paced the platform and leaned out to stare north down the tracks as far as he could. Nothing. Supposing the train was late? He paced some more. What would he say to Sally? He tried to remember the things she had said in her last brief letter. What did she expect of Mark? He wished he'd had time to get a haircut. He ran a finger around the inside of his collar and under the place where the sling was buckled. Still no train. He looked around him. Three people had formed a line at the ticket window, and there were more folks on the platform. A man in shirtsleeves was stacking luggage on a dolly. Johnny paced some more.

The train's whistle surprised him. He stood back, a yard from the edge of the platform, and braced himself against the wind of the monster as it lumbered in and ground to a stop. The platform came to life. People hurried toward the passenger cars, and the porter wheeled his luggage-laden dolly down to the baggage car. Johnny held his breath and watched the people who disembarked. What if Sally wasn't on this train? Every woman who got off received his intense scrutiny. They were all too old, too young, or claimed immediately by family members.

Except one.

Johnny froze when the black-garbed woman turned his way. Wide eyed, she looked a little scared, but determined. Her stark dress proclaimed her a respectable widow, not too prosperous, but decent. The sun glinted on the burnished hair that peeped from beneath her modest black hat.

As he stepped closer, her gaze settled on him. She looked like a little blackbird, all somber from head to foot—except for her face. When he looked into her blue eyes, Johnny forgot all about the mourning clothes. She was pretty enough to stop a locomotive.

CHAPTER 7

S ally stepped hesitantly toward the tall man with his arm in a sling.
He looked so young. Could he really be Mark? She hadn't expected
a beard. But he was the only man within sight not intent on claiming
baggage, giving directions, or boarding the train. And he was staring
at her.

"Mr. Paynter?" she asked.

"Y–yes." He stepped forward and after an awkward moment, he
held out his left hand. "You must be Mrs. Golding."

She smiled. So formal. "I believe we had made it to first names in
our letters. Shall we go back to Sally and Mark?"

"Fine with me." But he looked as though the words would choke him.
In fact, if asked by a friend, Sally would have said he looked petrified.

His hand enclosed hers. It was rough from hard work, but warm.
In fact, everything was warm. The sun beat down on her, and her small
veiled hat offered next to no protection. She had forgotten how intense the Texas sun could be. The train hadn't stopped long enough
this morning for her to find a place to change, and she'd had to keep
wearing her tired black dress. After three days of travel, she was certain
she didn't look her best.

"Did you have a pleasant journey?" Mark asked.

"Yes, thank you." They were both silent for a moment, and then
she couldn't stand it. "Or perhaps I should say, it was not overly unpleasant. I'm sure it could have been worse."

Mark chuckled then. His whole face changed when he laughed,

and Sally suddenly knew she had made the right decision.

"What happened to your arm?" she asked.

He sighed and glanced away and then back to her eyes. "I had a driving accident last night. Smashed up the wagon."

"Oh my!"

"It's all right," he said. "My ranch hand has gone to hire a buggy, so I can drive you out to the ranch."

"I see." But she didn't. Mark had mentioned nothing about a ranch hand in his letters. He had also written that he would have everything prepared for the wedding on her arrival. Best to be direct, Sally decided. "Will we have the ceremony first?"

"Uh, well. . ." Mark swiveled his head and looked toward the hitching area beside the station. "I thought you might want some time to. . . to get to know me better before we make things permanent. And then there's this." He looked down at his injured arm. "I had to see the doctor, and I didn't have time. . . ."

Sally laid a hand gently on his sleeve. "Mark, I'm ready to marry you now."

"Oh, well, uh. . .I guess we can, if. . ." His gaze darted about the front of the depot.

He was watching for someone. The ranch hand, obviously. "I didn't know you'd hired a man."

"Oh. I uh, needed some help, and. . ." He lifted his hat and wiped his forehead with his shirtsleeve then put his hat back on, but not before Sally noticed his thick chestnut hair. "Cam's an old friend. I met him at—well, at another ranch I used to work at. I'm planning to increase the herd soon, and I thought it would be—"

As he talked, his face seemed to wobble and then go hazy. If only it weren't so hot! Sally's knees shook, and she knew her body was about to betray her. She reached toward him.

"Mark, I. . ."

As she fell, his strong arm came around her and supported her.

———

Johnny did the best he could, but the injury and the sling hindered him from sweeping Sally up into his arms. Luckily, a sturdy bench sat not three yards away. She seemed not to have completely lost consciousness, and he was able to guide her to the bench, supporting her heavily with his good arm.

He sat her down so that she leaned against the wall of the depot and ran back to pick up the small basket she had dropped on the platform. When he returned and sat down beside her, she was patting her face lightly with a handkerchief. Strands of her golden hair stuck to her damp forehead and neck. Her face was flushed, and she avoided his gaze. Johnny wished he could set her at ease, but he didn't have much experience with fainting women.

"I'm so sorry," she said, still not looking at him. "What must you think of me, swooning like that?"

"Well, I—I guess I think you're unwell. What can I do?"

"I'm not ill," she said. "Not really. It's just that it's so hot, and I'm. . . well, if you want the truth, I'm hungry."

Johnny let out his pent-up breath. Hunger he could handle. "Sorry. I didn't think about you not having much to eat on the train. There's a hotel right across the street. Let me take you over there when you're able, and we'll get some. . ." He hesitated, not sure what to order for a famished lady. "Some sandwiches, maybe? And some tea?"

"That sounds heavenly." Sally's gentle, rolling voice reminded him of home and his mother. Ma never raised her voice unless she absolutely had to.

"You can rest at the hotel while I. . .while I see to things."

"What things?" she asked.

"Well, the. . .the preacher, I guess. If you really want to go ahead with it. . ."

"I do, Mark. I feel that we've gotten to know each other very well through our correspondence. Don't you?"

Johnny's mouth was dry. He wanted to tell her that he'd only seen half of the correspondence in question, but he couldn't do that. He looked deep into her somber blue eyes. How could he disappoint her, when she had gone through so much to get here?

But still, it wasn't right. Sally was a God-fearing woman. He knew that from her letters. If he told her he'd been lying. . .

On the other hand, didn't she deserve the truth?

Johnny's head spun. If he didn't do something, one way or the other, he'd be the one swooning on the platform. He would feed her, and then they would talk. That was it. He jumped up.

"Can you walk now? I think we should get you out of the sun and order some luncheon."

"I would appreciate that so much! I confess, my funds ran low, and I tried to economize. Perhaps too much."

"I should have sent you more money." As soon as it came out of his mouth, Johnny clamped his jaws shut. He was adding to the lie. *Stop talking, you idiot!* He held out his left hand. "Let me help you."

Sally took his hand and pulled on it, levering herself up off the bench. She turned and tucked her hand snugly in the crook of his good elbow.

"Now, you tell me if you feel woozy," Johnny said.

"I will. Thank you."

He led her through the depot and out the front door, onto the main street. Still there was no sign of Cam and the rig.

Halfway across the street, he paused and looked back. "Oh, your luggage."

"We can go back for it later," she said.

"Sure." A wagon was coming down the street, but it wasn't Cam. Johnny drew Sally on toward the front steps of the hotel. It felt fine having her hold on to his arm like that, even though the warmth of her dainty, black-gloved hand made his arm sweat. A fellow lounging on the hotel porch straightened when he saw them—saw Sally, really. He didn't glance once at Johnny, but he tipped his hat and murmured, "G'day, ma'am," as Sally passed.

"This is a small town," Johnny said as he held the door open for her.

"I don't mind," Sally said. "I was getting quite tired of St. Louis."

That wasn't exactly what he'd meant, but he didn't disillusion her. The thought that had flashed through his mind was that in Beaumont, it wouldn't take five minutes for everyone in town to hear about the beauty who had gotten off the train and waltzed over to the hotel on Mark Paynter's arm. If he was going to break the engagement, he needed to do it soon. Every minute he spent with her made it harder.

The dining room wasn't busy in the middle of the afternoon; only two tables were occupied, and those by travelers who had gotten off the train. Johnny took Sally to a small table near the side wall and pulled out a chair for her.

"Thank you." She sank into it and closed her eyes for a moment.

He watched her anxiously, but her eyelids fluttered up again, revealing those captivating blue eyes. She smiled at him.

"Won't you have a seat, too, Mark?"

Johnny took the chair opposite her and set his hat on his lap. He tried not to stare, but she was quite pretty, even with a smudge on her cheek, limp hair, and dusty dress in a severe black fabric. He could only imagine how attractive she would be when she'd had a chance to clean up. He hoped she wouldn't wear black all the time.

"May I bring you something?"

Johnny glanced up. A middle-aged woman with her iron-gray hair in a bun stood next to the table.

"Uh, yes, thank you. A pot of tea and. . ." He arched his eyebrows at Sally. "Sandwiches?"

"That would be fine," Sally said.

"We've got some chicken and dumplin's left from dinner," the woman told her.

Sally's face nearly glowed with anticipation. "That sounds lovely, if you don't mind, Mark."

It sounded good to Johnny, too, but he decided he'd better find Cam and straighten things out with him. Fast.

"Sure. Uh, none for me, but if you have any cake or. . ."

"Fresh pies," the woman said.

"I'll enjoy a piece of pie with you when I come back," Johnny said to Sally.

"When you come back? Where are you going?"

"You know—to make sure everything's ready."

"Oh, yes." Her cheeks flushed, and Johnny wanted to linger. Watching Sally's expression change was more entertaining than a roundup.

He stood and fidgeted with his hat. "I shouldn't be too long." He looked back at the serving woman. "Do you have a place where Mrs. Golding can wash up and rest for a while?"

"Certainly. We have a small parlor she may use."

"Good." He shot one more glance at Sally.

She gave him an uncertain smile. "I'll be waiting."

He nodded and headed out the door.

Across the street, in front of the train station, Cam was just climbing down from the seat of a light wagon. Johnny hurried toward him.

"Cam! Where have you been?"

Cam turned and eyed him for a moment then grinned and slapped the flank of a thin bay horse. "Gittin' the rig, boy. Gittin' the rig."

"All this time?"

Cam shrugged. "What time is it?"

Johnny suspected Cam had spent at least an hour in the nearest saloon. At least he had remembered to go for the rig.

"It's way past train time. I've got Sally over at the hotel, chowing down. Now, while we pick up her bags, you help me figure out how to break it to her that we're not getting married."

Cam blinked owlishly at him. "What? Is she homely?"

"No, she's not homely. She's downright pretty."

"Then what's the problem?"

Johnny sighed. "I was brought up to think marriage was sacred and permanent. I don't want to go into it lying. It's not that I don't like Sally. She seems very sweet. And very trusting. But I feel guilty. I can't do it to her."

Cam's forehead wrinkled. "Do what?"

"Marry her. And I can't do it to Mark's memory, either."

Cam held up one hand, fingers outstretched. "Whoa there. Didn't we have this conversation last evening?"

"We did. I haven't changed my mind."

"You seemed like you did."

"Well, I've changed back. Cam, I feel too guilty. This is a lifetime commitment we're talking about. We didn't come here looking for a lifetime commitment. We came looking for a place to hide for a few weeks, or maybe a few months. Not for the rest of our lives."

Cam stood there for a long moment, frowning. "The way I see it, you can't afford not to marry her."

"I don't care. I'd rather tell the truth and pay her way back to St. Louis—if I had enough cash—"

"Which you don't."

"Which I don't. But if I come clean, maybe she'll understand."

"Oh, sure," Cam said. "She'll understand, all right. She'll understand that you expect her to fend for herself, that you're abandoning her penniless in a strange town. She'll understand that you led her to believe you were somebody else. You can't do that to a respectable lady. If you tell her Mark is dead, who do you think she'll go tell the story to? I'll tell you who. The sheriff, that's who."

"Cam, hush." Johnny looked around to make sure no one had overheard him. "You've been drinking."

Cam cleared his throat. "Not too much."

"Yes, too much."

"I'm not drunk."

Johnny had to admit he wasn't staggering drunk, but he was louder than usual, and if anyone heard him reasoning out why Johnny should keep living a lie, they would both be in hot water.

"You've got to keep quiet."

Cam nodded, smiling. "So do you. That's the whole point. We need to keep quiet about what happened to Mark. So let's do that. I'll go in and fetch Mrs. Golding's baggage. You go find the preacher."

"Hadn't I ought to put on the good clothes first?"

When he'd come around to agreeing with Cam, Johnny wasn't sure, but they fetched the jacket and clean shirt from the horses and went back to the station. Cam asked the stationmaster and was directed to an outhouse where Johnny could change. It wasn't ideal, but it was better than removing his sling and work shirt on the main street.

"Looks like it'll fit." Cam stood in the open doorway as he worked the sleeve over Johnny's swollen arm.

"It's tight."

"You'll live." Cam buttoned the front. "Now the jacket."

For some reason, putting that on hurt more than changing his shirt. At last, Cam situated the sling for him again, and Johnny tried to find a position that reduced the screaming pain in his arm to a livable ache. They walked around to the front of the station together, and Cam stowed his work shirt in the rented wagon.

"You couldn't get a buggy?" Johnny asked.

"Nope. The livery's got one, but it was already spoken for."

"All right. I s'pose there's nothing for it but to go talk to the preacher," Johnny said. "But what if he—"

Suddenly, Cam turned his back to the station door. "Don't look now."

Involuntarily, Johnny glanced toward the door of the depot. The sheriff was just coming out.

"Well, hello, Mark! This must be your new cowpuncher."

CHAPTER 8

A fternoon, Sheriff." Johnny glanced at Cam and nodded. "This is my hired man, Cam Combes."

"I'm Sheriff Jackson."

"Howdy." Cam shook his hand.

"So, what are you boys up to?" the sheriff asked.

"Why, Mark just fetched his bride-to-be off the train, and I was about to go in and get her luggage," Cam said.

Johnny felt his face heat up beneath his whiskers.

"Getting married?" The sheriff smiled, almost chummy.

"Uh, yeah." Johnny couldn't quite meet his gaze.

"I guess that explains the duds, but not the sling. What happened?"

"Oh, a driving accident," Johnny said.

Jackson nodded. "So, is the bride from around here?"

"No. Well, her family's from north of here. But she's been living in St. Louis."

"Oh, well, good. A Texas girl. So am I invited to the wedding?" Sheriff Jackson asked.

"Sure," Cam said jovially. "He'll need another witness."

Johnny managed a weak smile. "Sure."

"Thanks. When's the hoopla?"

"Any minute," Cam said.

Johnny flinched. "Well, not that quick. I've got to make sure the preacher's ready."

Jackson smiled. "Have you got a ring for the lady?"

Johnny's jaw dropped. "A ring." He glanced at Cam. "We forgot to get the ring."

"Well, you haven't got time to save up coupons from Arbuckle's coffee. But you can get one at the mercantile," the sheriff said. "They have a case of jewelry near the counter."

"I'll get it while you settle things with the parson," Cam said. "We'll probably be ready in an hour, Sheriff."

"Think so?" Jackson arched his eyebrows at Johnny.

"Uh, well, maybe. I guess."

"At the church?"

"Yeah, that's right," Johnny said.

"Good enough."

"Hey, Boss, I'll go get those bags," Cam said. "Nice to meet ya, Sheriff." He scooted up the steps and into the depot.

"Well, I. . .uh. . .guess I'd better go see the preacher." Johnny looked anxiously down the street toward the steeple.

"He's probably in his house there by the church," Jackson said. "I'll see you in an hour or so."

"Right." Johnny squared his shoulders and walked determinedly down the dusty street. Thanks to Cam and the sheriff, there was no backing out now. As he approached the church, he noticed the neat little frame house to one side. That had to be the parsonage. He pulled in a deep breath and walked up to the door.

He hesitated once more. If the minister knew Mark well, Johnny's charade would be over in minutes. And what if Mark had gone to see him recently—without a beard—and asked him to stand by to perform his wedding?

He couldn't see another option, so he knocked soundly on the door panel.

The man who answered his summons was thin and wiry, in his fifties, Johnny guessed. His hair was cut short, and his gray eyes missed nothing.

"Hello. Mr. Paynter, isn't it?"

"Yes, sir."

"What can I do for you?"

Johnny exhaled in a puff. "I, uh, I'm getting married, sir. That is, I want to. If you're willing to tie the knot."

"Be glad to, if she's a respectable Christian lady."

"Oh, she is, Reverend. Guaranteed."

The minister nodded and peered up the street. "Where is she?"

"I left her at the hotel with some refreshment. She just came in on the train."

"I see. And do you want the ceremony right away?"

Johnny gulped. "Yes, sir. In a half hour, maybe?"

"That's fine. Step inside for a moment, and let me write down the names. I'll need to know them for the service, and I'll have to make out a certificate when we're done."

Johnny followed him into the kitchen, where a plump woman in an apron was kneading bread dough.

"Myra, you've met Mr. Paynter?" The minister said.

She glanced at him. "Oh my, yes, but he's grown a beard since I last saw him." She winked at Johnny. "You haven't been in church for a few weeks, Mr. Paynter."

"Uh, that's right. I'm sorry. Couldn't help it."

She eyed his sling. "Well, I see you have an excuse. And I don't blame you for not wanting to shave one-handed."

Johnny decided not to correct her mistaken ideas and followed the preacher into the next room.

"There, now, what's the bride's name?" The pastor sat down at a desk and took up a pen.

"Uh, Sally Golding. She's a widow."

"Is that her maiden name?"

"Uh. . ." Had Sally mentioned her family name in her letters? He couldn't remember. "I'm sorry, it slips my mind. I've never met her folks, you see. But they're living up near Fort Belknap."

"She can tell me at the church, I guess. And Mark Paynter."

"With a *Y*," Johnny said, and spelled his last name. "But, uh, I wondered if you could do me a favor, sir?"

"What's that?" The minister looked up at him.

"Well, uh. . .I wondered if you could say 'Mark John Paynter' when you do the marrying?"

"Certainly. And I'll ask Mrs. Golding if she wants her full name on the certificate as well."

The minister wrote a few words on a sheet of paper.

"Do you have witnesses lined up? My wife can step in if you don't, and—"

"The sheriff's coming," Johnny said. "Him and my ranch hand. They'll be coming along in a while, and I need to go and fetch Sally."

"Good, good. I'll see you and Mrs. Golding at the church in half an hour, then."

"Thank you, sir."

Johnny made his escape through the kitchen, calling good-bye to the minister's wife as she covered her bread dough with a clean towel. Outside, he walked over to the low fence that bordered the cemetery and leaned on it. He made himself take several deep breaths. At least his legal name would be in there somewhere. He couldn't stand it if he thought the marriage wasn't real. He felt as though he ought to confess the lies he'd told the preacher, but he wasn't sure God would listen to him right now.

Slowly he turned and trudged toward the hotel.

———

Sally poured herself another cup of tea from the ivy-sprigged teapot. The hotel's luncheon had proved more than satisfactory. Now, if she could say the same thing about her intended groom.

Something wasn't right. She could feel it. Mark was nervous, and something more. She'd built her hopes upon the tone of his letters, but talking to him was almost like conversing with a different man. She certainly hadn't expected to be left waiting at the hotel. She had imagined going straight from the depot to the church.

Obviously, she had imagined too much.

"Would you like dessert, ma'am?" The unsmiling serving woman was back. Sally suspected she was the hotel owner's wife or spinster sister. Surely no businessman with any sense would hire such a dour woman to represent his service.

"Thank you, but I'll wait for my fiancé," Sally said.

The woman raised an eyebrow, and Sally wished she hadn't spoken so frankly. She pushed back her chair. "I believe you said there's a washroom?"

"Yes. I'll show you where it is."

A glance in the mirror plunged Sally's spirits to new depths. No wonder Mark had the jitters. Three days of travel had taken their toll. Her face was dirty, and her hair resembled a bird's soggy nest after a rainstorm.

"May I get a jug of hot water, please?" she asked the woman.

"Of course."

When she emerged a few minutes later, the hostess was waiting. Sally had learned her name was Mrs. Lane and her husband owned the hotel.

"Our small parlor is this way," Mrs. Lane said. "When your fiancé returns, I'll show him in."

She took Sally to a cozy room furnished with a horsehair sofa, two side chairs, and a small table. On the table, an oil lamp sat on a tatted doily. A framed drawing of a steamboat, which Sally thought was quite good, and an amateurish oil painting of a field of bluebonnets completed the décor. The double-hung window faced the backyard of the building, overlooking a stable.

Sally sat on the sofa and tried to be patient. What was Mark up to?

He had seemed anxious for the ranch hand to show up. She supposed that he needed an employee if he planned to buy more livestock. Still, she had expected that the two of them would live alone on the ranch. This would take some adjustment. Just as well he had hired a man, in light of his broken arm.

She stifled a yawn. Sleep on the train had come in snatches, and she could do with a nap. She wished Mark had taken a room for her, but of course, that would cost more, and the ranch wasn't far away. A book to read would be nice, or something else to distract her, but the sparsely furnished parlor held no reading material.

Her luncheon had settled, and she wished she had accepted a piece of pie. But Mark had said they would eat dessert when he returned.

After a few minutes, she opened her handbag. She had stitched it of scraps left from the mourning dress she had sewn for a woman in St. Louis. The pouch wasn't roomy, but it was big enough to hold her ticket stub, a handkerchief, the twenty-one cents she had left, and Mark's last letter. She took out the envelope and unfolded the sheet of paper.

My dear Sally. How precious those words had been. *I cannot tell you how happy I am that you have agreed to come and be my bride.*

What had changed since Mark penned those words?

She told herself to stop worrying. He was nervous. His life was about to change drastically. And he had broken his arm. He was probably in pain the entire time she was with him.

She sighed and put the letter away. "Lord, help me to do and say what's best for both of us." As she whispered the words, the root of her anxiety struck her squarely between the eyes. She was afraid Mark would call off the wedding.

Her chest tightened, making it hard to breathe. If only she could loosen her corset! She had spent three days bound in the thing, and her discomfort was probably contributing to her anxiety. "Lord, thank You for getting me here. Help me to trust You to—"

The parlor door opened, and she turned eagerly toward it.

A strange man stood in the doorway. He was shorter than Mark, and a little stockier. He held a wide-brimmed hat in his hand, and his dark hair tumbled over his forehead. His keen brown eyes sized her up, no mistaking that.

"Sally Golding?"

"Yes?" She stood, her heart pounding.

The man smiled. "I'm Cam Combes, Mark's ranch hand. Pleased to meet you, ma'am."

"H—hello." Sally stared at the smiling man in work clothes. Had Mark sent his hired hand to tell her the wedding was off?

———

Johnny took a deep breath before the door of the small parlor to which Mrs. Lane had directed him. He wanted to see Sally again, but at the same time, he dreaded the meeting. This was it—his last hour as a single man.

He pasted on a smile and opened the door.

"There's Mark now." Cam stood up with a mug of beer in his hand and raised it in his direction. "What took you so long, pal?"

"Oh, uh, well, the preacher. . .you know."

Sally's smile looked a little wobbly. "Is everything arranged?"

"Yes. We're to meet him at the church in half an hour."

"We weren't sure when you'd return, and Mr. Combes was famished, so we ordered the pie," Sally said.

Johnny's gaze swept over the table. At least Sally was drinking milk, not beer with Cam.

"That piece is yours." Cam nodded toward an untouched slice of apple pie on a plate. "Do you want some beer?"

"No, I'll get some—" He almost said coffee, but then he remembered Mark didn't like coffee. Had he told that to Sally? "I'll get some of that milk."

"I'll get it for you. Sit down." Cam set his mug on the table and scuttled out the door.

"So." Johnny eased down onto the sofa next to Sally. "You met Cam."

"He's very charming."

"Oh." Johnny wasn't sure what to say. He'd always known Cam had a way with the ladies. He could talk to anyone easily anytime, about any topic, whereas Johnny tended to freeze up around people he didn't know, especially females. "He's good with a rope, too." There.

"Is everything all right, Mark?" Sally asked softly.

"Yeah, sure."

"You did want a piece of pie, didn't you?"

He nodded and picked up the fork with his left hand. The sugary pastry hit his stomach hard. Maybe he hadn't ought to eat any more until after the wedding. But his eating seemed to put Sally at ease. She had picked up her plate and was taking a forkful of her half-eaten slice. He made himself take another bite.

Sally smiled at him, and his insides went all squishy again.

"Are you nervous?" she asked.

"Some. You?"

"A little," she admitted. "I'll be glad when it's done. Mr. Combes said—"

"Call me Cam," came the deep, cheerful voice from the doorway. "Short for Cameron. I'm not apt to answer to Mister." He handed Johnny a tall glass of frothy milk. "I settled up with the hotel lady. We can just pull out when we're done here."

"Thanks." Johnny took a big gulp from the glass. Half of it went up his nose, and he thumped the glass down on the table, coughing.

"Are you all right?" Sally asked.

Johnny wiped his nose with the back of his hand. Sally thrust a black handkerchief between his fingers, and he used it to advantage.

"Thanks." His eyes watered, and inside his head felt like someone had stuck a poker up his nostril.

"Well, eat up," Cam said. "We don't have long."

Sally looked anxiously at Johnny. "I don't suppose. . ."

"What is it?" he asked.

"I suppose it's silly, but I have another dress in my valise. I had hoped to change out of my traveling things before the ceremony."

"Of course," Johnny said.

Cam jumped up. "I'll run right out and get it, ma'am. The leather bag?"

"Yes."

Cam hurried out the door.

Johnny ate the rest of his pie and drank the milk, knowing Sally was watching him. This one-handed business could be downright awkward.

He wiped his mouth with his napkin and hoped he didn't have crumbs in his beard. "I hope you're feeling better now."

"Much better, thank you," Sally said with a gentle smile. "All I needed was a bit of solid food in my stomach."

Cam came back with a leather satchel, and Sally rose.

"Oh, thank you. That's exactly what I need. If you'll excuse me, I'll try not to take too long."

Cam ducked out and came back with another glass of beer.

"Did you need to get that?" Johnny asked.

He shrugged and sat down.

Johnny got up and paced the parlor. Cam's sobriety wasn't his only concern. How much of their limited funds had his friend spent at the saloon?

"It's going to be fine," Cam said. "And she's not half bad looking."

"Stow it," Johnny said, glancing toward the doorway.

Less than ten minutes later, she was back. He could hardly believe the transformation. She had not only changed into a fresh dress the color of pine needles, but around her neck hung a square-cut green stone in a gold setting, on a fine gold chain. The only remnant of her mourning attire was the black gloves. She had left off the depressing black hat and done something to her hair that made it look shimmery. He supposed she had brushed out the dust and cinders and re-pinned her updo. Whatever she had done, he was struck by the beauty of his bride.

"Don't you look lovely, Mrs. Golding!" Cam stepped forward, grinning.

Johnny realized he'd been staring.

"Thank you," Sally murmured to Cam, but her eyes were on Johnny.

"You do look lovely," he said.

Her smile almost melted him. "You look nice, too, Mark."

Cam and Sally seemed all too eager to get over to the church, but he didn't resist. As promised, Cam had the rented wagon waiting outside, and a trunk bound with straps was in the back. Cam added Sally's valise. Reckless and Paint were still tied down near the bank.

"Should we get the saddle horses?" Johnny asked.

"I'll get 'em after the ceremony," Cam said. "Come on."

Johnny offered Sally his hand to help her up into the wagon. She smiled down at him and mouthed, "Thank you."

As Johnny walked around the horses' heads, Cam stopped him. "I got the ring."

"Good."

"They said if it doesn't fit, she can bring it back and exchange it later."

Johnny nodded. "How much was it?"

"Five dollars. They put it on your account at the store."

Johnny winced, but he couldn't do anything about it at this point.

On the short drive to the church, Sally looked around. "What a charming little town. I didn't realize it had so much industry."

"Rice mill," Johnny said. "Lumber mills, too. There's a lot of river traffic." He drove up in front of the church and halted the horse. The minister stood in the doorway, beaming at them.

"Hello, Mrs. Golding. I'm Pastor Lewis."

Johnny tried to file the name away in his mind. Mark would surely have known that.

"Hello." Sally took the preacher's hand. "Pleased to meet you."

With his other hand, Mr. Lewis held out a posy of wild roses and greenery. "My wife asked me to bring these to you. If you already have a bouquet, we can use these as an altar decoration."

"Oh, thank you. How very thoughtful. I didn't have one." Sally took the roses and held them to her nose.

Johnny kicked himself mentally. He should have thought of flowers. But where would he have gotten them? Mark didn't have a flower garden, and he couldn't have stolen them from someone's yard in town.

"Aren't they lovely?" Sally asked, holding them up for him to inspect.

"Yes." Johnny nodded at the minister. "Would you please thank Mrs. Lewis for us?"

"Of course."

"Howdy, boys." Johnny swung around to see the sheriff walking toward them.

"Well, hi, Sheriff," Cam said. "This is Mrs. Golding, soon to be Mrs. Paynter."

"How do you do?" Sally said.

"The pleasure's all mine, ma'am. I'm the local sheriff, Lionel Jackson. People call me Fred."

Sally laughed. "Are you and Mark friends, Sheriff?"

"Not much, but he invited me to come today."

"You can't ask for a better witness to this auspicious event," the minister said. "Shall we go in?"

Somehow Johnny managed to stay upright during the ceremony. Sally didn't bat an eye when the Reverend Lewis said, "Do you, Mark John." In turn, Johnny learned that Sally's real name was Sarah Aileen.

He barely heard the rest of the minister's words but repeated them when instructed to do so. Sally held his hand so tightly he thought he might lose a finger before they were done. It was the first indication that she might be somewhere near as frightened as he was, and that made him feel a smidgen less nervous.

"I now pronounce you man and wife." Reverend Lewis smiled at him the way he might at a small boy who dropped his penny during the offering. "You may kiss your bride."

That jolted Johnny back to earth. Sally was also smiling, but he could swear tears glistened in her eyes. He hoped she wasn't going to cry. His mother had said once that women always cried at weddings, but he thought she meant other people's weddings, not their own.

He leaned toward Sally, feeling awkward as he still held her right hand in his left, and he couldn't use his other wing for balance. Her lips were quite a ways down, but Sally rose on tiptoe to meet him, and they executed a quick smack. Immediately, Cam slapped him on the back.

"Gentlemen," the minister said somberly, "It gives me great pleasure to present Mr. and Mrs. Mark Paynter. Just let me sign the certificate, and you can be on your way."

They shook hands all around, and between them Johnny and Cam put together two dollars for the minister's fee. That about cleaned them out, Johnny surmised. The sheriff offered hearty congratulations and said he'd better get back to work.

"Thank you, Mr. Lewis," Johnny said.

"Glad to do it," the minister replied.

Cam walked out to the wagon with them. "What do you say we tie ol' Reckless to the back of the rig? Then you two can go on home."

"What about you?" Johnny asked.

"Thought I'd stay in town for supper. I'll see you in the morning." Cam headed off down the street toward where they had left the horses.

Johnny looked at Sally. "Well, uh. . .are you ready to see your new home?"

Her gentle smile warmed him. "I'm looking forward to it enormously, Mark."

Johnny gulped and held out his left hand to give her a boost onto the wagon seat. That can't-breathe feeling was back. What on earth would they ever talk about on the six-mile drive without Cam to keep the conversation rolling?

CHAPTER 9

"So, um, yeah, it's pretty small." Mark looked around at the inside of his cabin as though he suddenly saw it through her eyes.

Sally patted his arm. "You warned me. Don't worry about it. Like you said in one of your letters, if we get a good price for the cattle. . ."

"Right. Well, listen, I'll bring in your things. Uh. . ." He looked toward the corner where a narrow bunk stood against the wall. "You can sleep there."

Sally's stomach plummeted. "And what about you? Where will you sleep?"

"I, uh. . ." He shifted his arm in the sling a little. "I guess with this and all. . .well, I thought maybe I'd sleep on the floor for now."

She didn't know what to say, and she hesitated too long.

Mark said quickly, "I should have built a bigger bed before you got here, I know. We actually were going to build a. . . Well, I got so caught up in the work, and—and—"

"Don't worry about it," she managed to say smoothly. "We'll get by. Where does Cam sleep?"

"He's staying in the barn. We need to fix it up better for him, but it'll do for now."

She nodded. "All right, then. If you can bring in my satchel first, I'll get out an apron and get to work on supper. May I have full run of the kitchen?"

"Sure. It's not much, but we did lay in a few supplies." Mark looked sheepishly toward the other end of the cabin. "I've got a garden out back, but there's not much right now. A few green beans and carrots and some crooknecked squash. Most of the spring garden's about done, and it's been awful dry this year. We'll plant more later on, after we get past the worst of the heat."

"I'll see what you've got on hand. If we're lacking something I need, will we be able to get more supplies soon?"

"Uh, probably. Sure." But he looked doubtful. Sally decided she would make do with whatever he had, no matter how meager. For now.

Somehow, she had expected him to have everything ready and to stock up on foodstuffs. Had things taken a turn for the worse financially? She hoped her train ticket hadn't cleaned him out.

He hurried out to the wagon and a moment later returned with her leather satchel.

"Thank you." Sally nodded for him to set it on the bed, where she opened it. Mark began taking a few folded clothes out of a rough cupboard, made from wooden packing crates.

"You can use this if you want. I don't have a dresser."

"That'll be fine," Sally said.

Without comment, Mark headed for the door again. "You'd best leave my trunk until later," she said. "Your arm. . ."

He hesitated in the doorway then nodded. "I'll get you some water."

She removed her hat and got out her best apron, one she had pieced from the scraps left from her various sewing projects.

She walked determinedly to the kitchen area. The situation wasn't as bad as she'd feared. She found plenty of flour, cornmeal, oatmeal, and sugar, as well as baking powder, salt, pepper, lard, and a few canned goods. The dishes were scanty. She regretted selling off her few household furnishings after David's death, but she'd had no place to store them, and she had desperately needed the money they brought.

At a thump behind her, she turned. Mark had set a wooden bucket half full of water on the floor near the worktable.

"I'll bring in some eggs," he said.

"Fresh eggs will be lovely."

He nodded. "And it's nearly time to milk the cow."

"A cow? Wonderful! Do you have any meat?" she asked.

"There's bacon in a crock in the root cellar out back, and I could kill a rooster. We've got three, I think. And Cam and I thought we'd butcher a bull calf after you got here."

"It's awfully warm for that."

He shrugged.

"Do you fancy chicken pie tonight?"

"Sounds good. I'll bring you the bird in a little while."

Satisfied, Sally set about building up the cook fire and starting the piecrust. She would make a cake, too, but that would be a surprise. *Our wedding cake,* she thought with a wry smile. And this evening maybe she would have a chance to write to her mother and give her the news.

Mark didn't seem to stand still long enough for her to ask him any more questions. He was in and out, bringing her half-a-dozen eggs and a few sticks of firewood at a time. After that, he didn't appear for another hour, when he suddenly turned up with a dressed chicken and half a bucket of fresh milk.

More than once, she had eyed the narrow bed. Each time, she had turned her back on it. Had she come here to marry a man who wouldn't share his bed with her? The broken arm was more than an excuse, to be sure, but that hadn't happened until last evening, according to the story Mark had told her on the way to the ranch. He'd had weeks to build a wider bed. Why hadn't he done it? Was it just an oversight? That seemed unlikely. But she couldn't believe he'd had no intention. . . . No man would write such intense, heartfelt letters as Mark had if he didn't mean to have a true marriage. And he had spoken of children.

She looked up at him as he set the bucket containing about a gallon of milk on the worktable.

"Thank you, Mark."

"I can strain it for you."

"I can do it. I'm sure you have a lot to do outside."

"Not so much. I've done most of the chores."

The rays of sunlight slanting in through the tiny window told her it was getting late. "I believe Cam said he won't be here for supper?"

"Right."

He didn't look happy. Sally's heart ached. She didn't want to upset him, but she needed more than this. She put her hand lightly on his shirtsleeve.

"Mark, what's wrong?"

"Nothing."

She held his gaze for a long moment. "You don't seem glad that I'm here."

"Aw, Sally." He ducked his head as though embarrassed. "I don't want you to feel that way. I'm glad."

"Truly?"

He nodded.

"Well, good. Because I've looked forward to this day for so long. I. . .I feared I might have disappointed you. You can be honest with me, Mark. If I'm not what you imagined, or what you'd hoped for. . ."

"You are. You're more than I hoped for." His free hand found hers, and he gazed into her eyes. He didn't look confident, though. If anything, he seemed frightened.

"You're not scared of me, are you?"

"What?" He chuckled, but his voice cracked. "Well, maybe just a little. Sally, I—" He swallowed hard. "Are *you* disappointed?"

"Not at all."

He let out a deep sigh. "I want everything to be the way you wished for it to be, but I feel like I haven't done a very good job of that. Cam and I tried to get ready, but—"

"You and Cam?"

He looked at her again, anxiety radiating from his brown eyes. "I told you he's an old friend of mine, didn't I?"

"You mentioned it."

"Well, when he came by looking for work, I couldn't turn him away."

"I wouldn't expect you to," Sally said.

Mark nodded. "He's been a big help. With the cattle and such."

"I hope he can help you enough. You need to rest that arm."

"Yeah, the doc said that, too."

"Did he give you any medicine?"

"Some powder. I'm supposed to put it in my coffee or water."

Sally put her hands on her hips. "Well, why didn't you tell me? Where is it? I'll fix you some now."

He fished in his pocket and came out with a small bottle. "Here. A teaspoon, the doc said."

"Does it hurt now?"

"Some. Milking the cow. . ."

She opened her mouth wide as she realized her own failure. "I never thought. How did you ever do it? Mark, I know how to milk a cow. I'll do it next time."

"I expect Cam can do it in the morning. I just used one hand and didn't strip her dry. We usually get about twice that much." He eyed the pail ruefully.

"Should I go out and—"

"No, she'll be fine."

Sally sighed. "All right, but there's something we need to get straight. I'm your wife now. That means we're partners, and I'm not afraid of hard work. If you need anything—whether it's because of your arm or something else—you tell me." She eyed him sharply. "How did you dress that chicken?"

He chuckled. "I held it down with my foot."

She shook her head. No wonder it had taken him so long. "I'm ashamed of myself for not thinking about it. At least I know I married a resourceful man. Now, you sit down, Mark Paynter, and I'll bring you that medicine. No more chores for you tonight."

She thought they understood one another now. After taking his dose, Mark sat for a while, but he seemed restless and went outside again while she cooked the chicken and made it into a pie. She feared he got his supper much later than usual, but he ate two helpings.

"That was really good," he said, laying down his fork. "Worth waiting for."

"Thank you. There's cake in the oven."

"You made a cake, too?"

"Thought we could celebrate. If you don't want sweets every day, it's all right."

"I love sweets. So does Cam."

She tried not to show her disappointment at his comment. Why did Cam have to enter into every conversation?

She rose and refilled Mark's coffee cup before cutting the cake. "I didn't have time to make boiled icing, so I put a crumb topping on it." She set a generous slice before him, on a small china plate she'd found in the cupboard.

"Smells mighty fine." He lifted his fork and took an experimental bite. "Tastes fine, too."

Sally smiled and cut herself a piece. She sat down next to him. "Now, tell me what we'll be doing tomorrow. Will you be working with the cattle? Or shall we tend the garden?"

"I thought maybe I'd help Cam fix up his room out in the barn. Hated to kick him out of the house."

"He was sleeping in here?" Sally asked.

"On the floor. But he ought to have a proper bunk and a mattress."

"So should his employer."

Mark's face went red. "We can tend to that, too. But I want Cam to have a nice place of his own, so he'll be happy working here."

That made sense, but Sally had heard about all she cared to of Cameron Combes. "All right. If you two work out there, I can milk the cow and feed the chickens and get my trunk unpacked."

"We'd better get that inside," Mark said.

"Cam hasn't returned?"

"No sign of him."

"Well," Sally said, "as long as it doesn't rain, the trunk should be all right in the wagon."

"Oh, we have to return that tomorrow," Mark said.

"Maybe that would be a job for Cam."

He gazed at her for a long moment and then looked away. "I expect so."

Sally kept an ear tuned to hear the hired man return, but no one rode up to the ranch all evening. While she washed the dishes, Mark puttered about, moving things an inch here and there. He offered to sweep the floor, but she couldn't imagine him doing a good job with one hand. Still, he had killed that rooster. . . .

She put the thought aside and kept at her kitchen work. She scrubbed the table and the sideboard around the dishpan. She washed every dish they'd used and put away the leftovers, carefully covered so they could use them the next day.

"I suppose we have mice," she said with a half smile. All country homes had mice, unless they had a cat.

When Mark didn't respond, she looked over at him. He had fallen asleep sitting at the table.

"Mark." She touched his shoulder gently.

He sat up, blinking. "Oh, sorry."

"Never mind. I'm finished with my work. I thought I'd get a bath before I retire, if you don't mind."

She watched his face anxiously. He flushed to his hairline and stood, holding on to his injured arm.

"Do you have plenty of water?" he asked.

"I think so. I filled the boiler earlier, and it's warm now. There's a bucket of cold, too."

"I'll get the tub." Without another word, he went out the door.

Sally got her best nightdress and her hairbrush out of her satchel. Mark came in with a round washtub and set it on the kitchen floor.

"I'll be outside."

"Towels?" she asked.

He hesitated and then brought two from the kitchen. "That's the best we have, I'm afraid. Not very big."

"Thank you," Sally said. "I'll set the buckets outside when I'm done."

The water wasn't very deep in the tub, and she kept her bath short, but being out of her corset at last and washing off the grime of her journey felt wonderful. She scrubbed her skin thoroughly then dried off and slipped on her gown. She hesitated but then went ahead and washed her hair in the same water. Rinsing it in cold jolted her, but at least it wouldn't smell of smoke.

At last she sat on a bench near the stove and brushed out her hair. She wished Mark was here, watching her, seeing the cascade of gold. But he was so shy, he probably wouldn't even think of such a thing. She sighed as she continued her brushstrokes. How could a man seem so open on paper and be so reticent in person?

When her tresses were mostly dry, she took the empty water bucket to the door and set it out on the step. She looked toward the barn, but she didn't see any light out there, or any sign of Mark in the twilit yard. Where had he gone?

Back inside, she set her satchel off the bed and hesitated. If he truly intended to sleep on the floor, she ought to set out some bedding for him. But would doing that confirm that he had no other option?

CHAPTER 10

Paint's hooves beat a tattoo in the darkness. Johnny sauntered to the corral gate and waited. A minute later, Cam drew up and hopped off the pinto's back.

"You're awful late," Johnny said.

Cam jumped. "You scared me." He glanced toward the cabin. "What you doin' out here?"

"Waiting for you. I didn't expect you to spend half the night at the saloon."

"Figured you two would want some time alone."

"Cam, this isn't right."

"Hold on," Cam whispered. "You didn't tell Sally?"

"No, but I wish I had. I'm miserable, and I don't think she's much better."

Cam pulled off the saddle and flopped it onto the top rail of the fence. "What happened?"

"Nothing. I killed a rooster one-handed, and she cooked it, and we ate supper, and—"

"I didn't think about you doing all that stuff with your arm hurtin'."

Johnny shrugged. "In the morning, you'll have to help me get her trunk in."

"Does she need it tonight?"

"I don't think so."

Cam looked again toward the cabin. "You should be inside."

Johnny wasn't sure what to say, so he stood there fidgeting while Cam took off Paint's bridle.

"Why aren't you?" Cam asked.

He shrugged. "I gave her the bunk."

Cam stopped walking, the bridle slung over his shoulder, and stared at him. "You've got to be joking."

Johnny shook his head.

"Look, I know it's a small bunk, but—"

"I figure Mark would have built a better bed if he'd lived that last few days before she came, but he didn't. Anyway, I told her I'd sleep on the floor."

"Was she mad?"

"Not exactly."

Cam eyed him keenly. "She expects more from Mark."

Johnny said nothing. The whole point was he wasn't Mark, but Cam knew that, and if he said it, his friend would only go into a tirade about how he couldn't change things now.

Cam clapped him on the shoulder. "Go on in, Mr. Married Man. I'll see you in the mornin'."

———

Sally heard the horse come in, and then the men's low voices out near the corral. She held her breath and listened, but she couldn't make out their words. After a few minutes, the door opened stealthily. She waited, her heart tripping, but Mark didn't come near the bed. She heard rustling in the dark. She was certain she heard when he took off his boots, and the moment when he settled down on the pallet of blankets she'd made for him.

She wished she hadn't done it. Then maybe he would have come over and asked her what he was supposed to sleep on. Or at least he might have needed to light the lantern to find some bedding. Setting out the bedding was a tacit agreement that he wouldn't share her bed tonight. Had she made the biggest blunder of her life?

All was quiet, but she was wide awake, and she knew he wasn't asleep. This was not the way she wanted to start her new marriage. What if she said something? She wasn't sure she dared. David would have gone into a rage if she had questioned one of his decisions. She lay silent for a minute, holding back a sob. Above all, she didn't want her new husband to think she was trying to control him. That would be a big mistake.

Her pulse pounding, she lifted her head off the pillow. "Good night, Mark."

After a long moment of utter silence, he said, "Good night, Sally."

———

Mark was up and gone already when Sally awoke in the gray predawn. He had bundled up his bedding and left it in a semi-neat mound on the floor. She hurriedly dressed, keeping an eye on the door and wishing she had her trunk inside.

As soon as she was decent, she folded his blankets and stacked them on the foot of her bed.

A timid knock came at the door.

"Come in."

Mark opened the door and entered, carrying a basket. "Morning." He glanced at her once and quickly away, but she saw the relief in his expression. He must have shared her anxiety that he would interrupt her while she was dressing.

"Good morning." Sally smiled her best smile. "Are those more eggs?"

"Yes. Got seven this time."

"I'll cook them up for you boys." She wished she hadn't said *boys*, but Mark didn't seem to mind.

"Cam's milking the cow. I'll bring in some water, and some coal for the stove."

She made a quick trip out back to the necessary and then donned her apron and set to work. Cam brought in a full bucket of milk while she was mixing biscuit dough.

"Oh, thank you," Sally said. "I can use some of that."

Cam set it on the worktable. "Good morning, Mrs. Paynter. Looks like it's going to be a scorcher."

"Call me Sally. How are you, Cam?"

"Fine and dandy. Anything I can do for you?"

"You could put a little coal on the fire. I hate to heat up the house, but I can't bake if I don't."

"I wonder if Mark and I shouldn't set up an outdoor oven for you," Cam said.

"That would be helpful," Sally said. Overheating the kitchen had seldom been a problem in St. Louis, but she remembered that her mother often did her baking outside in summer, to keep the house cooler.

"I'll talk it over with Mark and see what he thinks."

When they all sat down to breakfast a short time later, Cam steered the conversation to ranch work and improvements the men could make to the buildings.

"I know you plan to increase the herd of cattle," Sally said to Mark. "When will you be getting the new stock?"

Mark hesitated, and she wondered if money was a problem.

"I'm not sure," he said. "But I thought we'd take what we already have farther up into the hills next week. The grass will be better up there, and it will be about played out in the pasture here."

"Meanwhile, we can work on my quarters in the barn and maybe start building one of those outdoor ovens like the Mexicans use for Sally."

Mark eyed him cautiously. "There's something else I've been meaning to get at for a while."

"What's that?" Cam asked.

"Well, I'm not sure we can do everything right away." Mark shot a glance at Sally and then looked down at his plate. "I aim to build another room on this cabin, so's we can have a bedroom separate from the rest."

"Now, I think that's a capital idea," Cam said. "And while we're at it, we should build a decent bedstead for you and the missus."

Sally's face burned. She jumped up and lifted her plate and silverware. "Anyone want more biscuits?"

"I'd take another," Cam said.

She hastened to the worktable and stood for a moment with her back to them, trying to calm herself and willing the blood to leave her cheeks. Cam was a charming man, but he was a bit more blunt than she cared for.

Mark and Cam continued their conversation while she filled her dishpan with warm water and began to do up the dishes. She couldn't hear everything over the clinking of pottery and pans, but she caught the words *lumber*, *sawmill*, and *money*.

When they rose, Mark brought his dishes over. "Where would you like your trunk?"

"Oh, right there at the foot of the bed, I guess." She turned to look at the scanty floor space. "Thank you."

They brought it in, and Sally kept busy while they arranged it.

Cam drove away in the rented wagon with his pinto tied behind it. He was back in an hour. All day the men kept busy. Even with his arm in the sling, Mark hammered, carried, and held boards in place for Cam. After the noon meal, they put a harness on Mark's horse and ground drove him around the barnyard to get him used to pulling in harness then repeated the process with Cam's paint.

Sally determined not to slack or feel sorry for herself. She arranged her things. The little house was so clean that she didn't feel she needed to scrub everything. She did some extra cooking and went out back to survey the vegetable plants in the garden, where she salvaged some beans and root vegetables. The early garden was about done, but a few things still produced.

At midafternoon, she followed the sound of hammering to the barn, carrying a tray with cake and cool milk. She found them in a small room inside the barn, where they were constructing a bunk bed between saddle racks and a feed bin.

Mark smiled when he saw her in the doorway. "That looks terrific." He and Cam came over to take the food and cups from the tray.

"Mighty good," Cam said after his first bite of cake. "Mark, you picked yourself a winner."

Sally smiled. "Thank you, Cam. I'm stewing what's left of the chicken for supper." She turned to Mark. "Do you have any seeds for planting a second garden?"

Mark hesitated. "Look in one of the crocks in the kitchen. I think I put the leftover seeds there."

"Thank you." She smiled at him. "When do you think I should plant the next round?"

"Uh. . ." Mark looked toward Cam.

"Not yet," Cam said.

Mark nodded. "If you plant now, it'll come up during the worst of the heat, and everything will die off."

"Wait a few weeks," Cam said. "Maybe the middle of August."

Sally hated to wait that long. She wanted to see new plants popping up through the soil. But she supposed they were right. Meanwhile, they would be without fresh vegetables for a while.

"Once we get this bunk squared away, we'll lay out where to build the addition to the cabin," Mark said.

"Are you sure you want to?" Sally asked. "Maybe you should wait until your arm heals."

"No, I want to get it done."

She took that as a good sign. Mark wanted them to have their own bedroom and therefore privacy. "Thank you."

He nodded gravely, and she wished Cam wasn't there. She longed for her husband to take her in his arms and hold her while he described his dreams for the place. But Mark seemed to be a shy man, much more so than she had guessed during their correspondence. She hoped that was the only reason he held back. She looked at their handiwork.

"Well, Cam, you'll have a bed. Maybe later, you can make some more furniture."

"I'm thinking I'll build a bunkhouse in the fall, if we make a profit this year," Mark said.

"A bunkhouse? Do you anticipate hiring a lot of men?"

"Not right away, but Cam will need a bigger place than this."

She nodded, wondering how much Mark felt he owed his friend. "Just don't overdo it," she said, eyeing his sling. Should she have made him more willow bark tea?

"I'll see that he doesn't," Cam said.

———

The following morning, Johnny worked with Reckless in the harness for two hours while Cam worked on the farm wagon. After dinner, they hitched the horse to the repaired wagon.

"I'll drive him," Cam said.

"No sense two of us getting stove up if he takes exception to this," Johnny said.

"If he does, you can't pull hard enough with one arm to slow him down." Cam shook his head. "You'd just be going in circles until you ran into something again. I'll do it."

Reckless stood quivering in the harness while Cam climbed to the seat. Johnny patted his horse's neck with his good hand.

"Now you behave yourself. Cam's not going to hurt you."

Reckless's ears shifted, one back toward Cam and the creaking wagon, the other forward toward his master.

"I mean it," Johnny said softly. "Nobody's chasing you. You're just going to help us out. Be a good fella." He gave one final pat and stepped back. Sally had come from the house and stood beside him.

"Think he'll wreck the wagon again?"

"I sure hope not," Johnny said.

"All right, crow bait," Cam said in his most winsome voice. "Show the lady what a handsome fellow you are." He clucked, and Reckless stepped gingerly forward. They went the length of the barnyard.

"Now comes the tricky part," Johnny said, and Sally clutched his arm as though she was in mortal fear.

Cam turned the horse in a wide, slow circle and headed back toward them. When the wagon was aligned straight, he clucked to Reckless and fluttered the reins on the horse's flanks without popping them. Reckless snorted, shook his head, and picked up a trot. He high-stepped and twitched his ears, but he didn't bolt. Cam made him trot over close to where Johnny and Sally stood then pulled gently on the lines.

"Whoa."

Johnny grinned and reached to scratch Reckless's forelock. "What a good horse."

"I'll take him down the road a ways and turn around past the boulder," Cam said.

Johnny nodded. "Take care." He watched the wagon roll slowly down the dirt road. When it was out of sight, he turned to Sally. In the sunlight, her calico dress was a bright maroon with a small gold-and-black print. It brightened up the drab barnyard.

"What?" Sally asked softly.

He realized he had been staring.

"Nothing. You look nice."

She smiled. "Thank you."

Johnny's chest tightened. He ought to compliment her more. Her smile made things look so much brighter—so much more doable. Maybe they could make this marriage work.

"We want to take the wagon into town and get some lumber for the spare room."

"You're going to start on it already?" Her blue eyes sparkled.

"That's the plan. Maybe you should tell me what you'd like?"

Her cheeks flushed pink, and she gazed up at him, her lips parted. "Really? Oh, Mark, thank you! Suppose you show me where you're aiming to put the door."

She took his hand, and Johnny's heart cannoned. He gulped and walked with her to the cabin. Inside, all was shadowy, but Sally's presence beside him was solid and real. She smelled good. Her soft hand warmed his rough one. Her hair brushed his beard as she turned her head. Johnny caught his breath.

"Where will it be?" she asked.

"I was thinking over there, where the coal scuttle is now. What do you think? We could go off the back, if you want, but that would cut into the garden spot."

"No, don't do that. I'd like it off to the side. Or even the other side, near where the bed is."

Johnny looked over toward the bunk, conscious that he was still holding her hand. His face heated on principle. "I hadn't thought of putting it there. We could. Then I wouldn't have to move the stovepipe."

"It would be farther from the stove, but that might be a good thing," Sally said. Suddenly she stepped directly in front of him and gazed up into his eyes. "Mark, you are glad I came, aren't you?"

"Yes."

How she got into the crook of his arm, Johnny wasn't sure, but he pulled her in close, and her hands sneaked around to his back. She laid her head against his chest. He'd never felt anything so glorious.

"We'll put it wherever you want," he said.

"And a window?"

"Yes, a window. Two if you like." It was reckless, since he wasn't sure he could pay for it.

Outside, the wagon's creaks and Reckless's trotting hoofbeats came closer. Paint nickered from the corral.

"Guess Cam's back already," Johnny said.

Sally pushed up on her toes and kissed his cheek. "This will work."

Those three words lingered in his ear, and he squeezed her hard, just for a moment. He wished Cam wasn't here. He wished he didn't have to think about lumber and green horses and financing a building project.

He let go of her and stepped back.

"We'll be going in town. Do you want anything from the store?"

Sally laughed, a low, musical laugh. "Dozens of things, but I can get along with what we have. Mark, I don't want to spend money if we don't have it."

He hesitated. "Tell me two things you'd like."

"All right, more sugar and some cocoa powder."

"I'll get 'em."

"Thank you. That's real nice."

He went out into the sunshine grinning.

Cam was turning the wagon slowly at the end of the barnyard.

"Everything go all right?" Johnny called.

"Right as rain. You ready to go to town?"

Johnny met him near the well and swung up onto the wagon seat. He looked back at the cabin. Sally stood in the doorway. She smiled and waved. A breeze caught a tendril of her golden hair, and it waved, too. Johnny lifted his hand in salute. In spite of the pain in his arm, he couldn't hold back his grin.

"You're a lucky man," Cam said.

"She's going to make us a chocolate cake."

"Real lucky."

Johnny turned forward and sat grinning and thinking about his bride.

He wasn't much help in loading the lumber, but Cam insisted it was all right. The sooner his arm healed, the sooner they would finish their building projects. Johnny still hadn't told him that he was sleeping on the floor, but he thought Cam might have guessed.

Johnny was more useful in holding boards for Cam to nail in place. They spent several days on framing the walls for the new bedroom and laying the floor. When that was completed, Cam put him to work sanding the four bedposts for Sally's new bed. Johnny could hold a piece of wood steady by leaning on it or bracing his foot against it, and then he could sand with one hand.

After three days of work, during which the room slowly took shape, Cam set off alone after breakfast to fetch the windows.

"Now, don't let Sally peek in there today," he told Johnny before driving off. "We want her to be surprised when she sees it, with the glass windows and the new bedstead and all."

"Oh, she'll be surprised all right," Johnny said. Cam had measured the bed frame himself, cautioning Johnny to make it wide enough for two people, but not too wide. "We'll need a double mattress." He frowned at Cam. "We don't have much money left in the bank, but get some ticking."

"Sure," Cam said. "Sally can stitch it up, and we'll fill it with fresh hay for her."

Johnny watched him drive off, a little nervous. *Why couldn't Mark have taken care of all this before. . . ? Before what?* Johnny sighed. If his brother had lived, he probably would have done exactly what he and Cam were doing now—made the cabin a nicer place for Sally.

The thought of his brother as Sally's husband made Johnny feel like an interloper. Mark should be the one Sally did things for, the one she hugged around the waist when she was happy with him. Mark should be the one who would share the new room with her.

Johnny wasn't sure he could bring himself to move in there when it was finished. Maybe Sally could put her things in there and he could keep the bunk in the corner.

But he knew that wouldn't wash. Cam would have fits, and Sally. . . How would she feel? Would she be disappointed? Angry? Hurt? Confused?

Johnny walked over to the fence and gazed out at the cattle that grazed so peacefully. Mark had probably had a good stash of food, and maybe some cash when he was attacked. He'd have been in pretty good shape, or he wouldn't have offered a woman his support and protection. Where did they stand now? As near as he could tell, he had about forty dollars total and three people to take care of. Where had Mark expected to get more money? He'd told Sally he intended to buy more cattle. Had the outlaws gotten the money he had set aside for their purchase?

"Mark!"

He turned toward the cabin. Sally was there in the doorway, her patchwork apron picking up the red of her calico dress and the gold of her gleaming hair. She waved, and Johnny raised his hand to wave back.

"I've got fresh gingerbread and whipped cream."

A piece of something inside him slipped into a chink. How could she be so cheerful, when he found it hard to even smile? Yet she plunged into the work of the ranch and did special things for him. She'd mixed the medicine for him those first few days, when his arm hurt so bad. She baked up sweets and folded his bedding every morning. The cabin stayed neat as a pin, even though they barely had room to turn around. Sally didn't complain, either. He'd caught her fetching her own pail of water yesterday, and she'd said she didn't mind, since his arm was still mending. Johnny had determined that she would never be short on water once he was healed.

He walked toward the house and caught the spicy scent of the gingerbread. It overcame the smells of grass and dust and the smoke from the chimney, and it made his stomach flutter.

"Smells like my ma's kitchen," he said as he crossed the threshold.

Sally smiled. "Have a seat."

His father had tried to take good care of Ma. Johnny needed to do the same for Sally. He hated that he lied to her. They'd never spoken of the secret things she had put in her letters, but he felt a great compassion for her. Someday maybe they could talk about really important things. Family. Children. God.

She had cut two big slabs of gingerbread and put them on Mark's ironstone plates.

He had to stop thinking of everything as Mark's. If he didn't, someday he'd slip up.

"That looks real fine," he said.

"Doesn't it? I admit I can't wait to eat some. And I'm glad you were close by, because the cream would break down if we didn't eat it right away."

Cam would miss out, but Johnny didn't care. This was something Sally had done for him. She had deliberately waited until Cam had gone and they were alone on the ranch. Should he be nervous? He didn't want to be. He sat down in his usual chair.

She poured coffee for both of them and sat down opposite.

"Should we pray?" he asked. It wasn't a meal, and he wasn't sure how she felt about praying for snacks.

"God tells us to give thanks for everything," she said gently.

Johnny closed his eyes. "Lord, we thank You for this gingerbread. . . and for. . .for Sally being here to make it." He opened one eye. Her eyes were closed, but she was still smiling. She had no idea how hypocritical he felt, praying when he knew he was a liar. "Amen."

"Amen." Her eyelids flew up.

Johnny caught his breath. Her eyes surely did set a man reeling.

"Mark, I wanted to do some washing this afternoon, but I couldn't find any laundry soap."

"Oh, yeah." He and Cam had finished the last of it in their frenzy of cleaning to prepare for her arrival. But after her journey, Sally probably wanted to give her wardrobe a good soaking. "I ran out and should have asked Cam to get some more. I'm sorry."

"It's all right. I can wait a few more days."

Gazing into those eyes made him want more than anything to please her.

"How about if we go to town tomorrow, just the two of us?"

"Will you be up to it?" she asked.

"I think so. Reckless is driving pretty well now. You can go to the mercantile and pick out whatever you want."

"For soap?" Sally asked.

"Soap and anything else you think we need." Though how he would pay for it, he didn't know. He would have to ask the storekeeper how much he owed already. How had Mark expected to support himself and Sally with such a small herd of cattle?

She was smiling at him. "I'd like that a lot, if you're not too busy with the building project to take me."

"Oh, well. . ." Johnny rubbed the back of his neck. "If Cam comes straight back with those windows, we can put them in this afternoon." Besides, Johnny was the boss now. If he wanted to take his wife in town, he could.

Sally's smile made the gingerbread taste even better. She reached over and gave his hand a squeeze, and a jolt of fire shot through him.

"Thank you, Mark. That's very thoughtful of you. And if your arm starts to hurting, I can drive."

That wasn't going to happen, but Johnny didn't think they needed to discuss it. He took a big bite of gingerbread.

CHAPTER 11

———◆———

Sally sang softly to herself as she prepared the noon meal. The kitchen was sweltering hot, and perspiration soaked her calico bodice. She recalled that her mother used to serve a cold dinner on hot days and cook only in the early morning and the evening. Until she had an outdoor oven, perhaps she should follow that practice.

Cam drove up when the sun was high overhead, and Mark ambled out of the barn and joined him.

Sally went to the doorway. "Dinner is ready."

Mark waved, and Sally went back to the stove to put the food on the table.

A few minutes later, the two men came in with droplets falling from their hair. Sally smiled, glad they were the kind who washed up before meals.

"Sit right down. I've got everything ready."

Cam took his seat and said, "I reckon we can finish the windows today, ma'am. Mark said you'd like to go into town tomorrow."

Sally wished he hadn't phrased it that way. "Mark asked me if I'd like to go."

Cam nodded. Was he thinking it wasteful to go to town two days in a row?

"I'll bring that ticking in after we eat."

"Ticking?" Sally asked.

Cam looked at Mark and raised his eyebrows.

"Uh, for the. . .the new mattress," Mark said. His cheeks went deep red, and he reached for the water pitcher. "We. . .uh. . .we're building a new bedstead for the addition."

"I see." Sally couldn't look at either one of them. She jumped up. "I forgot the salt." She hurried over to the cupboard but took her time fetching the saltshaker. Would Mark share the new furniture with her, or would she live in solitary splendor?

She liked Mark. A lot. When they were alone, he seemed as thoughtful and sensitive as he had in his letters. Maybe even more sensitive. Certainly more shy. She felt as though he was courting her, which wasn't bad, except that they were already married. She hoped this stage wouldn't last long. Maybe he was waiting for the new room to be finished, to guarantee them more privacy. Or for his arm to heal. Or for him to feel more comfortable with her, or with marriage in general. She sighed. There were so many forces at play, she couldn't sort out his motives. Cam was a big help, especially since Mark had been injured, but Sally couldn't help feeling the hired man stood between them and kept them from being as open and spontaneous with each other as they would be if they were alone on the ranch.

The next day, Mark informed her at breakfast that he would take her to town as soon as she was ready. He had helped Cam do the chores that morning, and Cam would stay behind to put some finishing touches on the new room. For one thing, they hadn't cut a door between the cabin and the addition yet. Sally hadn't seen the inside of it since the walls went up. The "boys" had climbed in and out one of the framed window holes until the first window was in place. Part of what Cam planned to do today was to set in the second casing, but he'd have to cut the doorway first, or he'd seal himself into the new room.

"Don't know as I'll have time to make a door today," Cam said.

"We can hang a curtain until it's done." Sally could hardly wait to move into the new bedroom.

As soon as the men cleared out after breakfast, she did up the dishes and put on her bonnet. She took her purse from the shelf beside the bunk. Before going out, she paused to finger the ticking. It was the standard, striped cotton used for pillows and mattresses. Mark had said he would fill it with sweet hay for her when she had sewn up the shell. She smiled and headed outside.

Reckless was in harness, and Mark stood at his head, stroking the chestnut's nose. He smiled when he saw Sally, and she smiled back. Things were getting better, even though she still didn't feel really married. *All in good time,* she told herself.

"Is your arm all right?" she asked him after the first couple of miles.

"It's fine." Men could be stubborn, she knew, but she hoped he wouldn't overdo it.

In Beaumont, he pulled up before the bank. "I reckon I'd better go in and get some cash."

"They won't give you credit at the mercantile?"

He frowned. "That's just it. They've given me quite a bit, and I don't like to keep stacking up bills."

She nodded. Financial responsibility was a good trait in a man, one her first husband hadn't known.

"Sally." He almost looked old when he said it—at least, he looked a bit worried, frowning and serious.

"What is it?" she asked softly.

"I don't know how it's going to go this year with the cattle and all. And I don't have all that much in the bank."

"Then we'll be frugal," she said readily. Was he worried that she would overspend? She needed to put his mind at ease. "We can get by, I'm sure. And if you can't increase the herd this year, then it will have to wait until next year. I'm used to living small, Mark."

His lips twitched in an almost smile. "Sure."

She glanced across the street. "Shall I go over and look at the merchandise while you're at the bank?"

Mark hesitated and then nodded. "That'd be fine."

He got down and gave her a hand as she climbed from the wagon.

"Now, don't you be worrying." Sally smiled and walked across to the mercantile. Before entering, she turned and looked back. She had known there was something between them, something holding them apart. Was it money, or the lack of it? Because she meant every word about that. She could eke out a living on next to nothing. She was glad he had brought up his concerns. But still, she wasn't convinced that was the whole of it. There must be something else. She sighed and went into the store.

Johnny walked up to the teller's cage, glad no one else was in line. The man he faced was the same one he had dealt with the day he withdrew money for the doctor and the preacher.

"Mr. Paynter," the teller said with a smile.

Another man behind the divider looked up from his desk and shoved his chair back.

"Mr. Paynter."

"Yes, sir?" Johnny peered through the grille at him. Did he know this man? More likely his brother did. His somber black suit, white shirt, and necktie bespoke prosperity and business. Johnny pegged him for the bank's president, manager, or owner.

He walked over close to the teller and lowered his voice. "Just wanted to make sure you knew the payment came into your account from the stockyards in Fort Worth."

"Oh," Johnny said. "Thank you."

The banker nodded. "I know springtime's difficult sometimes, and you ranchers are always watching to make sure your payments come in on time."

"Yes, sir."

The man nodded and walked back to his desk.

The teller smiled again. "How much did you want to withdraw, sir?"

"Uh. . ." Johnny wondered how much was in there now. He'd better not be too optimistic. "How about fifty dollars?"

"That would be fine, sir. If you have your passbook, I'll update that for you."

"Sure." Johnny had a hard time getting the bankbook out of his breast pocket with his left hand.

A moment later, the teller handed it back to him with fifty dollars in paper money.

"Thank you." Johnny walked out of the bank and went to lean against the side of his wagon. He stuffed the money into his pocket and carefully opened the bankbook. Six hundred and forty-two dollars, and that was after his withdrawal. His heart skipped a beat. No wonder Mark's herd was so small. He'd sent a bunch of steers off to the stockyards this spring.

Good old Mark. Johnny could hardly believe it, but the bankers wouldn't lie to him. There was someone else he ought to thank. He lifted his eyes skyward.

"Lord, I'm not sure You're speaking to me," he said softly, "but thank You. I don't deserve this, and that's certain. But Mark would have used it to build up the ranch and make a nice home for Sally. And that's what I intend to do with it. I hope You're not too mad at me."

He put the bankbook in his shirt pocket and walked across the street. Sally could buy whatever she wanted now.

When he walked into the mercantile, she was gazing at bolts of cloth. He stood still for a moment, watching her. Her fingers caressed the fabric then she pressed her lips together and moved on to the groceries. Johnny walked up behind her.

"Howdy. Finding what you need?"

She whirled around, her cheeks tinged with pink. "Oh, hello. I found the laundry soap already, and I thought I'd see what they have for spices. Mr. Minnick said he could help me anytime."

"Good. And I thought you might need a couple yards of cloth for a door curtain, if Cam and I don't get the door made right away."

Susan Page Davis

"That's good thinking." Sally looked back toward the display of material.

"How about you get some extra," Johnny said. "Would you like a dress length?"

"Oh, I don't need that, Mark." Her hand fluttered at her throat.

"It's all right." Besides her mourning dress and the green one she'd been married in, he had only seen her wear one calico dress. He wasn't sure whether she had more or not, but she was a seamstress. Surely some new fabric to work with would please her. He leaned toward her and whispered, "I got paid for some cattle I sold. You can buy out the store if you want."

He pulled back and was pleased to see the surprise on her face. "Is it those cattle you sent to market last month? You told me about driving them to the railway."

"Yeah," Johnny said, thinking rapidly.

"I figured you'd already been paid."

"Well, I. . .I wasn't sure when I'd get it."

"So we're not—" She glanced around, her cheeks pinker than before. "I guess that's something to talk about on the way home."

He nodded. "But get whatever you like for cooking, and for clothes. If you need anything—"

"Thank you." She pressed his hand and looked up into his eyes so intensely that Johnny's stomach flipped.

"I'll just. . . I'll be over looking at the hardware," he said. "Cam said to get hinges and a latch for the new door."

"All right."

He walked over to where the tools hung on a wall over bins of nails and other small hardware. From reading her letters, he knew Sally had been pinching pennies for years. He was glad he could relieve her of that anxiety. But would she go overboard now? Maybe he shouldn't have given her such broad permission.

When she approached him shyly twenty minutes later, she held a few notions in her hand.

"I've got thread and elastic and some buttons here. If you're sure, I'll get two yards of calico for the curtain, and another six for a dress. And I wondered, do we have linens that will fit the new. . ." She looked down, flushing again.

"That's a good thought. Maybe get something for that?"

"Muslin," she said. "Unless. . .well, linen's nicer. But it costs more."

He walked over to the yard-goods display with her. When he saw the prices, he almost laughed. She was talking about a few cents per yard difference.

He reached out with his good hand and felt the different materials. "Get the linen," he said.

"All right."

Shopping with Sally for the next half hour was pleasant. Johnny wondered why men complained about taking their wives to the store. He had laid out the hardware he wanted and added the metal parts he would need to make a windlass over the well. Sally asked the storekeeper to cut the lengths of cloth for her. Together, they listed off the soap and a few grocery items they'd thought of.

"Anything else?" Johnny asked. "More dishes, maybe?"

"We can get by with what you have, at least for a while."

He nodded. "All right, but you be thinking about it. Sometime I want to get you a nice set of dishes."

She smiled. "Christmas, maybe?"

"Or sooner." He didn't know her birthday. He'd have to coax that out of her sometime.

"Oh, maybe a clothesline?" Sally said.

"Sure." The few things Johnny and Cam had laundered since they'd been at the ranch, they had flung over the corral fence to dry, but that wouldn't do for a lady. "I should have had one a long time ago."

By the time they'd finished, they had two crates of stuff, and they were both laughing over something the storekeeper had said.

"Oh, and I'd like to bring my bill up to date." Johnny reached into his pocket for the money he'd gotten at the bank. He glanced apologetically at Sally. "Sorry, but putting it in my wallet was too hard with one hand. Would you mind helping me?"

Her eyes were wide as she took the bills from him.

"Well, let's see now." The storekeeper turned a few pages in a ledger on the counter. "You owed twenty-seven dollars and ten cents, and with all this stuff. . . Looks like thirty-nine fifty total."

Johnny let out the breath he'd been holding. That could have been a lot worse. He handed over forty dollars. Mr. Minnick gave him back fifty cents.

"Let me help you load those boxes." He came from behind the counter.

"I can get this one." Sally picked up the crate that held the cloth and soap and a few other items.

"You shouldn't do that," Johnny said.

She smiled. "Hush. I'm not a weakling, and you have a broken arm."

Sheepishly, Johnny trailed them outside and across to the wagon, where Reckless waited patiently. After Mr. Minnick had gone back to the store, he told Sally, "I'd like to go by the feed store and pay on my bill there, too. They were kind enough to give me credit."

"Certainly."

He drove down the street and went into the feed store by himself. The owner hailed him at once and came over with a grin.

"Hey, I heard you got married, Paynter!"

"Uh, that's right."

"Congratulations."

"Thanks. I wondered how much my bill is. Thought I'd pay you some today."

"I like the sound of that."

Johnny followed him to the tiny room he used as his office. The bill stood at twenty-one dollars. Johnny gave him the ten remaining in his pocket and promised to pay the rest soon.

"No hurry," the owner said.

Sally was looking at some papers when he got back to the wagon.

"What's that?" he asked, picking up the reins.

"The pattern for my new dress." She turned her head so he could see her face beneath the brim of her bonnet. She looked prettier than ever, because she looked ultimately happy.

"I'm glad you found one you like." He headed Reckless toward home. "Cam will be glad to know I got that money for the cattle."

"Cam?" Sally frowned. "Why would Cam care? Have you been discussing your finances with him?"

Johnny eyed her uncertainly. Had he done something wrong? "I sort of told him things had been a little tight lately."

Sally said nothing.

Johnny thought quickly. "I wasn't sure I could pay him at the end of the month. You don't think I should talk to him about stuff like that?"

"It just seemed odd to me that you would tell a hired hand about your finances."

"Well, he *is* an old friend."

Sally folded up the flimsy sheets of paper on which the pattern was printed and tucked them into an envelope. "I'm sorry." She looked over at him earnestly. "I know everyone's different, and I shouldn't have questioned you on that. My parents were always short of money, but they would never discuss it with anyone outside the family. I guess their attitude rubbed off on me."

"It's probably a good one," Johnny said. "I just didn't think about it with Cam. I mean, it's been him and me for the last. . .well, for a while now."

"You were close friends before he came here?" Sally asked.

"Close enough. We worked together. Got along all right. Didn't always agree on everything, but he's a stout fellow. If you get in a fight, you want him on your side."

"I'll keep that in mind."

Johnny laughed. "The boys used to say, if you get in a brawl in town, make sure Cam's with you."

"Oh, did you get in a lot of those?" Sally's face was sober, but her eyes twinkled just a bit, and Johnny had the feeling she was teasing him.

"No, not many. I usually kept clear of saloon fights. But you're right. I need to get used to. . .us. We're a family now."

Sally looked down at her hands in her lap. "Well, the start of one, anyway."

Johnny felt his own face heat. "Right. And I suppose there's things married folks hadn't ought to air with anyone else. Is that how you see it?"

She nodded and gazed up at him. "It is, Mark. Thank you for understanding. And I'll try to understand better about you and your friend."

They rode on in silence for a while. Finally Johnny decided to ask her flat out about some things.

"Sally, I was wondering, is there anything else you'd like to do, or anything I should know about?"

Her gentle smile warmed him. She tucked her hand through the crook of his arm.

"I did wonder if we'd be able to go to church."

"Well, sure." Johnny tried to think what day it was. Sally had come on a Tuesday. . . . "Is tomorrow Sunday?"

"Yes."

"It kind of snuck up on me."

"That's all right. If you don't want to go this week. . ."

"No, I'll go. Just remind me in the morning, so I can be ready in time."

"Have you and Cam been going?"

"Uh. . .not the last few weeks. In fact, not since Cam got here. We've been real busy."

"I understand," she said, "but you did tell me in your letters that you went nearly every Sunday."

"I try," Johnny said weakly. Would anyone at the church realize he wasn't Mark? "I don't know if Cam will go, though. We can ask him."

"It would do him good," Sally said with a wry face.

"Why do you say that?"

"Oh, Cam's a charming fellow when he wants to be, and I guess he's a steady worker, but I've heard him comment a couple of times about stopping in at the saloon, and I did smell beer on him when he came home from town yesterday."

Johnny didn't know what to say. He did recall a few times back in Colorado when Cam came back from his night off staggering and belligerent. He didn't think Cam had ever joined the few that went to church during his time at the Lone Pine Ranch. But maybe it was better not to volunteer that information.

"Well, we can ask him."

"We certainly can." They rode along in silence. A few clouds studded the sky, keeping the sun's heat from being unbearable. The wagon raised a dust, but Reckless behaved as though he'd been a driving horse for years, and the journey was peaceful. Sally didn't take her hand away from his elbow, and Johnny liked the feel of it. He wished his other arm wasn't in the sling. He might be able to hold her hand.

"Mark?"

"Hmm?"

"I know you're a godly man," she began.

Johnny gritted his teeth. He did believe in the Almighty, and in His Son, Jesus, but he wouldn't have pegged himself as godly. Especially not now. Godly men didn't lie to their wives, or to preachers or lawmen. He started to protest, but Sally went on.

"I wondered if you'd like to read the scriptures together in the evening. I'd. . .I'd like to have a Christian home."

"We can do that." Johnny remembered when Ma used to read from the Bible to him and Mark.

"Thank you."

He nodded. "And if there's anything else you want, you tell me."

Sally squeezed his arm a little. When they came in sight of the ranch, though, she took her hand away. Hammer blows resounded from the far end of the house.

"Sounds like Cam's at it," Johnny said. He got down and helped Sally to earth. She paused for a moment, looking up at him. He couldn't help thinking how perfect she was for Mark. Could he make his brother's ideal match happy?

"Thank you for this time with you," she said, not quite meeting his gaze.

Johnny dared to touch her sleeve. "I enjoyed it."

Her smile held him for a moment, until Cam's boisterous voice called, "Thought I heard the wagon. How'd it go?"

Sally turned toward him. "Just fine, Cam. We have some supplies to carry in."

He walked over and peered into the wagon bed then whistled. "That's a lot of stuff, Boss."

"It's all right," Johnny said. "Help me with those crates, will you?"

Sally was already halfway to the house. He wished they could have talked longer.

Cam smiled impishly at him. "Looks like you and the missus are getting along pretty good."

"Yeah, I guess so."

"Great. Because I got the windows all squared away. If you want to get the hay for the mattress this afternoon, and if Mrs. Paynter has a mind to stitch, you can occupy your new abode tonight."

Johnny swallowed hard. "That'd be good." But inwardly he wondered. Sally liked him. She wanted them to be a family. He liked her. His arm wasn't hurting so badly now. Should he continue to make excuses?

"I got the door ready to hang, too. You can help me after we put this stuff away and take care of the horse."

"Sure." Johnny walked to Reckless's head and began to remove his bridle. "Sally and I are going to church in the morning. And in case you're wondering, that's my normal habit. I just haven't gone the last few weeks, since you came here, because we had so much work to do."

Cam paused with the first crate on the edge of the wagon bed. "That right?"

Johnny nodded. "I'd appreciate it if you didn't tell her any different, and at least be polite if she invites you to go along."

Cam swung the crate out and turned toward the cabin. "That's fine, as long as I can say no."

CHAPTER 12

Cam set the crate of cloth on the table and rummaged under the calico and linen. "I've got the hinges and the latch set. Anything else I should take out of here?"

"I think that's it," Sally said. She took off her bonnet and turned to hang it up and stopped to stare at the new doorway in the wall. "Oh."

Cam grinned. "As you can see, I was pretty busy while you two were gone. I got the doorway cut and the windows trimmed, but I still need to put the bedstead together and build the door."

"I got some extra calico for a curtain. You don't have to finish the door today."

He shrugged. "We'll see how it goes. I'm sure you and Mark would like to get settled as soon as possible."

She wasn't sure what he meant by that and decided not to ask. Sometimes Cam said things that hinted at the unseemly. She hung up her bonnet and took her apron from its hook.

"Mark said he could stuff the mattress as soon as you're done stitching it up."

"I'll settle that with Mark," she said brusquely and opened the cupboard to get some cornmeal. It was nearly noon, and she didn't have dinner ready.

She hoped Cam would go out and leave her alone in her kitchen, but he hovered, removing items from the crates. He carried the laundry soap to one of the shelves and stowed it then went back to the table and took out a sack of rice.

"I'll take care of those things," Sally said.

"No trouble."

She forced a smile. "A woman likes to arrange her kitchen to her own liking."

He eyed her uncertainly for a moment and then let the sack fall gently back into the crate. "All right, then."

The door opened, and Mark came in. Sally turned back to her task, relieved.

"There's some pretty fresh hay in the loft," Mark said. "We can cut new if you'd rather, but it would take two or three days to dry out."

"What's in the barn will be fine, so long as it smells fresh," she said.

Mark nodded. "Then I reckon I can throw some down for you, and then Cam and I will work on the door until dinnertime."

Sally refused to let Cam steal the joy she took in preparing dinner for her own husband. She wasn't even sure what it was about Cam that bothered her, short of his very presence. A newlywed couple ought to be alone. She was sure Mark would open up more if it was just the two of them.

She put together a hasty noontime meal, made easier by some of the canned goods they had purchased. Once the men had gone back to work, she laid out the mattress ticking and pinned the edges for the seams. This would be a long, boring task, but she didn't mind. It was for her own home, her own husband. She hummed as she worked, against a counterpoint of hammering and sawing from the barn.

She was halfway around the edge, making small, tight stitches, when Mark came to the front door.

"Cam and I are ready to bring the door in. I forked down plenty of hay for you."

"Thanks." She smiled at him, and Mark smiled back.

A few seconds later, he and Cam walked through, balancing the new door between them. They tipped it to get it through the front doorway then watched the edges, trying not to bump anything. Mark was walking backward, and Cam kept calling directions to him.

"A little to your left. No, your right. Sorry. Look out for the—"

Thud.

Mark looked sheepishly down at the pan that had fallen from her worktable.

"No harm," Sally said. "I meant to put that away earlier."

The door was soon hung, and the men spent the next half hour fussing over the latch. Cam crossed the room with a hammer in one hand and a can of small hardware in the other.

"May I see the finished room?" Sally asked.

"Oh, well, Mark and me are going to do some finish work in there. Whyn't you wait a bit?"

"All right." Sally kept stitching. Mark and Cam went out and in, and she feigned disinterest, but she noticed that on several trips, they carried boards and other pieces of wood from outside into the new room. At last they seemed to have everything they wanted. More pounding ensued and clattering and muffled exclamations.

"It doesn't fit right," Mark said once, to which Cam replied, "Yes, it does. I tested it in the barn."

More pounding followed. As Sally placed the last few stitches, she distinctly heard Cam swear and decided it was time for her to go out and stuff the mattress. She smoothed out the ticking, turned it, and folded it. With the unwieldy bundle in her arms, she went out into the harsh sun.

In the barn, she found a pile of sweet-smelling hay, as Mark had promised. She set to work filling the tick and prodding the hay into the proper shape and firmness. Perspiration dripped from her brow and trickled down her cheeks and her back. She took one break and went to the well for a drink of water. Even the well water wasn't very cold, but it was far cooler than the air. She made a trip to the outhouse. When she came out, she could still hear the men hammering away, so she went back to her task.

After what seemed an eternity, she had all the hay she could fit in the tick, and she went back to the house for her sewing basket. Her arms ached, and her bodice was saturated with perspiration. She was sure dust had caked on her face, but she didn't mind. She was nearly done, and it felt good.

She stitched closed the opening through which she had stuffed the mattress and put her needle away. She couldn't resist stretching out full length on the ticking. She didn't feel any bad lumps, and she let out a big sigh. She hadn't felt so comfortable in days.

———

"All done," Cam said at last.

"I'll tell Sally." Johnny went into the main room, but she wasn't there. "She must be filling the tick," he called to Cam. "I'll go get her."

He ambled out to the barn, surprised at how low the sun was. Sally would be starting supper soon. He liked knowing his wife would cook for him and make sure he had a good supper.

"Sally?" he called outside the barn. She didn't answer, and he stepped into the shade under the roof. There was the new mattress, with Sally lying on it fast asleep. He stood over her, grinning. Just like Goldilocks. Her hair fanned out on the striped ticking. Her face was smudged with dust, and she looked like a child. An adorable child. He sank to his knees beside her and reached out to touch her shoulder.

"Sally."

Her eyelashes fluttered, and she looked up at him then tried to push herself up, her face flushing.

"I must have dozed off."

"It's all right. Must be a comfy mattress." He winked at her, and she gave him a timid smile.

"It surely is, Mark. I hope you'll try it tonight."

Johnny swallowed hard. "Well, I dunno. . . ."

Her smile disappeared. "What time is it?"

"Nigh on suppertime."

"Oh no. I didn't start the sweet potatoes."

He helped her up. "I'll carry this in for you. Are you ready to see your new room?"

"I've been waiting with bated breath."

He laughed, knowing that wasn't true.

"Well, figuratively," she amended, brushing the hay and dust from her skirt. "Am I filthy? I feel as though I am."

"Not too bad, but if you'd like a bath tonight, I'll fetch extra water."

She frowned. "You've been working all day. You'd better let Cam lug the water, and that mattress, too."

Johnny tried to stand it on edge, but he couldn't manage with one arm. "Guess I'd better ask him to help me."

He laid the mattress down and dared to seize Sally's hand. "Come on. I want to be there when you see it."

They hurried across the yard to the cabin, and she didn't pull her hand away. Johnny refused to think about how it made him feel to walk with her like this, her warm fingers curled around his.

They walked through the dim main room and stopped before the closed door. Sally surveyed the planed boards and the wrought-iron hinges and thumb latch.

"It looks nice."

Johnny smiled and squeezed her hand. "Open it."

Sally put her hand to the latch and squeezed it then slowly pushed the door inward. She took two steps into the room and stopped. Cam stood near the far window with a piece of sandpaper in his hand. Johnny dodged around her so he could see her expression. She was smiling.

He looked over at Cam and grinned.

Cam stepped forward. "We had some trouble putting the bedstead together, ma'am, but it's fine now. And we'll bring in the mattress for you whilst you're cooking supper."

"Thank you," Sally said softly. She glanced at the row of hooks on the inside wall then walked to the near window and looked out through one of the four small panes. "I can see the garden."

"That's right," Johnny said, "and from the other window, you can see the road toward town. That way, if you hear someone coming, you can look out and see who it is before they tie their rig up."

She turned toward him, her face aglow. "You've done a wonderful job, boys."

Johnny could hardly contain his pleasure at hearing her words of praise. "And we put baseboards all around," he added. "It'll keep out the drafts and some of the vermin. Don't know if you want the walls painted."

Sally looked around at the plain, pine-board walls.

"I thought maybe later on, if the money's not too tight, you might want to plaster and wallpaper," Johnny added. His mother had told him once that wallpaper was a sign of permanence. If a woman wallpapered her parlor, she was staying put.

"That might be nice," Sally said, "but this is fine for now. Very fine. Thank you both."

"We'll get that mattress in," Johnny said, "and you can put your new linens on it. Come on, Cam."

When they carried the straw tick through a couple of minutes later, Sally was bustling about the kitchen. She had stirred up the cook fire, and it already felt hotter in the house. Johnny wished there was a way to cool things off for her. He'd have to think about that outdoor oven soon.

They situated the mattress on the bed frame.

"There." Cam patted his side as smooth as could be expected. "You and the missus will have a fancy place to sleep tonight."

Johnny felt his cheeks fire up, as they always did when Cam mentioned his private life with Sally.

"Maybe I can filch the tick off the bunk bed," Cam said.

Johnny considered that. "All right, but we'd better ask her first, not just do it." He had had some vague idea that he might sleep out there on the narrow bed, now that Sally had this fine room, and not tell Cam he was still, for all practical purposes, a bachelor. "I reckon we should build a bunkhouse by fall."

Cam grinned. "Thinking you'll prosper come fall roundup? Maybe you'll need to hire some more hands."

"I doubt that."

In the kitchen, Sally was stirring some kind of batter in an earthenware bowl.

"Ma'am, do you mind if I take the mattress off that there little bed?" Cam asked.

"Oh, help yourself, Cam." Sally leaned over the worktable, frowning at a sheet of paper. "Two eggs."

"I'll help you," Johnny said.

"Naw, I can get it," Cam said. He folded the bedding from the bunk. When he'd gone out with his prize, Johnny sat down on a stool on the opposite side of Sally's worktable.

"Need anything?"

She glanced up at him and smiled. "Not right now, thanks. But I would take you boys up on the offer of bathwater later."

"Sure. We'll fill the boiler for you."

Sally went to the cupboard and came back with two eggs, which she cracked into her mixing bowl. Johnny looked over his shoulder to make sure Cam wasn't coming back inside yet.

"Listen, Sally. . ."

She stopped stirring and gazed into his eyes. "What is it?"

"I've been thinking about what you said. I've decided not to tell Cam how much money we have."

She smiled a little when he said *we*.

"He asked me, when we were working today, why I charged so much at the mercantile, when he knew I was about broke. So I told him that. . . that a payment came in for the cattle. But I didn't say how much."

She nodded. "That's probably wise, Mark. Now he'll know you

can pay him for his work, but he won't know all your business. Even though he's a friend, I think it's good for an employer to keep a little distance between himself and his workers."

Johnny nodded slowly. He and Cam had lived closer than most brothers for the last few weeks, but still, he knew they were as different as a peach and a cactus. For a while their future had depended on each other. He wouldn't have made it out of Colorado alive without Cam's warning and urging to make haste. And Cam wouldn't be surviving now without him. At least not comfortably.

But if none of that business at the Lone Pine had happened, Mark would still be dead, and someone would probably have contacted him, and he supposed he would have inherited his brother's property. They hadn't found any papers in the house indicating otherwise.

That put him in mind of something else. He ought to write a will, bequeathing all of this to Sally. That was what Mark would have wanted, and Johnny knew at once that he wanted it on paper. If anything happened to him, there should be no question about who owned the ranch. The way things stood now, Cam could open a can of worms if he died.

But would a will he signed with Mark's name be legal? Johnny clenched his teeth together. It would be as legal as this marriage.

"You look powerful somber," Sally said.

"Just thinking."

"Care to share your thoughts, Mr. Paynter?"

The subtle reminder of their bond only made Johnny more uncomfortable. He should be telling her everything. A man shouldn't keep secrets from his wife. Though Sally's tone had been light, her face was dead serious.

"I. . .I need to write a will."

She blinked. "That's an odd thing to say. You don't expect to leave this earth soon, do you?"

Johnny rubbed the back of his neck and wished it wasn't so hot in here. "No, but you never can tell, can you? I just meant I want to make sure that if something should happen, you would get the house. The ranch. Everything."

"I'm your wife. Wouldn't I get it anyway? I mean, this is Texas."

He hesitated. When it came down to it, Sally had lived in Texas a lot longer than he had. She knew the laws better. "I guess so. I just wasn't sure what would happen if I didn't have a will."

"I suppose it would be better to have it on paper," she said.

He nodded. "I'll get started on that extra hot water. And can I move your things into the other room for you?"

"That'd be nice."

Hauling the water one bucket at a time was hard work, but somehow Johnny didn't want to ask Cam to help get his wife's bathwater. It took him quite a while, and Sally had to help him heft and tip each pail up when he brought it to the kitchen, but at last both the stove's reservoir and the boiler were full.

Supper was ready then, and he didn't move her things until afterward. Sally had kept most of her clothing and personal belongings in her trunk so far. He would have to get Cam to help him move that into the bedroom, but he could take her satchel in, and her things from the little cupboard.

She was in there before him, shaking out the snowy new bottom sheet. Without asking, Johnny went to the other side of the bed and tucked in the edge.

She smiled big. "Thank you."

He cleared his throat. "We'll bring your trunk in later."

"I'm in no hurry."

He went out to the main room and brought the box cupboard in. It was light, with only a few things inside.

Sally stood by the row of six hooks. "I'll leave you half."

"Two is plenty," Johnny said.

"All right, then, I'll hang up my Sunday dress."

"My ma always brushed hers on Saturday night," Johnny said. "Us boys' pants and jackets, too. She'd starch our Sunday shirts real stiff and press 'em." He gulped. "We don't have a flat iron. I'm sorry. I should have thought of it when we were in town."

Sally turned her bright smile on him again. "Well now, I'm real happy to tell you that I can save you some money. I'm a dressmaker, you know. I've got an iron in my trunk."

Johnny laughed. "No wonder it's so heavy."

Sally laughed, too. "You made a joke, Mark! I think you're making progress."

"What do you mean?" The way she said that made him feel like there was something wrong with him. Other than being a bold-faced liar.

She walked over and stood facing him, her arms crossed. "We can have a good life together, Mark Paynter. And we can have good times. Happy times. It's up to us to make them." She reached up and touched his cheek, sliding her warm fingers into his beard along the side of his jaw. "You've got to believe that."

Johnny's stomach went all wobbly. "I do," he said quickly.

She held his gaze a moment longer. "All right. Well, maybe you can open that trunk and bring me the green dress, while I spread the quilt out."

"Sure." He escaped into the main room, feeling he had disappointed her. What did she want? He knew what he wanted. He'd been tempted to pull her into his arms and kiss her. But if he did that, and then she found out he wasn't Mark, how much would she hate him? This wasn't a game, and when he kissed her again—if he ever did—it had to be when she knew the truth.

He unbuckled the straps that encircled her trunk and opened the lid. Green dress, she'd said. Something blue and soft was on top. A shawl, maybe. He hadn't seen her wear that yet. He pushed it carefully aside, thinking how pretty Sally would look in that cloud of fluffiness, with her blue eyes gazing into his.

Underneath was the sturdy, dark green material of the dress she'd worn for the wedding. He lifted it out. That was the dress, all right, the color of the pines in the Colorado mountains. He wondered if she had made it herself. The front was all full of tucks and folds, with shiny mother-of-pearl buttons right down the middle. As he lifted the skirt free of the trunk, something beneath it shifted. It looked like a packet of letters, similar to the one Mark had kept, only this batch was in Mark's handwriting.

Johnny's hands clenched around the folds of the green dress. Sally had kept all of Mark's letters, the same way he had kept hers. She was familiar with Mark's handwriting, which was nothing like Johnny's. What would he do when she noticed that his writing was not the same as it used to be?

His broken arm would help for another month or so. No one expected him to do much writing while it healed. But there would come a day when he had to write something, and Sally would be there to read it.

Maybe he could tell her that the broken arm had changed it somehow. It had made his bones heal back differently, and that made his handwriting different. Sloppier, for sure. Mark had always written more neatly than he did. Johnny figured he stood a fairly good chance of getting Sally to believe it.

More lies.

He hated himself for even thinking it, for planning to lie to her again. But if he didn't, she would unmask him. Even if he wrote a simple will to benefit her, or if he went off on a cattle drive and sent her a note to tell her he was all right, she would know, or at least suspect. But he couldn't go the rest of his life without writing anything.

He sat down on the hard boards of the bunk with the dress spread across his knees. This wasn't right. It hadn't been right from the start, and it still wasn't. But if he told her, would she be more hurt than if he didn't? She probably wouldn't want to stay with him, but what would she do? Would she go back to her folks? She hadn't when her first husband died. Would she be too mortified to face them again if she learned her new marriage was a fraud?

"Mark?" Sally came to the doorway of the new bedroom, smiling. "There you are. I thought maybe you'd gone out to the barn."

He stood and walked across the room, holding out the dress. "No, I'm here. This is the dress you wanted, isn't it?"

"That's the one." She took it and held it up with a satisfied glint in her eyes.

"I was recalling how pretty you looked in it," Johnny said. "Did you stitch it yourself?"

"Uh-huh."

He looked at it again. "You're really good at sewing, aren't you?"

"I'm not bad. And I meant what I told you before. . . . If we ever truly go broke—I mean, if something terrible happened and we lost all the cattle or something—I might be able to help earn some money by sewing again."

"Thanks. I hope you won't ever have to worry about that."

"So do I, but I wanted you to know that I can if we need it."

He nodded. The last thing he wanted to do was ask Sally to support him. He'd already done enough to ruin her life, if she only knew.

He was tempted again to kiss her, and he turned toward the door. "I'd best see if Cam needs anything else."

That evening, while Sally took her bath in the new room and he leaned on the corral fence watching the calves, and later, when Sally got out her Bible and read aloud from the book of Romans, he kept brooding about Mark's letters. If he could read those letters, it would certainly help him out some. He would know what Mark had promised her and what Sally had expected when she got off the train in Beaumont. And he might learn a few other things from his older brother—like how to win a woman's love.

He knew Sally liked him, but that was only because she thought he was Mark. Deep down, he wanted her to like Johnny, too—all right, to love Johnny. Because he already understood why Mark was attracted to her. Just reading her letters, he had fathomed that. Now that he'd been living under the same roof with her for several days, he truly wished he were Mark so that he wouldn't have to disappoint her.

CHAPTER 13

S ally patted her hair into place and eyed herself critically in the small hand mirror she'd brought along from St. Louis. Maybe someday, she and Mark would have a fine ranch house and a big, beveled mirror. For now, the little cabin with its rough addition and her brass-framed hand glass would have to do.

She hoped she would pass muster with the ladies at church. Mark had seemed to like her green dress. He'd really opened up a little yesterday. Or so she had thought, until it was time to retire.

She frowned and reached for her small pendant with the green stone. It was the only piece of jewelry she owned besides her two wedding rings and an onyx mourning brooch her aunt had sent her after David's death. She was married now, and she would not wear the brooch again, but the pendant held happier memories. Her father had traded supplies for it and a turquoise necklace for her mother to some Comancheros. Sally was only twelve years old at the time. Her mother had said it was a waste to trade for jewelry, but the men offering it needed supplies, and they didn't have much else to trade. They claimed Sally's was an emerald, but her father said it probably wasn't real. Later, they'd heard the Comancheros traded people as slaves, and her father regretted doing business with them. But Sally loved the square green stone on its gold chain.

As to Mark, she had lain awake for hours last night, debating whether or not to touch him or to say something. He had kept to his side of the new bed and didn't seem inclined to cross the invisible line between them. Sally didn't know what more to do. If her father were here, she'd ask him to have a frank talk with her husband. But there was no one. She certainly couldn't discuss the topic with Cam. Her hopes had slowly waned until his even breathing told her he had drifted into sleep, and she had held back the tears that hovered so close to the surface.

She sighed and fastened the clasp to the necklace. Best not to get upset thinking about it now. If they didn't leave for church soon, they would be late.

Mark was waiting in the dooryard. He had Reckless brushed and harnessed. Her husband looked even nicer than he had the day they got married. She couldn't help smiling as she walked toward him. Surely if she kept praying about it, they could work things out. He was a very nice man, and he seemed willing to do anything to assure her comfort—except the one thing that would make her feel truly married.

His velvety brown eyes smoldered as he gazed her way. Sally took her time walking over to where he stood by the wagon.

"You look. . .real fine," he said.

"So do you, Mark. Very nice."

"Thanks."

With his good hand, he helped her onto the wagon seat. Sally arranged her skirt and shawl and set her Bible in the wagon bed behind them, while he climbed up and gathered the reins.

"You couldn't talk Cam into going?" she asked.

Mark shook his head. "I don't think he's of a mind for it."

"That's too bad. You did want to go, didn't you?" She hoped he wasn't just driving into town and sitting through church for her sake.

"Of course. I shouldn't have quit going so long."

"I'm glad you're taking me." She slipped her hand beneath his elbow. Of course, he had to hold the reins, but he squeezed her hand against his side a little with his arm. Encouraged, Sally set about to keep him talking. "What's the minister like?"

"Oh, he—" Mark frowned. "Uh, he's all right. You met him."

"Yes, but only for our wedding. How are his sermons? Is he fiery or pedantic, or. . ."

"Um, I guess I'd say. . .he's about average."

She smiled. "Mark Paynter, you're a hard man to get information out of, do you know that?"

"Sorry. I know he spends some time preparing his sermons."

"That's good. A preacher ought to study God's Word a lot."

"Well, sure."

"And I know he's married," Sally said. "What's his wife like?"

Mark seemed to have to think hard about that one. "She. . .uh. . . she cooks a lot. Bakes bread."

Sally laughed. "What's her name?"

"Uh. . .Myra, I think."

"Well, that's something. Will you introduce me to her?"

"Sure."

"Maybe she'll give me her bread recipe."

He eyed her sidelong, as though wondering whether she was serious.

"Do they have children?" Sally asked.

"Uh. . .I'm not sure. I don't really know them very well."

"I see." Sally would just have to get to know Mrs. Lewis and ask her about the family.

They arrived at the church on time, and Mark was settling Reckless with a measure of oats when the bell pealed. He took her Bible from the wagon and handed it to her then offered his arm.

Sally felt very self-conscious as they walked to the steps. Everyone seemed to be staring at her. Two women were talking just outside the door. One of them, a middle-aged woman dressed in lavender, turned and smiled.

"Mr. Paynter! Won't you introduce me to your lovely bride?"

Mark hesitated and then drew Sally forward.

"Surely, ma'am. Uh, this is Sally. And Sally, this is Mrs. Lewis, the preacher's wife."

Relieved at the woman's overt friendliness, Sally extended her hand. "I'm so pleased to meet you, Mrs. Lewis."

"We're very happy to have you here, my dear."

"Thank you. And thank you for the bouquet you sent to the church last week. It was lovely and much appreciated."

Mrs. Lewis waved a hand as though it was not worth mentioning. "Now, we have just a minute before the second bell. Let me introduce you to a few of our ladies." She smiled coyly at Mark. "You won't mind sharing her, will you, Mr. Paynter?"

He looked a little dazed, but he shook his head and let Sally go. There followed a round of breakneck introductions. Women, from girls barely old enough to put their hair up to elderly matrons, seemed to appear from out of thin air. Sally would never keep the names straight, so she stopped trying and basked in their warm welcomes and felicitations.

"I have to say you caught the handsomest bachelor in the congregation," one very pregnant young woman said. "Almost as good a catch as my husband, Bill."

"Oh, thank you," Sally said, unsure whether or not to comment on her assessment of Mark's looks.

Mrs. Bill pulled another youngish woman toward her. "This is my sister-in-law. We're both named Mary, so if you want one of us just yell, 'Mary Hood,' and one of us is sure to come running."

"Or both," said the other Mary.

Sally laughed. "Thank you. Glad to meet you both." The second Mary seemed more reserved than the first, but she gave Sally a shy smile from beneath her chip bonnet.

Sally tried not to be too obvious in observing the women's attire and decided that, poor as she was, she was among the better dressed. This was due to her own sewing skills, she was certain. Although her current wardrobe was small and serviceable, her dresses were well cut and tastefully trimmed.

The bell tolled again, and the ladies hurried to round up their children and join their husbands inside. Mark was waiting for Sally where she had left him. She took his arm and entered the small, dim building. People filled nearly all the benches, but the first Mary and a young man Sally assumed to be Bill squeezed over, leaving enough room on the end for the Paynters.

Every church was different, Sally realized, but this one seemed more like home than any church she had found in St. Louis. In spite of the warmth inside the little building and the closeness of the eighty or so people in it, she wouldn't have traded the next hour for anything. Pastor Lewis led them in singing a few familiar hymns, and when he began his sermon, Sally felt something inside her chest nestle down in contentment. After more than a year of the Reverend Mr. Winters's rants, Pastor Lewis's homily soothed her.

Mark was watching her. When she glanced over at him, he looked straight ahead, but she caught him at it again later. She smiled and turned her attention back to the minister.

When the sermon was over, people thronged them in the aisle, introducing themselves to Sally and congratulating Mark on his marriage. Everyone seemed happy for him, though most of them called him "Mr. Paynter."

One very tall man pumped Mark's hand and said, "Hey, Mark, you ol' cuss. You still want that young stock we talked about?"

Mark seemed at a loss for words momentarily. "Uh, sure. Yes."

"Great. Ride on over tomorrow anytime. I'll cut 'em out for ya." The man nodded and headed for the door in the wake of a woman in a voluminous yellow calico dress. Mark followed him with his eyes, frowning.

He glanced at Sally, and she whispered. "That's great. He's holding some cattle for you."

"Yeah," Mark said.

A red-haired woman of about thirty tapped Sally on the shoulder.

"Hi. I'm Liz Merton. Just wanted to welcome you and invite you to the ladies' group on Wednesday afternoon."

"Oh," Sally said. "Where is it held?"

"At my house this time. We're making a quilt for the missionary barrel."

"Sounds like fun," Sally said. "Can I bring anything?"

"Just your sewing basket and yourself." Liz giggled. "I live on Flood Street, just past the bank."

"Flood Street?" Sally asked.

"Uh-huh. On account of the lower end floods every spring. Second house on the right, with a sweet potato plant in a pot on the porch steps."

"All right. Thank you." Sally would have to make sure Mark didn't mind, but she looked forward to a chance to get to know the ladies and exercise her stitching skills on something prettier than mattress ticking. The six-mile drive into town wouldn't be too burdensome.

By the time they got out the door, Sally had a request for her dress pattern and a dinner invitation for herself and Mark the next Sunday.

Pastor Lewis greeted them heartily. "Well, well! So good to see the newlyweds being faithful on the Lord's Day."

"I enjoyed the service very much," Sally said, shaking his hand.

"Thank you kindly, Mrs. Paynter. I bring what the Lord gives me each week." He grinned at Mark and stuck out his hand to him. "Mr. Paynter. Hope to see you again soon."

"Probably so," Mark said. Once they reached the ground in the churchyard, he looked all around and sighed deeply.

"Is something wrong?" Sally asked.

"I don't see that feller."

"Which one?"

"The one with the young stock. The truth is, I can't remember what his name is. I've met him a few times at church, and he said he had some calves to sell me, but I'd sort of forgotten, and now I can't recall his name."

"Oh dear." Sally glanced about and spotted Liz Merton. "Wait just a minute. Or better yet, get Reckless ready to go. I'll meet you at the wagon."

She dashed off before he could protest. A bearded man who looked at least ten years older than Liz was handing her up onto the front seat of a farm wagon. Two boys sat in the back.

"Oh, Mrs. Merton," Sally called, running the last few steps.

The man turned and waited expectantly.

"Mrs. Paynter," Liz said with a broad smile. "This is my husband, Dan Merton."

"Ma'am," he said, touching the brim of his hat.

"Is there something I can help you with?" Liz asked.

"Yes. I wondered if you could tell me someone's name. I've met so many people today, I'm afraid I'm confused."

"Surely. Who is it?" Liz and her husband both gazed over the emptying churchyard.

"Well, he's left now," Sally said. "But he was really tall, and he had a beard."

"Sounds like Caxton," Mr. Merton said.

"I believe his wife was wearing a yellow dress," Sally added.

"Poke bonnet?" Liz asked.

"Yes."

"Definitely Eph Caxton." Liz nodded firmly.

"Thank you so much." Sally dashed off before they could ask why she hadn't simply appealed to her husband for the man's name. Panting, she arrived at their wagon. Mark was just fastening the last buckle. "His name's Eph Caxton."

"Eph Caxton. I don't s'pose your friend told you where he lives?"

Sally drooped low in her seat. "No. I'm sorry. I would have asked, but I thought she'd wonder why I was so interested in him."

"No matter. I'll find out. But thank you."

———

Johnny whistled as he puttered around the barn and corral the next morning. He had put a bug in Cam's ear, and of course Cam was more than willing to ride into town and discover the whereabouts of the Caxton ranch. Johnny figured Cam could play the "I'm Mark Paynter's new ranch hand and I don't know where anyone lives" card for some time yet.

He would be glad when his arm had healed enough to let him do basic chores like milking the cow, carrying buckets of water, and digging fence-post holes. The pain wasn't sharp now, but it still ached, and the doctor had been firm about letting it heal thoroughly before he tried to do too much with that arm. Sally and Cam split the chores quite cheerfully, and Johnny found other things that he could handle one-handed. Riding fence, for instance. If he was going to put a new bunch of young stock in his pasture, he'd better go all the way around the fence and make sure it was secure.

Sally came from the house with the water pail. Johnny ambled toward her and met her at the well. He wished he could pull the full bucket up for her. He had done it a few times with his left arm only, but he found it extremely difficult. Usually he wound up having to use his right hand, too, and that made his arm hurt. Building a windlass for the well would be one of his first projects after he was healed.

"I wish I could be the one doing that," he said as she hoisted the bucket hand over hand.

She smiled. "It's all right. You'll soon be mended, and then I'll gladly give the job over."

"Anything else I could do for you today?"

She cocked her head to one side and considered. "Could you tighten the clothesline? I put it up, but it's slack. I know there's a way to fix it, but I don't have the knack."

"That's easy. In fact, I can teach you to do it less than a minute."

"Really?"

Johnny grinned. "Really. Any woman as smart as you can learn something like that easy enough."

Sally hefted the bucket of water the last few inches and set it on the edge of the stone berm around the well. "I don't know about that. I don't think of myself as smart."

"Sure you are," Johnny said. "Look at how you make things. Most women can cook and sew, but you make art out of it."

Her eyes widened. "Thank you. That may be the nicest thing a man ever said to me. But still. . ."

"What?" He took the bail of the bucket with his left hand and started walking toward the cabin.

"If I were smart, I wouldn't make so many mistakes." Her whole face darkened when she frowned.

Johnny eyed her cautiously. He didn't know of any mistakes she'd made except marrying that no-good first husband of hers. Unless she was counting him as a mistake.

"You read and write real well, too," he said.

A smile flickered on her lips. "Let's see if you can teach me how to take the slack out of that line."

He set the pail inside by the stove and rejoined her in the yard. They walked behind the house. Sally had tied one end of the clothesline to a bent nail on the corner of the new addition and the other to a post Cam had set for the purpose. Cam should have gone ahead and strung the line for her, but apparently he'd left the task for Sally and gone on to something else.

The cotton rope sagged all right. When Johnny put his hand on it and pushed down, it went halfway to the ground.

"We need another piece of rope," he said. "Did you have some left over?"

Sally nodded. "I cut it off. Was that the wrong thing to do?"

"No, that's fine, if it's long enough."

"I'll get it." She grabbed handfuls of her skirt and bustled around the corner. A minute later, she was back with a six-foot length of the rope.

"Perfect." He took it and tied the ends together. Holding a loop on one side of the clothesline, he wrapped the rest of it twice around the line and slid it through the hole of his loop. Tugging the other end of it tightened the looped rope around the clothesline. He tied the dangling end of the looped piece to the clothesline about a foot below his knot. "Now you can slide this up the clothesline, and it will pull up the slack." He demonstrated, pushing his slipknot up the line. The looseness of the clothesline tightened, with the shorter piece of looped rope now taking the slack and the long piece taut.

Sally stared at it with her mouth open. "That's amazing."

Johnny laughed. "Not to a sailor."

"You're not a sailor."

"No, but my father was once. He taught me to do this."

"Let me try it."

"Sure." He untied the shorter rope and handed it to her. Sally went through the steps slowly, glancing at him often for encouragement. "That's just right," he said when she had tightened the clothesline once again. "I told you you're smart. You're quick at learning things. I think my pa had to show me two or three times before I could do it."

Her smile was deeper now. She stood on tiptoe and kissed his cheek, just above the corner of his mouth. "Thank you. It makes me happy when you say things like that."

Johnny warmed through and through. It was another of those moments when he longed to kiss her properly—not like the little peck he'd given her at the wedding. But he knew he shouldn't. In order to have the right to do that, he'd have to tell her everything. Things were just too complicated.

Hoofbeats drummed on the road, and he took Sally's hand and pulled her around to where they could see the horse approaching. Cam, of course, galloping Paint for all he was worth.

"Do you think something's wrong?" Sally asked.

"Probably not," Johnny said. "That's just Cam for you—runs breakneck into everything."

"Yes, I've noticed that. He's an act-first-think-later man."

That was a pretty good assessment, but Johnny didn't say so. He strode over to the corral gate to meet Cam. When he looked back, Sally had turned toward the cabin door.

"Well?" he demanded before Cam was out of the saddle.

"Good thing you didn't ask at church. That man's our nearest neighbor."

"What, that place with the windmill?"

"Yup. We ride past it every time we go to town." Cam swung down and stood with his arm draped over the saddle. "Now all the cow-punchers around think I'm the idiot on this spread."

Johnny scowled. "I'm doing the best I can, Cam."

"Of course you are." Cam laughed. "So what's the plan now, Boss?"

Johnny clenched his teeth together. Sometimes Cam's humor didn't sit well. "You want to ride over there now?"

"Might as well," Cam said. "Go in and tell the missus. I'll get Reckless ready for you."

"I can do it."

Cam held up a hand in protest. "Hey, Boss, I'm not questioning your ability, but we need you to rest your arm, remember? The doc said if you started throwing around saddles and swinging ropes, it wouldn't heal right."

"He didn't say that."

"Maybe not those exact words. How are things going with Sally, anyhow?"

"Not bad. I fixed her clothesline for her."

Cam sighed, shaking his head. "Boy, if I had a wife like that and an hour alone with her, I'd do more than fix her clothesline."

Johnny glared at him, not sure where to start in on him. "You went to the saloon, didn't you?"

"Where else would I get information?"

"Oh, I don't know. The post office, maybe, or the mercantile?"

"What, and make it look like that was the only reason I went to town? I did stop at the post office, though. I mailed Sally's letter to her folks."

Johnny nodded, thinking about Cam's big mouth and trying to concentrate on Caxton's ranch and the young stock.

"There wasn't anything for you," Cam said.

"That's good." Receiving mail addressed to Mark could only bring complications. Johnny huffed out a breath.

"Now go kiss your wife good-bye and let's move," Cam said.

"Watch it."

Cam's eyebrows came together in a scowl. "What did I say?"

"Just watch how you talk about Sally."

For a moment, neither of them said anything; then Cam shrugged. "Sure." He walked into the barn and came out with Johnny's saddle and bridle.

Johnny went to the cabin and paused in the doorway. Sally was humming as she kneaded bread dough at her worktable. Her hair was pulled into a braid that shimmered even in the dull kitchen, catching rays of light that streamed through the small window. She had rolled up her sleeves, and with her flushed cheeks, she made the most charming picture of domesticity Johnny had ever beheld.

He took a step forward, and she looked up. "That Mr. Caxton—he's a close neighbor. The place with the windmill. Cam and I are going to ride over there now."

"Oh." She came toward him, wiping her hands on her apron. "I hope I didn't bruise your reputation by asking his name. I didn't tell the Mertons you wanted to know. I expect they'll just think I was curious and didn't want to ask you."

Johnny nodded. It made sense, and he was glad she had covered for him, instead of laughing at him the way Cam did.

"You keep close about the place, won't you," he said.

"Of course."

He swallowed hard. "Don't know if you heard anything at church, but there were outlaws in these parts a few weeks ago. They. . .they've been known to attack ranches and steal stock and supplies."

Her eyes widened. "I see. Thanks for warning me."

"I would have written to you about it, but. . .but it was. . .you were already preparing for your trip."

She nodded. "Should I keep to the house, then?"

"No, but be aware. If you hear someone coming, don't assume it's us until you see us."

"All right." She took another step toward him, hesitant but expectant.

He could smell the bread dough on her hands and the soap she'd used to wash her hair. Again he wanted to reach for her. She held his gaze, yearning for something. Johnny bent his head and carefully placed a kiss on the softness of her cheek. "I don't know when we'll be back," he said, low.

"But today."

He straightened and nodded. "Surely. But maybe not by noontime."

"Then take some biscuits."

She whirled away from him and the spell was broken. Quickly she wrapped half-a-dozen biscuits left from breakfast in a napkin and handed it to him.

"Thanks." Johnny went out the door, thinking of Cam's words. If he had a wife like Sally. He slowed his steps toward the barn and looked up at the unbroken blue sky. "God, am I crazy?"

CHAPTER 14

Sally baked a cake and two kinds of cookies while her bread rose. She had stew ready at noon, but the men didn't appear, so she set the kettle on the back of the stove to simmer. It would taste even better at suppertime, or whenever they returned and wanted to eat it.

After having a bowl herself, she set about doing laundry. The grueling job took most of her afternoon, but with satisfaction she viewed her full clothesline as the sun moved westward. It hardly sagged at all, and none of her clean wash touched the ground.

She took the bread out of the oven, wishing Mark were there to taste it still warm. These loaves had an especially nice, crispy crust, and the smell was heavenly. The only drawback was the temperature in the house, since she'd kept the fire going all day for her baking. She covered the loaves with a linen towel to keep the flies off and added a bit of water to the stew.

As she folded Mark's second-best shirt, she heard the sound of many animals coming. It had to be Mark and Cam. She tossed the shirt on top of the wicker basket and ran out to the road. Dozens of calves were milling toward her, some lowing and others darting about, looking for an escape. Sally ran across the barnyard to the pasture gate. Mark saw her and waved for her to go ahead. Sally opened the gate wide. The cattle in the pasture were grazing down near the creek, and there was no danger of them getting loose.

Mark and Cam got around the rabble-rousers and shooed them with the rest of the bunch toward the opening. Within minutes the gangly calves were bolting past Sally into the field. When the men pulled their mounts to a halt, she pushed the gate and hopped on, riding it to the gatepost, where she hooked it securely.

Mark was down off Reckless by the time she'd finished. He dropped the chestnut's reins and ambled toward her, laughing.

"Good job, Sally girl!" He slid his uninjured arm around her and gave her a little squeeze. It felt great.

"Good job yourself," she said. To distract him and Cam from her fierce blush, she looked out at the herd that was now exploring its new home. "That's a lot of young'uns."

"Ain't it, though?" Cam grinned down at her from the back of his pinto. "Some of 'em didn't like leavin' their mamas, but we got 'em here."

"You got something for us to eat?" Mark asked, smiling into her eyes. He sounded happier than at any time since she'd arrived.

"I surely do. Of course, I only let cowpunchers sit at my table if they've washed up."

Mark laughed again, and Sally wished she could press that moment between the pages of her Bible and keep it forever.

—————

Johnny took down the Bible the next evening while Sally finished putting away the clean dishes. Cam drained his coffee cup and stood.

"Guess it's time for me to head out to the barn. 'Night, folks."

"You can stay, Cam," Sally said.

"Thanks, but not this time." He shuffled out and shut the cabin door.

Sally frowned at Johnny with mournful eyes. "I wish he'd stop to listen to the scriptures now and again."

Johnny nodded. Cam was a harder case than he'd realized. He'd never thought about his friend avoiding church back in Colorado. A lot of men never went. But hardly any of them would be rude to a woman by refusing her invitation to sit and listen for a few minutes. And afterward, who knew what they might talk about this evening? He'd been purposely putting off the Bible reading until later in the evenings for this very reason—so they wouldn't drive Cam out. But tomorrow they'd be pushing the herd into Mark's north pasture to take advantage of the new grass there, and they needed to get to bed early.

Besides, Johnny didn't want to miss this time with Sally. Pastor Lewis had mentioned Sunday that a man was the head of his family, and it was up to him to set the spiritual climate in the home. Johnny had never dreamed he had such a responsibility, now that he'd taken a wife. He didn't want to shirk his duty.

During their evening readings, he'd learned Sally thought deeply about scripture. She had opinions on what some verses meant. A few of them, she looked at in ways he'd never thought of. At first he felt guilty for letting his own faith lapse, but now he just wanted to get back to where he thought about God every day and tried to follow Him. To where he could talk to Sally about those things easily, without always feeling like a hypocrite.

They'd been reading in Proverbs, and they seemed to jump all over the place on different topics. The trouble with that was, whatever they read each evening, something in it seemed to punch Johnny right between the eyes. Like the bit that said a lying tongue was one of the things God hates most. That gave Johnny pause. Maybe God would never forgive him for all the lies he'd told Sally.

But sometimes they read something that almost made him happy. Like the place that said finding a wife was the same as finding something good. Ol' Mark had gotten it right on that score. But did it work the other way around? Johnny was sure that Sally had found a treasure in Mark, but she wasn't married to Mark. What kind of bargain did she get in him? Those kinds of thoughts made him determined to do good things for her and make life easier for her whenever he could. Of course, when his arm was strong again, that would be a sight easier.

One verse they talked about a lot that evening was Proverbs 17:17, where it said, *"A friend loveth at all times, and a brother is born for adversity."*

"My father used to say it meant your brothers are there for you during hard times," she said.

"Really?" Johnny said. "I always thought it meant brothers fight a lot."

She smiled. "I guess it does sound that way. Did you and Johnny fight all the time?"

He swallowed hard, knowing he would have to be careful. "Not really. He was. . ." How had Mark viewed him? "Mostly, he was a bother. But when he got big enough so we could do things together, we had some good times."

A flood of memories rushed back. He'd always looked up to Mark. When he was little, he'd wanted to do everything his big brother did, and he'd followed Mark around relentlessly. One of his favorite memories was when their father took them up into the hills to cut firewood. They'd stayed overnight and worked hard all day long. It was fun camping with just Mark and their dad. Now Mark was buried in an unmarked grave not far away, and Johnny was sitting in his chair, talking to the woman who should have been Mark's wife.

His throat tightened, and he blinked back unexpected tears. He shoved back his chair and went to the stove. The coffeepot simmered as usual, and he poured himself a cup of coffee, though he didn't really want it. Fixing it gave him an excuse to turn his back on Sally for a minute or two.

He cleared his throat. "You want anything?"

"No, thanks."

He carried his cup back to the table and sat down across from her.

"You should write to your brother," she said. "Maybe he could come and visit us."

"I don't think that's possible." Johnny took an experimental sip of the coffee. It was very hot, so he blew on the surface.

"Well, you should at least keep in touch." After a moment's silence, she said ruefully, "Of course, I'm not much of a one to talk. I didn't write to my folks for a long time, and when I did, I didn't tell them everything. But I did write as soon as I was settled here. I told them where I am now, and that I married a fine Christian man who has his own ranch." She smiled at him. "I'm so much better off now, Mark. Thank you."

"You don't owe me anything."

She started to speak but closed her mouth and just smiled. Johnny nodded toward the book. "Read another."

"All right."

She bent her head over the Bible and read the next verse, but Johnny didn't hear it. She had told her mother and father that he was "a fine Christian man." He felt a little sick.

———

The next Sunday, Johnny and Sally again made the drive into Beaumont for church. The cattle were moved and had settled down; Sally seemed to be happy tending to her housework and cooking. Johnny was content.

After the service, they walked over to the parsonage for dinner with the Lewises. Johnny hoped no touchy topics came up in the table talk. He was a bit surprised when Sheriff Jackson joined them for the meal. The sheriff took off his gun belt and hung it near the door with his hat before sitting down with them.

"Didn't realize you were a regular parishioner, Sheriff," Johnny said after the minister asked the blessing.

"Try to be," the lawman replied. "I don't always make it."

"You've been busy lately." Pastor Lewis passed the platter of fried chicken. "Have you learned any more about that outlaw gang?"

Jackson frowned as he picked out a plump chicken leg and speared it with his fork. "Nothing this week. They made some trouble in Victoria a while back."

"The same gang?" the pastor asked.

"Pretty sure. The leader's a big man they call Flynn. He fits the description Frank Simon gave me of the man who shot him."

"We visited with the Simons yesterday," Mrs. Lewis put in. "Frank's starting to feel a little more pert."

The pastor scooped some green beans onto his plate. "I'm afraid it will be a long time before he's fully recovered, if ever."

"I'd sure like to run those fellas in." The sheriff accepted the bowl of green beans and took a helping.

"Nobody feels safe with them on the loose," Mrs. Lewis said.

"Mark mentioned outlaws to me, but I didn't realize the trouble was so bad," Sally said.

"Oh, yes." Mrs. Lewis shivered. "You want to lock your doors if your man's not at home with you."

The minister smiled at Sally. "I'm sure you're safe at your ranch, Mrs. Paynter, but a bit of caution is never misplaced." He turned the talk deftly to his sermon of the morning, and Johnny was glad. Whenever the topic of the outlaw gang surfaced, he thought of Mark, murdered in his own home.

Mrs. Lewis brought up the subject of the upcoming church picnic, and Sally happily agreed to help organize the event. A few minutes later without revealing too much of his own ignorance, Johnny was able to glean some information from the sheriff about the way the local ranchers shipped their beef to Fort Worth and how they cooperated in spring and fall roundups.

Jackson didn't linger when the meal was finished. He excused himself and put on his hat and gun belt. "Unfortunately, the saloons don't close on Sunday, and I have to make my rounds." He smiled at Mrs. Lewis. "Thank you kindly for the dinner, ma'am. That was mighty good chicken."

Myra Lewis beamed at him. "You're very welcome. Come by anytime, Fred."

Jackson nodded to the pastor, Johnny, and Sally. "Nice talking to you folks. I imagine I'll see y'all soon."

Johnny breathed a little easier when he was out the door.

On the way home, Sally caught him totally off guard with one of her innocent remarks.

"That's a nice graveyard beside the church. They keep it looking pretty. Sometime I'd like to go in there and read some of the tombstones."

"Why?" Johnny asked.

She laughed and gave a little shrug. "Just curious. This is my town now. I'd like to know about the people who started it and the families who have put their roots down here."

Her words only reminded Johnny of the lonely grave on the knoll behind the barn. Would Mark be forgotten? That seemed silly, since he was living as Mark. More likely Johnny would be forgotten. Either way, it didn't sit right with him. Not telling Sally—not letting her grieve Mark—wasn't right. The way things were now, he couldn't grieve his brother, either. Someone needed to remember Mark—the real Mark.

When they reached home, he helped Sally down.

"It's so hot," she remarked, brushing a strand of golden hair off her damp forehead. "I hope it's cooler inside."

"Why don't you take a nap?" Johnny asked. "We had a big dinner, and there must be something left from last night. You don't need to cook supper and heat up the cabin."

"That sounds wonderful," Sally said. "But Cam—"

"Cam will survive. He went for days on end eating nothing but canned beans and jerky on his way here. He's used to living spare."

"Oh my."

Be careful, Johnny told himself. He'd almost said, "Cam and I went for days on end. . . ." Was it the guilt that made him so careless? He supposed it was a combination of that and the heat and his fatigue, along with a pinch of strain from trying all afternoon not to blurt out the wrong thing at the Lewises' house or on the way home.

He glanced at the corral. Cam's paint horse was gone. He hoped his friend was out riding the range, not in town at one of the saloons.

"I'll be out in the barn if you need me," he said.

Sally nodded and headed for the cabin.

He'd meant to be gentler, more courteous. Sally gave him nothing but kindness. Why couldn't he do the same?

He went into the barn and poked around in the pile of wood scraps left from the recent building efforts. He found two pieces of pine left from the bedstead that might be shaped into a cross. He could fit them together and carve the crosspiece. It wouldn't be as nice as an engraved stone, but at least there would be something to mark his brother's passing.

He found that he could hold the knife without too much pain. He was pretty good at carving, at least he was before he'd broken his arm. It was healing, and he ought to be able to do some close work without damaging the bones.

Bracing the flat board with his left hand, he carved very slowly, wanting to make something beautiful. His right arm began to ache, but he kept at it, one small cut at a time.

An hour later, Cam rode in. When he brought his saddle into the barn, he saw Johnny and pulled up short.

"Whatcha makin'?"

Johnny kept on shaving the extra wood from the vine he was carving. "A cross."

Cam stepped closer and stood for a moment watching him. "You can't do that, you know."

"Can't do what?"

"Put it on Mark's grave."

"Why not?"

"That's a foolish question."

Johnny's jaw clenched. "I'm not going to put his name on it."

"Even so, when she sees it, she'll ask questions. Are you ready to deal with that?"

He was right. It would mean more lies.

"Don't do it." Cam's voice was quiet, almost pleading.

Johnny stopped working and closed his eyes. "I've already decided. I'm going to do this."

"You can't."

"Yes, I can." Johnny met his stare then. "We've already dishonored him enough. I *will* mark his grave."

Cam scowled. "Come on, chum. Take your lumps. Act like a man."

"It's too late. A real man would have told the truth and faced the consequences."

Cam pulled in a slow, deep breath. His chest puffed out, and his shoulders squared. "Are you ready to go back to Colorado and turn yourself in, then?"

Johnny sat still, the knife in his hand. What would happen if he did that now? "I'm innocent." At once the guilt swamped him. "Of that crime, at least," he added quickly.

"So, you'd just volunteer to be hanged for something you didn't do." Cam shook his head. "Fine. Go ahead and put it up. Just don't look at me when Sally starts nagging you with questions."

Cam plunked his saddle on its rack and marched out of the barn.

Johnny sat for a long time, looking down at the cross and the half of an ivy vine he'd carved. He wanted to pray and ask God what to do, but he couldn't. His hands began to shake, and the knife fell into the hay on the floor.

He lowered his head and squeezed his eyes shut tight.

CHAPTER 15

A week later, Johnny rode in at noon, tired to the bone. He'd cast aside the sling completely, and his arm ached. He wasn't sleeping enough, but he couldn't help it. At night, he lay awake, staring up at the ceiling while Sally slept. Sometimes he thought she was awake, too, but they never broke the silence at night.

He and Cam hadn't spent a lot of time together this week. They each managed to find chores that took them to different parts of the ranch, which suited Johnny just fine. He'd spent a lot of time riding Mark's fences and studying the deed to figure out exactly where the boundaries lay. Cam had fixed the gate between the pastures. Today he'd taken the wagon into the hills to try to find some firewood.

When he turned Reckless out in the corral, Johnny noted a strange red roan there, still saddled, but no sign of Cam's paint or the wagon. A rifle stuck up from a scabbard on the off side of the saddle. The back of Johnny's neck prickled, and he drew his revolver as he looked toward the house.

At that moment, the door opened, and Sally waved to him.

"Glad you're back. The sheriff's here."

The relief left Johnny a little wobbly. He holstered his gun and walked toward the house. He wanted to ask Sally what Jackson wanted, but she'd already ducked back inside, leaving the door open.

He took his hat off and used it to beat his clothes a little, getting out some of the dust. When he climbed the steps, he could see Jackson inside, sitting at the table with the one china cup in front of him. He really needed to get Sally to pick out some dishes.

"Howdy, Sheriff." He stepped inside and hung his hat on its peg near the door. "Been waitin' long?"

"No, just a few minutes," Jackson said. "Mrs. Paynter told me you were likely to be in soon for your dinner."

"I've invited the sheriff to join us," Sally said, and Johnny noted she had set the table for three. Cam had said that morning he wouldn't be back until dark. She moved to the stove and shuffled a couple of pots around.

By the time Johnny sat down, she had a cup of water ready for him. He took a swallow. It was cooler than the inside of the cabin, so she must have drawn it from the well recently.

"What can I do for you?" he asked Jackson.

"Well, I got some circulars in. They come once a month or so, from the U.S. Marshal's office."

Johnny nodded and sipped his water.

"There's one that I thought you might know something about. It came out of Colorado."

Johnny thumped his cup down on the table, louder than he'd intended. "Colorado?"

Jackson nodded. "You been up there lately?"

Johnny shook his head. This was it. His chest felt like a bear was squeezing it.

The sheriff took a folded paper from beside his plate and handed it across the table to Johnny. "Is this man a relative of yours?"

Johnny stared down at the paper, unable to focus for a moment. Sally came and stood behind his chair, looking over his shoulder. He made himself read the words. *Wanted for murder in the state of Colorado—John Paynter, age 28, brown hair, brown eyes, medium height. Reward $500.* At least there wasn't a picture.

Sally sucked in a breath and clapped her hand down on his shoulder. "Oh, Mark!"

Johnny looked up at the sheriff, his heart racing. "That's my brother's name."

Jackson nodded. "I thought maybe. I'm sorry."

Johnny laid the flyer down. "He didn't murder that man, no matter what they say at the ranch."

Jackson's eyes narrowed. "What man is that, Mark?"

Johnny made himself breathe slowly, but he couldn't meet Jackson's gaze.

After a moment, the sheriff leaned toward him a little. "Look, Mark, I realize this is unpleasant, but your brother has a price on his head. Have you seen him since this murder took place?"

"No."

"Got a letter, maybe?"

Johnny shook his head. He had to be careful, but his thoughts swirled in his mind, crashing into each other. Sally's hand on his shoulder tightened. He made himself look Jackson square in the eyes.

"I haven't seen or spoken to my brother in more than two years, and the last letter I got was—" The image of Cam burning his letter to Mark flickered at the edge of his mind. "It must have been more than a year ago."

"Then how do you know he's innocent?"

Johnny picked up his cup and drained it. He swallowed, still trying to frame an answer. "I just know."

Jackson cocked his head to one side. "Because he's your brother?"

"I know him. He didn't do it."

"What did he say in his letter last year?"

"Told me he was working on an outfit in Colorado. The Lone Pine, I think it was called."

"Did he mention the foreman?"

"No. He said he liked it fine. A lot of trees, he said, more than he was used to."

"Why did you say he didn't kill that man? The poster doesn't say it was a man that was murdered."

"I don't know. I just. . . My brother's a good man. If someone has accused him, they've got it wrong."

"All right. Look, Mark, I'm sorry I upset you with this news. If you hear from your brother, it would be in your best interest to tell me."

Johnny nodded slowly.

"And if you think of anything else, or if you ever want to tell me anything, just come to my office." Jackson stood.

"Oh, Sheriff, aren't you going to eat with us?" Sally asked.

"Thank you kindly, ma'am, but I think I'd better get back to town and give you folks some time to talk things over."

They both watched him go. When the door shut behind him, Sally squeaked out, "Mark?"

He shoved back his chair and turned to face her. She threw herself against him, and he closed his arms around her. Why did she have to hear? Why couldn't Jackson have come out to the barn to meet him and tell him in private?

Sally sobbed. Johnny reached up a shaky hand and stroked her golden hair. She lifted her tear-streaked face.

"We should pray for your brother."

He caught his breath but managed a curt nod.

Sally nestled against his chest and held on to him. "I'm so sorry, Mark."

He held her another minute, but all he could think of was that she was wearing a brand-new dress—the one she'd sewn from the calico he bought her—and his filthy clothes were getting dust all over it.

———

Mark stayed away from the house all afternoon. Sally watched for him, even though he'd said he was riding to the high pasture to check on the stock. She couldn't stop thinking about his reaction when the sheriff produced the wanted poster for his brother. It had been a shock, anyone could see that. Poor, dear man. His own brother!

A shadow of disloyalty hung over her. She wanted to be able to tell Mark that he was right. His brother would never do such a thing. But she didn't know Johnny, and a lot of men had done murder without the slightest indication in advance that they were capable of the act. Or maybe it wasn't murder. Maybe he'd accidentally killed someone and run away, and they were looking for him. He would go on trial if he was caught, and the truth would come out. Yes. It could even be self-defense.

As she folded laundry, churned butter, and set out ingredients for a cake, she prayed, sometimes in her heart and sometimes out loud.

"God, You know what really happened in Colorado, and we can't change it now. Please comfort Mark. Don't let him grieve so over his brother." But she knew she would do the same if she got word that one of her brothers was wanted for murder.

A longing came over her to see her family, especially her mother. She would write home again, once this latest business had settled down. Wouldn't it be wonderful if Ma and Pa could come visit? She clung to that thought. She had no one here to discuss woman talk with. She was getting to know the church ladies, but she wasn't close enough to any of them to bare her soul. And she wouldn't, anyway. She couldn't do that to Mark.

No, even her mother couldn't know that her husband barely touched her, even in the quiet darkness of their bedroom. Today's embrace was rare, brought on by a crisis.

Tears poured from her eyes, and she pulled her apron up to wipe her face.

Lord, You know I love him, and I believe he loves me, too. What's wrong with us? With me? Why won't he truly make me his wife?

She'd wondered thousands of times in the last month. Mark treated her respectfully and performed countless small kindnesses for her. Now and then she saw a longing in his eyes. It wasn't the hard, fierce passion

David used to turn on her, but a sweet, sad yearning. She had to believe Mark wanted more from their marriage, as much as she did. He could be the kind of husband she'd longed for, she knew he could. Why wouldn't he act on that desire?

The air was hot and humid—too hot for her to add more heat to the cabin. She would wait and bake after supper. She hung up her apron, donned her bonnet, and carried a basket outside.

She stopped at the well and pulled up a pail of water. Even the well water didn't get cold on hot days. The heat would get worse as the summer wore on. By the end of July, she would look back on these balmy June days as paradise.

The spring garden was dying, with only a few carrots and a yellow squash or two left. Sally picked them and placed the basket inside the front door. She had forgotten how different the rhythm of life was in Texas, and she had never lived this far south before. She would have to ask the other women what they did to keep cool.

She walked over to the corral fence and leaned on it, thinking about Mark. His arm was better; he had even brought in fuel and water for her the past few days, and he had milked the cow this morning. That was no longer the excuse for the barrier between them, if it had ever been.

They read scripture together every evening and talked about it. Sometimes he read, and Sally sewed while she listened. On other nights, Sally read, and Mark sat in his chair whittling. He'd carved her a wooden spoon during their devotions last week.

She had even heard him pray a few times. True they were not deep, profound prayers, but she didn't expect him to be a preacher. And today when she had suggested they pray for Johnny, he had agreed, but then, once they'd sat down together, he'd held her hand and said, "You pray, Sally. I can't."

So she had asked God to protect his brother and let the truth be told. Mark didn't seem to take exception to anything she'd said. She'd figured he was just too choked up inside to voice his own prayer. She hoped he was praying now, off on his own someplace, where no one but God would hear him.

David had never prayed to her knowledge, through the entire time of their marriage, and he had disdained her regular reading of the scriptures. She had even hidden her Bible during the last year of David's life, for fear he would destroy it. He blamed many of her shortcomings on what he called her sanctimoniousness.

Sally let out a big sigh and rested her head on the rail. She had tried to present a calm and cheerful spirit to David and not nag him or sermonize to him, but he had still said she was too religious. For that reason, she had tried to be unobtrusive about her faith with Mark. But he had welcomed her suggestion of Bible reading together, and she didn't force him to go to church. He seemed to want to be there. From the letters he had sent her in St. Louis, she knew he was a true believer. Maybe she should take those letters out and reread them, to remind her of how strong his faith was.

Because sometimes these days, Mark seemed to falter.

She walked to the barn door and looked in. She seldom entered the barn, because that was Cam's domain. Just thinking of him cast a pall on her. That first day she'd arrived, she'd found him charming, but the better acquainted she got with him, the less she found to like.

She turned away and walked around the other side of the barn. A slope rose behind it, and she wondered what she'd be able to see from the top. A few trees grew in the pasture, along the creek. Were there any on the other side of that knoll?

She wandered slowly up the low hill through bluestem grass, stopping now and then to pick a wildflower. As she reached the top, she noticed something to one side, among the weeds. She walked toward it, curious at first, then satisfied when she realized what it was, and then curious again.

She stood looking at the three-foot cross, built of pine still fresh and yellow. A vine twined along the crosspiece, and the whole thing had a coat of shellac, but nothing else. The grass in front of it was shorter than that around it, and she could tell someone had been here recently. The stems were bent over around the cross.

Troubled, she walked back down the hill to the cabin.

Mark and Cam arrived home within minutes of each other, though they came from different directions. Sally wished she'd had a chance to talk to her husband alone, but maybe this was part of God's plan. She waited until they had eaten their first servings of beans, bacon, carrots, and bread and caught each other up on what they'd accomplished that day.

Cam held out his coffee cup expectantly, and she rose to refill it. When she came back to the table, he smiled at her. "Thank you."

She nodded and resumed her seat. Had Mark told him about the sheriff's visit? She didn't think that was possible, unless they had met out on the range somewhere and discussed it, but their talk didn't hint at such a meeting. She had watched out the window while Cam unharnessed his horse, and Mark hadn't lingered to talk to him then.

"I was wondering," she said, and they both stared at her. Sally cleared her throat, suddenly nervous. "There's a cross on the hill yonder. I wondered what it's for. It looks like a grave."

Neither man spoke for a moment, and then Cam said, "That's a cowhand—the fella who had my job before I got here."

Sally eyed him with misgivings but tried not to show it in her face. Mark hadn't mentioned Cam in his letters, and he certainly hadn't mentioned any previous employees. In fact, in one of his letters Mark had stated that he hadn't hired anyone yet. If she allowed that he'd taken Cam on in the last few weeks before her arrival, that still didn't account for the man buried on the knoll.

She looked at Mark, but he looked away and helped himself to another large spoonful of beans. Sally watched him for a moment.

Cam turned back to Mark. "So, next time you go into town, maybe you should talk to that fella at the feed store about getting a windmill. Caxton said he ordered his there."

"That'd be kind of expensive," Mark said. "We'll see how the water in the creek holds out. It looks all right so far."

"But if you wait until it goes dry, it'll be too late."

So that was how it was. Sally stood and carried her dishes to the worktable and poured hot water into her dishpan. Cam, at least, seemed determined to put the subject of the grave behind them. But nighttime was coming, and Cam would be in the barn.

As the time approached, her conscience began to peck away at her resolve. Was it right for a woman to ambush her husband on a touchy topic when he was otherwise good and kind?

She brushed her long hair until it gleamed in the lamplight. Holding up her mirror, she considered the features she was given. She wasn't the most beautiful woman in Texas, but she certainly wasn't the homeliest, either, and she was the only one on this ranch. While her twenty-eight years gave her a maturity, that could be an advantage. If she'd married Mark ten years ago, her confusion would have driven her to tears every day.

Besides, Mark was legally bound to her. So what was holding him back?

By the time he knocked on the bedroom door, she had decided not to pounce on him with the question of the cross, but to try to open a general discussion on their marriage.

He entered almost humbly, glancing at her, where she sat on the edge of the bed in her nightdress. He nodded and closed the door then sat down to take off his boots.

"Mark?" she said cautiously.

"Yeah?" His first boot thumped to the floor.

Her heart beat faster. "Is something wrong?"

Silence.

After a long moment, the second boot dropped on the rag rug.

She turned and looked at his back. He was just sitting there. Sally climbed onto her hands and knees and clambered across the bed. She touched his shoulder, and he jerked a little.

She let out a small puff of air, trying not to let the hurt drive her away from him. "I don't know how to *be* with you," she whispered. "I thought you wanted a wife, and I've tried—"

"You're a wonderful wife," Mark said.

Sally let that sink in. "Then why. . ." She couldn't say it. Her face flamed just thinking about it. Instead, she blurted out, "I know something's wrong. Please tell me. *Please.*"

His shoulders trembled. "There's nothing wrong, Sally."

Tears sprang into her eyes. "I feel like there is."

He shook his head.

"There must be. Don't you trust me?"

"Sure I do."

"Then what is it? Do you wish you hadn't brought me to Texas?"

"No! I'm glad you came."

"Then what is it? I love you so much, but—" She stopped, appalled at what she'd said. Was she turning into a weepy, clinging shrew? The tears flowed freely now, splashing down on her cotton nightdress.

He bent over, and after a moment she realized he was putting his boots on again.

"Mark?" She sat up straight, her heart ripping in two. "Where are you going?"

He shoved his foot down hard and stood. "I'm sorry."

"For what?"

"I just. . . I'm not ready, Sally."

She stared as he walked out of the room without looking her way and shut the door. She pivoted and flopped on her pillow.

"Dear Lord, what is wrong with this man? Does he have some morbid fear of marriage?"

That was crazy. How could he have written those tender letters if he secretly feared intimate contact? There must be some other explanation. Her thoughts swirled, but they always came back to one thing: something about her repulsed Mark, no matter what he said.

She buried her face in the pillow slip, trying to keep her sobs quiet.

CHAPTER 16

Johnny paced back and forth on the grass in front of the corral, where his steps wouldn't make much noise.

God, this is a nightmare. What do I do?

He gazed up at the array of stars in the cloudless sky. More than anything, he wanted to be honest with Sally, but how could he, when he was in this deception up to his neck?

She was in there crying—he was sure of it. That made him the worst kind of scoundrel. Sally was a lovely, innocent, well-meaning woman. Johnny grabbed handfuls of his hair and pulled until it hurt. He had never aspired to be a ladies' man, but neither had he intended to be a cad. She deserved better than this.

"What are you doing out here?"

Cam spoke from the opening to the barn.

Johnny turned slowly and eyed him across the barnyard. He didn't want to talk to Cam, but he didn't want his friend yelling at him, either, which Cam probably would do if he didn't go closer.

His wooden legs carried him slowly across the dusty yard until he stood three feet from Cam. "Couldn't sleep."

Cam snorted. "With a woman like that, you ought to be able to think of better things to do than stroll around the barnyard."

Johnny's fists clenched. "Shut up, Cam."

"Oh! Trouble in the marriage made in heaven?"

Johnny thought of several things he might say. He also thought of knocking a few of Cam's teeth down his throat. He turned and walked quickly back to the cabin. Inside, he shut the door and stood still, trying to calm his breathing.

The bunk was gone, but a couple of quilts were still folded up in the corner. Johnny shook out one of them and spread it on the floor. Taking his boots off without making any noise was tricky, especially since the pulling motion brought back the ache in his arm. He toed off the first one, but the second took longer. When it finally slid off his foot, he sat panting on the quilt. Carefully, he set the boot down nearby, without making a sound, and then he lay down on his back.

He wished he had a pillow. Odd how he'd slept on the trail for weeks without one and hardly noticed, but now, in his house, its absence rankled him. He rolled over.

Light made a slit at the bottom of the bedroom door. The lamp was still on in there. Sally was probably still awake. Maybe still crying.

Maybe he should just go out and tell Cam what was going on—that he hadn't consummated the marriage and that Sally was hurt and confused.

He knew what Cam would say. *What are you waiting for, idiot?*

He supposed he could live with Sally as her husband, the way most people did. But once he did that, he couldn't undo it. He would have to keep the secret from her forever if he crossed that line, and would that be a true marriage? It wouldn't be the kind of marriage he wanted—or the one Sally wanted, either.

Lord God, I love her. And I know You don't take to liars. How can I lie to the person I love most?

The only other option he could see was to tell Sally everything and let the chips fall where they may.

He rolled toward the wall so he couldn't see the stripe of lamplight. As long as he kept his hands off Sally, he had the option of confessing the truth to her. He wasn't ready to give that up yet. But if he told her now, she would probably leave him. He wouldn't blame her one bit.

"Show me what to do, Lord," he whispered to the corner of the rough board walls.

———

In the morning, Sally rose with a heavy heart. Mark had not come to bed. She had heard him come in, or so she thought, a short time after he had left her, but he had not returned to their room.

She dressed in the early morning light and opened the door cautiously. The front room was empty. Trying not to dwell on last night, she went about her usual breakfast preparations.

About an hour later, Cam came in with a pail of milk.

"Morning." He grinned as he set the pail on the floor near her worktable.

"Where's Mark?" Sally asked.

Cam's smile faded. "Oh, he said he was going to ride up to check on that new young stock. He didn't think he'd be back until suppertime."

Sally turned her face away and busied herself with the eggs she was frying. Hadn't Mark checked the young stock recently? Besides, the ranch wasn't big enough to take all day to ride around. And Mark hadn't taken any food with him; she would have heard him if he'd rummaged around in the kitchen this morning.

Cam poured himself a cup of coffee and carried it to the table. "Guess it's just you and me this mornin'."

Sally slid the eggs onto the platter with the bacon. She set it in front of Cam and went back for the biscuits and butter. When everything was on the table, she sat down.

Cam pitched right into the food, but she paused and bowed her head to ask a silent blessing on the food. *And my husband,* her heart cried out. *Protect him and bring him home safe!*

She opened her eyes. Cam was watching her as he chewed. He swallowed and took a drink of coffee and said, "Really good eats, Sally."

"Thank you." She put an egg and two pieces of bacon on her plate and picked up her fork.

"Look, maybe it's none of my business," Cam began, "but if you and Mark—"

"You're right," Sally said firmly. "It's none of your business." She rose and went into the bedroom and shut the door. She walked to the window that looked out on the road and stood staring through the glass. How much had Mark told Cam? And what gave a cowpuncher the right to give his boss's wife advice?

She could hear him out there, finishing his breakfast. His silverware clinked on his plate now and then, and after five minutes or so, his chair scraped back over the floor. She held her breath and analyzed his footsteps. Cam took his dishes to the dishpan and then lifted the lid to the stove's firebox. A moment later, he walked across the room. The front door opened and closed.

She let out her breath. This would be a long day. If Cam came to the house for his dinner, she would hand him a basket packed with a cold lunch

----

Johnny rode up a draw until the shadow of a bluff shielded the ground from the direct morning sun. He dismounted and took off Reckless's bridle so he could graze. The young stock was fine, but he didn't want to go back to the house and face Sally.

Two things kept picking at him, like coyotes gnawing a bone. Sally had found Mark's grave, and she had said she loved him.

Did she really love him, Johnny, the man she'd lived with this past month? How could she? He hadn't treated her fairly. She ought to hate him. If she was truly in love, then Mark was the object of her affections. She loved the man she'd glimpsed through the letters, and she was holding out hope that the man she had married would live up to the promise.

Cam had been right about the grave. He never should have made the cross. To salve his own conscience, he had hurt Sally deeper than before, and he'd spurred her imaginings.

Sally was a smart lady. He had no doubt about that. Would she put it all together and realize she was living with a fugitive?

He went over the clues she might have noticed and all the lies he had told to cover them. He couldn't even tell her that he loved her. When she learned about the other business, she would think that was a lie, too.

He stared up at the sky, cloudless blue above the rocky walls. This might be one of the few places on the ranch where he could find shade. The willows along the creek were too close to the house. Sally had started exploring, and she might find him there.

So it had come to this. He loved his wife, but he was hiding from her. "Lord God, I hate this. I know You hate it, too."

He wasn't sure how long he lay there. The sun eased its rays over the edge of the bluff, almost blinding him. He sat up. Reckless had worked his way down the draw a hundred yards or so. Johnny tried to whistle, but his mouth was too dry. He got up and walked slowly toward the horse with no solution to his problem.

The days dragged by with nothing resolved between them. Johnny had stayed away most of the daylight hours, when he should have been working around the home place. He'd promised Sally an outdoor oven and a windlass for the well. Half-a-dozen other projects awaited him.

Johnny guided Reckless home at suppertime on Saturday. He had asked Cam that morning to make sure there was plenty of fuel and water in the kitchen. While he was quite capable of taking care of those jobs himself, Johnny didn't want to risk another heart-to-heart with Sally.

He'd continued sleeping in the main room, and she seemed to accept that. She'd left a pillow and another blanket out where he'd find them. She packed up sandwiches and cookies and biscuits each evening—things he could carry easily and eat for dinner when he was off with the herd or in town. And she hadn't cornered him again.

That was how Johnny felt when he thought about their last conversation—cornered. She'd waited for him to come into the bedroom that night, because she figured he couldn't run away. Well, he had, but he took no satisfaction in that, or in the fact that he hadn't answered her questions. A wife had a right to know the things Sally had asked about.

His heart felt like a lump of lead in his chest. The position of the sun told him she would have supper prepared, but he wasn't ready to face her again. He turned Reckless to his right. They would take a slightly longer route home. He wanted to stop by Mark's grave.

He let the horse walk slowly up the hill. No sense making him work harder than necessary in this heat. He spotted the top of the cross, above the grass heads, and pointed Reckless toward it. When he came even with it, he edged Reckless around so he could see the front.

Johnny drew in a sharp breath. Grass was growing over the top of the grave, but it was sparse, and the dirt showed through. A clever person would know this grave wasn't old. Lying at the foot of the cross was a bunch of daisies and cardinal flowers. They were starting to droop, but in this heat, they couldn't have been there more than a couple of hours.

Sally.

Nobody else would do that, and she didn't even know who was buried there. Had she been prodding Cam for more details? For all Johnny knew, Cam could have spun a yarn about the imaginary ranch hand buried here. He'd better find his friend and talk to him before supper.

Johnny pivoted Reckless and loped for the corral. Cam was at the well, drawing a bucket of water. Johnny trotted over to him and swung down from the saddle.

"Hey," Cam said.

The door of the cabin creaked open, and Sally stood there, eyeing them soberly. "I'm glad you boys are both here. Supper's ready." She looked tired. Thin and wrung out.

"We'll be right in," Cam said with a smile.

Sally glanced at Johnny and nodded. She withdrew and shut the door.

Johnny leaned toward Cam. "Did you say any more to her about the grave?"

"No. Why?"

"She's been up there, putting flowers on it."

Cam's eyes narrowed. "I told you it'd bring trouble when you built that cross."

"I know. It was a mistake. I wanted to make sure you hadn't told her anything else about it."

Cam shook his head. "I'll leave that up to you, Boss."

"Don't call me that."

They glared at each other for a moment.

"Sorry," Johnny said. "We're friends. I'm not really your boss."

"Yeah, you are. That's the only way it can be now."

Johnny thought about that for a moment. "Are you just saying that so that I'll pay you?"

Cam laughed. "No. I'm saying it because it's true. Whatever you tell Sally now is true, and you've told her you hired me. Therefore, I work for you, and you're my boss."

Johnny didn't like it, but it made sense. If he intended to stay married to Sally, then Cam was no longer just a friend trying to help him avoid injustice. "Fine. Collect your pay on the last day of the month."

"I'll do that," Cam said. "Now, take care of Reckless. We'd better go in."

"Yeah." Johnny squared his shoulders. Going into that cabin was getting harder every time.

CHAPTER 17

The silence between them on the ride to church almost crackled in the hot, stagnant air. They had driven more than halfway to the little church when Sally said, "My pa says there's an electrical storm coming when the air's all breathless like this."

"Some folks can feel it comin' on," Mark said.

He didn't offer another word on the rest of the ride, and neither did Sally. She was too tired to turn the weather comments into a discussion, or to bring up another topic. If only she could sleep through the night, she wouldn't feel so dull in the morning. But Mark was still bedding down on the floor, and she was still tossing and turning and crying out to God half the night.

The sermon might as well have been made of India rubber. It bounced off her and veered away. She was sure it completely missed Mark, judging by his stony expression. He barely moved a muscle during the hour Pastor Lewis spoke.

When it was over, they joined the line in the aisle to shake the minister's hand. Liz Merton squeezed between two people to ask Sally, "Are you going to the ladies' group Wednesday?"

Sally hesitated and glanced toward Mark, but he had stepped forward with the line, apparently unaware of Liz's question.

"I'll have to see if my husband can let me have the wagon that day," Sally said.

Liz nodded and patted her arm then disappeared into the throng. Sally caught up with Mark just before he reached the reverend on the top step. She stepped through the doorway and braced herself against the sun.

"Hello, Mrs. Paynter." The pastor smiled and shook her hand. "Another hot one today."

"That's the truth," Sally said.

Mark managed a civil reply to the pastor's comment as they shook hands.

At the bottom of the steps, Sheriff Jackson walked over and greeted Mark. He was smiling, so Sally didn't think he had anything to say about Mark's brother, and she hung back a little.

The two Mary Hoods, whom Sally had learned were known as "Mary Bill" and "Mary Pete," found her and launched into a discussion of baby names.

"Bill doesn't want to name him William, because he's Bill Junior already, and it's too confusing," Mary Bill explained, one hand protectively resting on the mound of her abdomen.

"Yes," said Mary Pete. "My Pete says we can't have any more Bills or Marys in this family, or we'll all go loco. I suggested John, after General Hood, but Bill doesn't like it."

"Too plain, he says," Mary Bill chimed in, "and besides, his sister's got a John already."

"I see," Sally said. "But what if it's a girl?"

Mary Bill's face beamed. "Lucinda. We're agreed on that, at least."

"Yes, and I think it's lovely," Mary Pete said, "but as sure as you settle on a girl's name, it will turn out to be a boy."

Sally glanced toward Mark and found he was looking at her, too. Apparently the sheriff had moved on.

"Excuse me, ladies," she said, smiling at the sisters-in-law. "Seems Mr. Paynter's ready to go. I hope to see you both on Wednesday."

Sally joined Mark, and they walked to the horse shed together. Mark harnessed Reckless to the wagon. When he'd climbed to the seat and started them rolling out the lane, he said, "What's on Wednesday?"

Sally was so relieved that he'd spoken, she laughed aloud. "The monthly ladies' group. We hope to finish the quilt this time. We're meeting at Mrs. Bill Senior's—that would be the young ladies' mother-in-law's house. Do you think I'll be able to use the wagon? I know you've needed Reckless a lot lately."

Mark frowned, and she feared he would say no. She didn't mind so much missing the group, but it would mean he was still planning to be gone on these all-day odysseys he'd taken to, ever since she'd asked him about the cross. Last month, he'd driven her into town for the meeting at Liz's, but he probably wouldn't want to spend that much time alone with her again this week.

"We should buy a driving horse," he said.

She stared at him. "Really? That would be wonderful, but can we afford it?"

"I think so. Maybe."

She half expected him to say he would see what Cam thought, but he didn't, and she was glad.

"If we do," she ventured, "we ought to get one that rides or drives well. Then you could give Reckless some rest now and then."

"That's sound thinking. On most ranches, the punchers have at least three horses each. And in this heat, we'll need them. Don't want to overwork Reckless and Paint."

"They're good horses."

He nodded and kept on driving, looking straight ahead. Sally didn't want the conversation to end.

"What happened to that horse you had that you called Ranger?" she asked.

He flicked her a glance. "Oh, I . . ." He hesitated and then said, "He was stolen."

"What? When?"

"Shortly before you came."

"Why didn't you tell me?"

He winced, and Sally regretted speaking the way she had.

"Sorry. I was just surprised. You mentioned him in your letters, and. . ." A sudden thought occurred to her. "Was it those outlaws?"

"I'm not sure."

She eyed him carefully. "You didn't want to worry me, I suppose."

"No, I didn't. I'm sorry. I should have told you. And folks are right about being careful when you're home alone."

"All right." Her troubled thoughts churned. Why had Mark not mentioned this when they had discussed the outlaw gang with the Lewises and Sheriff Jackson? Maybe he had reported the theft earlier and not seen a need to bring it up again.

He was frowning again, and she decided it was best to speak of something else.

"Do you mind if I take the day and go on Wednesday?"

"Maybe Cam could drop you off and get supplies while you're quilting."

"Cam?" Tears sprang into her eyes, and she blinked them back. She didn't want Cam squiring her around the county while Mark rode herd or whatever it was he did out there. "I'd rather stay home," she said softly.

He still didn't move, and she wasn't sure he'd heard. After a long moment, he pulled in a deep breath. "You got something against Cam? Tell me if you do."

"Not really. I'd just rather drive myself—or have you beside me."

"Well. . .we'll see."

It was something, and she seized on it. "Oh, please, Mark. I plan to do up all the laundry tomorrow, and I'll bake on Tuesday, even if it's sweltering. Please, can't you go along with me? I'd like it ever so much."

His lips twitched. "What's so great about having me take you?"

She smiled and sneaked her hand inside his elbow. "The girls will all see you bringing me, that's what. I'd like for them to see that, the same as I liked writing to my mother about how you fixed the new room for me, and I liked having people at the store see you buying me yard goods."

He glanced down at her. "That meant something to you?"

"It meant a lot. It meant my husband's taking care of me, and the handsomest man in Beaumont wants me to have nice things."

His lips twitched. "I do, Sally. I want you to be happy. Seeing you smile is just about the prettiest sight I ever saw."

Sally began to hope that he would drive her on Wednesday and that she might be able to make slow progress in other directions.

———

That afternoon Mark built a fire ring on the dry earth at the edge of the garden behind the cabin. He piled enough of their precious stock of firewood to keep a fire going all day. Next he built a frame to suspend the big wash kettle from and got out the kettle and filled it with water. He also filled the copper boiler and four extra pails of water.

Sally watched with satisfaction at first, but as the afternoon wore on, she became uneasy. By suppertime, she knew he was preparing everything she would need so that he wouldn't have to come home all day. What drove him so? Was he really doing anything, out there in the grazing land?

She rose before dawn on Monday, before she heard him stir. By the time she had her dress on and had opened the door, he was folding up his blankets.

They gazed at each other across the room.

"I'll fix your breakfast," she said.

"No need."

"I want to. Let me do this."

He nodded and set the blanket down. When she turned around again, he was out the door.

She stirred up pancake batter and fried some eggs and sausage. If he rode out without eating, she would give up.

Mark had told her once that he didn't like coffee, but he seemed to drink it fairly often. Cam couldn't get enough. She filled the pot and set it on the stove. The kitchen was already uncomfortably hot. At least Mark had readied things so she could do the wash outside.

She had a platter of pancakes ready when he and Cam came in. They both sat at the table, and she took over the sausage, sorghum, eggs, coffee, butter, and a dish of applesauce.

"Fine breakfast," Cam said.

"Thank you." Sally sat down beside them and bowed her head.

After a moment's silence, Mark said quietly, "Lord, we thank You for this food. Amen."

"Amen." Sally opened her eyes and smiled. "What are you boys up to today?"

Mark said nothing. Cam glanced at him and then said, "Well, Mark's going to clean out the spring. We're concerned the water's starting to slack off. And I'll be working around here, so if you need more water or anything like that, I'll be handy."

She couldn't bring herself to say thank you.

All morning she worked at the fire, first struggling to heat the water and then washing the clothes. She had quite a pile of towels and table linens, too. By noontime, she wished she hadn't undertaken so much. In spite of all the water Mark had drawn, her multiple rinses required more. She finally sat down for a few minutes to rest before getting dinner. She still had one load left of the men's grimy work clothes.

The kitchen wasn't any cooler, but at least she was out of the sun. She put her arms on the table and laid her head down. Her skin felt leathery, and her eyes ached. Maybe she'd gotten too much sun, despite her bonnet. She could hear Cam sawing in the barn and wondered what he was making. Surely she could rest a couple of minutes before she started cooking.

"You all right?"

She sat bolt upright. Cam stood beside her, by the table, his hand on her shoulder.

"I must have dozed off." She glanced toward the window, trying to judge the position of the sun. "It is noontime?"

"Yup, but if dinner's not ready, it's not a problem."

She was very aware of his hand still resting solicitously on her shoulder. "No, no, I'll get you something." She jumped up, shoving the chair back and a little toward him, forcing him to let go. "I'm sorry, Cam. It will just take me a minute. There's a bit of ham left from last night, and I've got a little bread left. Would you like a sandwich? Or I can make gravy in about five minutes." She shot a guilty glance toward the stove. She hadn't replenished the fire inside. "Or ten."

"A sandwich is fine. I can make it myself. You oughta just sit there and relax, young lady. I could see you've been working hard all mornin'."

"Oh, well, that's Monday for you. Washing always takes awhile."

"Whyn't you sit right down again," Cam said, walking toward her. "Let me bring you something for a change."

"No, that's all right. I'll get it." Sally reached for the tin box on the shelf where she kept bread. The half loaf was in her hand when she felt him touch her again. This time, his fingers found her bare skin at the back of her neck.

"I don't mind, Sally."

She jumped and whirled toward him. "Don't touch me."

Cam stepped back, a look of innocence throwing her into confusion.

"Sorry," he said. "I didn't mean anything. I just wanted to get the bread down for you."

Sally took a breath, trying to sort things out. For a few seconds, she had felt that Cam was a threat to her. Was she wrong? She was tired, and she hadn't liked Cam almost from the start. Was she imagining something that wasn't there?

She made herself pull out a smile. "Why don't you get yourself a cup of milk? There's coffee on the stove, but I suppose it's cooled off. Anyway, I know where everything is, and it will be quicker if I fix us both sandwiches by myself."

"Sure, Sally. Whatever you say."

Something in his tone rankled her. He sounded like a man hoping to appease an angry child.

She worked swiftly while he brought in the jug of milk and poured a tin cup full. She was determined to finish the meal preparation as soon as possible. A couple of minutes later, she plunked Cam's plate in front of him. "There you go. I'm going to go stoke my laundry fire. I put some more water on to heat, and I want it to be warm when I finish eating."

"I'll do it for you," Cam said.

"No, I'm fine. Go ahead and eat."

Sally dashed out the door before he could stop her. She slowed immediately as the sun beat down on her. She hadn't grabbed her bonnet. She'd have to move slowly and not stay out here long, but she had already determined that she wouldn't go back inside until after Cam came out. She didn't like being in there alone with him, whether justified or not.

As she had feared, the fire had died down to almost nothing. She stirred the ashes and found a few coals. The woodpile had shrunk considerably, but there was enough to heat this last cauldron, at least to warm it. She could rinse their trousers and shirts in cold water.

She picked up two sticks of dry, twisted wood. How far did Mark and Cam have to go to find even this poor fuel? Using the stove made more sense, except that firing it up on a day like this would make it far too hot for them to sleep inside. They could leave the windows open all night, and the cabin still wouldn't be cool by morning. Maybe someday Mark would remember the idea of an outdoor oven.

Of course, Cam had been the one to bring that up first, and for that reason, Sally wouldn't mention it. If one of them broached the subject, she would encourage them to go ahead with the project.

The feathery bark on the gnarled sticks caught fire suddenly, and the blaze leaped high. Sally jumped back, but not quickly enough. The hem of her skirt flared up in orange flames, with acrid smoke stinging her eyes.

"Oh!" Sally went to her knees and slapped at the burning cloth. The flames spread around the edge of the skirt, faster than she could quell them. The material seemed to melt away as a long, orange plume raced up the side of her skirt.

"Cam! Cam!" Her hands hurt as she clapped them over the worst part of the fire.

Rough hands grabbed her from behind and shoved her down.

"Roll!"

He pulled her over onto her side. Sally's brain processed Cam's presence and his command, and she rolled in the powdery dirt. Her calf screamed with pain, but she kept thrashing until he pressed heavily on her arm and back.

"Stop now, Sal. It's over. It's all right."

She sat up, gasping and reached toward him. He grabbed her hands to pull her up, and she let out a little shriek.

"My hands!"

He turned them palm up and stared at her reddened flesh.

"What else?"

"My leg."

"Your skirt's still smoking. Stand up. We have to get it off."

She stared at him. She would not disrobe in front of Cam, even if it killed her. But the water in her kettle was too warm to douse herself in.

"No. Get me a bucket of water."

He opened his mouth and closed it then snatched an empty bucket from beside the fire pit. He wheeled and headed for the well.

Sally examined her skirt, separating the layers of burnt cloth carefully with her tender fingers. Her palms screamed with pain, but she had to make sure her skirt wouldn't flare up again. At least it was her old, threadbare calico, not the new one. The fire had burned her leg, too, but Cam would never know how badly. She would make sure of that.

He came with the water, and she thrust both hands into the soothing coolness. After only a few seconds' relief, the stinging, searing pain returned.

"Pour it over my skirt, please."

Cam blinked and then stood back a pace. He swung the bucket, drenching the side where the flames had done the most damage. Sally braced herself for the shock of it, but it didn't jar her as much as she had expected.

"I'm going in." Her lips trembled, and her legs shook, too. She hoped she could make it inside without collapsing. "Can you bring me more water?"

"Of course. But won't you let me carry you?"

"No!"

She limped toward the house, trying to hold together the edges of her tattered skirt. She gave that up after Cam turned away to go back to the well.

Her hands throbbed mercilessly when she tried to lift her skirt to mount the steps. She held them up and looked at them. Blisters were forming, and the rest of her palms were angry, red welts. Her fingertips also held blisters in various stages of development. She staggered up the steps, taking the risk of tripping on her hems.

She had reached the bedroom door when Cam came in behind her.

"Here, let me—"

"Don't touch me." The words she had spoken a quarter of an hour earlier struck her with a force that made her shiver. "I can take care of myself," she said. "Just set the pail inside my room, please."

She stood aside while Cam obeyed. He came out and paused before her.

"Leave me," she said.

"I'll go find Mark."

"No. He doesn't want to be here." She wished she hadn't said that. The appraising look in Cam's eyes told her he parsed her words and reached conclusions, ones she didn't want him to make.

"Are you sure you'll be all right?"

"Yes."

He nodded. "I'll be outside. Call for me if you need anything. Anything at all."

"Thank you."

She waited until he went out. In her bedroom, she closed the door and tried to unbutton the waistband of her skirt. Her seared fingertips sent lances of pain through her when they encountered the hard button. She clenched her teeth and forced the button through the buttonhole. From there, she was able to ease what was left of the skirt down, followed by her cotton petticoat. Ma always wore woolen skirts when she worked over an open fire. Sally should have followed her example, though in this heat she might have swooned wearing wool. She had brought one old winter woolen dress from St. Louis, thinking she would probably never wear it in Texas.

She stepped out of the circle of charred fabric and sat down on her bed. At once she wished she had asked Cam to fill her wash basin. She would not call him back, not for anything.

She got up slowly and hobbled to the water bucket. Bending over, she immersed her hands in the water for several seconds and then splashed a handful on her calf. A large red patch discolored the outside of her left leg below the knee. A smaller spot, about two inches long and half an inch wide, went deeper. The skin was peeling away. She wondered if Mark had any burn salve. If not, she would put butter on it—but she wouldn't go out to the kitchen for it now. Cam could walk into the main room at any moment, and she wasn't dressed.

She took a cloth from the washstand and soaked it then limped back to the bed. Cautiously, she worked her way onto the mattress and lay back on her pillow. Her hands and leg hurt so fiercely she wanted to cry out. Tears gushed from her eyes. If Ma were here, she would know what to put on the burns, and she would fix some soothing tea.

Dear God, please help me.

She lay staring at the board ceiling and tried not to scream.

CHAPTER 18

—◆—

Johnny rode wearily into the barnyard. He was getting home later than usual, and the sun was already lowering. He'd spent half the day cleaning the spring and the other half bringing in some cattle that had broken through a weak place in a stretch of fence on his farthest boundary line. After two hours of chasing them up and down the hills, he'd finally gotten them inside the fence. Then had come the job of repairing it so they couldn't get out again.

Cam was standing near the corral gate, obviously waiting for him. Before Johnny had even hit the ground, he blurted out, "Sally's hurt."

"What happened?"

"Burned herself doing the laundry."

Johnny's breath whooshed out of him. "How bad?"

"She said she can take care of herself, but I looked in the cabin a little while ago, and she hasn't started the stove or anything. Her hands are the worst, I think, where she tried to beat it out."

Johnny dropped Reckless's reins and ran for the cabin. The front door was wide open, but the bedroom door was shut. He threw it open. Sally raised her head from her pillow and blinked at him.

"Mark?"

He stepped over a heap of discarded clothing, went to her side, and knelt by the bed. "Sally, are you all right?"

She looked around as though dazed, then back at him. "I must have slept."

Her hair was damp, clinging in strands to her forehead. He pushed it back gently. "How bad is it?"

She raised her hands and stared at her palms. In the dim light, he could see that they were swollen. A blister the size of a silver dollar disfigured her right palm, and smaller ones had formed on her fingers. He took her wrist gingerly and turned her left hand toward him. It was even worse.

"Oh, Sally, I'm so sorry!"

"My skirt caught. It happened so fast."

"Your skirt?"

She nodded, and he noticed the tear streaks on her cheeks. "My leg hurts, but my hands. . ."

She hadn't put the quilt over herself, but one of the linen sheets covered her from her waist down. He pushed it aside.

"Don't," she choked.

His face heated. "I need to, Sally. It's all right."

He'd never seen a woman's bare limbs before. He tried not to think about that but just concentrated on her burn. If this were his own leg he was looking at, what would he be thinking?

"Do you have any salve?" she asked.

"I. . .there might be something in the barn." Tears spilled over his eyes, and he swiped at them with his cuff. "I'm sorry. I should have been here."

"Cam. . ." She stared at him, her lips trembling. "If Cam wasn't here. . ."

"Thank God he was."

She nodded slowly.

"I'll find something to put on the burns."

"It's suppertime, isn't it?" Her hoarse voice tore at him.

"Don't think about that. I don't want you to get up."

"But I only gave Cam a sandwich this noon."

"We won't starve." Johnny pushed to his feet. "What can I get you first?"

"A glass of water. And a basin full, so I can bathe my hands again."

He looked toward the doorway and saw a bucket of water sitting there. "Can we use that?"

"Not for drinking. I put my hands in it before."

"All right. I'll get some fresh."

He ran outside. Cam was leaning against the well berm.

"Cool water for Sally," Johnny said.

Cam waved in acknowledgment.

Johnny went back inside and carried the bucket in the bedroom over to the washstand. He set aside the empty pitcher and poured a couple of quarts of water into the bowl.

"Can you sit up?" he asked.

"Help me."

Sally still wore the bodice of the dress she'd had on that morning, with her muslin chemise hanging down below it to her knees. Even so, Johnny could tell it mortified her that he was seeing her in this state of undress.

A quiet knock on the doorjamb made him cover her again quickly. Cam stood there with another pail of water.

Johnny took it from him. "Get me a cup?"

Cam fetched one and put it in his hand.

"Thanks," Johnny said. "You're on your own for supper."

"I can fry up some bacon."

Johnny nodded. He shut the bedroom door and dipped a cup of water for Sally. After setting it on the stand beside the bed, he grasped her wrists and pulled her up gently. She caught her breath, and her face went white.

"What hurts?" he asked.

"My leg." She closed her eyes, and he thought she might have fainted. After several seconds, her eyelashes fluttered. "I'm sorry. Just help me get it over the edge of the bed, will you? It's stiff and it hurts a lot, but if I could sit up, I think I could bathe it."

"I'll do it," he said.

"No."

"Yes. And I'll dress it, too." Careful not to touch her hands, he got one arm around her and eased her to the edge of the bed until she sat with her lower legs hanging down. Johnny brought over the cup of fresh water. "Ready?"

She reached for it instinctively but then drew back her hands. "Could you—?"

He put the rim to her lips and tipped the cup carefully. She drank half of it down and drew back.

"Thank you."

Johnny set aside the cup and took a damp cloth that hung beside the washbowl. He rinsed it and wrung it out. "Now let me see the leg." Kneeling beside her, he swabbed her wound tenderly. She gritted her teeth but said nothing.

"My mother used to put honey on burns," he said. "But we don't have any."

"Butter?" she asked.

"Milk, I think. I'll see if we have any salve. If not, I can soak some gauze in milk and wrap your hands." He eyed her carefully. "Maybe you should see Dr. Neale."

"It's not that bad."

"Isn't it? You seem to have a lot of pain."

"I can bear it."

Johnny frowned. "I'll make you some of that tea."

Sally lifted her chin. "Willow bark. I should have thought of it. And do we have any regular tea? I think my mother used that in poultices, too."

"No, but I could send Cam for some."

"It's late. The stores will be closed."

"Tomorrow then."

She nodded.

A few minutes later, he settled her back on her pillow with the sheet laid lightly across her legs. "I'll be back."

In the kitchen, Cam had fired up the stove. The heat was oppressive.

"Have we got any salve for burns?"

"Not that I know of. Vinegar might help."

Johnny winced. "That would hurt."

Cam shrugged.

"I'll have you go in to Doc Neale's tomorrow and get something," Johnny said. "And if she's worse, you can fetch the doctor himself."

"Burns can get infected easy," Cam said.

"Yeah." Johnny sank down on a stool. "You should have come and got me."

"Didn't want to leave her alone. Besides, she said. . ."

"What?"

"She told me not to get you. Said you wouldn't want it."

"That's stupid. She didn't say that."

"Something like that." Cam frowned as he turned the bacon in the skillet. "She said you didn't want to be here. And I guess she's right, the way you been acting." Cam looked over at him and shook the fork at him. "Look, I don't know what's going on with you two, but if it was up to me—"

"Nothin's going on," Johnny said. "Absolutely nothin'."

"Yeah. That's about what I figured."

Johnny met his gaze for about five seconds and turned away. He tried not to stomp too hard as he headed for the door, so he wouldn't disturb Sally.

———

Liz Merton came on Thursday. Sally was much better then, up and about. The burn on her leg was healed over, and the skin had peeled a couple of times. Her hands were still tender, especially the left one, and she kept it bandaged during the day but left it open to the air at night.

"We missed you yesterday," Liz said, "and then Dan ran into the doctor in town. I was so sorry to hear you'd burned yourself. Are you going to be all right?"

"I think so." Sally beckoned her inside, and Liz set a basket on the table. "I brought you some grape jelly and a pecan pie."

"You dear," Sally said. "If my hands didn't hurt, I'd hug you."

"Well, I can hug you," Liz said, and she did. "Sit down, honey."

"Mark got me some black tea in town. The doctor says it's good for poultices—draws the fluid out of burns. But I like to drink it, too. Would you like a cup?"

"I'd love it," Liz said. "I see your kettle's steaming. Let me get it."

Sally directed her on where to find the cups, tea, and other things she needed.

"Is it just your hands, then?"

"There's a place on my leg, but it's a lot better now. Dr. Neale sent some salve for the places that weren't blistered, and that worked fine. It takes the heat out of it somehow."

"He's a good one, Doc Neale." Liz brought their cups over and set Sally's in front of her. "Can you drink it by yourself?"

"I manage now." Sally laughed, remembering how helpless she had felt on Monday and Tuesday. "Mark had to help me at first."

"If I'd known, I'd have come and stayed with you."

"Thank you." It would have been so much easier if she'd had a woman handy to help her. The worst humiliation—other than Mark seeing her without her skirt and petticoat—had been when she'd finally begged him to loosen her corset for her late Monday night. She could tell such a thought had never entered his mind, and she wished she hadn't had to put it there, but she'd grown increasingly uncomfortable and had swallowed her pride at last. He'd done what was necessary and then disappeared until morning. She didn't blame him.

She felt dowdy now, receiving Liz without her stays in place, but she couldn't manage the unwieldy garment alone yet, and she would die before she asked Mark to put it on her.

Liz sipped her tea. "Tell me what happened."

"I wasn't paying enough mind to my skirts, that's all. I was doing laundry outside, because it was so hot in here."

"That will do it," Liz said with a nod. "Open flames and long skirts."

"Yes. It was so quick."

"Was Mark here?"

"No, but our hired man was. He came to my aid, or I'm sure I'd have suffered worse." It was true, she reflected. She owed Cam her life, or at least a large measure of lessened pain. If Cam hadn't been here. . . On the other hand, if Cam had been off on the other side of the ranch instead of Mark, and if Mark had been home, she probably wouldn't have gone out to tend her fire during the dinner hour, and she certainly wouldn't have been so distracted.

She enjoyed a chat with Liz, during which Sally gleaned much information about the other church members, and especially about the Mertons' family life. Liz had three children who were all in school for another two weeks and then would have two months off during the hottest part of the summer.

"Now, I'm going to start dinner for you and your menfolk," Liz said, rising and taking their teacups to the worktable.

"You don't need to do that," Sally said.

"I insist. Dan works all day at the rice mill, and he won't be home for dinner today. What were you planning to serve?"

After a little more cajoling, Sally guided her in cooking the plucked and dressed chicken Mark had brought her that morning and preparing rice and greens.

"Did you get to set your bread this week?"

"No," Sally admitted, "but you mustn't. You've done so much already."

"Hmm." Liz looked around the little cabin and nodded. "I think I'll stop by the Hoods' on my way home. I expect Mary Pete could come out here tomorrow and give you a hand with that."

"Oh, that's too much trouble!"

Liz shook her head. "Nonsense. She's a lively girl and would probably love to get out from under Mrs. Hood's eye for a while. Not that she doesn't get along with her mother-in-law, but you understand. A woman likes to get off on her own once in a while and have her own adventures."

Sally smiled. She had never been forced to live with a mother-in-law, and right now such an arrangement would probably be a blessing. But memories of living in Effie Winters's household were still vivid.

"If she truly wants to and is able, I won't say no. Thank you so much, Liz."

"I enjoyed every minute." Liz took off Sally's patchwork apron and hung it near the dish cupboard. "If you're not up to coming to church this week, I'll try to visit you again on Monday. If there's anything that's too bothersome for you with those poor hands, just leave it for me or Mary Pete. I mean it." She kissed Sally on the cheek.

"Thank you. And for the pie and the jelly."

"That's nothing." Liz squeezed her and picked up her bonnet and basket.

Sally followed her into the yard and watched as Liz climbed into her buggy. "Good-bye!"

"Don't let that rice boil dry!"

Mark and Cam drove toward them along the road. They'd gone to Beaumont for more barbed wire and staples that morning. They waved to Liz, and Mark pulled the wagon over so she could pass them.

A minute later, he jumped down from the wagon in the yard. "Well, you had a visitor."

"Yes, we had a lovely chat, and Liz brought a pie."

"Sounds good," Mark said.

Cam climbed down and went to the horse's head. "I'll tend to Reckless."

Mark grabbed a sack from the back of the wagon and walked with Sally to the cabin. "Everything all right? How are your hands doing?"

"Fine, thanks to Liz. She got our dinner for us."

"That was nice of her." He held the door open for her and carried his sack to the table. "I stopped by Doc Neale's. He sent a little pot of a new cream he just got in." He fished in the sack and pulled it out. "Says to tell him if it works better than the other stuff, and if it does, he'll order more to have on hand for patients."

"Can you open it, please?"

Mark unscrewed the top, and she leaned over to sniff it.

"Smells all right." She stuck her right index finger in it and took enough to smear across all her fingers.

"Want me to dress your palms with it?"

"Maybe after we eat."

"I got you more tea, too, in case you want to make more poultices."

She smiled up at him. "Thank you. That was very thoughtful—and we're nearly out, since Liz and I had a pot between us." There was so much more she wanted to talk to him about, and Mark seemed to be in an open, soft mood, concerned for her well-being. But at that moment, Cam came in and hung his hat on a peg next to Mark's.

"Something smells good."

"Oh, I'd better get the rice off. Liz warned me not to let it go dry, and I've probably done just that." Sally hurried to the stove and lifted the lid on the pan of rice. "Perfect. If you boys would carry things over, we'll serve right from the pans today. Fancy serving dishes, but it will save you washing more. Mark, the chicken's in the oven. It should be done now."

The two men willingly went about setting the table and arranging the food. Cam poured coffee all around, and they sat down. Without a mention from her, Mark bowed his head and offered a brief prayer. Again, Sally felt he was making an effort to make things easier for her and to be a good husband. But when would they be able to talk about things that mattered? She still wanted to know about the poor man buried on the knoll, but another topic had hounded her this week.

Though Mark had stayed close to home Tuesday and Wednesday and done any chores she needed done, he still kept away from her at night. She longed for private time in their bedroom, where she could know Cam wouldn't overhear them.

The more she replayed Monday's events in her mind, the more she longed to tell Mark how Cam had frightened her before she was burned. Would that upset Mark? Or would he offer her reassurances that his friend wouldn't do such a thing? Somehow she knew he would not confront Cam about the incident. And what could she give as evidence? Maybe it was better that she hadn't told her husband. But if Cam ever put one whisker out of line again, she would hold him accountable.

CHAPTER 19

Johnny finished the windlass and tested it to be sure it worked right. Sally would be pleased, but then, she was always grateful when he did things for her. They had lived for the past several weeks in quiet camaraderie—at least he saw it that way. The tension seemed less between them since Sally was burned. She thanked him for sticking closer to home and letting Cam handle most of the jobs that required being away for hours on end, and she seemed to have accepted the pattern of their lives.

He pulled a bucket of water up from the well and carried it over to the stoop, where he'd built a rough washstand. While he was washing his hands, Sally came to the doorway. Her hands were healed over now but still tender. He didn't let her pull up full buckets with the rope anymore—that had spurred him to building the windlass, and whenever he was aware that she needed water, he drew it for her. But he wouldn't always be around.

He didn't let her do the laundry, either, or anything else over the open fire. He and Cam had talked to other ranchers and people in town about an outdoor oven. So far all he'd come up with was a stone fireplace with a grate on it. That was an improvement, but still dangerous. Sally had said she could wear her skirts shorter, but he wasn't sure he wanted her working over the flames again, ever.

He turned and gazed at her as he dried his hands. She was a picture, all right. Prettier than that first day he'd seen her, and that was saying a lot. Texas, despite its heat and wind and hardship, seemed to agree with her. The dress she wore today was the one she had sewn from the blue print cotton he'd bought her that first week.

"Do you know what day it is?" she asked.

Johnny shook his head and hung the towel over the railing. "Can't be Sunday again already."

"No, it's Thursday, but that's not what I meant. We've been married two months, Mark. It's our anniversary."

"Oh." Was he supposed to have done something special? He must have shown his dismay, because she smiled a bit. His heart still quickened when he saw that, though he'd constantly tried to discourage the thoughts of holding her and kissing her—just plain loving her—that still plagued him.

"It's just a day," she said, but he could tell it was more to her.

"I'm glad you're feeling well now. Come and see the windlass."

She walked out to the well with him, and he demonstrated for her how easy it was to wind it and bring up a pail of water. He'd taken extra care to sand the handle so she wouldn't get slivers in the new skin of her palms.

"Thank you." She gazed at him again, but she didn't smile.

She seemed troubled, and Johnny began to feel uneasy. He wanted to ask if there was anything wrong, but he was afraid she'd say yes, and he didn't want to hear that. He wanted everything to be calm and peaceful between them, the way it had been lately.

———

The next morning, Mark rode out after breakfast without so much as a good-bye. Sally heard the hoofbeats and looked out the window in time to see Reckless's hindquarters disappear on the road toward Beaumont.

No one had brought in the milk yet, which set her teeth on edge. Mark wouldn't leave the cow unmilked, so Cam must be doing that now. She did up the breakfast dishes and settled down with her sewing. Her hands still hurt when she flexed them, but with her thimble and a leather palm patch, she'd begun sewing again for short periods each day.

She had discovered a new yard-goods shop in town and a possible source of income. Mrs. Ricks, who ran the shop, had taken a liking to Sally's newest dress. She had started a conversation that ended with Sally agreeing to make her a dress in a complicated new pattern when she felt up to it. In exchange, Mrs. Ricks would give her a dress length of silk. Word would get around town, and Sally knew she would soon get more orders if she wanted them.

Her feelings on that subject were in chaos. One minute she wanted to succeed and tell Mark she could add to the ranch's income. The next, she was ready to give it all up and go home to her mother. What kind of life was she living here, anyway, with a husband who wasn't really a husband at all?

Of course, telling her parents would be difficult. That held her back, even on days when she was most frustrated with Mark. She had formed a pattern of her own, Sally realized. With David, she'd never told her family about the bad times. Now she did the same thing with Mark. Her mother had answered her first two letters, joyful that Sally was now closer to home and excited to think they might visit each other. Sally wasn't sure she was ready for the humiliation of revealing how things really were.

She was studying Mrs. Ricks's pattern and the way the ruffles fell across the dress's basque in the diagram when Cam came in with the milk. He set the bucket on her worktable.

"I wondered if you wanted some meat for dinner," he said, leaning against the table.

Sally kept her eyes on the pattern. "We've a bit left from last night. Will Mark be home to eat?"

"Not sure. He was going to go talk to a few of the ranchers about getting together for fall roundup."

Sally laid the tissue pattern across her lap. "Goodness! Is it coming up soon?" It was mid-July, and she hadn't thought of much lately besides getting through each painful day and keeping cool.

"Not for a couple of months, but he wants to make sure he's got everything in place when the time comes."

Sally nodded. Regardless of her tumultuous feelings, ranch life went on.

"I can wring a chicken's neck for you if you want," Cam said.

"Oh, don't bother."

"Doesn't take much, just a quick twist. Not hard at all."

She shuddered. "No, thank you. Not today. I'll make out with what I've got."

"Suit yourself." Cam ambled outside and left the door open, as was Sally's habit, to let the breeze through.

She sat staring after him, feeling a little sick. Cam almost seemed to enjoy the thought of killing a chicken. That man was a strange mixture of charm and peculiarity. Sometimes he made her flesh crawl.

She spent the next two hours laying out Mrs. Ricks's pattern on the fabric and cutting out the pieces; then she put the project away and concentrated on making last night's leftovers into an appealing meal.

Cam came in for dinner at noon, and Mark had not returned. When they sat down together, Sally was afraid the conversation would be stilted, but Cam began telling her about his adventures that morning in rounding up a few of the young steers that had managed to squeeze under the fence where it crossed the creek, and by the end of his tale, he had her laughing.

"Mark should really buy you a horse," he said. "Then you could come out and see what really goes on out there."

"He's talked about it," Sally said.

"I expect you'd be good at helping with the stock." Cam gave her an appraising look. "You'd probably have fun, too."

"I was quite a tomboy when I was a girl." Sally stood. "More coffee? I really should get back to my sewing."

He stayed away from the house for the next three hours, for which she was thankful. She worked until her hands ached too badly to continue and made herself a cup of willow bark tea. As she sat in the path of the warm breeze to drink it, Cam bounded in through the doorway, holding the black body of a five-foot snake.

Sally jumped up and backed behind the table before realizing the snake was missing its head.

"Found this fellow in the feed bin," Cam said. "Thought maybe you'd cook it up."

"N—no thank you." Sally's hands shook as she pulled out the chair farthest away from Cam and the reptile. "Please take it away."

He laughed. "Aw, come on, you're a Texas girl!"

"I don't eat snakes."

"Mark would eat it. He and I roasted one on the trail one time. Mighty tasty it was, too."

Sally swallowed hard. "Why don't you cook it, then? Outside. You and Mark can eat it tonight if you've a mind to. I'd as soon not have it in my kitchen."

"Well, what do you know? I had you pegged wrong, Sal." He stood there grinning, and she wanted to throw something at him.

"Just get it out of here, please."

"Awright, awright."

He went, laughing, and Sally stood for a long moment with her hands clenched around the chair back. When she at last spread her fingers, her hands hurt terribly. She sat down where she was, facing the door, and pulled her teacup across the table. No more sewing for today, and perhaps she would use Dr. Neale's salve again, though she'd forsaken it for the last few days.

She brought her Bible to the kitchen and read for the next half hour, letting her doctored hands rest on the tabletop. After a while, she was able to put the headless serpent out of her mind and focus on the words before her.

At last she heard a horse approaching, and she leaned to watch through the doorway. Mark and Reckless appeared as they slowed to a halt near the corral. She rose and fixed a bowl of cottage pudding for Mark and added a little fuel to the fire to heat up the coffeepot.

She began to fear he wouldn't come into the cabin, but after about ten minutes, his form blocked the light from the doorway.

"Hello," she said. "Did you eat dinner?"

"Mrs. Caxton fed me."

"Good. I made some cottage pudding, if you'd like some."

"Thanks." Mark hung up his hat and gun belt and made his way to the table.

"Coffee with it, or milk? There's plenty of milk."

"I'll take some of that," Mark said.

She poured him a glass full and sat down across the table from him. He took a bite of the pudding.

"What's the word?" she asked, trying to keep her tone light and cheerful.

"I saw the sheriff in town. He said the outlaws are about again. He may get up a posse and go after them."

The thought of being alone if a gang came to the ranch terrified Sally, but she would probably be more frightened if she knew her husband was out chasing them. She pushed the thought aside, not to be deterred from her purpose. Mark ate in silence, and when his bowl was empty, he looked over at her and smiled.

"That was good. Thanks."

"Mark, there's something I need to say."

He sobered and cocked his head to one side. "Go ahead."

"Please don't leave me here alone with Cam again."

They gazed at each other for a moment. "What are you saying?"

"I'd rather be here alone than with Cam. Leave me your rifle if you need to go somewhere, and I'll be fine."

"But those outlaws. . .and Cam saved your life."

"Maybe so. Or maybe not. I don't know. But I do know that I don't want to be here alone with him ever again."

Mark took a swallow from his glass of milk. He set the glass down. "Did he do something?"

"Not really."

"He told me about the snake just now. You didn't like that."

"It's not just the snake. It's true I don't like them, but he seemed to enjoy frightening me with it."

"He's like a kid that way."

"That way and. . .others."

"What do you mean?" Mark's eyes narrowed. "What else?"

She felt her face flush, and she couldn't hold his gaze. "Nothing specific."

"There must have been something."

"Sometimes. . ." They sat in silence again. Mark's patience outlasted her, and she blurted, in a low voice, "Sometimes I'm afraid of him. And I mean him, not the snake."

Mark frowned. "What sort of things does he say?"

"It's not always what he says. It's the way he says it. Take this morning, for instance. He asked if he could wring a chicken's neck for me."

Mark's lips twitched.

"Yes, it's funny, isn't it?" Sally's anger made her voice rise, and she made herself take a deep breath.

"Sorry."

"Well, then he went on to tell me how easy it was to do, and I could almost imagine him doing it to. . .to a person, Mark. Call me fanciful if you want, but that man scares me."

"Sally. . ."

"And the day I was burned. I didn't tell you, because everything was so hectic, but. . .he touched me, Mark."

"What?" Alarm tightened his face. "To check your burns?"

"No, before that. In the house." She glanced toward the dish cupboard. "I was getting down the luncheon things. He came up behind me. Too close. And he touched my neck."

"It couldn't have been accidental?"

She hesitated. "He said it was, and he apologized in an offhand way, but it didn't feel like that when it happened." Sally buried her face in her hands for a moment. She could still feel Cam's fingers on the back of her neck, almost a caress. She shuddered. When she looked at Mark again, he was sitting still, staring into space. "Look, I know he's your friend." Sally shook her head helplessly. "He's not like you, Mark. He drinks, and he—"

"He's never come near you after he'd been drinking, has he?" Mark's voice rose.

"No."

"Good. I've tried to make sure of that."

"Then you don't trust him."

Mark let out a deep sigh. "I don't know as I'd go that far, but I've tried to keep any. . .unpleasantness. . .away from you. I'll have a word with him."

In that moment, Sally knew she had made up her mind. She stood. "I'm afraid a word isn't enough. I've decided to visit my parents. I'd like to take the train to Abilene tomorrow."

Mark's stunned expression wrenched her heart, but maybe this was what he needed.

"I'll pack this evening," she said. "I'd appreciate it if you'd drive me to the depot tomorrow."

"How long will you be gone?"

She hauled in a deep breath. "I don't know, Mark. Our marriage doesn't seem to be working. It isn't a real marriage at all."

He said nothing but watched her guardedly. She hadn't intended to hurt him, but nothing else seemed to work with this man.

Sally pushed the chair in. "If you want me to come back here—and truly make a life with you—you can contact me there. I'll leave you the address."

"Sally. . ."

She waited, praying he would have sense enough to walk around the table and take her into his arms. Short of that, even a simple "Don't go" would be enough. She waited, searching his brown eyes for the spark of love and determination she needed from him. But she saw only hurt.

"I'm sorry." He got up and walked slowly out the door, fumbling for his hat as he passed the pegs.

Sally stood watching him go, tears streaming down her cheeks.

———

Johnny walked over to the corral. He had just unsaddled Reckless and turned him loose after a long ride. He didn't want to ask the horse to work again. But he didn't feel like talking to Cam, either. How could he admit that he'd failed miserably and Sally was going away?

Reckless was grazing. He needed the rest and nourishment. Johnny turned away and walked around the end of the barn and on up the hill.

Mark's grave would have been indistinguishable except for the cross. The grass and weeds had grown enough to obscure where they'd turned the earth to bury him. Johnny doubted Sally had been up here since she'd burned herself. He crouched beside the cross and touched the carved vines. Mark's name should be there, or on a more permanent stone marker. He sat down in the grass.

"She's leaving me, Mark. I haven't done right by you or by Sally. It sounds like she might not come back. I don't know what to do." It occurred to him that she might hope he would fire Cam and send him away. Would she stay then? Cam could get a job on another ranch, if not here, then back in Colorado, or even up Wyoming way.

But what if he did that, and she still wouldn't stay? Cam wasn't the reason she gave for leaving. And if they both went, he would be all alone here with no one to talk to but his horse and his brother's grave.

There was God.

Johnny glanced up at the cloudless sky. He took off his hat and lay back on the ground.

After a long minute, he said, "I don't know what to do. I don't even know what's right anymore."

He heard a voice inside his head. His conscience, Ma would have said.

That's a lie. You do *know what's right. And you know what's wrong.*

The sun beat down on him, too hot. He sat up and put his hat on.

"If I tell her now, she'll leave for sure," he said aloud.

The thought came, almost as strong: *If you don't tell her, she'll leave anyway. Tell her and let her go knowing the truth.*

What if he told her, and Sally ran and told the sheriff? He thought about that for a long time. At last he rose. Even if he was accused of killing Mark, that would be better than Sally not knowing the man she really loved was honest and true and faithful to her. And dead.

His boots dragged through the grass, but he made himself keep walking toward the house.

———

Sally folded Mrs. Ricks's unfinished dress carefully and wrapped it in the brown paper that had been around the cloth when she brought it home. She would have to stop by the yard-goods shop before she went to the train station and return it with her apologies.

She hoped Mark wouldn't mind leaving home early enough tomorrow to allow for that errand. As usual, when something unpleasant happened, he had walked out the door. To be fair, his behavior wasn't as bad as David's had been. David would be in a saloon now—after he'd punished her for suggesting she might leave him.

Life with Mark was in some ways infinitely better than life with David. So why couldn't she stand it?

Tears gathered in her eyes, but she brushed them away and opened her trunk. She would not back down on this. She'd stuck with one husband through thick and thin, and she'd barely survived. This time she'd been more careful, had waited longer before committing herself. She'd made sure Mark was a man of faith and integrity.

Or so she had thought.

Questioning Mark's motives was futile. She had done that a thousand times. The most likely explanation she had come up with was that he knew she had miscarried twice before. Was that it? He didn't want that to happen again? She hadn't been able to voice the thought to him. And before she came, he had written that he hoped for children, so that couldn't be it. No, she kept coming back to that unknown factor, the reason he didn't want to be with her. Not knowing why ate at her. She couldn't stay any longer unless she knew, but the few times she had asked, he had run from her.

She placed her sewing patterns in the trunk and put one extra dress, her hairbrush, and her Bible in the satchel. She looked around the spotless bedroom to be sure she hadn't forgotten anything. If she left one item, Mark would hope it meant she'd be back. But she wouldn't be. Not unless he agreed to change his demeanor toward her.

His footsteps in the outer room froze her for an instant with her calico bonnet in her hands. He was back sooner than she had expected. Good. Maybe he was ready to talk.

Dear Lord, this is our last chance. Please let him want to talk things out. I don't know how else we can live together. And I do want to, truly. But I just—

She broke off her prayer. Since when did she make excuses to God? It struck her in an instant that she was doing the wrong thing and that she hadn't given Mark a fair chance to explain himself. True, she had asked him a few times what was wrong and had waited weeks for his answer. Did that mean she should stop waiting and pick up and leave?

"What are you doing?"

She jumped and whirled to face Cam, who stood in the doorway eyeing her open trunk and the satchel on the bed. Her lungs refused to pull in air.

"I'm packing." She cleared her throat. This could be the last time she would speak to him. "I'm going to visit my family. Mark is taking me to the depot."

Cam took a step into the room. "I could take you, if you'd rather not talk to Mark."

She gave him a look she hoped would wither his confidence. "Why would I rather talk to you than to my husband?"

"I don't know exactly, but you two don't seem to enjoy talking to each other much."

She felt her cheeks go crimson. She wanted to deny his assertion, but she couldn't. Still, that didn't mean he could walk into her bed-chamber and poke his nose into private matters.

"Where's Mark?" she asked.

"Somewhere out yonder." Cam glanced toward the empty hooks on the wall and the dresser crate that was now empty. "Guess you're not figuring on coming back here. You having regrets?"

Sally raised her chin and glared at him. "How dare you!"

Cam smiled and shifted his weight to one foot. "I dare because I think that's what you want, Sal. You want a man that speaks his mind, don't you? Not one like Mark, that holds things inside and won't tell you what he's really thinking." He took a step toward her. "Maybe you married the wrong man."

Sally gasped. The audacity of the man. She raised her hand to slap him, but Cam caught her wrist. His smile widened, and a jolt ran through her. This was exactly why she had asked Mark not to leave her here with Cam. This was the moment she had feared.

"Let go of me," she managed.

"Are you sure that's what you want?"

She dropped her bonnet and shoved his chest, but when he staggered back, he pulled her with him. Sally let out a scream, wondering who would hear her.

CHAPTER 20

Johnny tore for the house. That was Sally! Maybe a snake had gotten into the cabin. He glanced into the open front of the barn as he passed, but Cam wasn't there. Had he heard Sally's scream and gone to her aid?

He pounded up the steps and through the open door. Muffled sounds came from the new bedroom.

"Stop it!"

Johnny pulled up and listened.

"Let me go!"

"Not just yet."

Ice water washed over Johnny. That was Cam.

Sally let out another scream, but it stopped abruptly. Johnny crossed the room in three strides. He grabbed Cam by the back of his collar with one arm and yanked him out of the new room. He shoved him across the cabin. Cam crashed against one of the straight chairs and fell, taking the chair with him.

Johnny hurried to the row of pegs by the door. His hand shook as he pulled his revolver from the holster hanging on the wall and leveled it at Cam.

"Get your stuff and ride out."

Cam looked up at him, dazed, and wiped a hand across his forehead.

"Hey, no harm done."

"I said get out." Johnny gazed at him over the gun barrel without blinking.

Cam stared back for a moment, appraising him. A muffled sob came from the bedroom.

"We'll talk about this later." Cam staggered to his feet.

"No," Johnny said. "We'll never talk about this. Don't you ever come back."

Cam threw him a dark look and shuffled outside. Johnny pulled in a deep breath and shut the door. He walked slowly to the bedroom doorway. Sally was huddled on the floor, weeping beside her trunk, her hands over her face. He laid his revolver on the crate that usually held her clothes and walked slowly over to her.

He knelt beside her and put his arms around her. She sobbed harder and burrowed her face into the front of his shirt. Johnny didn't know what to say, so he didn't say anything. He just held on to her and let her cry.

After a long time, she lifted her face and took a deep, shaky breath.

"You tried to tell me," he said.

"I didn't think he'd be so. . .vile." Her sobs erupted again, and Johnny pulled her in close. She was soft and trembly, and it was too hot to be this close to somebody else, but he held on.

When she sniffed and stirred in his arms, he said, "Got a handkerchief?"

She shook her head. "They're in my satchel."

He got up, reluctant to leave her, and walked around the bed. He peered into the satchel and found several ironed, folded hankies and took one out. She had risen, and she took it from his hand and sat down on the edge of the bed. He looked away while she mopped her face and wiped her nose.

"I'm sorry I didn't take what you said more serious, Sally. I should have listened harder."

She sighed and stared down at the floor. "I thank you for what you did just now. Truly. But a man's got to be honest with his wife. I love you, Mark, but I know you're keeping things back. I meant what

I said earlier. If you won't tell me everything, I will get on that train tomorrow."

He nodded slowly. "I was thinking the same thing—that I need to tell you the truth. And I'm sorry that I didn't before. Real sorry."

From outside came a faint shout.

"Johnny! This ain't over!"

Sally's eyelids flew up, and she stared at him. With his heart pounding, Johnny retrieved his gun from the crate top and hurried out to the front door. He opened it a few inches and peered out. Cam had his saddlebags and bedroll on Paint's saddle, and his holster strapped on his thigh. But he was already mounted, and as Johnny watched, he gathered his reins and loped out of the yard, heading toward town.

"What did he mean?"

Sally was right beside him, her eyes huge.

Slowly, Johnny lowered his revolver and turned toward her.

"Let's sit down."

She turned and walked over to the table, picked up the chair Cam had tripped over, and set it right. She plunked down in it. Johnny walked over and pulled out the one next to it.

"You want coffee?"

She stared up at him. "No. I want you to talk."

He swallowed hard, sat down, and laid the gun on the table.

"I'm sorry."

"You said that."

He nodded and took a deep breath.

"I'm not Mark."

They sat in silence for a long time. Sally never moved a muscle. What was going through her head?

At last he couldn't stand it any longer.

"I wanted to tell you, first thing. But Cam said—" He broke off and ran his fingers through his hair. What did it matter now what Cam had said? "I'm sorry."

She frowned, and he hurried on.

"We were up in Colorado, working at the Lone Pine Ranch, Cam and me. I was out riding fence, and I stayed the night in a line shack at the far edge of the ranch. The next morning I was about to head out when Cam came barreling up on Paint and said the foreman had been shot. He said they all thought I did it, and there was talk of lynching me." His pulse skyrocketed just talking about it, and he made himself breathe deeply.

"You're John, then."

"Yeah. But I didn't do it. I swear, Sally, I was nowhere near that man when he was killed."

He tried to swallow the lump in his throat and watched her for a sign that she was ready for more. Funny, he'd thought telling the truth would feel good.

Sally folded her hands together on the table and stared at them. "Where's Mark?"

The air whooshed out of Johnny's lungs. "He's buried, up on the knoll."

She met his gaze. "When? He wrote me. . . ." She shook her head.

"He was dead when I got here. I thought I could ride down here and stay with him for a little while until things at the Lone Pine got sorted out. But when Cam and I rode in, Mark was dead." He looked over at the spot near the door, where his brother had lain. "He was right over there."

He turned back toward Sally. The stark whiteness of her face startled him.

"How?" she gasped.

"Someone had. . .had shot him. There weren't any horses on the place, nor any money, and his foodstuffs had been ransacked. We found out later that outlaw gang had been through these parts. We reckon they robbed Mark and killed him, not long before we got here."

"Are you sure. . . ?" Her eyes narrowed. "How do I know you're telling me the truth now?"

That struck to the heart. Johnny squared his shoulders. "I won't ever lie to you again, Sally. That's what happened. You don't think I would—" He broke off, realizing how deeply her trust had been shattered.

She blinked and looked away. "No. I was thinking more of Cam."

"Impossible," Johnny said. "We rode in here side by side. The place was empty, except for poor Mark." He glanced involuntarily toward the spot where he'd scrubbed away the blood. "We buried him the same day, and—"

"And you decided to take over his life." Sally's voice was flat.

"Not at first. We rode into town a couple days later, and everyone thought I was Mark. I'd grown a beard in the weeks we'd been on the trail, and everyone said things like, 'Oh, you grew a beard,' but nobody thought I wasn't him. They gave me credit at the store, and the banker let me use Mark's account." He saw it now with the same horror and disgust he'd felt those first few days. If he heard about another man doing this, he would be the first to condemn him.

"So you decided to let them keep thinking that," Sally said.

"I didn't want to."

She made a little noise in her throat. "This was Cam's idea, wasn't it?"

Johnny gazed into her blue eyes, once so hopeful and trusting. How convenient it would be to blame everything on Cam. "We were both at fault."

"I need to think."

Sally rose and walked into the bedroom and shut the door.

———

Sally moved the satchel off the bed and sat down. He wasn't the man she'd fallen in love with, even though she'd felt something for him. It was more than a fondness or an attachment; she yearned for him to love her. And she wasn't even married to him. The wedding ceremony was a sham. How could he have done this to her?

Her face flamed as the realization came to her how vulnerable she had been. But he had respected her. She had the reason at last for the way he had acted. She had longed to consummate the marriage, but even after they built this new room and this very bed, Mark—no, John—wouldn't touch her. And she had resented him for it. What had that restraint cost him?

She sank to her knees with tears bathing her face and began to pray.

All was quiet outside. She was surprised she hadn't heard him ride away. That would be just like him. But Cam was gone now, and he had said he wouldn't leave her alone. The outlaws were raiding again.

The outlaws. If she could believe what he said, that gang had killed her beloved. Odd, how she had been drawn to the cross on the hill. The mystery of it had fascinated her. Now she knew why he didn't want to talk about it. Cam had been glib enough, though. A former ranch hand. It all fit into place now. John had built that cross and placed it there. He had buried his own brother, but he wasn't allowed to grieve for him or even to tell anyone about his passing.

An hour later, she ventured out cautiously to visit the privy. She caught a glimpse of John at the corral gate. She hoped he didn't see her flit around the corner of the cabin.

He didn't come in for supper. She cooked up rice and beans, along with biscuits and carrots. When dusk came, she went to the door. Nothing stirred. She walked out to the barn and called cautiously, "John?"

No one answered. His horse was still in the corral.

Sally walked slowly around the barn and up the knoll. She could see him from twenty yards away, kneeling in the tall grass by his brother's grave. She covered half the distance and stopped.

"I've got supper ready."

He raised his head and looked at her then slowly got to his feet. He clapped his hat on and walked stiffly toward her. Sally didn't wait for him but turned and walked back to the house. She filled his plate and set it on the table, but she didn't feel like eating.

He came in and hung his hat on its peg. He looked at the table, set for one.

"Coffee tonight?" she asked.

He shook his head and walked over to the table.

"There's more pudding." Sally shoved the pan a few inches across her worktable so he would see it. Her heart was too full and too heavy to talk to him now. She retreated into the bedroom and closed the door. She sank onto the bed again, weeping and trying not to let him hear.

CHAPTER 21

Johnny slept in Cam's bunk in the barn, with his revolver under his pillow. He had gone over to the bedroom door after he ate and called to her.

"Sally?"

"What?" Her reply sounded odd, a bit strangled.

"I'll be at the barn. I'm leaving my rifle out here for you. You might want to bar the door, just in case." In case of outlaws, he meant, but Cam's final words still rang in his ears. To hear Sally tell it, Cam scared her more than outlaws did, and it seemed there was something to that.

He could still hardly believe Cam had tried to molest Sally. How could he do that? Even if not for their friendship, what decent man would assault a woman? Especially one as good and devout as Sally.

He lay awake a long time. Cam wasn't the man he'd imagined him to be. He'd always known his friend had flaws, but when you worked on a ranch together, that didn't matter much. Everyone had their quirks. But he would never have guessed Cam would do something like this. The betrayal cut deep.

But not as deep as Sally's hurt. She knew now that the man she'd dared to love was dead, and that she had married a lying fraud accused of murder.

Would she leave tomorrow? He couldn't think of a single reason why she shouldn't.

If quantity counted for prayer, he had a good balance by the time the rooster crowed. Coming clean with Sally wasn't his only obligation.

He knew that now.

When he went out to milk the cow, she blinked at him and lowed sleepily, as though surprised he had come around so early, but she didn't object further. He smelled smoke and knew Sally was up, so he carried the bucket of milk to the cabin and tried the latch. The door opened readily. She was frying eggs and wearing her black mourning dress beneath her apron.

Johnny took the bucket over and set it on her worktable. Maybe he should put most of the milk in a jug and run it down the well. She wouldn't be making any butter today, and he wouldn't be able to use it all himself. He would let the cow go dry. The thought of batching it here without Sally or even Cam for company opened a hollow place in his stomach.

"Sally?"

She looked up at him, her spatula in her hand.

"I'm going to talk to the sheriff today. After I put you on the train, if you'd rather be gone before I do it."

Her upper lip quivered. "What will happen to you?"

"I don't know."

"Is it a crime, not to report a death?"

"I don't know that, either. But. . .you saw the wanted poster."

She nodded curtly, picked up a tin plate, and scooped the eggs onto it. "Take this. I'll get the biscuits and side meat."

She laid a fine breakfast. Their last together?

Johnny went for the coffeepot, but it wasn't on the stove. He stood staring blankly at the steaming teakettle.

"You said you didn't like coffee much, and since Cam has gone. . ." She looked up at him and faltered. "Oh. That was Mark, wasn't it?"

"We'll have tea this mornin'."

"I'll fix it."

She sat down with him a few minutes later. They stared at each other across the table. All those times he had said the blessing. . .

"I'll pray," Sally said.

Johnny bowed his head. He had wondered if he had a right to talk to God when he was living as a liar. Apparently Sally had the same thought. Everything was ruined, that was for sure.

"Lord, we thank You for this food, and. . ."

No words came for so long that Johnny squinted at her. She seemed to be all right. Finally, she blurted, "We don't know what we're doing or what we *should* be doing, Lord. Please have pity on us and help us get out of this awful mess."

Johnny stared at her openly then. She'd said *we* and *us*. Did she consider the problem belonged to her, too, and not to him alone?

She said, "Amen," and opened her eyes.

"Amen," Johnny said quickly.

They couldn't sit there gawking at each other all day, so he picked up the plate of eggs and held it out toward her. Somehow, they got through breakfast. Afterward, he helped carry the dishes over to the worktable.

"I guess I'd better bottle up that milk and run it down the well."

"It'll spoil if we don't," Sally said.

There it was again. We.

Johnny cleared his throat. "What time did you want to leave?"

She hesitated. "Soon. As soon as we can." She set down the dirty plates and stepped closer to him. "Are we really married, John Paynter?"

His stomach felt like it was tied in knots, but maybe it was just the big breakfast. He wanted to say yes more than anything. But Sally. . . Her eyes were so intent, almost fanatical. Was she wondering how to undo it if the bond was legal?

"I think so," he said. "I asked the reverend to put 'Mark John' on the license. But I don't know for sure if that's enough."

"Do you want it to be true?" she asked softly.

His heart leaped. Of course he did, more than anything! But was she saying she didn't mind the thought? Could she possibly be thinking they could mend things? That seemed wildly impossible, and yet she had asked.

"Yes," he said.

After a moment, she stirred. She put her hands lightly on his arms and stood on tiptoe. Her lips brushed his, and Johnny caught his breath. He looked deep in her eyes. That longing was there again. He pulled her slowly to him, and she came, soft as butter. He kissed her the way he'd wanted to for weeks. When he released her, she didn't let go of him. She twined her arms around his neck and leaned against him. He held her, wondering if this was the last time, but hoping, hoping.

She rubbed her cheek against his shoulder. "You need to tell Sheriff Jackson, first thing."

"I will."

She pushed away and gazed up at him, frowning. "I think. . .I think we ought to tell the preacher, too. Ask him if. . ."

"If we're really wed?"

She nodded.

"What if we are?" he asked.

She drew in a deep breath. "I won't be sorry. Not if you're really telling me the truth now."

"I am, Sally."

She nodded, not breaking the gaze, though her eyes swam with tears. "And if we're not. . ."

"What, then?" he asked.

"I guess. . ." She cleared her throat. "I guess that's up to you."

"You mean. . .you'd stay?"

"If you face up to it, yes. I'll stand beside you."

He couldn't say what was in his heart, but he kissed her again, joy shooting through him. Even if he went to jail and had to face the hangman, this was worth it, to know she didn't despise him and that she would willingly stay his wife.

She pulled away and laughed. "Can't keep doing that. We might not be married at all." She touched his cheek. "Besides, you need to hitch up the wagon."

"Yes, ma'am."

"You don't need to load my trunk." She smiled and slithered her fingers through his beard, tracing his jawline. "You might want to shave this off, Mr. Paynter."

"Oh, yes, ma'am."

"Not now," she said, "but soon."

He smiled the whole time he worked at getting the wagon ready.

———

"What do we do now?" Sally sat on the wagon seat, looking down at Johnny. The sheriff's office was empty, and a placard on the door said, IF YOU NEED HELP, SEE THAD BOLLINGER.

"Bollinger's the owner at the feed store. Could be he's a deputy or something." Johnny climbed up beside her and took the reins. "Go, Reckless." The horse stepped out, and they drove down the street until they reached the sprawling feed store, near the grain elevators. "Stay here." Johnny hopped down and went inside.

He was back a couple of minutes later and climbed up beside her. "Jackson's off looking for the outlaw gang. They raided a rice plantation yesterday and stole some stock and guns. Shot up the owner and his foreman."

"The same ones who killed Mark?" Sally asked.

"Probably. No telling when he'll be back." Johnny clenched his fists and stared off toward the river.

"You wish you were with him."

"I wouldn't mind hunting them down." He smiled bitterly. "Jackson probably wouldn't let me go, since I came to turn myself in."

She patted his arm gently, and he gazed at her.

"What now?" he asked.

"Can we visit Pastor Lewis?"

"You want to tell him, even though we can't find the sheriff?"

She hesitated. Her experience with ministers wasn't limited to the Reverend Mr. Winters, and she wanted to believe that Pastor Lewis would guard their privacy. "I think he'll keep it a secret if we want him to. Do we?"

Johnny sighed. "Can't forever, but. . .well, it'd probably be best until we see what Jackson has to say. I reckon we can ask Pastor Lewis to keep it quiet for now."

He drove toward the church and pulled up before the parsonage. "Maybe I should put Reckless in the church sheds."

"Surely it won't take that long."

He nodded and climbed down. Sally waited while he secured the horse to the hitching rail, praying silently.

Lord, I love my husband. Please don't take him away from me.

Myra Lewis opened the door to them and beckoned them inside, smiling. "Good morning, folks! How nice to see you."

"We wondered if the pastor's busy," Sally said. Johnny seemed tongue-tied, standing beside her with his hat in his hands.

"I'm sure he's not too busy to see you. Come on in." Myra led them into the parlor, where Pastor Lewis hunched over his desk. He turned around as they entered. When he saw who had come calling, he stood.

"Hello, Mrs. Paynter. Mark." He shook both their hands.

Johnny threw Sally a panicky glance.

Sally took a deep breath. "Sir, we have a matter of some delicacy to discuss with you."

"Certainly. Sit down, won't you? Myra, perhaps some coffee in about fifteen minutes?"

"Yes, of course." Myra smiled at Sally and left the room, closing the door behind her.

Some difference from Mr. Winters's house, Sally thought. Effie would insist on staying to hear the conversation. Her esteem for both Lewises rose a notch.

She settled on the sofa, and Johnny plunked down beside her, still worrying his hat.

"Now, how may I help you?" Mr. Lewis asked, sinking into an upholstered chair opposite Johnny.

Sally waited for her husband to speak. She didn't want to usurp his place if he wished to be the one telling the tale. In fact, she hoped he would take on the task. It was his story to tell.

Johnny looked at her again, shifted in his seat, and cleared his throat. "Well, sir. . ."

Mr. Lewis waited a couple of seconds then leaned toward him slightly. "Yes, Mark?"

"See, that's the thing of it," Johnny said. "I'm not really Mark."

The pastor sat unmoving for perhaps five seconds then said, "What?"

"Yes, sir. I'm Johnny, Mark's brother."

"Oh. Perhaps you could clarify that for me."

"I'll try. I reckon it started when I was punching cows up in Colorado, and my brother, Mark, was down here. I didn't know he was corresponding with Sally here." Johnny continued with his tale, and when he had finished with his confrontation of Cam and his confession to Sally, they all sat in silence.

A soft knock came on the parlor door, and the pastor called, "Come in, my dear." As he rose and took the tray from his wife, he smiled apologetically. "I'd ask you to join us, Myra, but the Paynters have a dilemma I don't feel free to share with you yet. I'm sorry."

"That's all right," Myra said, giving Sally a reassuring smile. "I'll be in the kitchen if you need anything else."

Sally noted that she had set out only three cups on the tray with the coffeepot, cream pitcher, sugar bowl, and plate of small raisin cookies. Apparently Myra didn't make the assumption that she would be included in her husband's business conferences.

"If you'd like Mrs. Lewis to be here," she began, but the pastor shook his head.

"When we've finished, if you feel comfortable with it, I'll share our discussion with Myra, but with something this. . .unusual. . .I think it may be best to have utmost privacy until you've decided what you are going to do."

"Thank you," Sally said.

"Yes, sir," Johnny said softly. "We do appreciate that."

Myra smiled again and backed out of the room, shutting the door.

"Well, now. Would you care to pour, Mrs. Paynter?"

"I'd be glad to," Sally said, "but while I do so, maybe you can tell us if I'm really Mrs. Paynter."

Pastor Lewis frowned. "Oh, I see."

"That's one of our main concerns," Sally said.

Johnny leaned forward and held out a hand toward the minister, as if reaching for assurance. "See, when we came to you for the wedding, remember I asked you to say my name as Mark John Paynter?"

"I do recall that."

Johnny nodded. "That's because I figured I couldn't marry Sally using Mark's name. Now, his middle name was Daniel, but I thought maybe if you said my name in there, before Paynter, then it would make it legal."

Mr. Lewis sat back and drummed his fingers lightly on the arms of his chair. "I see. Very clever of you."

"So," Sally said. "We really hope it's good and legal. Is it. . . ?"

Lewis eyed her closely. "Mrs.—Sally. You say you hope it's legal. Does that mean you wish to remain married to this man, even though he deceived you about his identity?"

Sally squared her shoulders. "Yes, sir, I do. I have feelings for him, and I believe he has repented of his lying."

"I have," Johnny said, almost inaudibly.

Sally looked over at him. He looked like an overwrought little boy, about to burst into tears of remorse.

"I didn't want to lie, sir, and I surely didn't want to hurt Sally. I didn't know what to do, and Cam. . . ." Johnny sat up straighter. "Well,

I won't blame him. I knew it was wrong to lie to Sally. And to you. I kept thinking about Ananias and Sapphira and how they tried to lie to God. But if I didn't let her think I was Mark, I'd have to tell her he was dead, and it had been a few days by then. I'd have to tell the law, and Cam was dead certain Jackson would arrest me and send me back to Colorado to be hung. That, or he'd accuse me of killing Mark." He huffed out a breath and let his shoulders sag. "But I'm going to tell him anyway, as soon as he gets back."

"We went to the sheriff's office first," Sally said. "John wishes to turn himself in."

"I'll do whatever Jackson tells me," Johnny added. "I didn't kill anyone, though."

The pastor made no comment on this but nodded at Sally. "Let's have that coffee, shall we?"

While she poured the three cups full, Pastor Lewis rose and went to his desk. He opened a drawer and took out a small book and came back, flipping the pages.

"Here we are. You're correct, Mr. Paynter, about the name. On the marriage certificate I sent to the capital, I wrote Mark John Paynter." He closed the book and picked up his coffee cup. "I could write to the registrar and claim an honest mistake, which it was, on my part. They would correct the record there."

"And would that make it legal?" Sally asked.

"Oh, I believe the union is legal now." Lewis took a sip of his coffee. "Come, drink it before it gets cold."

Johnny and Sally both reached for their cups. The coffee was strong and a little bitter, but Sally didn't add sugar. This moment was sweet enough.

"Of course, I can't help you with the other matters, but I believe we can lay the marriage question to rest." The pastor put his cup down and smiled at them. "If you have any doubts, you could repeat your vows today."

The thought almost stole Sally's breath away. She looked sidelong at Johnny. He was gazing at her, his face transfigured into hope, with just a tinge of anxiety about his eyes.

"I'd like that," she said.

Johnny grinned. "Yes, sir. Me, too." He thunked his cup down on the table.

"Then please join hands," Mr. Lewis said.

Johnny's grip was strong and sure this time. Sally couldn't help thinking about that first time. If she had known then what she knew now. . . He was right. She would no doubt have told the authorities and left town.

Mr. Lewis stood. "I don't think we need a witness this time, but if you'd like, I could call Myra in."

"Please do," Sally said. Belatedly, she arched her eyebrows at Johnny.

"Sure. Why not?" Johnny said.

The pastor went to the door and opened it. "Oh, Myra! Could you join us for a minute, please?"

When his wife entered the parlor, Mr. Lewis smiled at her. "My dear, Mr. and Mrs. Paynter wish to renew their wedding vows. Would you like to witness the occasion?"

Myra smiled as if nothing would please her more. "What a lovely start to the day."

CHAPTER 22

The ride home was quiet and about as sweet an hour as a man could want. As soon as they were outside the town limits, Sally scooted over close to Johnny and laid her head on his shoulder. He slipped his arm around her and pulled her even closer. It felt good. It felt right.

As they passed the Caxtons' ranch, they could see Mrs. Caxton out hanging laundry on the clothesline. Johnny gave a neighborly wave, and Sally sat up straight and proper for a few minutes. But she cuddled right down again as soon as they were out of sight.

"I love you, Johnny," she said.

His chest felt like it was outgrowing his shirt. She looked up at him expectantly, and he nodded. "Love you, too." There. He'd said it. She knew who he was, and she loved him. He guessed he could do anything for her. Mark would have said it, loud and often. Maybe it wasn't too late to learn some things from his brother.

"Thanks for marryin' me again," he said. It came out a little gruffly, but she flung herself practically into his lap. Johnny let Reckless pick his own way for a hundred yards or so, while he kissed her good and proper. He was starting to think this marriage business wasn't so terrifying after all, once you did it right.

After a minute, he realized the horse had stopped and was grabbing mouthfuls of grass at the edge of the road.

"Hey, you!" He straightened out the reins and clucked. Reckless set out again at a lazy jog.

"You could have sent me back to St. Louis," Sally said.

"Why would I do that?"

"I know you didn't want to marry me the first time."

He sneaked a sideways glance at her. "Did you really know it then?"

"I suspected, but you kept saying everything was all right. And you did take me to the preacher, and you had a ring, and. . ."

He shrugged. "Once I saw there was no way out of it—"

"Oh, you!" She pounded his arm with her fists, but if she'd have been serious, she'd have hurt him. She was like a kitten playing with a wad of paper.

He laughed and hauled her in so tight a body couldn't have peeled her off him with a crowbar.

The lane to the ranch came in sight.

"What do you fancy to name this place?" Sally asked.

"What, the ranch?"

"Yes. Mark said in one of his letters he didn't have a name for it yet." Johnny shrugged. "His brand is an MP."

"His initials."

"Yup."

"Maybe we should call it something with those letters. Then we wouldn't have to change the brand."

"Wouldn't have to change it anyhow," Johnny said. What a headache that would be. He didn't have to guide Reckless off the main road. They were close to home, and the chestnut knew it.

"I'll fix us some dinner," Sally said.

Johnny looked up at the sun. "I reckon the train's leaving about now. I'm glad you're not on it."

"Me, too."

He leaned in and kissed her again. "Sally, I love you. I don't know when I knew it, but it's been a while, and I felt so terrible to be hurting you."

"Hush, now. That's done with. But I understand now why you acted the way you did." Her face went deep pink. "I thank you, Johnny.

I know now it wasn't because you didn't love me." She touched his cheek and then gathered her skirts to climb down from the wagon.

When he had turned the horse out, he went inside. She had something simmering on the stove already. For the first time, he felt this was his home, and he had a right to be here.

She came out of the bedroom, and the black dress was gone. She was dressed in her new calico.

"You changed." Immediately, he felt stupid for saying it.

"That was for Mark," she said. "But it's our wedding day. Our true wedding day. I'll mourn Mark, but I don't think I'll wear that dress for him." She went to the stove. "It'll be a minute before this is hot. Could you get the leftover corn bread?"

He got it and set the table while Sally puttered around the stove.

"I want to have a headstone made for Mark," he said.

She nodded soberly. "That would be nice."

He filled their cups with fresh water and sat down. Sally brought over the stew kettle.

"I'll fry up some chicken tonight, if you want to bring me one."

"Sure." Sort of a celebration dinner, he guessed, but neither of them said that. As they ate, they talked of unimportant things. The livestock, the garden. "Remember I said I ought to have a will?" Johnny said.

"Yes."

"Now that I'm sure we're legal, I think I'll do it. Just in case."

"Don't talk about that."

He took a few more bites and then laid down his spoon. "I think we should. They could hang me, Sally."

Her lower lip began to tremble, and she put her hand to her mouth. "Do you have to bring it up now? I was doing pretty well."

He let out a big sigh. "I need to think about taking care of you. What'll you do if Sheriff Jackson locks me up?"

"I guess I'll stay here and run this ranch."

"I don't know as you could do it by yourself."

"Don't start, John Paynter."

She sounded angry, and he wasn't sure he ought to pursue the topic. He only wanted what was best for her if the worst happened.

"I want you to be safe," he said.

"If you're going to be. . .gone. . .for a while. . ." She glared at him fiercely, and he kept his mouth shut. "Then I guess I'll go and stay with my folks."

"In Abilene," he said.

"That's right. Near there. If they lock you up, you go there when you get out and ask for Jeremiah Vane. Everyone knows my father there. Or you could send him a telegram. I'd come back."

Johnny nodded, easier in his heart. "That sounds like a good plan. Because if I was gone long, you'd need to hire a couple of hands. It would probably be better if you sold off the stock."

"All right, but that won't happen."

"Talk to Eph Caxton if it does, and tell him you need to sell the cattle. Him or Hector Gluck."

"I will, but can we please stop talking about it?"

"Sure."

She reached across the table and took his hand. "I love you, Johnny. No matter what, I'm going to stick with you, and I'll do everything I can to make sure they treat you fair."

"Thanks." He understood why she hated talking about these things. Even thinking about it took away his appetite.

"I have an uncle," Sally said more urgently, and he focused on her face. "He used to be a Texas Ranger."

"So?"

"I wondered if it would do any good to contact him."

"What could he do?"

"I don't know." She shook her head. "Probably nothing. It was just a thought. If there's anything I can do to help, I want to do it. But. . ." She looked into his eyes intently. "Mostly I just want to be Mrs. John

Paynter while I have the chance. Johnny, I don't want to sleep alone tonight."

He stared at her, mildly shocked that she would say it, but glad. He squeezed her hand. "I reckon you won't, unless maybe the sheriff comes out here before sundown."

———

Sally awoke before dawn, at the rooster's first crow. She was glad Fred Jackson hadn't shown his face but felt slightly wicked for thinking that way. If the truth were told, she would be relieved when everything was settled, one way or another.

She sat up and looked at her husband. Johnny still slept, with that tousled little-boy look, and she smiled. She reached toward him, but before she could brush his hair back off his forehead, the rooster crowed again, and Johnny stirred. He opened one eye and looked at her. Slowly, he smiled and rolled onto his back.

"Good morning," Sally said.

"I hope the sheriff stays away a long time."

"I kind of hope that, too, but it's too stressful. We need to know."

"I guess you're right." He sighed and shoved the quilt back. "Thad Bollinger will tell Jackson I want to see him as soon as he gets back."

Johnny went out to milk the cow while Sally fixed breakfast. Afterward, he shaved off his beard. She went about her housework, trying not to make a fuss about it, but she kept stealing glances while he worked in front of her small mirror.

At last he turned to face her, his face bare. "Well, Mrs. Paynter?"

She couldn't help grinning as she walked toward him. "I married a very handsome man, sir. And you managed not to cut yourself."

He wiped the last of the soap off and kissed her, and she ran her fingers through his hair. He squeezed her so hard she could barely breathe.

"Maybe you'll let me trim your hair later," Sally said.

"I might confuse the sheriff if I look too respectable."

She tried not to think about the future too closely as she sewed and cooked that afternoon, alternately fretting and wanting to sing. Johnny stayed close to the home place, going from one small chore to another all day. At suppertime, they had heard nothing.

"I'd best ride into town tomorrow and see if the sheriff's come back," Johnny said that evening.

"Take me with you. Otherwise if he arrests you, I'll be stuck here with no horse."

"Guess it's time to buy another. I wouldn't want you stranded six miles from town."

"What if the sheriff's still not back?" Sally asked.

"I'll leave a note to make sure he knows first thing I want to talk to him."

Sally sighed. She had a few more days with Johnny at best. Something would change when Fred Jackson heard his story. It was bound to, and they were fooling themselves to pretend it wouldn't. She would do her best cooking while she had Johnny, and keep the house spotless. She had washed her hair that afternoon. If her husband went to prison, she wanted him to remember her at her best.

Their drive into town was fruitless, so far as the sheriff was concerned. He wasn't at his office, and Thad Bollinger hadn't heard from him.

"What if he never comes back?" Sally asked when they got back to their wagon.

"He's got to come back," Johnny said.

"Not if those outlaws get him."

Johnny frowned. "Fred Jackson's a smart man, and he took half-a-dozen men with him. We'll hear something soon."

"Has that man got a family?"

"I don't know."

Sally looked around at the busy main street. "Someone ought to be caring whether he's all right."

"I'm sure there's someone. Come on." Johnny brightened. "Let's stop at the livery and see if Mr. Benner's got any likely horses for you."

Johnny took a liking to a dainty black mare that stepped high and looked like she had some hackney in her.

"She could take you around in a buggy, pretty as you please," the liveryman said.

Sally frowned at her husband. "We don't have a buggy, just an old farm wagon. Don't get me a fancy horse. I may be needing a cow pony. Get me a horse that will work when I need him to."

"Yes, ma'am," Johnny said.

Benner led out a short-coupled, ten-year-old bay mare. "She's a good cow horse."

Johnny got on the mare and rode her out to the street and back. "You want to try her, Sal?"

"I've got a sidesaddle you can use," Benner said.

"Yes, please." Sally stroked the mare's nose and waited while Benner switched the saddles.

The mare had a smooth trot, and she seemed energetic and willing. When they got back to where Johnny stood, Sally slid to the ground.

"I like her."

"Does she drive?" Johnny asked Benner.

"She does. In fact, I rented her out to a gentleman Saturday with a buggy. Got no complaints."

"How much?" Johnny asked.

"Sixty dollars."

Johnny scratched his head. He surely did look handsome with his new haircut and shave. "You know, we might get a better deal from one of the ranchers. I think Bill Hood might have a mare he'd sell."

"Fifty," Benner said.

Sally stayed out of it and watched. She had to admit her husband was a good bargainer, at least when it came to horses. When Benner got down to forty-two dollars, Johnny led the mare to their wagon and tied her to the back.

Then came the bargaining for the sidesaddle, and Sally started to feel a bit uneasy. She pulled Johnny aside while the liveryman was dusting off the second one of two he had available.

"Why don't you just get me a stock saddle? He wants too much for those."

"No, I can't have you riding astride. Folks would be scandalized."

Sally laughed mirthlessly. "As if we won't give them any scandal as it is."

Johnny winced. "Let me do this. Please? For my bride."

"All right, but is this the best place to get a saddle?"

"It would be more at a saddle maker's," Johnny said.

"What about a catalog? Or my pa might be able to send me one. My old one's probably still hanging in his barn."

"All right, we'll hold off on the saddle."

And so they went home without one. Sally had ridden bareback half the time anyway as a child. No reason she couldn't do it around the ranch until she was properly outfitted.

Johnny held Sally's hand all the way home. Every little while, she looked over her shoulder at the new horse.

"I'm going to name her Lady."

"Suits her," Johnny said. He bent to kiss her, for about the tenth time since they'd left town.

Sally smiled up at him afterward. "What if those outlaws came along now, and you weren't paying any attention?"

"Guess we'd die happy." But he straightened after that and paid more mind to the road ahead.

Sally cuddled against his side and squeezed his hand. She would make sure he got plenty of kisses after they got home.

CHAPTER 23

Nearly a week had passed since their visit to the minister when Sheriff Jackson finally rode out to the Paynter ranch. Johnny was outside working on the brick oven he was building for Sally as the sheriff's red roan jogged into the barnyard.

"Howdy, Mark." Jackson dismounted and let his horse's reins trail. "Working hard in spite of the heat, I see."

"That's partly why I'm doing it." Johnny reached for the shirt he had discarded an hour earlier. "Making Sally an oven, so she can cook out here and not heat up the house."

"I'm sure she'll appreciate that. I heard you wanted to see me."

"Yeah." Now that he was here, Johnny wasn't sure how to start.

"Does it have something to do with that ranch hand of yours?" Jackson asked.

"You mean Cam? No."

"Oh." Jackson frowned. "I got some news from Denver while I was gone. Thought it might interest you."

Johnny's mouth went dry.

"Is Combes here?" Jackson looked around the barnyard.

"No. Come in and have some lemonade? Sally manages to keep it halfway cool."

"Sounds good."

They walked to the cabin. The door was wide open. Johnny yelled, "Sally! The sheriff's here." He mounted the steps and entered the dim main room.

"Hello, Sheriff." Sally came from the kitchen area, wiping her hands on her apron.

"Howdy, Miz Paynter."

"Did you catch those outlaws?" she asked.

"I'm sorry to say we didn't. Tracked Flynn and his gang a long ways, and then we lost 'em." He smiled apologetically. "I need to talk to your husband, though."

Sally gazed at Jackson then back at Johnny.

"You got any lemonade left?" Johnny asked, though he knew she did. She'd kept a batch mixed up and down the well since his last trip to town.

"I'll get it. Sit right down, Sheriff."

When she was outside, Johnny pulled out a chair for the sheriff and plopped down across the table from him. "You said you heard from Denver?"

"That's right." Jackson took a folded sheet of paper from the pocket of his vest and opened it. He laid it in front of Johnny. "This telegram. I'd sent to the marshal up there, you see, just checking up on that brother of yours."

Johnny stared down at the printed words. *John Paynter cleared. Now looking for Cameron Combes. Slater.*

He inhaled carefully, as if any disturbance would change the words before him.

"Slater being the marshal?" he asked.

"That's right. I expect I'll get more information by post, but I thought I'd save him some trouble by making sure Combes was still here. Odd how you haven't heard from your brother, but the man they're looking for in Colorado is right here in Beaumont."

Johnny's stomach felt a bit odd, and he doubted he could drink the lemonade. Sally seemed to be taking her time getting it, and he was glad she hadn't returned yet.

"Is he saying Cam's the one who killed the person they thought. . . ?"

"I'm not sure. But they're looking for him. Why didn't you tell me he was from up that way?"

Johnny shook his head, wondering where to start. "I didn't think it mattered."

"This got me thinking," Jackson said soberly. "Maybe Combes knows something about your brother. Have you asked him? Could be he's not being straight with you."

"Sheriff, I—"

Sally came in, carrying a stoneware jug. Jackson picked up the telegram and folded it.

"Sally knows all about what I wanted to tell you," Johnny said. "And I was wrong. It does have to do with Cam. Sort of. But we don't know where he is now." He put his elbows on the table, clasped his hands, and leaned his forehead against them for a moment.

"Something happen here?" Jackson asked, shooting a glance at Sally.

She had poured out the lemonade and brought over two glasses.

"Here you go, Sheriff. It's no warmer than our well water, and that's pretty warm. I wish we had some ice."

"Don't worry about that, ma'am. But what is all this about the hired man?"

Sally frowned. "Cam? Not much, except my husband told him to leave last week."

Jackson focused on Johnny again. "Why was that?"

Johnny took a deep breath. "He was bothering Sally. But that's not why I left you the message, Sheriff. There's a lot more to it than that."

Jackson picked up his glass and sipped his lemonade. "That's good stuff, Mrs. Paynter."

Sally smiled. "Thank you. I know you two have a lot to discuss. I'll go out to the garden patch." She laid her hand on Johnny's shoulder for a moment. "Just call me in if you need me for anything."

He nodded, unable to meet her gaze. She went out and closed the door.

Jackson leaned toward him. "All right, Mark, spill it. What happened here?"

Sally pulled all the weeds out of the garden and pulled up the dead plants from their spring harvest. They wouldn't plant the fall garden for a month or more, but she did everything she could to prepare the ground. She wished she had started a wash or something else she could do out here. She wandered around to the front of the cabin.

The sheriff's horse had browsed its way a hundred yards down the road. She went after it. The roan let her approach, and she was able to pick up a trailing rein without alarming the animal. She led it back to the corral. Reckless nickered and came over to say hello. Maybe she should unsaddle the roan. A glance toward the house told her nothing. With a sigh, she opened the gate and turned the sheriff's horse out with Reckless and Lady. At the last moment, she decided to take off its bridle, so none of the horses could step on the reins.

This compromise left her feeling better, and she hung the bridle over the gatepost. Now what?

The cabin door opened, and Johnny came out. The sheriff followed, fitting his hat on as he walked.

"I acted too soon, fella," Sally said to the roan, who was sniffing about, hoping to find some grass. "Guess we'll have to put your bit back in."

Johnny walked toward her, but the sheriff lingered near the well.

"We're going to walk up the hill," Johnny said when he reached her. "I'm going to show him Mark's grave. Do you want to come?"

"What did he say? Is he going to arrest you?"

"No. He believes me. But he thinks. . . He thinks Cam may be in that Colorado business up to his neck."

"I don't understand."

"They've cleared me, Sally. Jackson says they must have new

evidence. He doesn't have all the details, but the marshal up there is looking for Cam. Jackson says it could be Cam killed Red Howell and then told me the men on the outfit thought I'd done it, so that I'd run away with him. It kind of makes sense. I told Cam I had a brother in Texas, and he figured this would be a good place for him to go. Nobody could connect him with Mark, and if I brought him here, it might be a good place for him to hide for a while."

Sally stared at him. "You mean that man was a murderer all along? And he—" She felt a little woozy, remembering Cam's fingers on her neck.

Johnny seized her arms and held on to her. "You all right?"

She nodded.

"You need to sit?"

"No. No, I—Johnny, did you tell Sheriff Jackson what he did? Here, I mean."

Johnny's eyes went hard. "I told him that I heard you scream and when I went in the house, he had his hands on you." His grip on her arms softened. "I'm so sorry I didn't listen when you first told me he made you uncomfortable."

Sally's mind reeled. So many times Johnny had ridden off and left her here alone. Cam could have attacked her any time he wanted. She supposed he had held off out of respect for his friend. But how respectful had he really been to Johnny? His words last week implied he didn't think Johnny was much of a man. Did he know they hadn't consummated their marriage? She didn't think Johnny would tell that to anyone. It was difficult for him to talk about anything personal. But Cam might have weaseled it out of him. To hear Johnny tell it, Cam had been pretty much in control of their flight and their arrangements once they got here. Cam had persuaded him to take Mark's identity. Cam had convinced him that he had to marry her. All the time he'd been with Johnny, Cam had held the hangman's noose over him.

"He could have killed us and claimed he'd bought the ranch," she said.

"I. . .I don't think. . ." Johnny looked away. "Guess I don't know what he's capable of. But we don't know for sure that he killed Red Howell."

"But that's why Cam brought you here. To get himself to a safe place without you suspecting. Isn't that what the sheriff thinks?"

After a moment's hesitation, Johnny said, "It's possible."

Sally took a deep breath. "Right. Let's show him the grave, then."

Johnny took her hand, and they walked back to where Jackson waited.

"I took your horse's bridle off," she said.

"Thanks. You coming along with us?"

"Yes."

The men walked quickly, and Sally was winded by the time they reached the cross. They all stood gazing at it in silence. Sheriff Jackson pulled his hat off, and Johnny followed suit.

"Sally and I decided we'll get a stone marker made," Johnny said. "It's a real shame, what they did to him."

"And you're sure it wasn't Combes?"

"Absolutely. He was with me the whole trip, and we didn't separate that last day to hunt or anything."

"You didn't hear the gunfire?"

Johnny shook his head. "We must have come along a couple hours after them, is all I can figure. We got here midday—past noon, I reckon."

"They probably hit the ranch at dawn," Jackson said. "They got into town around eight o'clock. Some of the stores weren't open yet. Frank Simon was just unlocking the grocery."

"Mark was up and dressed when they hit." Johnny sighed. "I hope he got off a shot or two. There weren't any guns here. I figure they took 'em. And his horses."

"What else?" Jackson asked.

"A lot of his foodstuffs. And there was hardly a penny nor a bullet around the place. They got what they came for."

"I expect you're right."

"Sheriff, if you go after that gang again, I'd like to ride with you," Johnny said.

"If they set foot in this county again, I'll be after them. Counting your brother, they've killed three people in my jurisdiction—that I know of."

"Mark was a good man," Sally said, tears clogging her throat.

"I wish I'd known him better."

Sally eyed Jackson from under the brim of her bonnet. Probably best to leave well enough alone, but she wanted his assurance. "You're letting Johnny get on with his life, Sheriff?"

"The way I see it, he's not guilty of anything except maybe poor judgment."

Johnny cleared his throat. "He said he doesn't think a court would find me guilty of any crimes for not reporting Mark was dead."

"A lot of people die out here without getting a death certificate. And you'd be surprised how many people change their names." Sheriff Jackson put his hat on. "Now, you folks tell me if Combes shows his face again."

"We will," Sally said.

Jackson nodded and clapped Johnny on the shoulder. "I'll expect to see you in church every Sunday or know the reason why."

"I'll be there," Johnny said.

"Wait!" Sally plucked at the sheriff's sleeve. "What will we tell folks in town?"

"I'll put it about that Mark's passed on and his brother's living at the ranch. You'll have to tell people you're close with."

"Nobody seems to have known Mark real well," Johnny said.

Jackson nodded. "He was quiet, kept to himself. Now that you've shaved, you don't look as much like him. I didn't notice at first because I wasn't looking for a change. That's not good for a lawman, but it's the truth. Most folks will be hazy on when the switch happened. The people at church know you got married recently, though."

"Pastor Lewis knows all about it," Sally said.

"So Johnny told me. Maybe he can help out with telling the people at church. I think they'd be an understanding bunch, if it comes to telling the whole story. But I doubt you'll have to. Just quit calling yourself Mark." He looked sternly at Johnny, who nodded. "Oh, and you'll have to straighten things out at the bank. When you're in town next, let me know, and I'll go over there with you and vouch for you."

"Thanks, Sheriff," Johnny said.

"I'm Fred. If I ever have call to arrest you, you can call me Sheriff. But don't let that happen."

Johnny nodded and put his hat on. They walked down the hill slowly, with Johnny holding Sally's hand. Already she was planning how to get it across to Liz that her husband was Mark's brother, not Mark, but they didn't want a lot of gossip about it. Liz would help, she was sure.

When they got to the corral, Jackson bridled his horse and brought him out through the gate and checked his cinch strap.

"All right, folks, best of luck to you." He swung up into the saddle. "I'll let you know if I find out more about the Howell murder."

Jackson rode out, and they stood together, watching his roan until it rounded the bend. Johnny let out a big breath.

"Feeling pretty good, Mr. Paynter?" Sally asked.

"Yes, ma'am. Better'n I have in some time." He put his arm around her waist, and Sally turned toward him, forcing him to look into her eyes. "Lots better," he amended.

She slid both her arms around him, and they stood there for a long time, holding on tight.

———

"Writing to your folks again?" Johnny asked. Sally sat at the kitchen table with paper spread out and her pen skittering across it like a lizard.

She looked up at him and smiled. "Uh-huh. Ma said they might be able to come down next month for a week or two."

"That sounds good," Johnny said. "Where'll we put 'em?"

"In our room, I reckon."

"Guess we could sleep out in the barn."

She chewed on the end of her pen for a moment. "Would you mind?"

"No. Would you?"

"Not if it meant having Ma and Pa here."

He smiled. The last two weeks had been the happiest in his life, and he would do anything the keep Sally smiling. She was easy to please, and he loved to see that wide-eyed look of wonder and glee when he came up with some small surprise for her. When he'd dug up a few wildflowers from the high pasture and brought them down to plant in front of the cabin, she'd about hugged him senseless.

"We need to make a proper room for a couple of hands out there if we're going to increase the herd this fall. Maybe we ought to go in town this afternoon. I could get some lumber, and you could pick up some new mattress ticking and curtain material. And dishes. We'll need a proper set of china if your ma's coming."

Sally's lips curved upward. "I'd love a chance to shop again. Maybe Mrs. Ricks has some new stock. And she might have word of a new sewing job for me."

"I'll hitch up the horses right after dinner," Johnny said.

The new mare pulled nicely on her own, but he liked to pair her with Reckless so Lady wouldn't tire as easily. Together they made an excellent team. The mare was calm and obedient in harness, and Reckless seemed to catch her mood. Or maybe he was trying to impress her.

They were only a mile out of town when Eph Caxton came charging down the road on his bay gelding. He pulled up next to the wagon.

"Flynn's gang has struck again," he said without preamble. "Sheriff Jackson's getting up a posse."

CHAPTER 24

Sally tried to hold the tears back as she packed Johnny's things into his saddlebags. She didn't want him to go, but she would never say so. Johnny said he had to help the sheriff, who had been so good to him, but she knew the real reason. Those men had killed his brother. Johnny had to do this.

He had insisted she not pack too much. The posse would move fast, and they didn't want to be weighed down. She let him make his own bedroll and prepare his weapons while she stashed food that would keep on the trail, matches, a tin cup and plate, extra socks, and one clean shirt.

He came in from the barn and leaned on the far side of her work-table.

"Will someone have a coffeepot?" Sally asked.

"No doubt."

She added a small parcel of ground coffee. The other men would appreciate it if everyone contributed to the pot.

"I'll leave you my rifle," Johnny said.

"You'll need it."

"I can't leave you here without one. Not after what happened to Mark."

She gazed at him steadily. "Mark had a rifle when they came."

Johnny looked away. "I expect he did."

"Just go. But come back to me, Johnny."

"What about if you go and stay with Liz Merton or the Hoods?"

"I'll be fine."

That did nothing to ease his anxious frown. "I mean it, Sally. If you stay here, I'll worry the whole time I'm gone."

"And who would tend to our livestock?"

"At least ride into town with me. I'll buy you a gun at the mercantile."

"That's too big an expense," she said as she poured water into his canteen. "We need to save what we can for new stock."

"I won't be thinking about buying more cattle if I lose you, Sal."

Just for a moment, she glimpsed the agony he had felt when he discovered Mark's body. She set the dipper down and put the stopper in the canteen.

"All right. Saddle Lady for me."

"It'll have to be that old cavalry saddle."

"It will do."

When they got to Beaumont, mounted men were gathering in front of the sheriff's office.

"You go," Sally said. "I can buy it myself."

"No, I'll come with you."

In less than five minutes he had picked out a used Sharps rifle and two boxes of cartridges. The price was higher than she liked, but he insisted on a good repeating rifle. He loaded the gun for her in the store.

"She'll need a saddle scabbard, too," he told Mrs. Minnick. "Can't lug it all the way home with nothing to rest it in."

"I'll get it," Sally said. "You go on, Johnny. The sheriff probably wants to hit the trail."

He eyed her unhappily and nodded.

He'd kissed her at home, before they mounted up, and there were too many people in the store to put on a display. He seized her hand and pulled her outside, still holding the new rifle. He drew her to one side, where their horses would shield them from the view of most onlookers.

"I'll come back. We may be a few days, but I *will* be home."

"All right."

He glanced around and stooped to kiss her briefly then handed her the rifle. She let out a sigh as he untied Reckless and swung into the saddle. After he had joined the throng down the street, she ducked back into the mercantile.

Mrs. Minnick was selling ammunition as fast as she could set it on the counter. Sally got in line. When her turn came, Mrs. Minnick said, "Oh, Mrs. Paynter. I've got your scabbard right here, and your husband didn't pick up his cartridges. You want that all on your account?"

"Yes, thank you." Sally wouldn't think about how she would pay for things if Johnny was killed chasing outlaws. She would have to trust the Lord to bring him back in one piece.

She gathered everything and carried her unwieldy burden outside. She stared at her saddle for a moment, perplexed. Finally she laid the rifle and scabbard carefully on the ground and tucked the cartridge boxes in the pouch that hung from her saddle. She picked up the scabbard and eyed the straps.

"Need some help, ma'am?"

She turned and found one of the Hood boys behind her. "Oh, yes. Pete, isn't it?"

"Yes'm."

"I was trying to figure out how to attach this to my saddle. Mr. Paynter insisted on buying me a rifle before he left with the posse."

"Probably a wise decision." Pete took the scabbard and walked around to the off side and deftly attached it. "Take the rifle out when you get home, before you take off the saddle, eh?"

"I will. Thank you." Sally picked up the Sharps.

Pete took it from her. "Climb aboard, ma'am."

Sally mounted, noting that Pete turned away while she did so. She wondered if she'd shocked him by riding with a man's saddle, but Pete was a rancher, and he knew about the posse. He probably understood about making do.

"All set," she said.

He turned toward her and settled the rifle in its resting place. "There you go."

"Thank you. Are you going out with the posse?"

"No," Pete said regretfully. "Pa and Bill are going. I drew the short straw, so I'm minding home with the womenfolk and kiddies. Call on us if you need anything."

"Thanks," Sally said.

He frowned. "In fact, Ma and the Marys would probably beat on me if I didn't invite you to come stop with them while the posse's out."

She smiled. "Convey my thanks to them, but I'll be all right. I don't want to leave our place empty."

He nodded and ambled into the mercantile. Sally looked down the street. The mounted men were heading out. She sat still on Lady until they had passed. Johnny was riding beside Eph Caxton, and they both waved to her.

When they had left, the street felt hollow. Sally remembered her letter home and stopped at the post office to mail it, though now she had more news to send her parents. That would give her something to do tonight.

The ride home had never seemed so long. The scabbard chafed against her leg, despite her skirt and layered petticoats. Finally she urged Lady into a lope. No matter what she did, it would irritate her. She may as well get the ride over as quickly as possible.

Once home, she hopped down, stiff and sore. She unbuckled the scabbard and laid it down with the rifle still in it. She wrestled the saddle off and got it into the barn. Finally she went out for the bridle and turned Lady out to graze.

Back in the barn, she went to hang up the bridle. In the opening at the front of the building, she looked around to make sure no one was about then lifted her skirt. Her thigh had an angry red patch where the strap had rubbed. She picked up the rifle in its case and walked to the house. Some of that salve she had used for her burns might help.

The afternoon dragged. She wished she had gone to see Mrs. Ricks. If she had a sewing job to work on, she could at least feel productive in Johnny's absence. Her letter home occupied her for half an hour. Her parents knew about Johnny now. She had written a long letter spilling the whole story the day after Johnny told the sheriff. In their reply, they had expressed concern, but they trusted Sally's judgment on the matter. If they could just meet him, she thought, they would realize he was the right man for her.

By sundown, she had cleaned the entire cabin and baked as much bread as she thought she could use before it molded. Johnny would return to a cozy home he would be proud of.

She was fine, thinking those thoughts, until full darkness descended. After barring the door, she lit two lamps and pulled the calico curtains shut over the windows. She wished she could lock her mare in the barn, but the open pole building had only one room that was really enclosed—the harness room. If robbers came, they would find it easy to steal Lady.

She shivered. Johnny had shown her the place where Mark had died. Right over there on the floor, between the front door and the table. In a way, she'd been twice widowed. First David, then Mark. How horrid it would have been to arrive here expecting to be married and discover her fiancé lying there dead.

She turned away from the spot and brewed a strong cup of tea.

Lord, she prayed, *I thank You for bringing Johnny along so I wouldn't be alone when Mark died. I don't want to lose Johnny, too, Lord. Please. . .*

She didn't know what else to say, but she figured God knew her tattered heart. She fell asleep with the bedroom lamp still burning and her Bible open beside her.

The next morning, she hated to unbar the door and go out to milk. Her father had told stories of the Comanche attacks that used to be so common in Texas. Of course, those were past, now that all the tribes were on the reservations, but the outlaws might be out there waiting for her to expose her vulnerability.

She prayed and carried the loaded rifle with her to the barn. She checked inside to make sure no one had taken refuge there then went to the fence, where the cow was lowing. The rifle leaned against the wall beside her while she milked, and she carried it as she gathered the eggs and fed the chickens, but no one disturbed her.

Finding enough to occupy her for the day took some effort. She didn't want to stray from the house, so visiting Mark's grave was out of the question. She caught up her mending and added to her letter to her parents, telling them more about the posse and Johnny's purchase of the rifle.

By noon she was pacing the cabin. Tomorrow she would return to town. It was that or do laundry, and she didn't really have enough to make that worthwhile yet. Besides, to do the wash, she would have to spend hours outside, with no one to keep watch. There was always the danger of fire, too. The smooth new skin on her hands was a constant reminder of her washday mishap. Better to spend the day in town, near other people.

The sore on her leg still stung. The thought of riding Lady to Beaumont and back with the scabbard chafing her didn't appeal to her. She would have to harness the mare and take the wagon, but that wasn't so hard. Her father had taught her how when she was a girl.

Once the decision was made, she felt better. In addition to visiting Mrs. Ricks, she could ask around for news of the posse. Of course, it was too soon for anyone to have heard much, but you could never tell. Perhaps she would go by the Mertons' and have a cup of tea with Liz.

She slept a little better that night, though she roused once to the lowing of the cattle and again when a welcome rain pattered on the roof. It wasn't much of a storm, but it might be enough to keep the temperatures a little cooler.

In the morning, as soon as she had done the necessary chores and eaten breakfast, she hitched Lady and set out for Beaumont. She found herself looking frequently over her shoulder to scan the trail behind her. Out here on the road, she had no cover, and no defense but the rifle.

On impulse, she stopped in at the Caxtons' ranch. Rilla came to the door and welcomed her with a spark in her eyes.

"Come in, come in! I've had no one to talk to these past two days but the two old punchers Eph left behind, and they're no great shakes when it comes to conversation, believe me."

Sally laughed and climbed down from the wagon. She hadn't planned on more than a dooryard call, but Rilla seemed so eager for company that she went in and consented to drink a cup of coffee and eat a piece of apple cake.

"No news from the posse, is there?" Sally asked.

"Nary a word, but soon I hope."

The older woman was full of stories of ranch life, and she had Sally laughing inside of five minutes. She was one of those who had come around to offer food and help with the housework after Sally was burned, and she looked pointedly at her guest's hands.

"How are those hands doing now?"

"Much better, thank you," Sally said. "They're a little tender yet, but Johnny intends to plant our fall garden when he gets back, and I think I'll be ready to work it."

Rilla frowned. "I can't get used to him being his own brother." She brushed a hand through the air. "Oh, you understand what I mean."

"Yes." Sally took a deep swallow of her coffee. She didn't like going into much detail about Johnny's identity, but the pastor's brief explanation at church had left some questions in the community.

"You came to marry Mark, I understand." Rilla's brown eyes drilled into her.

"That's true," Sally said. "But under the circumstances, Johnny and

I decided it was best to go ahead. . . ." She took another quick sip. That wasn't strictly true. They had both made the decision to marry that day, but she hadn't been possessed of all the facts. This was the aspect she dreaded her neighbors knowing. They would think less of her, surely, if they knew she'd married a liar. But even worse, they would think less of Johnny for his deception. He may be ready to bear the consequences, but a streak of protectiveness goaded her to shield him from the community's criticism.

She set down her cup and smiled. "I find I made the right decision. Johnny is a good man."

"I'm sure he is." Rilla frowned. "It's just that Eph thought he was Mark for. . .oh, I don't know. Weeks."

"He was a little embarrassed that people thought he was his brother, but he wasn't sure how to straighten it out without causing more confusion." Sally pushed back her chair. "And now I must be going. Thank you so much for the refreshment, and for the conversation. I do miss living close to other women."

"We're not so far apart. We ought to visit more." Rilla got up and walked with her to the door.

"Come by anytime," Sally said. "But I shan't blame you if you wait until the outlaws are caught. To be honest, I didn't truly feel safe driving that road alone, especially knowing what had happened to Mark."

"Yes, it gives one pause, doesn't it?" Rilla stood on the stoop and looked toward the empty road. "We knew they'd raided in town, but not our closest neighbor."

"I'm sorry," Sally said. "We really should have told you sooner. Johnny understands that now, but I hope you won't hold it against him."

"Hmm, well, he's doing business with Eph, same as his brother did, and so far he's kept up his end of the bargain."

"Which he'll continue to do." Sally climbed into the wagon and waved. She turned Lady and trotted her out to the road. As she had feared, their neighbors weren't able to trust Johnny quite as much as they had Mark, and they were uneasy over the blurring of his identity when he came. She and Johnny would have to be such good neighbors that the Caxtons and the rest got over that.

In town, she went to Mrs. Ricks's storefront first.

"Sally! I'm so glad to see you." The owner fairly pulled her into the shop. "The new shipment came in three days ago, and I've already got three women who want dresses from the new silk blends. Oh, and Mrs. Drury wants two new cottons made up for her daughter—Anne is getting married soon, you know."

"No, I didn't," Sally said.

"Well, I can keep you in dressmaking orders from now to Christmas if you've a mind." Mrs. Ricks, a fashionable lady of about forty, led her to the shelves where her bolts of cloth were piled. "Most women just buy the material and sew their own dresses, but some would rather not, and women like Mrs. Drury just don't have time. Before the wedding, you know. She wants to stitch the wedding dress herself, but Anne needs two other dresses, or so her mother thinks, for her trousseau. And then there are those, like old Mrs. Leary, who can't see well enough to sew anymore."

"I'll be happy to take the patterns and materials for a couple of orders with me," Sally said. "My husband is gone with the posse, and I'll be glad for something to keep me busy."

"Bless you!" Mrs. Ricks pulled out a new pattern catalog and showed Sally the styles her customers had chosen and gave her a slip of paper with Anne Drury's measurements on it. Ten minutes later, as she was cutting the calico yardage for one of Anne's dresses, two ladies entered the shop.

"You have customers," Sally whispered. "Why don't I come back in an hour for all of this?"

Mrs. Ricks nodded. "Good morning, ladies! How may I help you today?" She sailed from behind the cutting table. Sally nodded to the newcomers and escaped out the door.

At the grocery, the mood was less encouraging. The owner and customers could talk of nothing but the outlaw gang and the posse.

"If they don't catch 'em this time, my wife wants to pack up and go back to Virginia," one man said. "No telling where they'll attack next."

"I admit I don't feel safe with half the menfolk off chasing them," said one of the ranchers' wives.

Another added, "Seems to me this would be the perfect time for the gang to circle around and hit the town again."

Without asking, Sally determined that nobody had heard a word from the posse since they had ridden out of town. She made her purchases and went outside. For several seconds, she stood undecided by her wagon. Johnny could be gone for a long time. Last time, the sheriff had followed the outlaws for more than a week.

She put her parcels in the wagon and walked slowly toward the post office. Her letter would reach her parents in a few days, telling them that Johnny had gone off to chase the outlaws. But she dreaded going back to the ranch alone. She would have to check the barn again when she got there, and make sure nobody had gone into the house. Though she considered herself a strong person, she would live in fear until Johnny returned. She didn't like that. Maybe she should have listened to him, and to Pete Hood, and gone to stay with one of their friends.

She turned toward the hotel, where the telegraph office was housed off the lobby. She wasn't sure what good it would do to hasten the message to her parents, but she would feel better if they knew today what was going on. If she got bad news about the posse, and the family hadn't even received her letter yet, they'd be shocked. She told herself that was reason enough to justify the expense of a short telegram:

JP with posse after outlaws 2 days. No word yet.

She counted the words and figured the cost and then took out "No word yet." That would be obvious, and it would save her ninety cents.

She gave the clerk the money and the message form.

"Do you expect a reply?"

She shook her head. "Not right away, anyhow. They live a ways out from town, and so do I."

The young woman nodded. "We'll have to send someone out if you get a return message."

"Does that cost extra?"

"How far out are you?"

"Six miles. The Paynter ranch."

"A dollar."

Sally frowned. "I'll come back tomorrow."

"Are you eating dinner in town today?"

She hadn't considered it, but she could. And she could go around to visit Liz, who lived not far away, on Flood Street. With any luck, Liz would offer her dinner.

"I'll check back here before I leave town."

She found the house easily. Liz and her two children were outside, taking laundry off the line.

"Sally," Liz called as soon as she spotted the wagon pulling up.

Sally jumped down and ran to meet her. "Hello. Is Dan gone with the posse?"

"No," Liz said. "He's needed at the mill. I take it Johnny has?"

"Yes. I was going a bit off my head out there alone, so I came into town."

"Eat with us," Liz said, much as Sally had expected. "Dan will be home soon, and I have a chicken in the oven. I just need to get in the rest of these clothes."

Sally greeted the children and helped fold the last few items. Liz excused her ten-year-old son to go and meet his father. The thirteen-year-old girl, Deborah, went inside with them.

"Debbie, take Mrs. Paynter's bonnet," Liz said. "Will your horse be all right out front?"

"I think so, though she'll be ravenous before we get home."

"I can have Dan give her some oats when he gets here."

"No, don't trouble him."

"It's all right." Liz bustled about her kitchen, refusing to let Sally help.

"Then I'll help Debbie lay the table," Sally insisted.

Deborah smiled shyly at her and opened the drawer where they kept flatware.

"All right," Liz said. "Isn't it nice that it's a little cooler today?"

"It sure is." Sally counted out the spoons and followed Debbie, who was placing the forks around the table.

"They say we're in for a drought." Liz chopped turnips so fast Sally could barely follow her hands' movement.

"I hadn't heard that. I know it's been dry."

"Well, Dan says it will hurt the ranchers. You have a creek out there, don't you?"

"Yes. But Johnny and—and Cam were talking about a windmill."

"Dan said you've lost your hand."

"Yes, Cam's gone. It seems. . ." She shot a glance at Debbie and decided the girl was old enough to know. "The sheriff says he's wanted for a crime. We didn't know. Johnny had already discharged him when the sheriff told us."

"Oh, dear."

"He's probably lit out for someplace a long ways from here," Sally said. At least, she hoped so.

Liz hesitated. "I wasn't going to mention it, but maybe it's best if you know."

"What?" Sally studied her face. Liz was usually cheerful, but this talk of the posse and the dry weather seemed to have sobered her.

"Dan heard at the mill—oh, it's just a rumor, but—well, someone heard the outlaw gang has added a fellow who looks like your hired man."

CHAPTER 25

F red Jackson took off his hat, wiped his forehead with his bandanna, and ran it around the sweat band inside the hat.

"I'm afraid they're out of my jurisdiction again."

Johnny stared across the rocky, almost barren hillside before them. "Aren't you allowed to go after 'em if you know they did something in your territory?"

The sheriff plunked his hat back on his head. "Could, but it's mighty hard trackin' out here. I'm thinking we should go to the nearest town and see what help we can get." He shook his head as he knotted his grimy bandanna around his neck. "Hate to lose 'em now."

"They've gotta have water soon," said Eph Caxton, easing his horse up alongside Fred's roan. "Isn't there a creek not far from here?"

"Maybe." Fred squinted against the sun and studied the rugged terrain. "We can't be more'n four or five miles from the river."

"They probably camped there last night," Johnny said. "We could head straight for the river and see if we could pick up their sign there."

After a moment, Fred nodded. "Awright. Can't think of a better plan. But if we don't find something soon, we'll check with the county sheriff and see if they've had any trouble over here."

Johnny set out before Fred could change his mind. They couldn't be more than a few hours behind the raiders, and he was determined not to lose them. As much as he longed to get back to Sally, he wanted to bring those killers down more. He wasn't a scout by profession and he wouldn't claim to be an expert, but he'd sure tracked a lot of cattle over ground like this. If the gang had gone this way, he would find them.

Reckless stumbled a little and recovered. Johnny patted his neck. "Easy, boy. We'll find you some water soon. We're going to get those outlaws, and then we'll head on home."

In less than an hour, they reached the river and dismounted to stretch their legs and let their horses rest. The others sat down to talk while they ate a cold lunch, but Johnny couldn't sit still. He ate the last of the food Sally had packed him while trudging along the riverbank. Had the gang found a crossing place and gone over the river? If so, Jackson wouldn't want to follow them. He'd made that clear.

Half a mile downstream from where they'd camped, Johnny found what he'd sought. The tracks indicated that at least six horses had come to the brink here and then circled away. They hadn't crossed the river or headed back the way they came.

Johnny hurried to where the others were finishing up their meal.

"Sheriff, I found some signs. I think it's them. There's one horse that's barefoot, and five or six shod."

"Same as we saw yesterday," Fred said, standing and brushing off his clothes. "Did they ford the river?"

"Nope. In fact, if we go the way they headed, we'll actually be going closer to home."

"Mount up," Jackson called to the others. He turned and nodded at Johnny. "I figured they had a hideout closer to Beaumont than this. Maybe they're heading back there. You lead us."

―――――

Sally lingered longer than she had intended at the Mertons'. It was so peaceful, sitting with Liz and Deborah while they quilted. She didn't have to worry about who would come along, or run to the window every time a horse passed outside. She felt safe and a bit lethargic.

When Liz stirred up her fire to prepare supper, Sally jumped up.

"I need to get going. I don't want to be too late getting home."

"Stay here tonight if you want."

"Thank you, but I've got a cow that will need milking."

She hurried out to bridle Lady and took a hasty parting from Liz. She went to Mrs. Ricks's shop and picked up the patterns and cloth she needed. Remembering her reason for putting off the homeward trip, Sally stopped once more before the hotel. Already the dining room was full of customers. The young woman at the telegraph office smiled at her.

"Oh, Mrs. Paynter. I was afraid you'd gone and we'd have to send a rider out after all."

"No, I stopped at a friend's house. Is there a reply, then?"

"Here you go." She placed an envelope in Sally's hand.

"Thank you." Sally hurried outside and set Lady into a brisk trot toward the ranch. Once she was away from the bustle of town, she tore open the envelope.

COMING FRIDAY ON TRAIN.

The sender was her father. She clutched the paper to her heart. She hadn't asked it of them, but they were coming sooner than planned. At least Pa was. No, he wouldn't come alone. Ma would be with him. Sally's plans for their visit occupied her mind for the next forty minutes.

The sun was low when she got home, and shadows shrouded the barn. Sally carried the rifle with her when she went in to hang up the harness. She checked all the crannies before she went to do the milking. As she approached the house with a pail of milk in one hand and the heavy rifle in the other, she wished fervently that she had left town sooner. When Johnny got home, it wouldn't be to a dark house. She would be waiting for him with a pot of hot coffee and warm lamplight.

She supposed it was silly, but she checked every place in the cabin big enough to conceal a person. With that done, she barred the door and then realized she needed water and fuel for her cook fire. Her hand shook as she lit the lantern. Where was the strength everyone thought she possessed?

After three more trips outside, she was satisfied with her supplies for the night. At last she set aside the Sharps, leaning it against the door frame. In two days, her parents would be here. She smiled.

That night she slept better than she had since Johnny left. At dawn, she rose and put on a housedress and apron. She had one full day to get everything ready. At least she had cleaned thoroughly the day before. Now she could concentrate on baking, and she supposed she should do up her meager laundry so she wouldn't have to worry about it for a while. She might even have enough cream to make butter.

She took extra caution when she lit the fire outside. Liz had advised her to shorten one of her skirts for just such tasks, and Sally had taken her advice. She ought to have remembered how Ma hiked her skirts up when she worked around an open fire. During her years in St. Louis, Sally hadn't needed to deal with that situation, and she had forgotten some of the frontier ways.

Once a wagon passed by on the road, but the driver didn't stop. In the early afternoon, two men from one of the outlying ranches jogged past, their horses headed for town. Other than that, Sally saw no one all day. But she didn't mind. She did her washing, baking, and churning, and then settled down to start on the first dressmaking project for Anne Drury.

On Friday, she could hardly wait until time to leave. She made herself work carefully at her morning chores and fixed the bedroom up as nice as she could, with a bouquet of wildflowers on the stand and clean bedding. When she went out to get the cow, she noted how low the water in the creek was, despite the shower they'd had a couple of nights ago. They needed a good soaking rain. She had to haul water to the corral for Lady, as she didn't want to put the horse out in the large pasture.

At noon, Sally ate up most of her leftovers so that she wouldn't be hungry in town. Finally she harnessed Lady and set out. The dust from the road had her coughing in short order, and she tied a handkerchief over her face to help keep it out of her nose and mouth. Maybe that windmill wouldn't be such an extravagance. She and Johnny would have to talk about it in detail once the outlaws were captured and he was safe at home.

The thought that he might not come home safe niggled at her, but she shoved it aside. Nothing could check her buoyancy today.

The train came in right on time, and she stood on the platform, scanning the open-air car and the windows of the enclosed passenger car.

She spotted her father first. His tall, lanky form, topped by a shapeless gray felt hat, was unmistakable. He descended the steps and reached back to help her mother. Ma's faded blond hair showed beneath a becoming veiled blue hat that nearly matched her traveling dress. Sally ran toward them.

"Ma! Pa!" She embraced her mother first then let her father pull her into one of his enormous hugs.

"Sally, Sally, look at you," her father said, shaking his head.

"What?" She shoved back a lock of hair. "Do I look spindly?"

"You look fine," her mother said. "All grown up, but then we knew you would be."

"Ma, I was three and twenty the last time you saw me."

"Oh, I know. But I still think of you as my girl."

Sally shook her head and plucked at her father's sleeve. "Do you have a trunk? How long are you staying?"

"No trunk, but two suitcases, and we thought maybe a week."

"Is that all?" Sally wanted to pout, but then her mother would be justified in thinking her childish.

"We'll see how it goes," her father said. "What's the word on the posse?"

"Nothing yet." She came to earth with a thud. They were here because her husband was in danger. When David died, they couldn't come to her, and she had faced the horrors of sudden widowhood alone. They wouldn't let that happen this time. Her throat tightened. "Let's get your bags. I have the wagon right over there."

"I see it," her father replied, "and I'll get the luggage. You and your ma go ahead over."

Sally took her mother's hand and drew her across the platform. "I can't wait to show Pa the ranch. Maybe he can help Johnny decide whether or not we need a windmill." She took her mother to the wagon and gave her a hand up.

"That's a nice-looking mare you have," Ma said, eyeing Lady's hindquarters.

"Thank you. She's steady, which is what I need. I don't want to have to worry about a skittish horse when Johnny's off on an expedition."

Her mother grasped her hands. "Sally, dear, tell me plainly. Is everything all right? It was so strange, what happened with the two brothers."

"Yes, it was, but we're square now. Johnny has told me everything, and he's promised not to lie to me ever again."

"And you believe him implicitly?"

Sally gazed into her eyes, hating that her mother had to ask, but that was what mothers did. "Absolutely. Ma, he's a good man. You'll like him."

"I'm sure I will. It just seemed so far-fetched. Your father and I talked about it for hours after your first letter came telling us that Mark was dead. My dear. . ."

"Yes?"

Ma let out a big sigh. "We're happy for you, of course, but we can't help wondering if all is as it should be, even now."

"Of course it's not the way I'd have liked to begin a new marriage, but I do trust Johnny. He had a moment of weakness when his friend told him he could be accused of murdering his brother, but that's past now."

"Hmm. Seemed like more than a moment."

"Well, the marriage is legal. Pastor Lewis said so. I'm not backing out of it."

Her mother nodded. "What about that other business, up in Colorado?"

"He's cleared of that, make no mistake. If he hadn't been, I doubt I'd have stayed here. But I believe he's being honest with me, Ma. And he's too gentle to kill a man."

"Any man can turn to violence if he's backed into a corner."

Her father came with the bags, and Sally let him take the reins, directing him out of town and along the road that led to the ranch. Sally answered several direct questions from her father, revealing the details she hadn't written of what had happened between her, Johnny, and Cam. When she had told them everything, she smiled at her mother.

"Let's talk about something else. How's Tommy doing?"

As they made their way homeward, she prompted them with questions, so that she could catch up on life at home and the doings of her brothers and sisters. She pointed out other ranches and urged her father to take special note of the Caxtons' windmill.

"If we really are in for a severe drought, this would be a good year to have a windmill," she said.

"It may be too late." Her father looked over the neighbor's apparatus. "From here, that looks like a good setup. But it would take time to get the parts and then put it together. I doubt you and John could have one operating in less than a month, even if you acted right away. And if the demand for the machinery is higher than normal this year, it might take even longer. You might have to get in line with your order."

"I didn't think of that. Is it dry up where you live?"

"Terrible," her father said. "Ranchers are trying to sell off their stock, but prices are too low. I'm afraid a lot of cattle will die if we don't get the rain we need."

The roof of the barn came in sight.

"That's our place up ahead."

They rolled into the barnyard, and Sally looked around. Everything seemed the same as it was when she left earlier in the day.

"Come on in," she said. "I'll show you where you'll sleep, and then I'll come out and put Lady away."

Her parents followed her inside.

"It's small," Sally said, "but Johnny has plans to add on later. I wrote to you about when he and Cam built this room." She threw open the door to the new bedroom.

Her mother walked inside and looked around. "This is nice, Sally."

"Thanks. I want you and Pa in here."

"We don't want to put you out of your room," Ma said.

Sally shrugged. "It's the only decent bedstead we have. I'll sleep out in the other room, like we did when I first got here."

"On the floor?" Ma frowned at her.

"It's not a problem. And when Johnny gets home, we'll move out to the hired man's room in the barn."

"You could stay in here with your mother," Pa suggested.

"No, you two will be in here." Even Sally could hear the stubborn edge her voice took on.

Pa smiled. "All right. I'll go get the bags, and don't you worry about the horse. I'll take care of her."

"Thanks, Pa. Just turn her out in the small corral. The harness hangs up inside the barn. There's a little harness room—where the bunk is."

"I'll find it." Her father went out.

"Do you want to freshen up?" Sally asked her mother. "There's water in the pitcher. And the necessary is out back."

A few minutes later, Ma joined her in the kitchen. "Mm, that smells good. What are you fixing for supper?"

"Chicken and dumplings," Sally said. "It's the meal I had at the hotel in town, the day I married Johnny, so I'm partial to it."

"We like it, too. Let me help you. Oh, and I brought you some pecans."

"Great." Sally looked up as her father brought in the suitcases.

"I put your mare in the corral," he said, carrying the suitcases toward the bedroom. "Is it possible Johnny and the posse would come here?"

"What do you mean?"

"Several horses are coming along the road—not from town. The other direction."

Sally wiped her hands on a linen towel and hurried to the door. She could hear it now, the drumming of hoofbeats. Her heart raced. Was it Johnny, with the sheriff and the posse, as her father had suggested? She couldn't imagine them galloping in here.

A cloud of dust hid the group of riders from her for a few seconds, but the leaders burst through and pulled up in the dooryard. At the sight of a distinctive pinto gelding, Sally caught her breath. She shut the door and threw the bar across it then grabbed her rifle.

"Pa! Have you got a gun?"

CHAPTER 26

Johnny, Fred Jackson, and the other men of the posse sat on their horses, gazing down at the clear tracks coming up out of a creek bed.

"You were right," Fred said. "They're heading back toward Beaumont. Just took a roundabout way, and they stopped to water here."

"We'd best do the same," Johnny said.

The men and horses were tired, their throats parched from the dust they stirred up.

Fred turned and looked at the others. "All right, men, water your horses and fill your canteens upstream of them."

Johnny frowned as he eyed the outlaws' trail.

"What's bothering you?" Eph Caxton asked. "We're heading home."

"Yeah, and those killers are heading toward our families. Again."

"Whyn't they just leave us alone?" Bill Hood Sr. said. "Beaumont ain't such a rich town."

"It's home for them, too," the sheriff guessed. "At least they seem to like the area. We haven't been able to drive 'em out."

"And they haven't got the money from our bank yet," Eph said.

Fred nodded. "My guess is, they'll keep on coming back here until we take 'em down."

Johnny dismounted and let Reckless wade into the shallow stream. The water was only three or four inches deep.

"This thing oughta be twice this deep," Bill Junior said as he let his buckskin sink its nose in the water.

While Reckless drank, Johnny walked a few yards upstream to

where some of the others were replenishing their water supply. When his canteen was full, he mounted the bank and walked to where the outlaws' tracks left the streambed. Their trail was plain.

Fred came to stand beside him.

"How come they've quit trying to hide their tracks?" Johnny asked.

"Maybe they think we're not followin' 'em or that they lost us back in the rocky country. I was never able to stick with 'em this long before."

"If they're circling around toward where they started, where do you reckon their hideout is?"

"I don't know. I suppose it could be over toward the pine woods or even on a ranch."

"You think a rancher's behind this gang?"

"Not really," Fred said. "I s'pose they could be hiding out on some remote part of a ranch. The marshal in Houston thinks Flynn has connections over that way. If that's so, I don't know what the attraction is for him over here."

"Too hot for him over there, maybe."

"Could be. But I don't see what we can do at this point except keep followin' 'em."

Johnny looked off down the trail the outlaws had left. "Doesn't make me feel any better that I left Sally alone at the ranch. If they keep on this course, they'll go right past my house. Again."

Fred opened his mouth and then closed it.

"What?" Johnny asked.

"Nothing. Let's move," Fred said. "Come on, we can be there in two hours if we ride hard. Put your mind to rest."

Johnny nodded and went to collect his horse.

———

Sally's father took the rifle from her hands. "My pistol's in the brown leather valise. Get it. And keep low." He went to the side of the front window and pulled the curtains together. "There's at least six of them.

Maybe eight."

Ma came toward him from the kitchen. "Jeremiah?"

"Stay back," Pa said.

Sally dashed into the bedroom. Pa had left the suitcases on the bed, and she opened his. Feeling carefully between the layers of clothing, she found his holstered pistol and a box of cartridges. She went to the bedroom windows and drew the curtains then took the gun and ammunition out into the main room. She held the pistol out to her father.

"You're sure these aren't friends?" he said.

Sally eased over to the side of the window frame and peeked out at the edge of the curtain. Two men were at the well, and the others were near the pasture fence.

"I only recognize one of them," she said, "and he's not a friend. It's Cam Combes."

"The ranch hand Johnny let go?"

She nodded. "If it was the posse, Johnny would be out there, and Sheriff Jackson, and the Hoods. People I know."

"Have you practiced your shooting lately?" her father asked.

"No. And Johnny just bought me that rifle when he left, because I made him take his along. I haven't even fired it. But I've got more cartridges."

"Let me hang on to the rifle, then. If things go sour, your ma can shoot that Colt almost as well as I can. Give it to her."

Sally took a deep breath and carried the pistol to her mother.

"What do you think they want?" Ma asked as she turned the cylinder to make sure the Colt was fully loaded.

"I don't know," Sally said. "But I don't trust Cam."

"Pray, ladies," her father said grimly.

Sally closed her eyes and opened them again. She could pray with her eyes open.

"Set the extra ammunition on the table," Ma said.

Sally placed the box where she could reach it easily, sending up disjointed bits of prayer in her mind. *Help us, Lord! Don't let Ma and Pa get hurt. Make me wise.*

"One of them's coming to the door," her father said from near the window.

"What should I do?"

"Don't unlock it."

At that moment, the front door rattled against the jamb.

"Sally? You in there?"

Her knees nearly gave out on her. She looked toward her father and hissed, "That's Cam."

"Get to the side and answer him," Pa whispered.

She stepped to her left so that her body was not in a direct line with the door.

"What do you want, Cam?"

"Where's Johnny?"

"Why?"

"I wanna talk to him."

"Go away," Sally said, as sternly as she could.

"You all alone in there?"

"Go away!"

"That's no way to treat an old friend. You got some food for me and the boys?"

"No."

After a pause he said in an amused tone, "You always have food in there, Sal. Come on. Open up. We need more than the milk and butter you had down the well."

Another voice said, "Somethin' smells good. What you cookin', ma'am? We'd sure like to have a bite."

The door rattled again in its frame.

"You keep away," Sally yelled.

"Aw, Sally, don't make me stave in the door," Cam said, smooth and congenial.

"If you do, you'll get a belly full of lead."

He laughed, and a chill ran through her. She glanced at her father, and he nodded somberly, as if to say, *You're all right, gal. I'm here with you.*

"I know Johnny better'n you do," Cam said. "Wherever he's at, he's got his rifle with him, and his revolver, too."

Sally opened her mouth to reply, but her father held up a hand to stop her. He gestured for her to get down. She sank to the floor and crept away from the door, toward the corner of the room where Mark's bunk had stood.

At that moment the back door, in the kitchen, thudded, and Ma let out a gasp. Sally craned her neck to see. That door didn't have a sturdy bar, just a thumb latch and a hook for a lock inside.

Pa took three steps to the edge of the worktable, and Ma flattened herself against the cupboard. The door shook again, and the hook screeched against its eye latch.

"Cover your ears," Pa said.

Sally hardly had her hands clapped to her head before the rifle roared.

All was very quiet except for the thunder in her ears. It faded gradually to a ringing. She lowered her hands and stared at her father. He stood with the rifle still aimed at the back door, but nobody seemed to be worrying about the splintered wood now.

Carefully, she eased up to the side of the small front window and peeked out beside the curtain. She hoped to see Cam and his companions mounting up to ride off. Instead, she saw them in conference near the barn, watching the house while they talked, one of them gesturing wildly.

Her father came to her side and looked out.

"I won't break your window first thing. Get me something to block it up with."

Sally grabbed a small biscuit tin off a shelf. He raised the front window a couple of inches, and she stuck the tin beneath the sash.

The men outside froze and looked toward the house. The tallest one, who seemed to be their leader, spoke, and they scattered, taking cover behind the wagon and within the shelter of the barn. One of them led several horses around the corner of the barn.

"They're digging in for a fight," Pa said. "Get back and stay low."

Sally's mother sat down in the shelter of the cookstove but kept the Colt pointed toward the back door. Gunfire erupted outside, and one of the boards in the wall between Sally and her father splintered. Pa waited a moment then rose enough to peek out the gap below the window sash. His rifle boomed.

———

Sheriff Jackson, at the head of the column, stopped his horse and held up his hand. The horses behind him stopped. Fred had cocked his head to one side, and Johnny listened hard. From a distance, he heard an unmistakable *pop-pop*.

He trotted Reckless up next to Fred's horse.

"Gunfire," Fred said.

Johnny nodded, scanning the horizon. He had never ridden in from this direction, but he was certain the sounds came from near his house.

"Let's go," he said.

"Wait."

Johnny shook his head. "I left Sally alone." He urged Reckless forward, and the tired chestnut set out in a lope.

Behind him, Fred yelled, "Head for the Paynter ranch, men, and be careful."

The irregular popping became blasts as Johnny got nearer. Reckless's ears flickered back and forth, as though he needed assurance that he was supposed to run toward the sounds.

———

Sally's father sent off a volley of shots then ducked down below the window frame to reload. She tried to yell to him to be careful, since bullets were coming through the board walls, but she couldn't hear her own voice.

Half a minute later, he repeated the stunt—peek out, pull the rifle up, fire, then duck down. Ma crouched by the stove, watching the back door, her lips moving.

Pa made his move for the third time. Peek, rise, fire. This time, he flew backward and sprawled on the floor. Sally stared in horror as he clutched his shoulder.

"Get the gun. Get the gun."

He said it over and over, but it took a while for Sally to hear him, and for the words to register.

As she grabbed the rifle off the floor, the back door splintered, and Ma's pistol roared. Ma fired again, and a huge figure, shadowy in the smoke, sprawled on the kitchen floor.

The front window shattered, and Sally turned toward it. A man's head and arms, supporting a rifle, appeared in the frame. She swung the rifle toward him without really aiming and pulled the trigger. He flew backward.

When she turned back toward her mother, two men barreled through the ragged doorway at the back. Ma got off one more shot before the next man grabbed her and twisted the Colt from her hand.

He held her mother close against him and leveled a six-shooter at Sally. She saw his lips form the words, "Drop it! Drop it!"

The other man, who wore a blue calico shirt, unbarred the front door to let the rest in. Cam was the first over the threshold. Sally stared at him, hatred rising up inside her.

"Drop it," the man holding her mother yelled again. "I'll count to three, and then I shoot this woman. One!"

Five armed men stood in her house. Sally stooped and laid down the rifle. Her father writhed on the floor, clutching his wound.

One of the outlaws knelt by the man her mother had shot as he came through the back door. "Flynn's dead."

"What do we do now?" another asked.

Sally tried to keep her face calm. Her mother had killed the gang's leader, and in spite of the grimness of the moment, she wanted to celebrate.

Cam marched over and stared at Sally. She looked away, unable to meet his malignant brown eyes.

Cam glanced down at her father. "Who is he?"

Sally didn't answer. Cam hadn't been in the area very long. If she didn't enlighten him, he would probably think her pa was a local rancher he hadn't met. But if she told him, he might take out his anger at her on her father. Johnny had thwarted him the last time they met, but Johnny wasn't here now. She swallowed hard but said nothing.

Cam stooped and grasped her father's jacket. He hauled Pa roughly to his feet. "Outside, old man. Now."

"Cam, don't," Sally said, involuntarily.

Cam shot her a glance and shoved her father to the door. "Wouldn't want to mess up your floor any worse than it already is, Sal."

"No!" Sally lunged toward him, but the nearest man caught her around the waist and hauled her back. As she struggled, Sally caught a glimpse of her mother's pale face.

"You tell Johnny this is from me." Cam shoved her father out the door and down the steps.

"Cam, he's my father!"

He looked back at her.

"Please," Sally said with a sob.

Cam's chin came up just a notch. "Well, since he's your pa." His smile did not reassure her. Cam looked at the men holding her and her mother. "Bring them outside."

The man holding Sally pushed her toward the door. Her shoulder slammed against the jamb, and she gasped. She hurried down the steps as fast as she could without stumbling, clutching her bruised shoulder.

Her mother staggered down the steps and lurched against her. Their captors brought them up short, and they watched as Cam marched Pa a few steps away while another man stood watching the road.

"Torch the house," Cam called to the man in the blue shirt.

Ma caught her breath, but Sally only pressed her lips together. If they would only spare her parents, she wouldn't care about the cabin.

The man holstered his pistol and went into the barn, reappearing a moment later with an armful of straw. Meanwhile, Cam prodded her father toward the well.

"Your Sally is a good girl," he said in Pa's face.

Pa said nothing but stared at Ma and Sally, his eyes full of remorse.

"Say good-bye," Cam told him, holding his gun to the back of Pa's head.

Still Pa kept silent.

Cam glared at him. "For her sake, I won't blow your head off. Over you go, Pops."

Cam shoved Pa against the berm of the well and overbalanced him without difficulty. Sally's heart clenched as her father disappeared over the edge. She heard the water splash, and knew the ringing in her ears had receded. She pulled against the man who held her, but his grip around her waist tightened.

"Hold still, missy." The barrel of his pistol pushed against her temple. "You want your ma down there, too?"

Her mother sobbed, but Sally steeled herself. This was her fault, for refusing Cam. She wouldn't make him angrier unless she had a weapon in her hand.

"Someone's coming," the lookout called.

Cam whirled toward him. "Get the horses."

The man in the blue shirt lit a twist of straw and threw it on the pile banked against the house. Sally's captor released her, giving her a shove. She landed in the dirt, and when she pushed herself up onto her knees, Ma lay beside her and the five outlaws were scrambling to mount their horses. She noticed as they galloped down the road toward town that one of them had earlier put his saddle on Lady, and one of their spent horses stood listlessly in the corral, its head hanging low.

"Jeremiah!" Ma leaped to her feet and ran toward the well.

The dust from the departing outlaws hung thick in the air as another bunch of horses tore into the yard. Johnny was in the vanguard, and he stopped Reckless so hard the chestnut almost sat on his tail.

"Sally!"

"It was Cam, with the outlaw gang." She stood and pointed toward where the fleeing horses had gone as Sheriff Jackson and a dozen other men galloped their horses into the barnyard.

"Can you get the fire?" Johnny asked.

Sally turned toward the cabin. The flames crackled as they devoured the straw, but they hadn't taken hold on the siding yet.

"Yes, but—"

As she turned back to Johnny, he waved and spurred Reckless off after the outlaws. He apparently had not noticed her mother, or assumed she was a neighbor woman. Ma was leaning over the berm, calling, "Jeremiah!"

"Is he drowned?" Sally ran to her mother's side. Why hadn't she run to Johnny and told him Pa was in the well? It had all happened so fast, and now the entire posse was gone, leaving a drifting dust cloud behind.

A splash came from below.

"Pa?" She squinted against the glare of sun on the surface of the water far below.

"I'm not drowned. Quite. I'm up to my neck, but I can hold my head up for a while. Get a ladder."

Her mother clutched her arm. "Have you got a ladder?"

"No. Maybe." What had Johnny and Cam used when they had built the new room? She turned toward the house, and the burning straw caught her eye. The flames had died down a little, but a small blaze was running along the edge of one of the lower boards. "We've got to douse the fire, then we'll get him out."

Her mother lingered to yell something down to Pa, but her words were lost to Sally. She and Johnny were going to need this cabin, and she wasn't ready to let it burn after all.

Without stopping to worry who would see her, Sally unbuttoned her skirt and let it drop to the ground. She grabbed it, using it to slap at the flames as she kicked the smoldering straw away from the wall.

Her mother ran to her side. "We need water."

Sally wasn't sure what the outlaws had done with the bucket she'd had her milk and butter hanging in. They must have taken it with them.

"There was a pail in the kitchen. I'll get it." Sally thrust her smoking skirt into Ma's hands and dashed for the steps. Inside, she staggered to a stop. To reach the bucket of water in the kitchen, she would have to climb over the outlaw leader's body. She walked over to it and nudged him gingerly with her foot. He didn't move.

She stepped over him and picked up the bucket of water. She ran outside, careful not to slosh too much, and threw the water against the wall. Her mother stepped in with the skirt and beat at the few remaining flames.

"I'll get more." Sally ran to the well and hooked the bucket onto the end of the rope. "Pa, you all right?"

"I'm still here." His face was a gray blob floating on the well water, but he sounded weaker.

"We've nearly got the fire out. Hang on, and we'll have you out of there soon." Quickly, she turned the handle on the windlass to run the bucket down. Pa grabbed it and dunked it full for her. Sally cranked it up as fast as she could and carried it over to where her mother had the fire all but extinguished.

"Drown that patch, where it's started to catch the grass," Ma said.

Sally succeeded, and Ma wiped her brow with her sleeve.

"That's done. Now, how are we going to get your father out of the well?"

"There may be something in the barn. Let's look."

Together they went into the barn, where Sally noted several cartridge casings on the floor. Her mother let out a little scream. She had found another fallen outlaw sprawled on the floor in the loose hay.

"Has he got a gun?" Sally asked.

"I don't think so," Ma said. "He looks dead."

"Then he won't hurt us."

Sally looked all around and up at the underside of the loft, hoping to find a ladder the men had used on their building project, but she didn't see anything that would help her. The ladder to the loft consisted of short planks nailed to the wall between the studs, so that wouldn't help.

"I'll have to go down the well rope."

"You can't," her mother said. "I'm not strong enough to haul you up alone."

The well rope would be too hard for her father to climb with his wound, and even if Sally and her mother could haul that much weight up with the windlass, she doubted he could hold on securely to the rope that long.

"Maybe I can make some loops from the clothesline."

"The clothesline?" Her mother frowned at her, but Sally turned and ran for the house. She hopped over the dead outlaw and seized a kitchen knife then ran out the back door. When she returned to the well, her mother was bending over the berm.

"Jeremiah! You stay awake, now." She turned to Sally. "He's weak. We've got to get him out of there."

Quickly, Sally knotted a length of clothesline around the well rope, the way Johnny had shown her. Not sure if it would skim the surface of the water or not, she made another loop above it and threw the rope down.

"Pa, can you reach that? Hold on to one of the loops."

"What?"

Sally made herself slow down and explain carefully what she wanted him to do. If only Pa were healthy, he could climb up out of the water using rope loops for steps, but his slowness in even grasping the rope told her he couldn't contribute much to the rescue effort.

He reached for the rope and sank below the surface then bobbed up again, coughing. With one hand he found and held on to the bottom loop she had provided, but he sagged low in the water, and his head, tilted back, barely broke the surface.

"He's lost a lot of blood," her mother said.

Sally looked down at him, knowing even with the loop to clutch, he wouldn't be able to stay above the water for long. "I'll have to go down."

"No!" Ma seized her arm. "Don't you dare! I could never get the both of you out."

Sally slumped against the edge of the well. "Then what'll we do? If we don't get him out soon, he'll drown."

CHAPTER 27

O nly two miles up the trail, the outlaws veered off the road and stormed into the Caxtons' barnyard with the posse singeing their heels. The ranch had a large pole barn where Eph stored hay and feed. The outlaws ran their mounts inside and took cover behind the barn walls, a wagon, and a smokehouse.

Fred Jackson signaled the posse to hold up as soon as he saw where the gang was headed, and the men gathered around him.

"Eph, who's at your place?"

"Rilla, the kids, and two hands. The hands might be out away from the house, though."

"All right. Let's be cautious. We don't want them to get into the house and use your family as hostages." Fred directed his men on how to surround the gang.

Johnny listened closely. He fidgeted to get into place, but it would be best if they had a plan.

"Most of all," Fred told them, "make sure of your target. Don't just let off a round because you saw movement. It could be one of us, or those two ranch hands, trying to help us."

Johnny joined Eph to ride stealthily down a path to the spring that supplied the ranch's freshwater. Eph said they would be able to circle around the smokehouse from there without being seen. Meanwhile, others positioned themselves closer to the house or beneath the windmill where they would have a clear line of fire at the barn.

Johnny and Eph left their horses near the spring. Gunfire opened near the barn. They sneaked closer, coming up behind the smokehouse. Johnny spotted one man at the side of the little building, leaning out to shoot around the corner. From the nearness of the reports, another must be close by, though Johnny couldn't see him.

"Wish I'd gone into the house to be with Rilla and the kids," Eph said.

"Well, watch yourself. We want to get you back to her in one piece." Johnny patted his shoulder.

Eph nodded. "You want to get the drop on this feller? I'll come in from behind that juniper." He pointed toward a bush.

Johnny nodded, and they separated. He tried to keep behind cover, but the closer he got, the fewer hiding places were available. Soon he was in a good position to shoot the outlaw, but it didn't seem fair. You didn't just come up behind someone and shoot him in the back.

A lull came in the shooting, and from the meager protection of a low boulder, he called, "Drop your gun, mister."

The outlaw jerked around to face him and let off a round. Johnny ducked as soon as he saw him move, and the bullet pinged against the rock, inches from his head. He stayed down, trying to absorb what he had just seen. The outlaw he had challenged was Cam.

Johnny hauled in a deep breath, trying to prepare himself. Cam would kill him if he had the chance.

He made sure the rifle was ready and prepared to spring up and shoot.

Another bullet ricocheted off the rock close to his head, throwing shards. One of them stung his cheek, and when he touched the spot, his hand came away bloody. Cam couldn't have made that shot, Johnny reasoned, crouching lower. The other outlaw he'd heard shooting must have targeted him now. He searched for the shooter and saw movement in the junipers a few yards away.

Still he hesitated. That could be Eph. And what was Cam doing now? The low evergreen branches parted, and a man raised a pistol, pointing at him. Johnny let off two shots and hit the dirt. He heard more shooting close by but didn't dare raise his head at first. Finally, he lifted his chin. The man in the juniper appeared to be lying still. He pushed to his knees.

"Mark! Behind you!"

Eph's cry sent Johnny diving behind his boulder once more. Several gunshots roared, too close. He held his pistol ready, his heart thumping.

"Johnny! You all right?"

He looked up. Eph held out a hand to help him rise. "I got him. It's your old ranch hand."

Johnny stood cautiously. From out front, a couple more shots sounded, and then he heard Fred Jackson call, "Give it up. We have you surrounded."

"Sorry I called you Mark," Eph said. "But I'm glad you listened."

"It's all right. Better check that fellow in the bushes."

The outlaw he had exchanged gunfire with lay dead, and Johnny followed Eph over to where Cam lay, bleeding from a wound to the chest.

"Hey there, Johnny." Cam smiled with gritted teeth. "I guess it was bound to come to this."

Eph stooped and picked up Cam's pistol. Johnny knelt beside him. He pulled off his bandanna and pressed it to Cam's wound, but he knew it was too late.

"Cam, what are you doing with this bunch?"

"Didn't have nowhere else to go. Seemed like a good idea at the time."

"You know Fred Jackson was set on getting this gang."

Cam let out a bark of a laugh. "Didn't think he was smart enough."

"Sounds like it's all over out there," Eph said, looking toward the corner of the smokehouse.

"Well, be careful," Johnny said. "If they're done shootin', bring the sheriff here."

Eph scouted around the corner and then walked out into the open.

Johnny leaned in close to his old comrade. "Cam, Fred got a wire from Denver saying they're looking for you for Red Howell's killing."

Cam's face twisted. "So, somebody figured it out."

"You mean it's true? I didn't want to believe it."

Cam grimaced and closed his eyes. "Like I said, it was bound to come to this."

"But you told me you'd go with me to help me."

"Just lookin' out for my hide. Look where it got me."

Johnny stared down at him. At last he said, "I'm sorry."

Cam's mouth twitched. "*You're* sorry? You dumb kid. You never shoulda listened to me."

Fred Jackson strode around the corner, with Eph in his wake.

"You all right, Johnny?"

"Yes, sir." Johnny stood slowly. "It's Cam Combes. I thought you'd want to know. He's shot bad."

"My fault," Eph said. "He was shootin' at Mark. I mean Johnny."

"Don't fret about it," Jackson said. "Whyn't you see if Rilla can make a place for him in the house? She's got Bill Hood in there already. Maybe she can take this'un, too."

"Bill's hurt?" Johnny said.

"One of 'em winged him." Fred crouched beside Cam and put a hand to his throat. "I'm not feeling a pulse."

Johnny froze. Had Cam slipped away while they stood here talking?

After a long moment, Fred looked up and nodded. "He's gone. Can we use your wagon, Eph?"

"Sure. There's one over yonder in the juniper, too." Eph nodded toward the other downed outlaw.

Fred stood with a sigh. "One of them said there's a couple of bodies back at your place, too, Johnny."

"What?" Johnny stared at him.

"That's what they tell me. Flynn and another man were killed when they attacked your house. Two of them here are wounded."

Johnny turned and ran for Reckless.

"Someone's coming," Ma yelled down the well.

Sally, up to her neck in the water, was holding her father with his head above the surface. She had brought a short board down to drape his arms over, and so far she had kept him from going under. But he had drifted in and out of sensibility, and she didn't know how much longer she could support him.

"Go get the rifle! It could be one of the outlaws." She stared up at her mother's shadowed face. Her voice echoed off the close walls of the well. There was barely room enough for her and her father. She held doggedly to the rope with one hand.

"I think it's your man," Ma said after a moment. "Hold on."

Sally grimaced as her aching hand cramped. Far away, as though from the end of a mine shaft, she heard Johnny say, "Ma'am, how do? I'm John Paynter. Where's Sally?"

A moment later, he poked his head over the berm. "Sally, gal, what are you doing down there?"

"Trying to keep my pa from drowning." She hadn't meant to, but she burst into tears, and the last, broken word came out with a sob.

"Your pa?" Johnny's head disappeared, and she heard a low, earnest discussion going on. After a minute, he was back. "I'm coming down."

"No," she yelled. "There's not room enough. We'd all be stuck in here like sardines in a tin."

After a pause, he said, "Can you hold on to the well rope, and I'll hoist you up?"

"I can't let go of Pa. He'll go under."

"Is he conscious?" Johnny asked.

"Sometimes, but he's hurt bad. He's awful weak, Johnny. You gotta get him out of here."

"I will, I will. Help's coming."

Sally's arms ached. She'd been down here at least half an hour, clinging with one hand to the rope. Her other arm encircled her father's shoulders and chest. Her feet kept losing touch with the bottom, causing her to bob. She had taken off her shoes before descending, and her toes felt rocks and muck when she let herself sink six inches or so. She tried not to flail around much, as she was uncertain how stable the bottom of the well was or if it would hold when pressure was exerted.

Her mother called down to her, "Hang on, Sally. He's gone to get his lasso."

A moment later, Johnny's rope, stiffer than the one they used in the well or the clothesline, appeared. A loop about four feet in diameter descended to her. Bumping the sides of the well.

"Am I supposed to put that on?" she yelled.

"No. If you can, get it around him under his arms. Then I can hold him steady while you climb out. I think."

"I'll try."

Sliding the loop over her father's head and shoulders was easy, but getting his arms through it was another matter.

"Pa, come on. Help me here. Let's get your arms through this. We're going to get you out."

He moaned when she took his arm and tried to change his position.

"Are you awake?" she asked. "Come on, Pa."

She worked first on his left side, as his wound was more toward the right. Even so, he flinched and moaned with each little movement.

"I hate to hurt you, but I have to do this." She struggled to work the rope over his arm and get it into the loop. Every time she moved, she hit the wall of the hand-dug well. The top six feet or so was lined in stonework, but down here the sides were just earth. Whenever her flailing arms hit the wall, clods of dirt tumbled into the water that was already murky with dirt and blood. At last she had his left arm through. Her father's head rested against her shoulder.

"Johnny," she gasped. "I don't think I can get his other arm in."

"All right, can I get a ladder down there? Is there room?"

"You mean a wooden one?" she asked.

"Yeah. There's one in the loft that Cam and I built."

So that was where he had stored it. She ought to have climbed up there and looked first thing. Wearily, she lifted her face to gaze up at him. "I think so."

"Hold tight. I'll go get it. Your ma's going to hold the end of the lasso to help you a little."

Sally couldn't see that it was any easier now to keep Pa's head out of the water, especially since he had slipped into unconsciousness. The board wasn't helping at all. She willed her numbing arms to hold on and her back and legs to keep supporting both of them.

A few minutes later, her mother called, "Someone's coming. Someone in a wagon."

"Thank You, Lord," Sally whispered. She could hear distant voices as Ma explained the situation to the newcomer.

Johnny reappeared above her. "Eph Caxton's here, Sally. He's going to help me get the ladder down. Stay over to the side now."

Mr. Caxton poked his head over the edge of the well.

"Miz Paynter?"

"Yes. Hello."

"I'm going to help your husband. We'll put the ladder down easy if we can, but we might have to take off the windlass. I misdoubt the ladder's long enough to reach bottom, though."

Sally pushed back against the side of her prison, holding her father as close to her as she could. The space was tight, but his legs had stopped helping support him long ago, and she knew he would sag beneath the surface if she loosened her grip.

Johnny and Eph managed to work the ladder into the well without dismantling the windlass. They let it down slowly until they held it by its top rung. The bottom hung a few inches above the top of the water.

"I'm going to let go," Johnny said.

The ladder plunked downward, wobbled, and stood against the

wall of the well. Sally felt her father's body move. The ladder must have hit his feet.

"All right now, let go of him," Johnny said. "Eph will hold his head up with the lasso."

"What if it doesn't work?" Sally asked doubtfully.

"Then we'll have to hurry."

She reached for the floating board and tried to rest Pa's head on it, but his face still flopped into the water.

"Hold him up," she cried. "Johnny, I can't do it. He'll drown if I leave him."

"Take it easy. Can you lay him on his back and put that board under his head?"

She wasn't sure it would work or if there was room enough to shift his position that much, but she tugged at him until he lay back against her shoulder again.

"Pa, wake up." She fumbled for the board and pushed it underwater and beneath his head. "Pa, can you hear me?" She pulled away from him, and his body floated for the moment.

"That's it. Hurry, now," Johnny said. "Climb the wooden ladder, but hold on to the rope."

Feeling slightly befuddled, Sally grasped the well rope and put her weight on the bottom rung of the wooden ladder. It wobbled and tipped but then seemed stable. She climbed to the second step, then the third.

"How's he doing?" she asked. The brightness above her made it hard to see any detail below.

"He's all right. Come on up until you can reach my hands."

Johnny leaned over the side and extended his arms down the well, but he was still several feet above Sally. She climbed another step. Water streamed from her clothing. The ladder had only two more rungs, and the top one was a good eight feet below the berm.

"It's not high enough," she said.

"Use the rope."

She balanced carefully, with nothing to hang on to this high up but the well rope. The loops were too low to help her. If she could reach them, they might make the difference.

"I made loops," she gasped. Johnny's face was only a few feet away now.

"Loops?" he said, frowning.

"Like on the clothesline. For Pa, but he couldn't use them."

"Hold on to the ladder," Johnny said. "Let go of the rope."

She released it and clung to the top of the ladder's sides, hunched over and shaking. Johnny cranked the well rope up with the windlass, while Eph kept the lasso taut around her father's torso. Johnny caught the lower part of the rope and slid the knots Sally had made upward along the wet rope.

"All right, now you can use these for steps." He let the rope fall back down where Sally could reach it. The lowest loop hung a foot above the ladder rung she was standing on.

She grabbed the rope and held it for a moment, feeling stupid and slow. After a couple of deep breaths, she guided the loop and carefully fitted her shoeless foot into it. She grimaced and clung to the rope so she could step up into the next loop with her other foot.

"Now move the bottom one up," Johnny said.

"My feet hurt."

"Can you reach me now?" He leaned over and stretched to grasp her fingers.

Sally let go of the rope with one hand and strained upward. Their hands met.

"Good girl! Give me your other hand."

The rope loop bit into her arch as she pushed up on her top foot and gripped his other hand.

"Yeah! On three," Johnny, said, grinning. "One, two, three!"

He hauled her up to the berm by brute force, and Sally plummeted out onto the dirt beside the well. Her mother immediately wrapped her in a blanket. It felt good, despite the searing sun.

"Let's get you inside and find some dry clothes for you," Ma said.

"We have to get Pa out." Sally pulled back against her guiding hand.

"I'm going down now." Johnny was already lowering himself over the edge of the well. "You go get dried out. Eph, you ready?"

"Ready," Eph said.

"Come," Ma whispered. "You're not decent."

Sally looked down at her dripping chemise and petticoat and drew the blanket closer about her. "All right, but you stay with Pa. Make them bring him in to our bed."

Sally picked up her shoes and staggered toward the house. The bottoms of her feet still hurt, and her arms and legs felt tired to the point of uselessness. Still, she managed to get inside the house. At the sight of the outlaw's body, she pulled up short. Did Johnny even know this man was in here? "Dear God, help us!"

She lurched to the bedroom and closed the door. As quickly as she could, she peeled off her drenched clothes and threw them in a pile on the floor. Her fingers, still stiff and uncooperative, balked at the corset strings, and she cast the garment aside and pulled on a fresh dress.

Knocking came at the door before she could take her hair down to comb it.

"Sally, dear, are you ready?" her mother called. "They've got him out. Johnny's carrying him inside now."

Sally opened the door. "They'll have to overlook my appearance." At least she had a complete dress on. She rushed to the bed and flung the quilt back.

"No, leave that," Ma said. "I'll have to strip his clothes off, and we don't want to get the mattress wet from them."

Sally helped pull it back in place as Johnny and Eph carried her father in and stretched him out on top of the quilt. Johnny began at once to pull Pa's shoes off, and Eph set to work on his shirt. Pa's face was stark white, and Sally could barely make out the movements of his chest as he breathed.

"Who's that feller out in the kitchen?"

Johnny's terse question reminded Sally of the earlier events.

"I believe it's Flynn."

Johnny dropped Pa's second shoe and stared at her. "Their leader?"

"Yes. And Cam seemed ready to take over that position when Flynn fell."

"Well, Cam won't be doing any more terrorizing," Johnny said. "If I lug Flynn outside to Eph's wagon, can you heat some water and make some strong tea for your pa?"

"Of course."

Ma moved into his spot and began to help Eph work the wet clothing off her father's body. Sally turned away and walked with Johnny the few steps to her kitchen.

"If I'd known, I would have stopped when we came through," Johnny said, gazing down at Flynn's inert form.

"I know, and I wanted you so desperately to help Pa. Guess I should have made that clear. But it happened so quickly."

He shook his head. "I didn't even know your folks were here. What's been going on while I was gone, Sally?"

"They came on the train to keep me company until you came back."

"Well, your pa has paid dearly for that decision."

"If they hadn't come, I'd be dead, or in the outlaws' camp. Pa held them off." She brushed a stray tear from her cheek. "They shot him through the window, and then Cam threw him down the well."

Johnny clenched his jaw and eyed the back door. "Looks like the leader busted in through the back—that right?"

Sally nodded. "Ma was right here by the stove with Pa's Colt, and she blasted him."

Johnny stared at her. "Your ma shot that man?"

"Yes."

"I saw another'un in the barn when I went to get the ladder," Johnny said.

"That must be the one that tried to come in the front window. Either that or Pa got another when he was shooting through the window."

"Come here, girl." Johnny pulled her in against his chest and held her so tightly Sally could barely breathe, but she didn't want him to let her go. "Seems I owe your folks a big debt."

"Where's Sheriff Jackson?" she asked.

"Taken the prisoners into town."

"So, the posse got them all?"

"There was three left standing when we got done over at Caxtons'."

"Cam was riding with them when they came here," Sally said. "He tried to get me to open the door. He didn't know I had Ma and Pa here—thought I was all alone."

"If I'd known that, I'd have killed him for sure," Johnny said. "As it was, I couldn't pull the trigger when I came face-to-face with him. I was so shocked, to think he would do this."

"Who shot him?"

"Eph. Good thing, too. He was drawing down on me."

"We'll have to thank him properly after things settle down," she said.

Johnny nodded. "I still can't believe it, hardly. I asked Cam about Colorado before he died. Told him about the notice Fred Jackson got. He admitted it, Sally."

"He killed that man up there?"

"Yeah. Why didn't I realize it right away?"

"You thought Cam was a decent fellow."

"It's funny in a way, because we were never that close at the Lone Pine. Cam wasn't one I'd have picked for my best buddy. But you work with someone day after day, and you get to know them, and you know they'll stand by you if something happens. And then something did happen, and I didn't think twice about trusting him."

"I guess that's something we can learn from." Sally put her hand on his back and rubbed it in small circles. Was it so different from her trusting Johnny the day he met her at the depot, because she thought he was Mark? She probably should have been more cautious as well. "I'm sorry. But I sure am glad you're the one who came back in one piece."

Johnny was silent; then he straightened. "When the shooting was done at Caxtons', one of the gang told us there'd been a fracas here. I lit out when I heard it."

"I'm glad you did. I couldn't have held Pa up much longer."

"Come on, let's get that water heating." Johnny opened the lid of the firebox. "I'll build up the fire. Can you get more water?"

"The well water's a mess now," Sally said. "And I dumped the bucket I had in here on the fire outside. There's a little in the teakettle, though." She picked it up and judged its weight.

"Make the tea, then."

The bedroom pitcher still held a quart or so of clean water, so Ma used that to clean her husband's wound. Meanwhile, Johnny and Eph loaded the outlaws' bodies into the wagon next to Cam's. Sally got her comb and hand mirror from the bedroom and put her hair to rights then walked out to where Johnny was covering the bodies with an old blanket.

"I'll ask the doctor to come out here," Eph said as he climbed to the wagon seat. "And I'll bring you a barrel of water later."

Johnny waved in acknowledgment. He took off his hat and slapped it against his thigh as he walked over to join Sally on the stoop. "Now, Mrs. Paynter, you have a lot more to tell me."

"Yes, I do," she said. "But you need some dry clothes, and I believe there's still chicken and dumplings on the stove, if it hasn't burned on or dried out."

"I don't care if it has," Johnny said. "I'll eat it anyway. And I need a proper introduction to your mother."

CHAPTER 28

D r. Neale made a return visit to the ranch two days after the attack and pronounced Jeremiah Vane well enough to take a little solid food and sit up if he felt like it.

Johnny joined Sally in the kitchen while Mrs. Vane had a final word with Dr. Neale.

"Looks like your pa will be all right," he said.

"In time." Sally picked up the bucket of water by the stove and poured half of it into the wash boiler on top. The well water was almost clear now, but they were still hauling what they drank from the Caxtons'.

"It's been a shock to see Pa so weak," Sally admitted.

Johnny nodded. Sally was as solicitous as her mother in tending Jeremiah, but he could tell it pained her to see her father in his present condition. "He's getting better, though."

"The doctor says he needs to stay in bed a couple of weeks, at least. He won't even consider letting him travel before that."

"We'll see how it goes," Johnny said. "I can't see him riding a train, even as far as Abilene, for a while. He needs to get his strength back."

She smiled. "You know, five years ago, before I left Texas, he was a strong man. He could load or unload a ton of freight in less than an hour. That's how I remember him. Now he seems to have aged more than five years."

"Sweetheart, he was shot two days ago. Give him time."

"I know." Sally walked to the table and sat down. "The day I met them at the depot, he had seemed older to me, but not *old*." She glanced at Johnny. "Was that the same day the outlaws came? It all seems such a jumble."

"I reckon it was. And the day I came home."

"Mmm. Well, Pa's hair is much grayer now. I don't think it was that gray before the shooting. And he's so frail."

"That will change, especially if you and your ma feed him up like Doc Neale said."

"I guess so. But I've sort of realized my folks are getting older."

"So are we, when you get right down to it," Johnny said.

"Well, yes, but. . ." She shook her head.

Dr. Neale came out of the bedroom, carrying his bag. "Well folks, I'm off."

"Won't you stay and have a meal, Doctor?" Sally asked.

"No time. I need to stop in at the Hoods' and check on old Bill and also on Mrs. Bill's new baby."

"Mary had her baby?" Sally cried.

"Yes, a healthy little girl."

"How is Mr. Hood doing?" As Sally talked, she went to her work-table and wrapped a couple of biscuits and a slice of cake in a napkin.

"He'll be all right if his wound doesn't get infected. Bill's a hard man to keep down, though. He's already fussing about all the work he can't do."

"Take this." Sally held out the napkin package. "You must get hungry, driving around to see everyone who's ailing."

"Thank you kindly," Dr. Neale said. "Sheriff Jackson's still got a wounded outlaw at the jail. He sent the others on to Houston. I hope we can get the last one fit enough to send him off."

"I sleep a little easier, knowing that gang's been caught," Sally said.

Johnny walked out to the corral with the doctor. When he returned, Sally was back at work in the kitchen. "I'll put dinner on the table in fifteen minutes for you and Ma and me."

Johnny nodded. "And I'll spell your ma while she eats. Do you need anything now?"

Sally glanced around the kitchen. "I hate to say it, but I could use more water."

Johnny grabbed the bucket and went out to the barrel near the stoop.

A short time later, Sally persuaded her mother to join her in the kitchen for the meal, while Johnny helped Pa eat his dinner.

"Pa's getting pretty good at feeding himself," she noted as she put a tray with two dishes of beef stew in Johnny's hands.

"I'll let him do as much of the work as he wants to," Johnny said.

He carried the tray into the bedroom, and Jeremiah, propped up on pillows, smiled wearily.

"Got a mind for some stew?" Johnny asked.

"Maybe a little."

Johnny settled him with his bowl and sat down in a chair beside the bed to eat with him. When Johnny finished his own bowl, Jeremiah was only halfway done with his. Each time the older man lifted the spoon to his mouth, it seemed to take a great effort.

"Want some help?" Johnny asked.

"No, I'm fine, but thank you." Slowly, Jeremiah managed to get another spoonful to his lips.

"It's probably good for you to do it yourself," Johnny noted, remembering how helpless he'd felt when his arm was broken.

A couple of minutes later, Jeremiah let the spoon rest in the bowl and sighed. "Guess I'm done for the time being."

Johnny took the bowl and set it over on the tray on top of the washstand.

"Sir, I just want to say how much I appreciate that you were here when Sally had the trouble with the outlaws."

Her father smiled faintly. "It's not like we planned it."

"Oh, I know, but. . .I'm just glad she didn't have to face them alone."

"So am I. Things would have gone badly. That is, worse than they did." Jeremiah looked down at his bandages. "The doc says I'm lucky. The bullet didn't hit anything vital. And they could have shot me again. I believe they would have killed me outright if Sally hadn't spoken up. She stood up to the fellow—the one they called Cam."

"She's a stout one, your Sally."

"She'll make you a good wife, son. I guess you know she's the kind that will stick by you, no matter what."

"Yes, sir, I've found that to be true." Johnny wondered how much Mr. Vane knew about Sally's earlier marriage. Or maybe he was only talking about her decision to stay with him after she learned of Mark's death.

Their gazes caught and held for a moment, and Johnny's gut tightened.

"You be good to her," Jeremiah said quietly.

"Yes, sir." Johnny took a careful breath. Now was the time for frankness. "I won't lie to her, ever again. Or to anyone else."

"That's real fine. I hope you mean it."

"Oh, I do, sir." Johnny hoped he wouldn't have to prove his honesty and dependability to Sally's family all his life, but he couldn't fault her father for being a bit wary.

Jeremiah sank back into his pillows with a sigh. "I expect I should telegraph my son and tell him what's happened."

"Sally sent me yesterday to do that very thing," Johnny said. "She and her mother worded it carefully so as not to cause undue alarm."

"Good. We don't want the boys showing up here on your doorstep, thinking I'm about to die."

Johnny chuckled. "No, sir, though I'm sure Sally would be glad to see her brothers. She's been a mite homesick, I think, and not just this summer."

"You'll have to bring her up to see us before too long."

"I can do that."

Mr. Vane's eyelids closed again.

"I'll let you rest, sir," Johnny said. Mr. Vane showed no sign that he'd heard.

Johnny rose carefully and picked up the tray. When he entered the kitchen, Sally and her mother were still at the table, lingering over coffee and cake.

"You sure do make a good marble cake," Mrs. Vane said.

Sally laughed. "It's your recipe. I just wish I could bake without heating up the house so."

"Soon," Johnny said, thinking of the half-finished oven outside.

They both looked up at him expectantly.

"He's sleeping." Johnny carried the tray to the worktable and eyed the water level in the boiler. He judged that Sally had enough hot water to do the dishes in. "I ought to ride out and see if the cattle are getting enough water, if you don't need me here."

Sally nodded. "Go ahead. I suspect the creek is nothing but a trickle now."

"What will you do if it dries up?" Mrs. Vane asked.

"That's the big question all the ranchers are asking," Johnny said.

Sally stood and gathered her dishes. "I'll walk out to the barn with you."

She and Johnny had slept out there in the harness room for the past two nights. Sally admitted she felt less secure there than in the house, but he reminded her that Cam and the outlaws could no longer hurt them. Johnny slept on the floor between her and the door, with his pistol beside his pillow.

As they crossed the yard, he whistled, and Reckless and Lady came trotting to the fence.

"I'm glad we got Lady back." Sally walked over to pat the mare's nose while Johnny got his saddle.

He brought it from the barn and plopped it on the top rail then opened the gate for Reckless. Lady tried to crowd through behind him.

"No, you stay in there, girl." He pushed her head back and quickly closed the gate. "Had a talk with your pa," he said as he spread the saddle blanket over Reckless's back.

"What about?"

"You, mostly. I don't think he quite trusts me with his daughter yet." Johnny reached for the saddle.

Sally's face crinkled. "He'll learn. Did he scare you?"

"Maybe just a little. But I figure I deserve it."

She smiled, and everything came right inside him. He let go of the saddle and stepped toward her. She came into his arms, and he kissed her, not caring if the world saw.

Lady nickered, stretching her long neck over the fence. Sally pulled away from him and laughed.

Johnny tugged her back against his chest. He wasn't ready to let go of her.

"I love you, Sal."

Her smile lit her face, and he determined to say those words more often. She stood on her toes and kissed him again.

"You don't mind having Ma and Pa in our room, do you?"

"Not so long as it's not permanent."

"Maybe we could build another room on the house," she said.

"For company?"

"Or a nursery."

He half closed his eyes and studied her face, trying to determine what she meant by that.

"Think we'll need one soon?"

"Maybe so. And Ma says she'll come back when it's time."

He wanted to crow, but he remembered what had happened in the past with her other babies. "Did you tell the doc?"

"I did mention it to him. He said to come see him in a month if I still think. . . And sooner if anything seems wrong."

"So, you're not sure," Johnny said.

"It's early, but. . .pretty sure." Her hands tightened on his back. "Johnny, I want this one to be right."

"So do I. No more lifting and lugging things for you, you hear?"

She laughed softly. "Doc said that after what happened with Pa—being in the well and holding him up so long—if I wasn't strong enough to carry, I probably would have lost it then. If there is a baby."

"There is." He pulled her head tight against his heart. "There is, and we'll pray every day that he grows strong and healthy."

Sally jerked a little, like a hiccup, and he leaned down to see her face.

"You're not crying, are you?" he asked.

"Maybe."

He smiled and rubbed her back. "If it's a boy, we'll name him Mark."

"I'd like that."

They stood there for a long time, until she gently pushed him away. "You'd better get going, Mr. Paynter, and see if those cattle have enough to drink."

He hated to leave her now, even for an hour, but she was right. He needed to make a success of this ranch, as well as his marriage.

"I'll be back soon," he said. "And that's a promise."

ABOUT THE AUTHOR

Susan Page Davis is the author of more than fifty novels in the romance, mystery, suspense, and historical romance genres. A Maine native, she now lives in western Kentucky with her husband, Jim, a retired news editor. They are the parents of six, and the grandparents of nine fantastic kids. She is a past winner of the Carol Award, the Will Rogers Medallion for Western Fiction, and the Inspirational Readers' Choice Award. Susan was named Favorite Author of the Year in the 18th Annual Heartsong Awards. Visit her website at: www.susanpagedavis.com.

Also available from Shiloh Run Press. . .

The OUTLAW TAKES a BRIDE

Unabridged Audiobook

OTHER BOOKS BY
SUSAN PAGE DAVIS

The Prairie Dreams Trilogy

The Bride's Prerogative

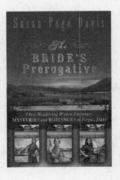

Available wherever great books are sold!